Max Havelaar: Or, the Coffee Auctions of the Dutch Trading Company, by Multatuli, Tr. by Baron A. Nahuÿs

Eduard Douwes Dekker

EDINBURGH: PRINTED BY THOMAS CONSTABLE,

FOR

EDMONSTON AND DOUGLAS.

LONDON	HAMILTON, ADAMS, AND
CAMBRIDGE	MACMILLAN AND CO.
DUBLIN	M'GLASHAN AND GILL
GLASGOW	JAMES MACLEHOSE.

Brebis Pt

Tega

Gebu   Watu...

A   G   A

Lebaluga

Sta...

Mt Slamet

Poomolingo

Poorachera

A   N   ...

Strayor

Bangoo

Mjiratjo

Silapi

Shilpadden
Bay

Karan

I

MAX HAVELAAR

OR THE COFFEE AUCTIONS OF THE DUTCH TRADING COMPANY.

BY

Multatuli.

Eduard Douwes Dekker

Translated from the Original Manuscript by

BARON ALPHONSE NAHUŸS.

EDINBURGH
EDMONSTON & DOUGLAS
1868.

PREFACE.

MAX HAVELAAR was published a few years ago, and caused such a sensation in Holland as was never before experienced in that country. The author wrote it under the pseudonym of Multatuli, but his real name, Eduard Douwes Dekker, formerly Assistant Resident of the Dutch Government in Java, at once became known. Full of fire, and overflowing with enthusiasm, the author presented it to his countrymen in the form of a novel,— a book wherein he made them acquainted with the incredible extortions and tyranny of which the natives of the Dutch Indies, "that magnificent empire of Insulind, which winds about the equator like a garland of emeralds," are the victims, and how he tried in vain, while still in the service of the Government, to put an end to the cruel oppressions that happen every day in those countries. Though some considered his book to be merely an interesting and captivating novel, the author maintained that it contained nothing but facts. He boldly asked the Dutch Government to prove the *substance* of his book to be false, but its truth has never been disputed. At the International Congress for the promotion of Social Sciences at Amsterdam, in 1863, he challenged his countrymen to refute him, but there was no champion to accept the challenge. In short, Mr. Douwes Dekker, who had been a functionary in the service of the Dutch Government for the space of seventeen years, rather understated than overstated the truth. Not a single fact was ever contested in Holland, and he is still ready to prove his statements.[1] In the Dutch Parliament nobody answered a single word, but Mr. Van Twist, ex-Governor-General of the Dutch Indies, who, on being appealed to by the Baron Van Hoevell, said that he could *perhaps* refute Max Havelaar, but that it was not his interest to do so.

The book proves that what was formerly written in *Uncle Tom's Cabin* of the cruelties perpetrated upon the

[1] Mr. Veth, the well-known learned Orientalist at Leyden, who made a special study of Indian matters, declared that Multatuli understated the truth, and quoted many authors, such as Mr. Vitalis and others, who had published accounts of scenes and facts much more shocking than he had depicted. Mr. Veth complimented Multatuli upon his moderation, saying that he displayed a mastership of art in not exhausting the subject.

slaves in America, is nothing in comparison to what happens every day in the Dutch Indies.

"Max Havelaar" is the name under which the author chooses to describe his experiences in the East; in the first chapters of the book he has just returned from India, and he meets an old school-companion, at that time a coffee-broker, a Mr. Drystubble. This Mr. Drystubble is very rich, and the author being just then very poor, the latter asks his old school-fellow to be security for the publishing of his book. At first Mr. Drystubble will not hear of this, but afterwards, when he perceives that it will be of some advantage to himself, he consents. Drystubble is a very characteristic person, knowing nothing beyond his trade, a great egotist, and is represented by the author with true wit and humour, in order to show the extreme contrast between himself and . . . . some of his countrymen, whom he may perhaps have met with since his return from Java. At that time the author wears a plaid or shawl, and Mr. Drystubble therefore speaks always of him as Mr. Shawlman. A few months after the publication of *Max Havelaar*, one of the most eminent members of the Dutch Parliament avowed that this book had struck the whole country with horror. In vain the Dutch tried to make a party question of it. The author openly declared that he belonged neither to the Liberal nor to the Conservative party; but that he placed himself under the banner of RIGHT, EQUITY, and HUMANITY. As soon, however, as he professed to be a mere friend of mankind, without bias to any political party, the official world avoided even to pronounce his name, and affected to have forgotten the man whose conduct had before been considered as a reproof, and whose influence menaced danger to people in place. Instead of accepting the challenge, it seemed more worthy to fight the battle out with the vile weapons of abuse and slander. Of course the reader will not regard Mr. Drystubble's nonsensical and hypocritical observations as the sentiments of our author. It is precisely Multatuli's intention to make Drystubble odious, and his philosophy absurd, though sometimes he speaks truth and common-sense—for he is a type of a part of the Dutch nation.

So much for the tendency of the book. Need I say that it will do honour to the literature of any language, and that it may be read as well for profit as for amusement? But *Max Havelaar* is immortal, not because of literary art or talent, but because of the cause he advocates. I think that every one who admires Harriet Beecher Stowe's immortal pleading, ought likewise to read Multatuli's accusation. I compare *Max Havelaar* to *Uncle Tom's Cabin*, but I do not compare Multatuli, the champion and the martyr of humanity and justice, to Mrs. Stowe, for I am not aware that that lady, with all her merits, has sacrificed future fortune, and all that makes life agreeable, for a principle—for right and equity—as has been done by Eduard Douwes Dekker. *Max Havelaar* bears evidence of having been written by a genius of that order which only appears at long intervals in the world's history. His mind embraces in its intellectual compass all mankind, regardless of race or caste. By the diffusion of this book a bond will be formed embracing all lovers of genius and justice throughout the world.

It was the intention of the author to have had his work translated into all the European languages. Unfortunately he *unwittingly* disposed of the property of his own book, and if it had not thus been "legally" withheld from the people of Holland, it is probable that I should not have been its translator ; but I have been constrained to make known as widely as possible the sad truth regarding the mal-administration of laws in themselves good, by the Dutch Government in her Indian dependencies. To the British nation the facts will be new, as the books published in England on Dutch India are few in number, superficial in character, and give no idea of the condition of the native population. I cannot judge of English politics or about British India, but however perfect British rule may be, it cannot be so perfect that it has nothing more to learn.

ALPHONSE JOHAN BERNARD HORSTMAR NAHUŸS.

THE HAGUE,
January 17, 1868.

TO

Everdine Huberte, Baroness Wijnbergen.

"J'ai souvent entendu plaindre les femmes de poëte, et sans doute, pour tenir dignement dans la vie ce difficile emploi, aucune qualité n'est de trop. Le plus rare ensemble de mérites n'est que le strict nécessaire, et ne suffit même pas toujours au commun bonheur. Voir sans cesse la muse en tiers dans vos plus familiers entretiens, —recueillir dans ses bras et soigner ce poëte qui est votre mari, quand il vous revient meurtri par les déceptions de sa tâche ;—ou bien le voir s'envoler à la poursuite de sa chimère . . . voilà l'ordinaire de l'existence pour une femme de poëte. Oui, mais aussi il y a le chapître des compensations, l'heure des lauriers qu'il a gagnés à la sueur de son génie, et qu'il dépose pieusement aux pieds de la femme légitimement aimée, aux genoux de l'Antigone qui sert de guide en ce monde à cet 'aveugle errant ;'—

"Car, ne vous-y-trompez-pas : presque tous les petit-fils d'Homère sont plus ou moins aveugles à leur façon ;—ils voient ce que nous ne voyons pas ; leurs regards pénètrent plus haut et plus au fond que les nôtres ; mais ils ne savent pas voir droit devant eux leur petit bonhomme de chemin, et il seraient capables de trébucher et de se casser le nez sur le moindre caillou, s'il leur fallait cheminer sans soutien, dans ces vallées de prose où demeure la vie."

(HENRY DE PÈNE.)

OFFICER. My Lord, this is the man who murdered Betsy.

JUDGE. He must hang for it. How did he do it?

OFFICER. He cut up her body in little pieces, and salted them.

JUDGE. He is a great criminal. He must hang for it.

LOTHARIO. My Lord, I did not murder Betsy: I fed and clothed and cherished her. I can call witnesses who will prove me to be a good man, and no murderer.

JUDGE. You must hang. You blacken your crime by your self-sufficiency. It ill becomes one who . . . . is accused of anything to set up for a good man.

LOTHARIO. But, my Lord, ... there are witnesses to prove it; and as I am now accused of murder . . . .

JUDGE. You must hang for it. You cut up Betsy—you salted the pieces—and you are satisfied with your conduct,—three capital counts——who are you, my good woman?

WOMAN. I am Betsy.

LOTHARIO. Thank God! You see, my Lord, that I did not murder her.

JUDGE. Humph!——ay——what!——What about the salting?

BETSY. No, my Lord, he did not salt me:——on the contrary, he did many things for me . . . . he is a worthy man!

LOTHARIO. You hear, my Lord, she says I am an honest man.

JUDGE. Humph!——the third count remains. Officer, remove the prisoner, he must hang for it; he is guilty of self-conceit.

(*Unpublished Play.*)

CHAPTER I.

I AM a coffee-broker, and live at No. 37 Laurier Canal, Amsterdam. I am not accustomed to write novels or works of that kind; therefore it took me a long time before I could resolve to order a few extra quires of paper and begin this book, which you, dear reader, have just taken in hand, and which you must finish, whether you are a coffee-broker or anything else. Not only that I never wrote anything that resembled a novel, but I even do not like to read such things, because I am a man of business. For many years I have asked myself what is the use of such works, and I am astonished at the impudence with which many a poet or novelist dares to tell you stories which never happened, and often never could have happened at all. If I in my position,—I am a coffee-broker, and live at No. 37 Laurier Canal,—made a statement to a Principal, that is, a person who sells coffee, in which I related only a small part of the lies which form the greater part of poems and novels, he

17   A

would immediately cease to employ me, and go over to Busselinck and Waterman, who are likewise coffee-brokers, —but you need not know their address. Therefore I take good care not to write any novels, nor to advance any false statements. I have always remarked that persons who do so are often badly off. I am forty-three years of age, I have visited the Exchange for the last twenty years, and, therefore, I can come forward whenever you are in want of a person of experience. How many firms do I know which have been utterly ruined! And generally, when looking for the causes of their failure, it appeared to me that they must be attributed to the wrong direction which most of them followed in the beginning.

My maxims are, and will always be, Truth and Common-sense; making, of course, an exception with regard to the Holy Scriptures. The origin of this fault may be traced to our children's poet, Van Alphen,[1] in his very first line, about " dear little babies." What the deuce could make that old gentleman declare himself to be an adorer of my little sister Gertrude, who had weak eyes, or of my brother Gerard, who always played with his nose? and yet, he says, " that he sang those poems inspired by love." I often thought when a child, " My dear fellow, I should like to meet you once, and if you refused me the marbles which I should ask you for, or the

---

[1] Hieronymus Van Alphen, author of *Little Poems for Children*, etc., was born in 1746, died in 1803.

initials of my name in chocolate—my name is Batavus —then I should believe you to be a liar." But I never saw Van Alphen; he was dead, I think, when he told us that my father was my best friend, and that my little dog was so grateful (we never kept any dogs, they are so very dirty); although I was much fonder of little Paul Winser, who lived near us in Batavier Street.

All lies! And yet in this manner education goes on: —"The new little sister came from the vegetable-woman in a big cabbage." "All Dutchmen are brave and generous." "The Romans were glad that the Batavians allowed them to live." "The Bey of Tunis got a colic when he heard the Dutch colours flapping." "The Duke of Alva was a monster."[1] "The ebb-tide (in 1672, I believe) lasted a little longer than usual, only to protect the Netherlands." Nonsense! Holland has remained Holland because our forefathers knew how to manage their affairs, and because they had the true religion—that is the reason. And then came other lies. "A girl is an angel." Whoever first discovered *that* never had any sisters. Love is a bliss; you fly with some dear object or other to the end of the earth. The earth has no end, and such love is all nonsense. Nobody can say that I do not live on good terms with my wife,—she is a daughter of Last and Co., coffee-brokers,—nobody can find fault with our marriage. I am a member of the

[1] See the History of Holland.

fashionable " Artis " club,[1] and she has an Indian shawl which cost £7, 13s. 4d., but yet we never indulged in such a foolish love as would have urged us to fly to the extremities of the earth. When we married, we made an excursion to the Hague. She there bought some flannel, of which I still wear shirts; and further our love has never driven us. So, I say, it is all nonsense and lies! And should my marriage now be less happy than that of those persons who out of pure love become consumptive, or tear the hair out of their heads? Or do you think that my household is less orderly than it would be, if seventeen years ago I had promised my bride in verse that I should marry her? Stuff and nonsense! yet I could have done such a thing as well as any one else; for the making of verses is a profession certainly less difficult than ivory-turning, otherwise how could bon-bons with mottoes be so cheap? Only compare their price with that of two billiard-balls. I have no objection to verses. If you like to put the words into a line, very well; but do not say anything beyond the truth; thus,—

" The clock strikes four
And it rains no more."

I will not say anything against that, if it is indeed four

[1] A club at the Zoological Gardens, whose motto is " Artis Natura magistra."

o'clock, and it has really stopped raining. But if it is a quarter to three, then I, who do not put my words in verse, can say, " It is a quarter to three, and it has stopped raining." But the rhymer, because it rains " no more," is bound to say " four." Either the time or the weather must be changed, and a lie is the result. And it is not rhyming alone that allures young people to untruth. Go to the theatre, and listen to all the lies they tell you. The hero of the piece is saved from being drowned by a person who is on the point of becoming a bankrupt. Then, as we are told, he gives his preserver half his fortune,—a statement that cannot be true, as I proceed to show. When lately my hat was blown by the wind into the Prinsen Canal, I gave the man twopence who brought it back to me, and he was satisfied. I know very well that I ought to have given a little more if he had saved my own self from drowning, but certainly not half my fortune; for it is evident that in such a case, falling twice into the water would quite ruin me. The worst of these scenes on the stage is, that people become so much accustomed to untruths, that they get into the habit of admiring and applauding them. I should like to throw all such applauders into the water, to see how many of them really meant that applause. I, who love truth, hereby give notice, that *I* won't pay half my fortune for being fished up. He who is not satisfied with less, need not touch me. On Sundays only I should give a little more, on account of my gold chain and best coat. Yes! many persons become corrupted by the stage, much more than by novels, for seeing is believing. With tinsel and lace cut out in paper, all looks so very attractive, that is to say, for children and men who are not accustomed to business. And even when they want to represent poverty, their representation is generally a lie. A girl whose father has become a bankrupt, works to support her family. Very well; you see her on the stage, sewing, knitting, or embroidering. Now, do count the stitches which she makes during a whole act. She talks, she sighs, she runs to the window, she does everything except work. Surely the family that can live by such work needs very little. This girl is, of course, the heroine. She has pushed some seducers down-stairs, and cries continually, "Oh, mother, mother!" and thus she represents Virtue. A nice virtue indeed, which takes a year in making a pair of stockings! Does not all this serve to give you false ideas of virtue, and of "labour for daily bread?" All folly and lies! Then her first lover, who was formerly a copying-clerk, but is now immensely rich, returns suddenly, and marries her. Lies again. He who has money does not marry a bankrupt's daughter. You think that such a scene will do on the stage, as an exceptional case, but the audience will mistake the exception for the rule, and thus become demoralized by accustoming themselves to applaud on the *stage*, that which in the *world* every respectable broker or merchant considers to be ridiculous madness. When I was married, we were thirteen of us at the office of my father-in-law, Last and Co.,—and a good deal of business was done there, I can assure you. And now for more lies on the stage :—When the hero walks away in a stiff, stage-like manner, to serve his native country, why does the back-door always open of itself?

And then this Virtue rewarded!—oh, oh! I have been these seventeen years a coffee-broker, at No. 37 Laurier Canal, and I have had a great deal of experience, but I am always much shocked when I see the dear, good truth so distorted. REWARDED Virtue, forsooth! just as if virtue was a trade commodity! It is not so in the world, and it is very good that it is not so, for where would be the real merit if virtue were always rewarded? Why then always invent such shameful lies? There is, for instance, Lucas, the warehouse-porter, who had been in the employ of Last and Co.'s father,—the firm was then Last and Meyer, but the Meyers are no longer in it,—he was really an honest man, in my opinion. Never was a single coffee-bean missing; he went to church very punctually; and was a teetotaller. When my father-in-law was at his country seat at Driebergen, this man kept the house, the cash, and everything. Once the bank paid him seventeen guilders too much, and he returned them. He is now too old and gouty to work, and therefore starves, for our large business transactions require young men. Well, this Lucas has been a very virtuous man—but is he rewarded? Does a prince give him diamonds, or a fairy nice dinners? Certainly not; he is poor, and he remains poor, and that must be so. I cannot help him. We want active young men for our extensive business; but if I could do anything for him, his merit would be rewarded in an easy life, now that he is old. Then if all warehouse-porters, and everybody else became virtuous, all would be rewarded in this world, and there would remain no special reward for the good people hereafter. But on the stage they distort everything—turn everything into lies.

I too am virtuous, but do I ask a reward for that? When my affairs go on well, as they generally do; when my wife and children are healthy, so that I have nothing to do with doctors; when I can put aside every year a small sum for old age; when Fred behaves well, that he may be able to take my place when I retire to my country-seat near Driebergen,—then I am quite satisfied. But all this is only a natural consequence of circumstances, and because I attend to my business. I claim nothing for my virtue; and that I am a virtuous man is evident from my love for truth, which is second only to my great inclination to my Faith—I should like to convince you of this, dear reader, because it is my excuse for writing this book. Another passion equally strong is my love of busi-

ness. I am a coffee-broker, at No. 37 Laurier Canal.
Well, reader, this book owes its existence to my inviolable
love for truth, and my zeal for business. I will tell you
how all this has happened. But as I must now leave you
for some time, being obliged to go to the Exchange, I invite you to a second chapter. Pray, take this with you;
it may be of service to you. Look here,—my card,—I am
the " Co.," since the Meyers went out—old Last is my
father-in-law :—

> *Last & Co.,*
>
> *Coffee=Brokers,*
>
> *No. 37 Laurier Canal.*

CHAPTER II.

Business is slack on the Coffee Exchange. The Spring
Auction will make it right again. Don't suppose, however, that we have nothing to do. At Busselinck and
Waterman's trade is slacker still. It is a strange world
this: one gets a deal of experience by frequenting the
Exchange for twenty years. Only fancy that they have
tried—I mean Busselinck and Waterman—to do me out
of the custom of Ludwig Stern. As I do not know
whether you are familiar with the Exchange, I will tell
you that Stern is an eminent coffee-merchant in Hamburg, who always employed Last and Co. Quite acci-
dentally I found that out—I mean that bungling business
of Busselinck and Waterman. They had offered to reduce the brokerage by one-fourth per cent. They are
low fellows—nothing else. And now look what I have
done to stop them. Any one in my place would perhaps
have written to Ludwig Stern, "that we too would diminish
the brokerage, and that we hoped for consideration on
account of the long services of Last and Co."

I have calculated that our firm, during the last fifty years, has gained four hundred thousand guilders by Stern. Our connexion dates from the beginning of the continental system, when we smuggled Colonial produce and such like things from Heligoland. No, I won't reduce the brokerage.

I went to the Polen coffee-house, ordered pen and paper, and wrote :—

"That because of the many honoured commissions re-
" ceived from North Germany, our business transactions
" had been extended "—[it is the simple truth]—" and that
" this necessitated an augmentation of our staff "—[it is the
truth: no more than yesterday evening our bookkeeper
was in the office after eleven o'clock to look for his spec-
tacles] ;—" that, above all things, we were in great want
" of respectable, educated young men to conduct the Ger-
" man correspondence. That, certainly, there were many
" young Germans in Amsterdam, who possessed the re-
" quisite qualifications, but that a respectable firm "—[it is
the very truth],—" seeing the frivolity and immorality of
" young men, and the daily increasing number of adven-
" turers, and with an eye to the necessity of making cor-
" rectness of conduct go hand in hand with correctness
" in the execution of orders "—[it is the truth, observe,
and nothing but the truth],—" that such a firm—I mean
" Last and Co., coffee-brokers, 37 Laurier Canal—could
" not be anxious enough in engaging new hands."

All that is the simple truth, reader. Do you know

that the young German who always stood at the Exchange, near the seventeenth pillar, has eloped with the daughter of Busselinck and Waterman ? Our Mary, like her, will be thirteen years old in September.

"That I had the honour to hear from Mr. Saffeler "—[Saffeler travels for Stern]—" that the honoured head of " the firm, Ludwig Stern, had a son, Mr. Ernest Stern, " who wished for employment for some time in a Dutch " house."

"That I, mindful of this "—[here I referred again to the immorality of employés, and also to the history of that daughter of Busselinck and Waterman ; it won't do any harm to tell it],—" that I, mindful of this, wished, with " all my heart, to offer Mr. Ernest Stern the German cor- " respondence of our firm."

From delicacy I avoided all allusion to honorarium or salary; yet I said :—

"That if Mr. Ernest Stern would like to stay with us, " at 37 Laurier Canal, my wife would care for him as a " mother, and have his linen mended in the house"—[that is the very truth, for Mary sews and knits very well],—and in conclusion I said, "that we were a reli- " gious family."

The last sentence may do good, for the Sterns are Lutherans. I posted that letter. You understand that old Mr. Stern could not very well give his custom to Busselinck and Waterman, if his son were in our office.

I am very anxious for a reply. But to return to my book. Some time ago I walked one evening through Kalver Street, and stopped looking into a shop where a grocer was diligently sorting a quantity of—

"*Java middling, fine, yellow, Cheribon coffee, slightly damaged,*"

which interested me much, for I am very inquisitive. Suddenly I observed a gentleman standing next to me in front of a bookseller's shop, whom I thought I had seen before, though I endeavoured in vain to recollect him. He, too, seemed to recognise me; for every moment we looked at one another. I must confess, that I really was too much interested in the adulterated coffee immediately to observe, what I saw afterwards, viz., that his clothes were very shabby; otherwise I should not have taken any notice of him; but all of a sudden I thought, perhaps he is a commercial traveller for a German firm, which is in need of a trustworthy broker. He had rather a German face, and appeared something of a traveller too; he was very fair, with blue eyes, and had something about him which made you think that he was a foreigner. Instead of a respectable winter-coat he wore a shawl or plaid, and looked as if he had just ended a long journey. I thought I saw a customer, and gave him an address card, " Last and Co., Coffee-brokers, 37 Laurier Canal." He took it, and holding it near the gaslight looked at it, and said,

" I thank you, but I was mistaken ; I thought I had the pleasure of seeing an old school-fellow, but... Last... that is not the right name."

" Excuse me," I said, for I am always polite, " I am Mr. Drystubble—Batavus Drystubble ; Last and Co. is the firm, coffee-brokers, at No. 37 Laurier Canal."

" Well, Drystubble, don't you know me ? Look me straight in the face."

The more I looked him in the face, the more I remembered having seen him before ; but, strange to say, his face made an impression on me as if I smelt foreign perfumes. Do not laugh at that, reader ; by and by you will see how that was. I feel quite assured that he had not a drop of perfumery about him, and yet I smelt something very strong, something which reminded me of——then I knew him !

" Was it you," I said, " who rescued me from the Greek ?"

" To be sure," said he, " and how are you ?"

I told him that we were thirteen of us in our office, and that we had plenty to do, and then I asked him how he had got on, which I felt quite sorry for afterwards, for it appeared that his pecuniary circumstances were not prosperous, and I dislike poor people, because it is for the most part their own fault, as the Lord would not forsake a person who had served Him faithfully. If I had only said, " We are thirteen of us," and " I wish you goodnight," then I should have got rid of him ; but these

questions and replies made it every minute more difficult
to shake him off. However, I must confess, that if I had
shaken him off you would not have had this book to read,
for it owes its existence to that meeting ! I like to look
at the bright side of everything, and those who do not
are discontented creatures : I can't bear them. Yes, yes,
it was the same person who had rescued me out of the
clutches of the Greek ! Don't think, however, that I
had been taken prisoner by pirates, or that I had had a
brawl in the Levant. I have told you already that I
went, after my marriage, with my wife to the Hague,
where we saw the Museum, and bought flannel in Veene
Street,—the only excursion that my extensive business at
Amsterdam ever allowed me. No ; it was on my account
that he gave a Greek a bloody nose, for always interfer-
ing with other people's business. It was in the year
1834 I think, and in September, the annual fair-time at
Amsterdam. As my parents intended to make a clergy-
man of me, I learned Latin. Afterwards, I often wondered why you must understand Latin to say in Dutch,
" God is good." Enough, I went to the Latin school, now
called the Gymnasium, and there was the fair,—in Amsterdam, I mean. On the Wester Market were booths ;
and if you, reader, are an Amsterdammer, and about my
age, you will remember that in one of them was a most
beautiful girl with black eyes, dressed as a Greek ; her
father too was a Greek, or at least he had the appearance

of a Greek. They sold all sorts of perfumes. I was just old enough to think the girl very beautiful, without having the courage to speak to her. Such an attempt would have been fruitless; for a girl of eighteen thinks a boy of sixteen a child, and there she is quite right. Yet we school-boys always went to the Wester Market to see that girl.

Now, he who stood before me with the plaid was once with us, though some years younger than the rest, and therefore too childish to look at the Grecian girl; but he was dux of our class,—for he was very clever, that I must confess,—and he was very fond of playing, romping, and fighting; therefore he was with us. While we looked from a distance at the Grecian girl (I think we were ten of us), and deliberated how we should set about making acquaintance with her, we made up our minds to put our money together to buy something. But then it was very difficult to know who should be so bold as to speak to the girl. Every one liked it, but nobody dared attempt it. We cast lots, and I was chosen. Now, I confess that I do not like to brave dangers; I am a husband and a father, and think every one who braves danger to be a fool: this you may read in the Bible. It is a great satisfaction for me to find that I think about danger and suchlike things exactly as I did many years ago. I have still the same opinion as I had on that very evening when I stood close to the Greek's booth, with the twelve pence we had put together in my hand. But because of false shame, I dared not say that I had not the courage to do it; besides, I had to advance against my will, for my companions pushed me, and soon I was standing before the booth.

I did not see the girl; I saw nothing. All became green and yellow before my eyes...I stammered out the First Aorist of I do not know which verb...

"*Plait-il?*" said she. I recovered a little and continued,—"Μῆνιν ἀειδε, Θεά," and "that Egypt was a present from the Nile."...I feel quite sure that I should have made her acquaintance if one of my companions had not at that moment given me such a punch in the back that I stumbled with much violence against the booth. I felt a grasp at my neck, a second one much lower, and before I had time to think about my position, I was inside the tent with the Greek, who told me in very intelligible French, that I was a "gamin," and that he would call the "police." Now, I was very near the girl, but it gave me no pleasure at all. I cried, and prayed for mercy, for I was much afraid. But there was no help for it; the Greek took hold of my arm, and kicked me. I looked for my comrades. We had just read that morning about Scævola, who put his hand in the fire——and in our Latin themes we thought it so fine and so elevated—— Pooh! nobody stayed to put his hand in the fire for me!! So I thought. But all of a sudden, our friend of the Plaid, or Shawlman, as we shall call him, rushed through the back entrance into the booth. He was then neither

B

tall nor strong, and only thirteen years old, but he was a brave and nimble little fellow. I still see the sparkling of his eyes; he gave the Greek a blow with his fist, and I was saved. Afterwards I heard that the Greek drubbed him soundly, but as I have a steady principle never to meddle with other people's business, I ran away immediately, and so I did not see it.

That is the reason why his face reminded me so much of perfumes, and how easy it is in Amsterdam to quarrel with a Greek.

Afterwards, whenever that man was with his booth on the Wester Market, I always went elsewhere to amuse myself.

As I am very fond of philosophical observations, I must be allowed to remark how strangely all things hang together in this world. If the eyes of that girl had been lighter, if her tresses had been shorter, or the boys had not pushed me against the booth, you would not now be reading this book: therefore be thankful for all that happened. Believe me, everything in the world is good, as it is, and those discontented men who are always full of complaints are not my friends. There you have Busselinck and Waterman...; but I must go on, for I have to finish my book before the great Spring Coffee Auction. To speak the truth—for I like truth—I felt it very unpleasant to meet that person again. I saw in a moment that he was not an acquaintance to be proud of. He looked very pale, and when I asked him what o'clock it was, he didn't know! These things a man observes who has frequented the Exchange for twenty years or so, and transacted business there.——I 've witnessed many a crash.

I thought he would turn to the right, and therefore I went to the left; but, lo, he too turned to the left, and so I was in for a conversation with him; but I bore in mind that he did not know what o'clock it was, and perceived at the same time that his coat was buttoned up to his chin, which is a very bad sign, so I did not speak much. He told me that he had been in India, that he was married, and had children. All very well; but this was not very interesting to me. At the *Kapelsteeg*,[1]—I never before went through that *steeg*,[2] because it is not considered respectable,—but this time I intended to turn to the right, and pass through the Kapelsteeg,—I waited till that little street was just behind us, to make him understand that his way was straight on, and then I said very politely—for I am always polite: one never knows whether he may not afterwards want to use a person:—" I am very much pleased that I have seen you again, Sir,...and...and, good-bye...I have to go this way." Then he looked like an idiot at me and sighed, and all of a sudden took hold of one of the buttons of my coat..." *Dear* Drystubble," said he, " I have to ask you something."

[1] *Kapelsteeg* = Butterfly Lane.   [2] *Steeg* = Lane.

I trembled all over. He did not know what o'clock it was, and had to ask me something! Of course I replied that "I had no time to spare, and had to go to the Exchange," though it was evening;—but if you have frequented the Exchange for some twenty years...and a person asks you something without knowing what o'clock it is...I disengaged the button, bade him farewell in a polite manner—for I am always polite—and went through the Kapelsteeg, which I otherwise never do, because it is not fashionable, and fashionableness I like above all things. I hope that nobody saw me.

CHAPTER III.

THE following day, when I came home from the Exchange, Fred told me that somebody had called to speak to me. According to the description it was Shawlman. How could he have found me out——oh, yes, I see, the card !

This made me think of taking my children away from school, for it is very annoying to be troubled twenty or thirty years afterwards by a school-companion who wears a shawl instead of a coat, and who does not know what o'clock it is. I have also forbidden Fred to go to the Wester Market when there are booths.

Next day I received a letter with a large parcel. I began at once to read :

" DEAR DRYSTUBBLE !" [I think he ought to have written ' Sir,' because I am a broker.] " Yesterday I called " at your house with the intention of asking you a favour. " I believe you are in good circumstances "—[that is true; we are thirteen of us in our office],—" and I should like " to use your credit to bring about a matter of great im-

" portance to me."—[Should you not think that he would
rather have given me a commission for the Spring Auction?]—"Through many misfortunes I stand somewhat
" in need of money."—[Somewhat! he had no shirt on his
back; this is what he calls somewhat!]—" I cannot give
" my dear wife everything that is necessary to make life
" agreeable, and the education of my children is, from
" pecuniary impediments, not as I should like it to be."—
[To make life agreeable——? education of children——?
Do you think that he wishes to take a season ticket for
his wife at the opera, and place his children in a
gymnasium at Geneva? It was autumn, and very cold,
—he lived in a garret, and without fire. When I received
that letter I was ignorant of this, but afterwards I went
to him, and I am still angry at the foolish style of his
letter. What the deuce!——Whoever is poor may say
it;——there must be poor people; that is necessary in
society. If he does not ask charity, if he annoys nobody,
I don't care for his poverty, but disguising the matter is
very improper. Now, let us see what more he has to
say.]—"As I am obliged to provide for my household, I
" have resolved to make use of a talent which, as I be-
" lieve, I am in possession of. I am a poet——"—[Pshaw!
you know, reader, how I and all reasonable men think
about that] " ——and writer. Since childhood I have
" expressed my feelings in verse, and afterwards, too, I
" always wrote down in poetry the sensations of my soul.

" I believe that I have made some valuable pieces, and I
" want a publisher for them.   This, then, is the difficulty.
" I am unknown to the public, and the publishers judge
" of works more according to the reputation of the author
" than the value of the contents."—[Exactly as we judge
of the coffee, according to the reputation of the trade-
marks.]—" The merit of my work can only be established
" by publication ; and the booksellers require payment in
" advance of all the expenses"—[There they are quite
right]—"which is at present not convenient to me.   I
" am, however, so convinced that my book would clear
" the expenses, that I could pledge my word for it, and
" as I am encouraged by our meeting of the day before
" yesterday,"—[That is what he calls being encouraged!]—
" I have resolved to ask you to be surety for me to a
" bookseller for the expenses of a first edition, even if it
" were only a small book.   I give you the choice of works
" for that first experiment.   In the accompanying parcel
" you will find many manuscripts ; from which you will
" see that I have thought, worked, and experienced
much "—[I never heard that he had any business at
all] ;—"and if I am not a stranger to the talent of ex-
" pressing myself well, my ill success will not be due to
" any want of impressions.   In hopes of a kind answer,
" I remain your old school-fellow"————[And he signed
this with his name ; but I make a secret of that, because
I do not like to bring discredit on any one.]

Dear reader, you can understand how foolish I looked in being made all at once a broker in verses. I am quite sure that if Shawlman—so I will continue to call him —had seen me by daylight, he would not have dared to ask me such a favour; for respectability and dignity cannot be concealed; but it was evening, and therefore I don't mind.

Of course, I would have nothing to do with this nonsense. I should have returned the parcel, but that I did not know where he lived, and I heard nothing of him. I thought that he was ill, or dead. Last week there was a party at the Rosemeyers, who are sugar-brokers. Fred went out for the first time with us; he is sixteen, and I think it right that a young man at that age should see something of the world; otherwise he will go to the Wester Market, or somewhere else. The girls had been playing on the piano and singing, and at dessert they teased each other about something that seemed to have happened in the front room while we played at whist in the back room—something in which Fred was concerned.

"Yes, yes, Louise," said Betsy Rosemeyer; "you did cry. Papa, Fred made Louise cry."

My wife said that Fred should not go out again if he was so naughty; she thought that he had pinched Louise, or something like that, which is not proper, and I, too, made preparations to say a few words about it,

when Louise said : "No, no, Fred was very kind ; I
should like him to do it again !"

"What then ?" He had not pinched her ; he had been
reciting, that was all. Of course the mistress of the
house likes to have some fun at dessert,—it enlivens the
company. Mrs. Rosemeyer thought that what had made
Louise cry would amuse us too, and therefore asked
Fred, who was as red as a turkey-cock, to repeat it. I
could not understand what he had done ; I knew his
whole *répertoire*, which consisted of the "Wedding-Party
of the Gods," the books of the Old Testament in rhyme,
and an episode from the "Wedding of Camacho," which
boys always like so much, because it is rather funny ;
and what there was in all this that could make any one
cry was a riddle to me ; it is true, a girl of that age
weeps very soon.—"Come, Fred ! Please do !"—and Fred
began. As I do not like to stretch the curiosity of the
reader, I will here at once state, that before leaving home
they had opened Shawlman's parcel, and Fred and Mary
had picked out of it a piece of sentimentality, which
afterwards gave me a great deal of trouble. This book
owes its existence to that parcel, and in due time I will
account for it quite becomingly ; for I like to make it
known that I love truth, and am a good man of business.
—[Last and Co., coffee-brokers, at No. 37 Laurier Canal.]

Fred recited a thing full of nonsense. A young man
wrote to his mother that he had been in love, and that

his sweetheart had married another—[there she was quite right I think]—yet that he nevertheless always loved his mother very much. Is that statement true or not? Do you think so many words are wanted to say that? At all events I had eaten a piece of bread and cheese, and nearly finished my second pear, before Fred finished his story. But Louise cried again, and the ladies said that it was very beautiful.

Then Fred, who, I believe, thought he had brought out a masterpiece, told them that he found it in a parcel sent to my house by the man with the shawl; and I explained to the gentlemen how that happened, but I said nothing about the Grecian girl, because Fred was present, neither did I speak of the Kapelsteeg. Every one thought that it was quite right on my part to get rid of that man. Presently you will see that there were other things in the parcel of more solid worth, some of which will appear in this book, because they concern the coffee-auctions of the Company.

Afterwards, the publisher asked me whether I would not add to the work the piece or poem which Fred had recited. I consented, but I wish it to be known that I am not responsible for the sentiments expressed. All stuff and nonsense. However, I withhold my observations from want of space. I will only remark that the poem was written at " PADANG," in 1843, and that this is of inferior mark—I mean the Padang coffee :—

Moeder! 'k ben wel ver van 't land,
Waar mij 't leven werd geschonken,
Waar mijne eerste tranen blonken,
    Waar ik opwies aan uw hand;
    Waar uw moedertrouw der ziel
Van den knaap haar zorgen wijdde
En hem liefdrijk stond ter zijde,
    En hem ophief als hij viel;
Schijnbaar scheurde 't lot de banden,
    Die ons bonden, wreed van een, . . .
'k Sta hier wel aan vreemde stranden
    Met mij zelf, en God . . . alleen, . . .

Maar toch, moeder, wat me griefde,
    Wat mij vreugd gaf of verdriet,
Moeder! twijfel aan de liefde,
    Aan het hart uws lievlings niet!

't Is nog naauwlijks twee paar jaren,
    Toen ik 't laatst op gindschen grond
Zwijgend aan den oever stond
Om de toekomst in te staren;
    Toen ik 't schoone tot mij riep
Dat ik van die toekomst wachtte
En het heden stout verachtte
    En mij paradijzen schiep;

Toen, door alle stoornis heen
    Die zich opdeed voor mijn schreên,
't Hart zich koen een uitweg baande,
En zich droomend zalig waande . . .

    Maar die tijd, sinds 't laatst vaarwel
Hoe gezwind ons ook onttogen,
    Onbevatbaar bliksemsnel,
Als een schim voorbijgevlogen, . . .
    O, hij liet in 't voorwaartsgaan,
    Diepe, diepe sporen staan!
'k Proefde vreugde en smart met één,
'k Heb gedacht en 'k heb gestreden,
'k Heb gejuicht en 'k heb gebeden, . . .
    't Is me als vlogen eeuwen heen!
    'k Heb naar levensheil gestreefd,
'k Heb gevonden en verloren,
En, een kind nog kort te voren,
    Jaren in één uur doorleefd. . . .
        *   *   *   *
'k Minde een meisje. Heel mijn leven
    Scheen mij door die liefde schoon;
    'k Zag in haar een eerekroon,
Als een eindloon van mijn streven,
Mij door God ten doel gegeven;—
    Zalig door den reinen schat,

Die Zijn zorg mij toegewogen,
  Die Zijn gunst geschonken had,
Dankte ik met een traan in de oogen ;...
  Liefde was met godsdienst één,
En 't gemoed, dat opgetogen,
Dankend opsteeg tot den Hoogen
  Dankte en bad voor haar alleen ! . . .

Zorgen baarde mij die liefde,
  Onrust kwelde mij het hart,
  En ondraaglijk was de smart,
Die mij 't week gemoed doorgriefde.
    'k Heb slechts angst en leed gegaêrd,
Waar ik 't hoogst genot verwachtte,
En voor 't heil waarnaar ik trachtte,
  Was mij gif en wee bewaard. . . .

'k Vond genot in 't lijdend zwijgen !
  'k Stond standvastig hopend daar ;
Onspoed deed den prijs mij stijgen, . . .
  'k Droeg en leed zoo graag voor haar !
'k Telde ramp noch onspoedsslagen,
  Vreugde schiep ik in verdriet,
Alles, alles wilde ik dragen, . . .
  Roofde 't lot mij haar slechts niet.

*   *   *   *

  Wat is min die eens *begon*,
Bij de liefde *met* het leven
't Kind door God in 't hart gedreven
  Toen het nog niet staam'len kon ! . . .
  Toen het aan de moederborst,

Naauw den moederschoot onttogen,
  't Eerste vocht vond voor den dorst,
't Eerste licht in Moederoogen ? . . .
  Neen, geen band die vaster bindt,
Vaster harten houdt omsloten,
Dan de band, door *God* gesloten,
  Tusschen 't moederhart en 't kind
En een hart, dat zóó zich hechtte
  Aan het schoon, dat even blonk,
  Dat mij niets dan doornen schonk,
En geen enkel bloempje vlechtte, . . .
  Zou *datzelfde* hart de trouw
Van het moederhart vergeten ; —
  En de liefde van de vrouw,
Die mijne eerste kinderkreten
  Opving in 't bezorgd gemoed,—
Die mij, als ik weende, suste,
Traantjes van de wangen kuste, . . .
  Die mij voedde met haar bloed ? . . .

*   *   *   *

'k Ben hier vèr van wat het leven
Ginds ons zoets en schoons kan geven ;
  En 't genot van d' eerste jeugd,
Vaak geroemd en hoog geprezen,
Kan wel hier mijn deel niet wezen ;
  't Eenzaam harte kent geen vreugd.
Steil en doornig zijn mijn paden,
  Onspoed drukt mij diep ter neêr,
En de last mij opgeladen
  Knelt me, en doet het hart mij zeer ; —
Laat het slechts mijn tranen tuigen,

Als zoo menig moed'loos uur
Me in den boezem der Natuur,
't Hoofd zoo treurig neêr doet buigen,...
Vaak als mij de moed ontzonk,
Is de zucht mij schier ontvloden :
" Vader ! schenk mij bij de dooden,
Wat het leven mij niet schonk !—
Vader ! geef me aan gene zijde,
Als de mond des doods mij kust,—

Vader ! geef me aan gene zijde
Wat ik hier niet smaakte... RUST !"
Maar, bestervend op mijn lippen,
Steeg die beê niet tot den Heer, . . .
'k Boog wel bei mijn knieën neer,—
'k Voelde wel een zucht me ontglip-
pen,—
Maar het was : " *nog niet, o Heer !*
Geef mij eerst mijn moeder weêr ! "

[The translator ventures with great diffidence, for he knows
how much beauty and tenderness have been lost in the translation, to give an English version of the Poem.]

O mother dear, I 'm far from home,
The land that gave me birth :
All hopeless and forlorn I roam,
A stranger upon earth.

'Twas in that home the dewy tear
First glistened in mine eyes,
Thy gentle hand dispelled my fear :
A mother's love ne'er dies !

'Twas there thy faithful soul watched
Thy helpless little child,   [o'er
Guiding the feet untried before,
With word and look so mild.

But Destiny destroyed the band
That joined us two in one ;
And now upon a foreign strand
I am, with God, alone !

Thy love, my mother dear, does still
In sorrow and in joy,
With undiminished ardour fill
The heart of thy loved boy.

At home, 'tis scarce four years ago,—
I stand upon the shore,
And think I see in future scenes,
Beauties unknown before.

At once the present I despise,
    And dreaming, think me blest :
I make myself a Paradise,
    Regardless of the rest.

I said farewell : I rue it now :
    'Twas all that phantom scene,
Which disappeared so soon ! O how
    Deluded I have been !

And time which fled with lightning's
    Deep traces left behind :   [wing,
It dried up the affections' spring—
    Destroyed my peace of mind.

I 've tested joy, I 've tested grief,
    I 've thought, and I have striven,
With earnest prayer have sought relief,
    But still I 'm tempest-driven.

I 've striven after bliss in life,
    I 've found and lost the power :
I am a child grown old in strife—
    Whole ages in an hour.

O mother dear, will you believe ?
    (God knows that I lie not),
O mother dear, as truth receive,
    That you are not forgot.

I loved a girl who seemed to be
    A treasure from on high,
By God Almighty given me,
    I knew not how or why.

And Him I thanked with happy tears,
    For making her my own,
My sighs were lost in transient joy,
    I prayed for her alone.

Yet love induced a weight of care,
    And trouble filled my breast ;
I found but pain and sorrow there,
    Where I had looked for rest !

I suffered gladly for her sake,
    In sorrows doubly dear ;—
No sacrifice but I would make
    So fate would leave her here !

Her image rooted in my heart,
    Till life's last sigh shall stand,
When *we* shall join no more to part
    In her dear fatherland.

But what is such a blighted love,
    To that with life begun—
A love implanted from above—
    Th' affection of a son !

The babe just taken from the womb,
    Draws from its mother's eyes
A light to guide him through the gloom
    That all around him lies.

He draws from out his mother's breast
    A stream that gives him life :
Her faithfulness insures his rest,
    Protects from early strife !

She treasures up his childish freaks,
  And soothes him when he cries,
Kisses the tears from off his cheeks
  With love that never dies !

O mother dear, will you believe
  Your son does love you yet ?
O mother dear, will you believe
  Your son does not forget ?

I'm far away from all but thought
  Of yonder better sphere ;
The joys of early youth I 've sought :
  I cannot find them here.

My lonely heart for ever mourns :
  I'm burdened heavily ;
My paths obstructed with the thorns
  Of long adversity.

In Nature's bosom oft have I
  Let fall a flood of tears ;

And even oft been heard to sigh,
  When overwhelmed with fears :—

" O Father, give me with the dead,
  What, living, I'm denied :
O Father, stretch me on the bed
  Whereon my loved one died !

" O Father, give me at their side,
  Of all thy gifts the best—
O Father, give me at their side,
  What here I yearn for—Rest ! "

But this rebellious hopeless sigh,
  Scarce uttered, died away ;
It went not up to God on high,
  And I knelt down to pray :—

" Not yet, my Father, take me hence,
  Though quivering on the rack—
O take me not, my Father, hence ;
  But give my mother back ! "

CHAPTER IV.

BEFORE I go on, I must tell you that young Mr. Stern has come; he is a good fellow. He seems to be active and clever, but I believe that he—as the Germans call it, " *Schwärmt.*" Mary is thirteen. His outfit is very nice, and he has got a copybook, in which to practise the Dutch style. I wonder whether I shall soon receive an order from Ludwig Stern. Mary shall embroider a pair of slippers for him,—I mean to say for young Mr. Stern. Busselinck and Waterman have made a mistake,——a respectable broker does not supplant, that's what I say. The day after the party at the Rosemeyers, who are sugar-merchants, I called Fred, and ordered him to fetch Shawlman's parcel. You must know, reader, that I am very precise in my family as to Religion and Morality. Now then, yesterday evening, just when I was eating my first pear, I read in the face of one of the girls that there was something in a verse from the parcel that was not right. I myself had not listened, but I saw that Betsy crumbled her bread, and that was enough for me. You

will perceive, reader, that I am a man of the world. I
made Fred hand over to me "the beautiful poem" of
yesterday evening, and very soon saw the line which caused
Betsy to crumble her bread. They speak there of a child
on the breast of its mother,—I say nothing of that;—but:
"which scarcely left the mother's womb,"—that I disapproved,—to speak about that, I mean,—so did my wife.
Mary is thirteen. Of "cabbage"[1] and such things we do
not speak; but to give all in this way its right name is
not necessary, as I am a great lover of morality. So I
made Fred, who knew it by heart, promise that he would
not repeat it again,—at least not before he was member of
Doctrina,[2] because no young girls come there,—and then I
put it in my writing-desk, I mean the verse. But I wanted
to know whether there was anything else of an offensive
nature in the parcel; I began to look and to inspect everything. I could not read all, for a great deal was written in
foreign languages which I did not understand, but at last
I caught sight of a treatise entitled "Account of the Coffee
Culture in the Residency of Menado." My heart leaped
for joy, because I am a coffee-broker, at No. 37 Laurier
Canal, and "Menado" is a very good mark. So this Shawlman, who made immoral verses, had been in the Coffee
trade. I looked at the parcel with quite a different eye. I
saw treatises in it which I did not completely understand,
but they showed a knowledge of business. There were

[1] See page 3.   [2] A club in Amsterdam.

statements, problems, computations, which I could not understand at all, and everything was done with so much care and exactness, that I, to speak plainly,—for I am a lover of truth,—thought this Shawlman, if perhaps the third clerk left,—a likely event, as he is old and dull,— could very well take his place. Of course I should like, first of all, to have testimony as to his honesty, religion, and respectability, for I will not take anybody into my office until I am satisfied on these points. This is a fixed principle with me. You have seen it in my letter to Ludwig Stern.

I did not care to show Fred that I began to take an interest in the contents of the parcel; and therefore I made him go away. I grew quite dizzy when I took in hand one treatise after another, and read the titles. It is true, there were many verses among them, but also much that was useful, and I was astonished at the variety of the different subjects. I acknowledge—for I love truth —that I, who have always been engaged in the coffee trade, am not in a position to criticise ; but without going so far as criticising, I can pronounce the list of the different titles curious enough. As I have told you the history of the Greek, you know that in my youth I was taught Latin, and though I avoid quotations in my correspondence— which would not be right in a broker's office—yet I thought, on seeing all these things : " De omnibus aliquid, de toto nihil," or " Multa non multum."

Yet I said this more out of anger, and a desire to speak in Latin of all this learning before me, than because I meant it. For if I examined something or other for a time, I was bound to confess that the author appeared to know all about it, and had even a great deal of sound argument in support of his opinions. I found in the parcel treatises and disquisitions—

On the Sanscrit, as the Mother of the Teutonic Languages ;

On the Punishment of Infanticide ;

On the Origin of the Nobility ;

On the Difference between the Ideas : " Infinite time," and " Eternity ;"

On the Theory of Chances ;

On the Book of Job—(there was something else about Job ; but in verse) ;

On the Proteïne in the Atmospheric Air ;

On Russian Politics ;

On the Vowels ;

On the Cellular Prisons ;

On the Ancient Hypotheses ;

Of the " *Horror vacui ;*"

On the Desirableness of the Abolition of Punishments for Slander ;

On the Causes of the Revolt of the Dutch against Spain, not being the Desire for Religious or Political Freedom ;

On Perpetual Motion, the Squaring of the Circle, and
   the Extraction of the Square Root of Surds ;

On the Ponderability of Light ;

On the Decline of Civilisation since the Commencement of Christianity ;

On the Mythology of Iceland ;

On the *Emile* of Rousseau ;

On Sirius as the Centre of the Solar System ;

On Import Duties as Useless, Indelicate, Unjust, and
   Immoral—(of this I had never heard before) ;

On Verse as the Most Ancient Language—(this I do not
   believe) ;

On White Ants ;

On the Unnaturalness of Schools ;

On Hydraulic Matter in connexion with Rice Culture ;

On the Apparent Ascendency of the Western Civilisation ;

On the Price of Java Coffee—(this I have put aside) ;

On the Secret Societies of the Chinese, etc. etc. etc.

And this was not all. I found, not to speak of the verses
—which were in all languages—many small treatises having no title ;—romances in Malay, war-songs in Javanese,
and what not. I found also letters, many of them in languages which I did not understand. Some were directed
to him, others written by him, or were only copies ; but
evidently made for some particular purpose ; for all were
signed by other persons, who testified that they agreed with

the original. I saw also extracts from diaries, notes and thoughts at random—some very much so. I had, as I said before, laid aside some treatises, because it appeared to me that they would be useful in my business, and I live for my business;—but I must confess that I was at a loss to know what to do with the rest. I could not return him the parcel; for I did not know where he lived. It was open now. I could not deny that I had looked at the contents —[and I should not have denied it, being so fond of truth], —because I had tried in vain to do it up exactly as it had been before. Moreover, I could not dissemble that some dissertations on Coffee interested me, and that I should like to make some use of them. Every day I read here and there some pages, and became more and more convinced that the author must have been a coffee-broker, to become so completely acquainted with all sort of things in the world. I am quite sure that the Rosemeyers, who trade in sugar, have not acquired such extensive knowledge.

Now I feared that this Shawlman would drop in unexpectedly, and again have something to tell me. I was now very sorry that I went that evening through the Kapelsteeg, and now felt the impropriety of passing through unfashionable streets. Of course, if he had come he would have asked me for some money, and would have spoken of his parcel. I should perhaps have given him something, and if he had sent me the following day the mass of MSS., it would have been my legal property. Then I should have separated the wheat from the chaff; I should have singled out what I wanted for my book, and should have burned, or thrown into the waste-basket, all the rest. This I could not do now; for if he returned, I should have to produce his property, and he, seeing that I was interested in a couple of treatises of his, would very soon have been induced to ask too high a price;—for nothing gives more ascendency to the seller than the discovery that the buyer stands in need of his wares. Such a position is therefore avoided as much as possible by a merchant who understands his business. I have another idea, previously mentioned, which may prove how a person who frequents the Exchange may yet be open to humane impressions;—it was this: Bastianus, that is the third clerk, who is becoming so old and stupid, has not of late been at the office more than twenty-five days out of the thirty; and when he does come, he often does his work very badly. As an honest man, I am obliged to consult the interests of the firm—Last and Co. since the Meyers have retired—to see that every one does his work; for I may not throw away out of mistaken pity, or excess of sensibility, the money of the firm. This is my prin- ciple. I would rather give that Bastianus three guilders [1] out of my own pocket, than continue to pay him every year seven hundred guilders which he does not deserve.

[1] Five shillings.

I have calculated that this man has drawn during the thirty-four years of his service—as well from Last and Co., as formerly from Last and Meyer, but the Meyers have left—the sum of nearly fifteen thousand guilders (£1250), and that, for a man in his station, is a large sum; which but few can command. He has no right to complain. I came to this calculation through the treatise of Shawlman on multiplication. That Shawlman writes a good hand, I thought he looked very poor, he did not know what o'clock it was—how would it do, I thought, to give him the situation of Bastianus? I should tell him in that case, that it would be his duty to "SIR" me. That he would know without telling, I hope; for a servant cannot call his superior by name, or he would catch it. He could commence with four or five hundred guilders a year.[1] Bastianus had to work many years before he got seven hundred,[2] and I shall then have performed a good deed. Yes, with three hundred guilders he could very well commence, for from his inexperience he would, of course, consider the first year as an apprenticeship, which would be quite right; for he cannot be equal to old hands; I am quite sure that he will be content with two hundred guilders.

But I was not easy about his conduct——he had on a shawl; and, moreover, I don't know where he lives.

A few days afterwards young Mr. Stern and Fred at-

---

[1] £30 to £40.   [2] £58 odds.

tended a book auction at an hotel, the "Wapen van
Bern." I had forbidden Fred to buy anything; but Stern,
who has plenty of money, brought home some rubbish:
that's *his* business. However, Fred brought news, that
he had seen Shawlman, who appeared to be employed at
the auction, in taking the books from the shelves, and
giving them to the auctioneer. Fred said that he looked
very pale, and that a gentleman, who seemed to have the
direction there, had growled at him, for letting fall a
couple of complete volumes of the "Aglaja;"[1] it was,
indeed, very clumsy of him to damage such charming
ladies' books. In the course of the scolding, Fred heard
that he got fifteen pence a day. "Do you think that I
intend to give you fifteen pence a day for nothing?" were
the gentleman's words. I calculated that fifteen pence a
day,—Sundays and holidays not included, otherwise he
would have spoken of so much a month or so much a
year,—make two hundred and twenty-five guilders a year.[2]
I am quick in my decisions—a man who has been in business for so long a time, knows immediately what to do,—
and the following morning I called on Gaafzuiger,[3] the
bookseller who had held the auction. I asked for the
man who had let fall the "Aglaja." "He had his dismissal," said Gaafzuiger; "he was idle, conceited, and sickly."

[1] "The Aglaja"—a Magazine for Ladies, published at Amsterdam.
[2] £18, 15s.
[3] "Gaafzuiger," a very characteristic name: *Gaaf* = talent, gift of
nature, endowment; *zuiger* = sucker.

I bought a box of wafers, and resolved immediately to give Bastianus another trial; I could not make up my mind to turn an old man so unexpectedly upon the streets. To be strict, but, where it is possible, forbearing, has ever been my principle, yet I never lose an opportunity of getting information which may be of use in business, and therefore I asked Gaafzuiger where this Shawlman lived. He gave me the address, and I put it down. I pondered over the book to be brought out; but as I like the truth, I must tell you plainly that I did not know how to manage it. One thing is quite sure: the materials which I found in Shawlman's parcel were important to coffee-brokers. The only question was, how to arrange the materials in a proper way;—every broker knows how important is the right sorting of the parcels. But to write, except correspondence with " Principals," [1] is rather out of my line, and yet I felt that I *must* write; because the future of the trade depended on it. The information which I derived from that parcel of Shawlman, is not such as Last and Co. can exclusively profit by; otherwise any one will understand that I should not take the trouble to have a book printed for Busselinck and Waterman's advantage; because whoever helps a rival in business is a fool;—this is a fixed principle with me. No, I saw that danger menaced the whole coffee-market—a danger that could only be averted by the united forces

[1] See page 1.

of all the brokers; but even these might be insufficient, and the sugar-refiners and indigo-merchants might have to help.

And thinking it over while I write, it seems to me that shipowners too are in some measure interested in it, and the commercial marine——

Certainly, that is true; sail-makers also, and ministers of finance; overseers of the poor, and other ministers; pastry-cooks, and shopkeepers; women, and shipbuilders; wholesale merchants, and retail dealers, and gardeners.—

It is curious how thoughts run on when writing,—my book concerns also millers, clergymen, vendors of Holloway's pills; liquor-distillers, tile-makers, and those who live on the national debt; pumpmakers, and rope-makers; weavers, and butchers; brokers' clerks, and shareholders in the Dutch Trading Company; in fact, on consideration, all other persons——the King too—yes, the King more than any! My book must go throughout the world. There is no help for it——I do not care if Busselinck and Waterman read it——I am not envious; but they are old women and sneaks, that's my opinion. I said the same this morning to young Mr. Stern, when I introduced him at "Artis:"[1] he may write home about it.

So it was, that a few days ago, I didn't know what to do with my book, but Fred showed me a way out of the dilemma. I did not tell him so, because I do not think

---

[1] See note, page 4.

it right to show anybody that I am under an obligation to him ; that is a principle of mine, and a true one. He said, that Stern was such a clever fellow, that he. made rapid progress in the Dutch language, and that he had translated Shawlman's German verses into Dutch. You see, the Dutchman had written in German, and the German translated into Dutch ; if each had stuck to his own language, much trouble would have been spared. But, I thought, if I have my book written by this Stern—— when I have anything to add, I can write a chapter from time to time. Fred may also help—[he has a dictionary of difficulties]. Mary may write the fair copy, and this is a guarantee against all immorality ; for, you understand, that a respectable broker will not give anything into the hands of his daughter that is contrary to Morals and Respectability.

I spoke to the young people about my plan, and they liked it. Only Stern, who, like Germans in general, has a smattering of literature, wanted to have a share in handling the subject. This I did not approve ; but because there would soon be a Spring Auction, and no order had yet come from Ludwig Stern, I did not like to oppose his wishes. So we agreed to the following conditions :—

1. That he should contribute to the work every week two chapters.

2. That I should make no alterations in his contributions.

3. That Fred should correct the grammatical errors.

4. That I should be at liberty to write from time to time a chapter, to give the book a respectable appearance.

5. That the title should be: "The Coffee Auctions of the Dutch Trading Company."

6. That Mary should make the fair copy for the press; but that we should have patience with her on washing-day.

7. That a complete chapter should be read every week at our party.

8. That all immorality should be avoided.

9. That my name should not appear on the title-page, because I am a broker.

10. That Stern should be at liberty to publish German, French, and English translations of my book, because, as he asserted, such works are better understood in foreign countries than at home.

11. That I should send Shawlman paper, pens, and ink. —[Stern insisted very much on this.]

I agreed to everything, for I wanted to finish the book. Stern was ready the following morning with his first chapter,—and here, reader, the question is answered, how it was that a coffee-broker—[Last and Co., No. 37 Laurier Canal]—wrote a book, something like a novel.

Scarcely, however, had Stern commenced the work when difficulties arrested him. In addition to the difficulty of selecting and arranging the materials, he met with, every moment, in the manuscripts words and expressions which he did not understand, and which puzzled even me. These were often Javanese or Malay; and abbreviations also occurred here and there, which we could not decipher. I perceived that we wanted Shawlman; and as I did not think it proper for a young man to fall into bad company, I would not send Stern or Fred to fetch him. I took some sweetmeats with me, which remained after the last party (for I always think about everything), and I went in search of him. His abode was certainly not brilliant; but equality for all men, and of their houses too, is a chimera. He said so himself in his treatise about "Pretensions to Happiness." Moreover, I do not like persons who are always discontented. It was in a back room in the Lange-Leidsche Dwarsstraat. On the basement lived a marine store-keeper, who sold all sorts of things, as cups, saucers, furniture, old books, glasses, portraits of Van Speyk, and so on. I was very anxious not to break anything, for such people always ask more money for the things than they are worth. A little girl was sitting on the steps before the house, and dressing her doll. I inquired if Mr. Shawlman lived there; she ran away; and her mother made her appearance.

"Yes, sir, he lives here. Your honour has only to go upstairs, to the first landing, then to the second, on to the third, and your honour is there. Minnie, go and say that there is a gentleman come. Who can she say, sir?" I said that I was Mr. Drystubble, coffee-broker, at No. 37 Laurier Canal, but that I should introduce myself. 1 mounted as high as they told me, and heard on the third landing the voice of a child singing, " Papa will come soon, —sweet papa." I knocked, and the door was opened by a woman or lady,—I did not know what to think of her. She looked very pale, and her features wore signs of fatigue. She made me think of my wife when washing-day is over. She was dressed in a long white gown or robe without waist-band, which descended to her knees, and was fastened in front with a black pin. Instead of a respectable skirt, she wore underneath a piece of dark linen covered with flowers,—which seemed to be wrapt round her body, hips, and knees very tightly. There was no trace of the folds, width, or amplitude becoming a woman. I was glad that I did not send Fred; for her dress seemed to be extremely immodest, and the strange-ness of it was still heightened by the gracefulness of her movements, as if she thought herself quite right in this way, and seemed quite unconscious that she did not look like other women. I also perceived, that she was not at all perplexed at my arrival : she did not hide anything underneath the table, did not move the chairs,—in a word, she did not do as is generally done, when a stranger of respectable appearance arrives.

She had combed her hair back like a Chinese, and bound it behind her head in a sort of knot. Afterwards I heard that her dress is a sort of Indian costume, which they call there *Sarong* and *Kabaai*, but I thought it very ugly.

"Are you Shawlman's wife?" I asked.

"To whom have I the honour to speak?" she said, and that in a tone which seemed to me as if she meant that I might have said *honour* too.

Now, I dislike compliments. With a "Principal" it is a different thing, and I have been too long a man of business not to know my position, but to give myself much trouble on a third storey, I did not think necessary. So I said briefly that I was Mr. Drystubble, coffee-broker, at No. 37 Laurier Canal, and that I wanted to speak to her husband.

She pointed me to a little chair, and took a little girl on her lap, that was playing on the ground. The little boy whom I had overheard singing looked steadily at me, having viewed me from head to foot. He also, though only six years old, appeared to be not at all perplexed. He was dressed in a very strange way, his wide trousers scarcely reached half-way down the thigh, and his legs were naked to the ankles.—Very indecent, I think. "Do you come to speak to papa?" he asked all of a sudden; and I saw at once that he had been badly brought up, otherwise he would have said "Sir." But as I was a little out of countenance, and wanted to speak, I replied—

"Yes, my boy, I am here to speak to your papa; do you think he will be in soon?"

" I don't know.   He went out to look for money to buy
me a box of colours."

" Be quiet, my boy," said the woman.   " Do play with
your pictures or with the puppet-show."

" You know, mamma, that that gentleman took away
everything yesterday."

It appeared that " a gentleman had been there and taken
away everything——" a delightful visit !   The woman appeared to be in trouble, for secretly she wiped away her
tears, whilst she brought the little girl to her brother.

" There," said she, " play a little with *Nonnie.*"—A
strange name.   And so he did.

" Well, my good woman," I asked ; " do you expect
your husband presently ? "

" I do not know,"—— she replied.

Then the little boy who had been playing with his sister,
left her and asked me :

" Sir, why do you call mamma ' my good woman ?' "

" What then, my boy ? " I said, " how must I address
her ?'

" Well—as others do.——You should say ' my good
woman' to the woman below, who sells saucers."

Now I am a coffee-broker—Last and Co., No. 37 Laurier
Canal : we are thirteen of us at the office, and, including
Stern, who receives no salary, there are fourteen.   Well,
my wife is not Madam, and ought I to call this creature
Madam ?   That is impossible ; every one must remain in

his own station——besides, the bailiffs took away everything. I thought "my good woman" quite right, and
made no alteration.

I asked why Shawlman had not called on me to ask for
his parcel? She seemed to know it, and said that they
had been to Brussels, where he had worked for the "*Indépendance*," but that he could not remain there, because his
articles caused the Journal to be so often refused at the
French frontiers; that a few days ago they had returned
to Amsterdam, where Shawlman expected a situation.

"That was certainly at Gaafzuiger's?" I asked.

"Yes, it was; but that would not do," she said.

I knew more about it than she. He had let the Aglaja
fall, and was moreover idle, conceited, and poorly——
therefore they had turned him out——"And," she went
on, "that he would certainly come to me one of these
days, and was, perhaps, just now going to my house to ask
for a reply to his request."

I said that Shawlman might come, but that he was not
to knock, that being so troublesome for the servant; if he
waited for some time, I said, the door would certainly be
opened, when somebody went out. And then I went
away, and took my sweetmeats along with me; for, to
speak the truth, I did not like the place. I did not feel
comfortable there. A broker is certainly not a common
porter, and I maintain that I am a very respectable man;
I had on my coat with furs, and still she sat as much at

her ease, and spoke as calmly with her children, as if she were alone. Moreover, she seemed to have been crying, and I cannot bear discontented persons: it was cold and unsociable there, because everything had been taken away, and I like sociability. While going home I resolved to give Bastianus another trial, not liking to give anybody his dismissal.

Now it is Stern's first week. Of course much is in it which I do not like; but I must obey stipulation No. 2, and the Rosemeyers are of that opinion; but I think that they flatter Stern, because he has an uncle at Hamburg in the sugar trade.

Shawlman had indeed been at my house; he had spoken to Stern, and given him some information about words and matters which Stern did not understand. I beg the readers to peruse the following chapters; then I promise afterwards something more substantial, composed by myself, Batavus Drystubble, coffee-broker (firm of Last and Co., No. 37 Laurier Canal).

CHAPTER V.

[COMPOSED BY STERN.]

ABOUT ten o'clock in the morning there was an unusual bustle on the principal highway which leads from the district Pandaglang to Lebak. "Principal highway" is, perhaps, too good a name for a wide footpath, which people called out of politeness, and from want of a better term, "the way;" but if you started with a carriage and four from Serang, the capital of Bantam,[1] with the intention of going to Rankas-Betong, the new capital of the Lebak district, you would be sure to reach your destination some time or other. So it *was* a road. It is true you often stuck in the mud, which in the Bantam lowlands is so heavy, clayey, and sticky, that travellers are often obliged to ask the assistance of the inhabitants of the villages in the neighbourhood—even of those who are not in the neighbourhood, for villages are not numerous in these regions ;—but if you did succeed at last in getting the assistance of a score of husbandmen, it did not take long

---

[1] A Residency (province).

to get horses and carriage again on firm ground. The
coachman smacked his whip, the running boys—in Europe
you would call them, I think, "palfreniers,"—but no, you
have nothing in Europe which can give you an idea of
these running boys.—These incomparable running boys,
with their short thin switches, tearing alongside of the
four horses, making indescribable noises, and beating the
horses under the belly to encourage them, till—the vexa-
tious moment arrived when the carriage once more sank
in the mud. Then the cry for help was renewed; you
waited till assistance was proffered, and then slowly re-
sumed the journey. Often when I passed that way, I
expected to meet a carriage with travellers of the last
century, who had stuck in the mud, and been forgotten.
But this never happened to me. Therefore I suppose,
that every one who went that way, arrived at last at his
destination. You would be mistaken, if you thought that
all the roads in Java were in the same bad state. The
military road with many branches, which Marshal Daendels[1] constructed with great sacrifice of men, is indeed a
masterpiece, and you are struck with wonder at the
energy of the man, who, notwithstanding many obstacles,

[1] Herman Willem Daendels was born at Hattem (province of Gel-
derland), October 21, 1762. His father was Burgomaster of Hattem.
In 1787 he went to France, and in 1793 he took part in the expedi-
tion into Flanders under General Dumouriez. Afterwards he entered
the service of the Dutch Republic, and in 1799 distinguished himself
in the campaign against the Anglo-Russian army in North Holland. He
tendered his resignation in 1801. In 1808 he was appointed Governor-

raised up by envious opponents at home, dared the displeasure of the population, the discontent of the chiefs,
and succeeded in performing a task, that even now excites
and merits the admiration of every visitor.

No post-horses in Europe, not even in England, Russia,
or Hungary can be compared with those of Java. Over
high mountain ridges, along the brow of precipices that
make you shudder, the heavy-laden travelling carriage
flies on at full speed. The coachman sits on the box as
if nailed to it, hours, yes, whole days successively, and
swings the heavy lash with an iron hand. He can calculate exactly where and how much he must restrain the
galloping horses, in order that, after descending at full
speed from a mountain declivity, he may on reaching that
corner * * *

"O God" (cries the inexperienced traveller),——"we
are going down a precipice, there's no road,——there's an
abyss!" * *

Yes, so it seems. The road bends, and just at the time
when one more bound of the galloping animals would
throw the leaders off the path, the horses turn, and sling
the carriage round the corner. At full gallop they run

General of the Dutch possessions in the East Indies. He was appointed Maréchal de l'Empire in 1807. From 1808-1811 he governed
those colonies. In 1811 he was recalled by Napoleon I., who had in-
corporated Holland. He took part in the campaign of 1812 in Russia.
In 1815 he was appointed Governor of the Dutch possessions on the
coast of New Guinea, where he abolished the slave-trade, and died in
1818.

up the mountain height, which a moment before was
unseen——and the precipice is behind you. Sometimes
the carriage is only supported at the bend by the
wheels on the inside of the curve: centrifugal force has
raised the outside ones off the ground. It needs a great
deal of coolness, not to shut one's eyes, and whoever
travels for the first time in Java, generally writes to his
family in Europe, that he has been in danger of his life;
but he whose home is in Java laughs at that.

Reader, it is not my intention, particularly at the commencement of this history, to waste time in describing
places, scenery, or buildings.—I am too much afraid of
disheartening you, by what would resemble prolixity; and
therefore, until I feel that I have won your attention, till
I observe in your glances and in your countenance that
the destiny of the heroine, who jumps somewhere from a
fourth storey, interests you, I shall not make her hover in
the air, with a bold contempt for all the laws of gravita-
tion, so long as is necessary for the accurate description of
the beauty of the landscape, or the building, that seems to
be put in somewhere to give occasion for a voluminous
essay on mediæval architecture. All those castles resemble
each other. They are invariably of heterogeneous architecture; the main building always dates from some earlier
reign than the wings which are added to it afterwards
under the reign of such and such a king. The towers
are in a dilapidated state. * * * Reader, there are no

towers. A tower is an idea, a dream. There are "half towers," and turrets. The fanaticism which wanted to put towers to the edifices that were erected in honour of this or that saint, did not last long enough to finish them ; and the spire, designed to point out heaven to believers, is generally supported by two or three low battlements on the huge base, which makes you think of the man without thighs at the fair. The towers of village churches only, with their spires, are finished.

It is not very flattering to Western civilisation, that the enthusiasm for an extensive work has very seldom prevailed long enough to see that work finished. I do not now speak of undertakings whose completion was necessary to defray the expenses: whoever wants to know exactly what I mean, must go and see the Cathedral at Cologne. Let him think of the grand conception of that building in the soul of the architect;—of the faith in the hearts of the people, which furnished him with the means to commence and continue that labour;—of the influence of the ideas, which required such a colossus to serve as a visible representation of unseen religious feeling—and let him compare that enthusiasm with the train of ideas, that some centuries afterwards stopped the labour.

There is a profound chasm between Erwin von Steinbach and our architects! I know, that for many years they have been occupied in filling up that chasm; at Cologne too they are again working at the Cathedral.

But will they be able to join the broken wire; will they
be able to find again in our days, what constituted the
power of prelate and builder?—I do not think so. Money
may be contributed, stone and lime may be bought, a
draughtsman may be paid to draw a plan, and a mason to
fix the stones——but the lost and still venerable faith,
that saw in an edifice a poem—a poem of granite, that
spoke very loudly to the people—a poem in marble, that
stood there as an immovable continual eternal prayer,
cannot be purchased with money. *   *   *   *

There was one morning an unusual bustle on the *frontiers* between Lebak and Pandaglang. Hundreds of saddled
horses were on the way, and a thousand men at least, a
large number for that place, ran to and fro in active expectancy. There were the chiefs of the villages, and the
district chiefs of Lebak, all with their followers; and
judging from the beautiful Arab steed, that stood there
in his rich caparison, a chief of great importance must be
there also. Such was the case. The Regent of Lebak,
RADEEN ADHIPATTI, KARTA NATTA NEGARA,[1] had left Rankas-Betong with a numerous retinue, and notwithstanding
his great age had travelled the twelve or thirteen miles
that separated his residence from Pandaglang. A new
Assistant Resident was coming; and custom, which has

---

[1] "Radeen Adhipatti" is his title, and "Karta Natta Negara" his
name.

the force of law in the Indies more than anywhere else, will have it that the officer who is intrusted with the rule of a district must be festively received on his arrival. The Controller, too, was present. He was a man of middle age, and after the death of the last Assistant Resident, being the next in rank, had carried on the government for some months.

As soon as the arrival of the new Assistant Resident was known, a *pendoppo* was erected in great haste; a table and some chairs brought there with some refreshments, and in that 'pendoppo' the Regent, with the Controller, awaited the arrival of the new chief. After a broad-brimmed hat, an umbrella, or a hollow tree, a 'pendoppo' is certainly the most simple representation of the idea "roof."

Picture to yourself four or six bamboo canes, driven into the ground, tied together at the top with other bamboos, on which is placed a cover of the large leaves of the water-palm, called in these regions *atap*, and you will have an idea of such a 'pendoppo.' It is, as you see, as simple as possible, and here it had only to serve as a *pied-à-terre*, for the European and native officials who were there to welcome their new chief.

It was not very correct of me to call the Assistant Resident the "chief" of the Regent. I must explain the machinery of government in these regions. The so-called "Dutch India"—[I think the expression inaccurate, but it is the official term]—as far as regards the relation of its population to the mother country, must be divided into two very distinct great divisions.

One of these consists of tribes whose kings and princes have been content to be tributary to Holland, but have nevertheless retained the direct government, in a greater or less degree, in their own hands. The other division, to which the whole of Java belongs, with a very trifling, perhaps only apparent exception, is totally and directly subject to Holland. There is here no question about tribute, tax, or alliance. The Javanese is a *Dutch subject*. The King of *Holland* is *his* king. The descendants of his former princes and lords are *Dutch* functionaries: they are appointed, transferred, promoted, dismissed, by the Governor-General, who reigns in name of the King. Criminals are condemned and punished by a law made at the Hague. The taxes paid by the Javanese flow into the Exchequer of Holland.

This book will treat chiefly of these *Dutch* possessions, which form an integral part of the kingdom of Holland. The Governor-General is assisted by a Senate, but this Senate has no power to modify his resolutions. At Batavia, the different branches of the Government are divided into departments, with Directors at their head, who form the link between the supreme direction of the Governor-General and the Residents in the provinces. Yet in matters of a political nature these Residents apply directly to the Governor-General.

The title of "Resident" dates its origin from the time when Holland acted the part of a protecting State rather than that of a feudal superior, and was represented at the Courts of the several reigning princes by resident functionaries. The Princes are gone; the Residents have become rulers of provinces; they have acquired the power of prefects. Their position is changed, but the name remains.

It is properly those Residents who represent the Dutch authority in the eyes of the Javanese population, who know neither the Governor-General, nor the Senators of the Indies, nor the Directors at Batavia; they know only the Resident and the functionaries who reign subordinate to him.

A Residency, so called—some of them have a population of one million souls,—is divided into three, four, or five departments or regencies, at the head of each of which is an Assistant Resident. Under these the government is carried on by controllers, overseers, and a number of other officers, who are required for the gathering of the taxes, the superintendence of agriculture, the erection of buildings, for the waterworks, the police, and the administration of justice.

In every department the Assistant Resident is aided by a native chief of high rank, with the title of Regent. Such a Regent, though his relation to the Government and his department is quite that of a *paid* official, always belongs to the high aristocracy of his country, and often to the family of the princes, who have governed in that part or neighbourhood as independent sovereigns. It is very politic in Holland to make use of the ancient feudal influence of the princes, which in Asia is generally very great, and is looked upon by most of the tribes as a part of their religion, because, by making those chiefs paid officers of the Crown, a sort of hierarchy is created, at the head of which is the Dutch Government, in. the person of the Governor-General.

There is nothing new under the sun. Were not the Margraves, the Burgraves, of the German Empire, appointed in the same manner by the Emperor, and generally elected from among the Barons? Without expatiating on the origin of the nobility, which is sufficiently evident, I wish here to insert the observation, that throughout the Indies the same causes have had the same effects as in Europe. If a country must be ruled at a great distance, you will need functionaries to represent the central power. Thus the Romans under their system of military despotism chose prefects from among the generals of the legions who had subjugated a country. Such districts thenceforth remained " provinces," and were ruled as conquests! But when afterwards the central power of the German Empire endeavoured to hold the people in subjection by other means than by material force, as soon as a distant region was considered to belong to the Empire from similarity of

origin, language, and customs, it became necessary to
charge with the management of affairs a person who not
only was at home in that country, but was elevated by his
rank above his fellow-citizens, in order that obedience to
the commands of the Emperor might be rendered more
easy by the military submission of the people to him who
was intrusted with the execution of those commands; and
in this manner the cost of a standing army was altogether
or in part avoided at the expense of the public treasury,
or, as it generally happened, of the provinces themselves,
who had to be watched by an army. So the first Counts
were chosen out of the Barons of the country, and if you
take the word literally, then " Count" is no noble title,
but only the denomination of a person invested with a
certain office. I, therefore, also think, that in the middle
ages the opinion prevailed, that the German Emperor had
the right to appoint " Counts " (governors of districts), and
" Dukes" (commanders of armies), but that the Barons
asserted that they were, as regards their birth, equal to the
Emperor, and were only dependent upon God, except as
regarded their obligation to serve the Emperor, provided
he was elected with their approbation and from among
their number. A Count was invested with an office to
which the Emperor had called him; a Baron considered
himself a Baron " by the grace of God." The Counts represented the Emperor, and as such carried his banners;
a Baron raised men under his colours as a knight. The

circumstance that Counts and Dukes were generally elected
from among the Barons, caused them to add the importance of their employment to the influence which they
derived from their birth; and it seems that afterwards,
especially when people got accustomed to the hereditary
nature of those employments, the precedence arose which
these titles had over that of Baron. Even now-a-days,
many a noble family, without imperial or royal patent,
that is to say, such a family as derives its nobility from
the origin of the country itself, a family which always
was noble, because it was noble—autochthonous—would
refuse an elevation to the title of Count. There are instances of this.

The persons intrusted with the government of such a
county naturally tried to obtain from the Emperor, that
their sons, or, in default of sons, other relations, should
succeed them in their employment. This also happened
very often, though I do not believe that the right to that
succession was ever proved, at least in the case of those
functionaries in the Netherlands, the Counts of Holland,
Zealand, Flanders, Hainault,—the Dukes of Brabant, Gel-
derland, etc. At first it was a favour, soon it became a
custom, at last a necessity; but never did that succession
become a law.

Almost in the same way, as to the choice of persons,--
because there can be no question of similarity of position,
— a native functionary is placed at the head of a district

of Java, who adds to the rank given him by the Government his autochthonous influence, to facilitate the rule of the European functionary representing the Dutch Government. Here, too, hereditary succession, without being established by law, has become a custom. During the life of the Regent this is often arranged; and it is regarded as a reward for zeal and trust, if they give him the promise that he shall be succeeded by his son. There must be very important reasons to cause a departure from that rule, and where this is necessary, a successor is generally elected out of the members of the same family. The relation between European officials and such high-placed Javanese nobles is very delicate. The Assistant Resident of a district is the responsible person; he has his instructions, and is considered to be the chief of the district. Still the Regent is much his superior—through local knowledge, birth, influence on the population, pecuniary revenues, and manner of living. Moreover, a Regent, as representing the Javanese element, and being considered the mouthpiece of the hundred thousand or more inhabitants of his regency, is also in the eyes of the Government a much more important personage than the simple European officer, whose discontent need not be feared, because they can get many others in his place, whilst the displeasure of a Regent would become perhaps the germ of disturbance or revolt.

From all this arises the strange reality that the inferior actually commands the superior. The Assistant Resident orders the Regent to make statements to him; he orders him to send labourers to work at the bridges and roads; he orders him to gather the taxes; he summons him to the Council, of which he, the Assistant Resident, is President; he blames him where he is guilty of neglect of duty. This peculiar relation is made possible only by very polite forms, which need not exclude either cordiality, or where it is necessary, severity; and I believe that the demeanour to be maintained in this relation is very well described in the official instructions on the subject, as follows, "The European functionary has to treat the native functionary, who aids him, as his younger brother." But he must not forget that this younger brother is very much loved, or feared, by his parents, and in the event of any dispute, his own seniority would immediately be accounted as a motive for taking it amiss that he did not treat his younger brother with more indulgence.

The innate courteousness of the Javanese grandee,—even the common Javanese are much politer than Europeans in the same condition,—makes this apparently difficult relation more tolerable than it otherwise would be.

Let the European have a good education, with some refinement, let him behave himself with a friendly dignity, and he may be assured that the Regent on his part will do all in his power to facilitate his rule. The distasteful command put in an inviting form is punctually performed. The difference in position, birth, wealth, is effaced by the

Regent himself, who raises the European, as Representative of the King of the Netherlands, to his own position; and the result of a relation which, viewed superciliously, would have brought about collision, is very often the source of an agreeable intercourse.

I said that such Regents had precedence over the European functionaries on account of their wealth; and this is a matter of course. The European, when he is summoned to govern a province which in surface is equal to many German duchies, is generally a person of middle or more advanced age, married and a father: he fills an office to gain his livelihood. His pay is only sufficient, and often insufficient, to procure what is necessary for his family. The Regent is "Tommongong," "Adhipatti,"[1] yes, even " Pangerang," that is, a "Javanese prince." The question for him is not that of getting his living; he must live according to his rank.

While the European lives in a house, *his* residence is often a *Kratoon,*[2] with many houses and villages therein. Where the European has a wife with three or four children, he supports a great number of women with their attendants. While the European rides out, followed by a few officers—as many as are necessary to draw up reports on his journey of inspection,—the Regent is followed by hundreds of retainers that belong to his suite, and in the eyes of the people these are inseparable from his high rank.

[1] Titles of nobility.   [2] Castle, palace, etc.

E

The European lives citizen-like; the Regent lives—or is supposed to live—as a Prince.

But all this must be paid for. The Dutch Government which has founded itself on the influence of these Regents, knows this; and therefore nothing is more natural than that it has raised their incomes to a standard that must appear exaggerated to one unacquainted with Indian affairs, but which is in truth very seldom sufficient to meet the expenses that are necessarily incurred by the mode of life of such a native chief.

It is no uncommon thing to find Regents in pecuniary difficulties who have an income of two or three hundred thousand guilders.[1] This is brought about by the princely indifference with which they lavish their money, and neglect to watch their inferiors, by their fondness for buying, and, above all things, the abuse often made of these qualities by Europeans. The revenue of the Javanese grandees may be divided into four parts. In the first place, their fixed monthly pay; secondly, a fixed sum as indemnification for their bought-up rights, which have passed to the Dutch Government; thirdly, a premium on the productions of their regency,—as coffee, sugar, indigo, cinnamon, etc.; and lastly, the arbitrary disposal of the labour and property of their subjects. The two last-mentioned sources of revenue need some explanation. The Javanese is by nature a husbandman; the ground whereon

[1] From £16,600 to £25,000.

he is born, which gives much for little labour, allures him to it, and, above all things, he devotes his whole heart and soul to the cultivating of his rice-fields, in which he is very clever. He grows up in the midst of his *sawahs*, and *gagahs*, and *tipars*;[1] when still very young, he accompanies his father to the field, where he helps him in his labour with plough and spade, in constructing dams and drains to irrigate his fields; he counts his years by harvests; he estimates time by the colour of the blades in his field; he is at home amongst the companions who cut paddy with him; he chooses his wife amongst the girls of the *dessah*,[2] who every evening tread the rice with joyous songs. The possession of a few buffaloes for ploughing is the ideal of his dreams. The cultivation of rice is in Java what the vintage is in the Rhine provinces and in the south of France. But there came foreigners from the West, who made themselves masters of the country. They wished to profit by the fertility of the soil, and ordered the native to devote a part of his time and labour to the cultivation of other things which should produce higher profits in the markets of Europe. To persuade the lower orders to do so, they only had to follow a very simple policy. The Javanese obeys his chiefs; to win the chiefs, it was only necessary to give them a part of the gain,—and success was complete.

[1] Rice-fields. The difference between *sawahs*, and *gagahs*, and *tipars* is in the mode of cultivation.
[2] Javanese village.

To be convinced of the success of that policy we need only consider the immense quantity of Javanese products sold in Holland; and we shall also be convinced of its injustice, for, if anybody should ask if the husbandman himself gets a reward in proportion to that quantity, then I must give a negative answer. The Government compels him to cultivate certain products on his ground; it punishes him if he sells what he has produced to any purchaser but itself; and *it* fixes the price actually paid. The expenses of transport to Europe through a privileged trading company are high; the money paid to the chiefs for encouragement increases the prime cost; and because the entire trade *must* produce profit, that profit cannot be got in any other way than by paying the Javanese just enough to keep him from starving, which would lessen the producing power of the nation.

To the European officials, also, a premium is paid in proportion to the produce. It is a fact that the poor Javanese is thus driven by a double force; that he is driven away from his rice-fields; it is a fact that famine is often the consequence of these measures; but the flags of the ships, laden with the harvest that makes Holland rich, are flapping gaily at Batavia, at Samarang, at Soorabaya, at Passarooan, at Bezookie, at Probolingo, at Patjitan, at Tjilatjap.

" FAMINE——? In Java, the rich and fertile, famine?" —Yes, reader, a few years ago whole districts were depopu-

lated by famine ; mothers offered to sell their children for
food, mothers ate their own children.——But then the
mother-country interfered. In the halls of the Dutch
Parliament complaints were made, and the then reigning
Governor had to give orders that THE EXTENSION OF THE
SO-CALLED EUROPEAN MARKET SHOULD NO LONGER BE
PUSHED TO THE EXTREMITY OF FAMINE.

"Oh! this angelic Parliament!——"

This I write with bitterness—what would you think
of a person that could describe such things without
bitterness ?

I have yet to speak of the last and principal source of
the revenues of the native chiefs, viz., their arbitrary disposal of the persons and property of their subjects. According to the general idea in nearly the whole of Asia,
the subject, with all that he possesses, belongs to the
prince. The descendants or relatives of the former princes
like to profit by the ignorance of the people, who do not
yet quite understand that their "Tommongong," "Adhipatti," or "Pangerang" is now a paid official, who has sold
his own rights and theirs for a fixed income, and that thus
the ill-requited labour of the coffee plantation or sugar
field has taken the place of the taxes which they formerly
paid their lords. Hence nothing is more common than
that hundreds of families are summoned from far remote
places to work, without payment, on fields that belong to
the Regent. Nothing is more common than the furnishing

of unpaid-for provisions for the use of the Court of the Regent; and if the Regent happens to cast a longing eye on the horse, the buffalo, the daughter, the wife of the poor man, it would be thought unheard-of if he refused the unconditional surrender of the desired object. There are Regents who make a reasonable use of such arbitrary powers, and who do not exact more of the poor man than is strictly necessary to uphold their rank. Some go a little further, and this injustice is nowhere entirely wanting. And it is very difficult, nay even impossible, entirely to destroy such an abuse, because it is in the nature of the population itself to induce or create it. The Javanese is cordial, above all things where he has to give a proof of attachment to his chief, to the descendant of those whom his forefathers obeyed. He would even think himself wanting in the respect due to his hereditary lord, if he entered his *Kratoon* without presents. These gifts are often of such small value, that to refuse them would be a humiliation, and the usage is rather more like the homage of a child who tries to give utterance to filial love by offering his father a little present, than a tribute to tyrannical despotism.

But the existence of such a good custom makes the abolition of a bad one very difficult.

If the *aloon-aloon*[1] in front of the residence of the

---

[1] *Aloon-aloon*—a square in front of a chief's residence, ornamented with beautiful trees,—called *waringi*.

Regent were in an uncultivated condition, the neighbouring population would be ashamed of it, and much force
would be required to prevent them from clearing that
square of weeds, and putting it in a condition suitable to
the rank of the Regent. To give any payment for this
would be considered as an insult to all. But near this
'aloon-aloon,' or elsewhere, there are 'sawahs' that wait
for the plough, or a channel to bring water, often from a
distance of many miles. Those 'sawahs' belong to the
Regent. He summons the population of whole villages,
whose 'sawahs' need labour as well as his.——There you
have the abuse.

This is known to the Government ; and whosoever reads
the official papers, containing the laws, instructions, regulations, etc., for the functionaries, applauds the humanity
and justice which seem to have influenced those who
made them. Wherever the European is intrusted with
power in the interior of Java, he is clearly told that one
of his first obligations is to prevent the self-abasement of
the people, and to protect them from the covetousness of
the chiefs ; and, as if it were not enough to make this
obligation generally known, a special oath is exacted from
the Assistant Residents that when they enter upon the
government of a province, they will regard this fatherly
care for the population as their first duty.

That is a noble vocation. To maintain justice, to protect the poor against the powerful, to defend the weak

against the superior power of the strong, to recover the
ewe-lamb from the folds of the kingly robber:—well, all
this makes your heart glow with pleasure at the idea that
it is your lot to have so noble a vocation;—and let any
one in the interior of Java, who may be sometimes discontented with his situation or pay, consider the sublime
duty which devolves upon him, and the glorious delight
which the fulfilment of such a duty gives, and he will not
bé desirous of any other reward.   But that duty is by no
means easy.   In the first place, one has exactly to consider where the *use* ends, to make room for *abuse*;—and
where the abuse exists, where robbery has indeed been
committed by the exercise of arbitrary· power, the victims
themselves are, for the most part, accomplices, either from
extreme submission, or from fear, or from distrust of the will
or the power of the man whose duty it is to protect them.
Every one knows, that the European officer can be summoned every moment to another employment, and that
the Regent, the powerful Regent, remains there.   Moreover, there are so many ways of appropriating the property
of a poor ignorant man.   If a *mantrie*[1] says to him that
the Regent wants his horse, the consequence is, that the
wished-for animal is soon found in the Regent's stables;
but this does not mean that the Regent does not intend to
pay handsomely for it some time or other.   If hundreds

[1] *Mantrie* = upper servant—properly an overseer of the building
department, and of agriculture.

of people labour on the fields of a chief, without getting
money for it, this is no proof that *he* makes them do so
for his benefit. Might it not have been his intention to
give them the harvest, having made the philanthropic
calculation that his fields were more fertile than theirs,
and would much better reward their labour?

Besides, where could the European officer get witnesses
having the courage to give evidence against their lord the
Regent? And, if he ventured to make an accusation without being able to prove it, where would be the relation of
elder brother, who, in such a case, would have impeached
his younger brother's honour? Where would he then find
the favour of the Government, which gives him bread for
service, but which would take that bread from him, which
would discharge him as incapable, if he rashly accused so
high a personage as an " Adhipatti " or " Pangerang ?"

No, no, that duty is by no means easy! This can be
proved by the fact—apparent to every one—that each
native chief pushes too far the limit of the lawful disposal of labour and property ; that all Assistant Residents
take an oath to resist this, and yet that very seldom a
Regent is accused for abuse of power or arbitrary conduct.

It seems also that there must be an insurmountable
difficulty in *keeping the oath:* " TO PROTECT THE NATIVE
POPULATION AGAINST EXTORTION AND TYRANNY."

CHAPTER VI.

THE Controller Verbrugge was a good man. When you saw him sitting there in his blue cloth dress-coat, embroidered with oak and orange branches on collar and cuffs, you could not have found a better type of the Dutchman in India, who, by the way, is quite different from the Dutchman in Holland. Slow as long as there was nothing to be done; far from that fussiness, which in Europe is mistaken for zeal, but zealous where business required attention; plain, but cordial to those around him; communicative, willing to help, and hospitable; very polite without stiffness; susceptible of good impressions; honest and sincere, without wishing to be a martyr to these qualities;—in short, he was a man, who, as they say, could make himself at home anywhere, yet without making any one think of calling the century by his name—an honour which, in truth, he did not desire.

He was sitting in the middle of the 'pendoppo,' near

the table, which was covered with a white cloth, and well
furnished with viands. Rather impatiently from time to
time, in the words of Mrs. Bluebeard's sister, he asked
the *mandoor*—[that is, the chief of police, and officials
under the Assistant Resident]—if there was nothing to be
seen. Then he got up, tried in vain to make his spurs
clatter on the hard clay floor of the 'pendoppo,' lighted
his cigar, and sat down again. He spoke little; but could
have spoken more, for he was not alone.——I do not refer
to the twenty or thirty Javanese servants, 'mantries,' and
overseers, who sat squatting on the ground in the 'pendoppo,' nor to the numbers who incessantly ran in and out,
nor to those of different rank, that held the horses outside, or rode on horseback;—the Regent of Lebak himself,
Radeen Adhipatti Karta Natta Negara, sat facing him.
To wait is always tiresome: a quarter of an hour seems
an hour; an hour half a day, and so on. Verbrugge might
have been more talkative. The Regent of Lebak was an
intelligent old man, who could speak on many subjects
with sense and judgment: one had only to look at him to
be convinced that most of the Europeans who came in
contact with him had more to learn from him than he
from them. His clear dark eyes contradicted by their fire
the weariness of his features and his grey hairs. What
he said was generally well considered, which is indeed
generally the case with cultivated Orientals; and you
perceived, if you were in a conversation with him, that

you had to consider his words as letters, of which he had
the copy in his archives, in order to recall them if
necessary. This may appear disagreeable to those who
are not accustomed to converse with Javanese grandees,
yet it is very easy to avoid in conversation all topics
that might become a stumbling-block, for *they* will never
abruptly give another direction to the course of the conversation ; because, according to Eastern ideas, this would
be contrary to politeness. Thus every one who has reason
to avoid speaking on a certain subject has only to speak
about insignificant matters, and he may rest assured that
a Javanese chief will not, by giving the conversation an
unwished-for turn, bring him upon ground which he does
not like to tread upon.

On the mode of dealing with these chiefs there are also
different opinions. I think that sincerity alone, without
any attempt at diplomatic prudence, deserves preference.
Be that as it may, Verbrugge began with an observation
on the weather and the rain.

" Yes, Mr. Controller, it is the rainy season."

Now Verbrugge knew this very well : it was January ;
but the Regent knew, too, what he had said about the
rain. Then again there was silence. The Regent beckoned
with a scarcely visible motion of the head to one of the
servants that sat squatting at the entrance of the 'pendoppo.' A little boy, splendidly dressed in a blue velvet
jacket and white trousers, with a golden girdle confining

his magnificent *Sarong*[1] round his waist, and on his head the pretty *Kain Kapala*,[2] under which his black eyes peeped forth so roguishly, crept squatting to the feet of the Regent, put down the gold box which contained the *Sirie*,[3] the lime, the *pinang*, the *gambier*,[4] and the tobacco, made his *Slamat* by raising both his hands put together to his forehead, as he bowed low, and then offered the precious box to his master.

" The road will be very difficult, after so much rain," said the Regent, as if to explain the long pause, whilst he covered the betel-leaf with lime.

" In the Pandaglang the road is not so bad," Verbrugge replied ; who, unless he wanted to hint at something disagreeable, gave that answer certainly a little inconsiderately ; for he ought to have taken into consideration that a Regent of Lebak does not like to hear the Pandaglang roads praised, even if they are much better than those of Lebak.

The Adhipatti did not make the mistake of replying too quickly. The little *maas* had already crept squatting backwards to the entrance of the ' pendoppo,' where he remained with his companions ; the Regent had made his

---

[1] A piece of linen. The Javanese women draw figures on such *Sarongs* wherewith they express some thoughts or emotion.—*Sarong*, a *sort* of petticoat.

[2] A handkerchief tied round the head ; a sort of turban. The Javanese never appears with uncovered head.

[3] Betel.   [4] *Pinang, gambier,*—different spices.

lips and few remaining teeth red with the juice of his betel, before he said—

" Yes ; Pandaglang is more populous."

To one acquainted with the Regent and the Controller, to whom the state of Lebak was no secret, it would have been quite clear that the conversation had already become a quarrel. An allusion to the better state of the roads in a neighbouring province appeared to be the consequence of the fruitless endeavours to improve the roads in Lebak. But the Regent was right in saying that Pandaglang was more populous, above all things, in proportion to the much smaller surface, and that, of course, united power rendered labour on the great roads there much easier than in Lebak, a province which counted but seventy thousand inhabit- ants on a surface of some hundred miles.

" That is true," said Verbrugge, " our population is not large, but——"

The Adhipatti looked at him, as if he expected an attack. He knew that " but " might be followed by something disagreeable for him to hear, who had been for thirty years Regent of Lebak. Verbrugge wished to end the conversation, and asked the 'mandoor' again if he saw nothing coming.

" I do not yet see anything from the Pandaglang side, Mr. Controller; but yonder on the other side there is somebody on horseback——it is the Commandant."

" To be sure, Dongso ! " said Verbrugge, looking outside ;

"he hunts in this neighbourhood; he went away this morning very early——ho! Duclari—Duclari——"

" He hears you, sir; he is coming this way. His boy rides after him."

" Hold the Commandant's horse," said Mr. Verbrugge to one of the servants. " Good-morning, Duclari, are you wet?——what have you killed? Come in."

A strong man about thirty years of age and of military appearance, though there was no trace of a uniform to be seen, entered the 'pendoppo.' It was Lieutenant Duclari, commandant of the small garrison of Rankas-Betong. Verbrugge and he were familiar friends, as Duclari had lived for some time in Verbrugge's house, pending the completion of a new fort. He shook hands with him, politely saluted the Regent, and sat down asking: " What have you here?"

" Will you have some tea, Duclari?"

" Certainly not; I am hot enough. Have you no cocoa-nut milk?—that is refreshing."

" I won't let you have it. If one is hot, cocoa-milk is, in my opinion, very unwholesome; it makes you stiff and gouty. Look at the *coolies* who carry heavy burdens over the mountains—they keep themselves active and supple by drinking hot water or *Koppi dahoen*—but ginger-tea is still better——"

" What?—*Koppi dahoen*, tea of coffee-leaves? That I have never seen."

"Because you have not served in Sumatra : there it is common."

"Let me have tea then—but not of coffee-leaves, or ginger.——So, you have been at Sumatra——and the new Assistant Resident, too, has he not ?"

All this was spoken in Dutch, which the Regent did not understand. Either Duclari felt that it was not very polite to exclude him in this way from the conversation, or he had another object in view, because all at once he commenced speaking Malay, addressing the Regent :—

"Does the Adhipatti know that the Controller is acquainted with the new Assistant Resident ?"

"No, I did not say so ;—I don't know him," said Verbrugge, in Malay. "I have never seen him ; he served in Sumatra some years before me. I only told you that I had there heard a good deal about him."

"Now, that is the same thing ; it is not necessary to see a person in order to know him——what does the Adhipatti think about it ?"

The Adhipatti at that moment wanted to call a servant. Some time elapsed before he could say, "that he agreed with the Commandant, but that still it was often necessary to see a person before you could judge of him."

"Generally speaking, that is perhaps true," Duclari continued in Dutch, either because he knew that language better, and thought he had done enough for politeness' sake, or because he wished to be understood by Verbrugge alone,

—" that may be true, generally speaking; but with regard to Havelaar you need no personal acquaintance——he is a fool."

" I did not say so, Duclari."

" No, you did not say so, but I say it, after all you have told me of him. I call any one who jumps into the water to save a dog from the sharks a fool."

" Yes, it was foolish, but——"

" And recollect that——epigram on General Van Damme ——that was not proper."

" It was witty——"

" Yes, but a young man may not be witty at the expense of a General."

" You must bear in mind that he was then very young —it was fourteen years ago—he was only twenty years old."

" And then the turkey which he stole ?"

" That he did to annoy the General."

" Exactly so. A young man may not annoy a General, especially one who is, as civil governor, his superior—— the epigram I think very funny——but then again that duelling——"

" He did it generally on behalf of another; he always was the champion of the weak."

" Well, let every one *fight* for himself, if fighting there must be. As for me, I think that a duel is seldom necessary; if necessary, I should accept it, but——to make a

custom of it——I'd rather not.   I hope that he is changed
in this respect——"

"To be sure, there is no doubt about that.   He is now
so much older, has long been a married man, and Assistant
Resident.   Moreover, I have always heard that his heart
is good, and that he has a strong sense of justice."

"Then he is just fit for Lebak——something happened
this morning that——Do you think that the Regent
understands us ?"

"I do not think so ; but show me something out of your
game-bag ; then he will think that we are speaking of that."

Duclari took his bag, pulled out two wood-cocks, and,
handling them, as if speaking about his sport, he communicated to Verbrugge that he had been followed by a
Javanese, who had asked him if he could do nothing to
lighten the pressure under which the population groaned ?
"And," he went on, "that means much, Verbrugge !   Not
that I wonder at the fact itself; I have been long enough
in the Residency of Bantam to know what is going on
here ; but that a common Javanese, generally so circumspect and reserved in what concerns the chiefs, should
make such a request to one who has nothing to do with
it, surprises me."

"And what did you answer, Duclari ?"

"Well, that it was not my business ; that he must go to
you, or to the new Assistant Resident, when he arrives
at Rankas-Betong, and there make his complaint."

"There they come," said the servant Dongso, all at once. " I see a 'mantrie' waving his *toodoong*."[1]

All stood up. Duclari not wishing it to appear that he had come to the frontiers to welcome the Assistant Resident, his superior in rank but not in command, and who was moreover a fool, mounted his horse, and rode off, followed by his servant.

The Adhipatti and Verbrugge, standing at the entrance of the 'pendoppo,' saw a travelling carriage approaching, dragged by four horses, which soon stopped, covered with mud, near the little bamboo building.

It would have been very difficult to guess what there could be in that coach, before Dongso, helped by the runners and a legion of servants belonging to the Regent's suite, had undone all the straps and buttons, that enclosed the vehicle in a black leathern cover, an operation which put you in mind of the precautions with which lions and tigers were formerly brought into cities when the Zoological Gardens were as yet only travelling *menageries.* Now there were no lions or tigers in the van; they had only shut it up in this way because it was the west monsoon,[2] and it was necessary to be prepared for rain.

Now the alighting out of a van, in which one has jolted for a long time along the road, is not so easy, as he would

[1] A broad-brimmed straw hat, affording protection from rain and sun.
[2] The rainy season.

think who has never, or but seldom travelled. Almost as in the case of the poor Saurians of the Antediluvian period, which, by staying too long, at last became an integral part of the clay, which they had not originally entered with the intention of remaining there, so with travellers who have been sitting too long cooped up in a travelling carriage, there happens something that I propose to call *assimilation*.——At last one hardly knows where the leathern cushion ends, and his individuality begins. Yes, I even think that one might have toothache or cramp in such a position, and mistake it for moth in the cloth, or mistake moth in the cloth for toothache or cramp. * * *

There are but few circumstances in the material world that do not afford to the thinking man the opportunity of making intellectual observations, and so I have often asked myself whether many errors, that have become common with us, many " Wrongs" that we think to be *right*, owe their origin to the fact, of having been sitting too long with the same company in the same travelling carriage? The leg, that you had to put there on the left, between the hat-box, and the little basket of cherries;—the knee, which you held pressed against the coach-door, not to make the lady opposite you think that you intended an attack on her crinoline or virtue;—the foot, covered with corns, that was so much afraid of the heels of the " commercial traveller" near you;—the neck, which you had to bend so long a time to the left because rain came in on the right side, all these are at last somewhat distorted. I think it well to change from time to time coaches, seats, and fellow-travellers. Then you can give your neck another direction, you can sometimes move your knee, and perhaps you may have a young lady near you with dancing-shoes, or a little boy whose feet do not touch the ground. Then you have a better chance of looking and walking straight, as soon as you get solid earth under your feet.

If anything in the coach that stopped before the 'pen-doppo' was opposed to the solution of continuity I don't know; but it is certain that it was some time before any-thing appeared.

There seemed to be a difficulty of etiquette, judging from the words: "If you please, Madam!" and "Resident!" Be this as it may, a gentleman at length stepped out who had in his attitude and appearance something perhaps which made you think of the Saurians I have spoken of. As we shall meet him again afterwards, I will tell you at once that his immobility was not only due to assimilation with the travelling coach, since, even when there was no van in the neighbourhood, he exhibited a calmness, a slow-ness, and a prudence, that would make many a Saurian jealous, and that in the eyes of many would be considered as tokens of a sedate, calm, and wise man. He was, like most Europeans in India, very pale, which, however, is not in the least considered in these regions as a sign of delicate health. He had fine features, that certainly bore witness of intellectual development. But there was something cold in his glance, something that made you think of a table of logarithms; and though his aspect on the whole was not unpleasing or repulsive, one could not help thinking that the very large thin nose on that face was annoyed because there was so little stir.

He politely offered his hand to a lady, to help her in getting out, and after he had taken from a gentleman who was still in the coach, a child, a little fair boy of about three years old, they entered the 'pendoppo.' Then that gentleman himself alighted, and any one acquainted with Java would immediately observe that he waited at the carriage door to assist an old Javanese *baboe* (nurse-maid). Three servants had delivered themselves out of the little leather cupboard that was stuck to the back of the coach, after the manner of a young oyster on an old one.

The gentleman who had first alighted had offered his hand to the Regent and the Controller Verbrugge, which they accepted with respect; and by their attitude you could see that they were aware of the presence of an important personage. It was the Resident of Bantam, the great province of which Lebak is a district,—a Regency, or, in official language, an Assistant Residency. I have often, when reading works of fiction, been offended at the little respect of the authors for the taste of the public, and more than ever with anything comical or burlesque ; a person is made to speak, who does not understand the language, or at least pronounces it badly ; a Frenchman is made to speak Dutch thus : "*Ka Kaurv na de Krote Krak*," or "*Krietje Kooit Keen Kare Kroente Kraakwek*." [1] For want of a Frenchman, a stammerer is selected, or a person "created," whose hobby consists of two words recurring every moment. I have witnessed the success of a foolish *vaudeville*, because there was somebody in it who was always saying : "My name is Meyer." I think this manner of being witty too cheap, and to tell you the truth, I am cross with you, if you think this funny. But now, I have to introduce to you something of that kind myself. I have to show you from time to time a person —I shall do it as seldom as possible—who had, indeed, a manner of speaking which makes me fear to be suspected of an unsuccessful effort to make you laugh ; and, therefore, I must assure you that it is not my fault, if the very sedate Resident of Bantam, of whom I am speaking, is so peculiar in his mode of expressing himself, that it is very difficult for me to sketch that, without giving myself the appearance of seeking to produce the effect of wit by means of *tic*.[2] He spoke as if there stood after each

---

[1] This is, when rightly spelt : " Ga gaauw naar de groote gracht," ═ Go quickly to the great Canal. "Grietje gooit geen gare groete graag weg,"═ Gertrude does not like to throw away any cooked vegetables.

[2] LITERALLY translated ═ convulsive motion.

word a period, or even a long pause; and I cannot find a
better comparison for the distance between his words than
the silence which follows the "Amen" after a long prayer
in church; which is, as every one knows, a signal of the
proper time to cough or blow one's nose.   What he said
was generally well considered, and if he could have per-
suaded himself to omit those untimely pauses, his sentences would have been, in a rhetorical point of view at
least, passable, but all that crumbling, stuttering, and
ruggedness, made listening to him very tedious.   One
often stumbled at it, for generally, if you commenced to
reply, thinking the sentence finished, and the remainder
left to your ingenuity, the remaining words came on as
the stragglers of a defeated army, and made you think
that you had interrupted him,—an idea which is always
disagreeable.   The public at Serang, such persons at least
as were not in the service of the Government, called his
conversation 'slimy,' but Government *employés* were more
circumspect.   I do not think this word very nice, but
I must confess that it expressed very well the principal
quality of the Resident's eloquence.   As yet I have said
nothing of Max Havelaar and his wife,—for these were
the two persons who had alighted from the carriage after
the Resident, with their child and the 'baboe;' and perhaps
it might be sufficient to leave the description of their appearance and character to the current of events and your
proper imagination.   But as I am now occupied with

descriptions, I will tell you that Madam Havelaar was not beautiful, but that she still had in language and look something very charming, and she showed very plainly, by the ease of her manner, that she had been in the world, and was at home in the higher classes of society. She had not that stiffness and unpleasantness of snobbish respectability which thinks that it must torment itself and others with "constraint," in order to be considered *distingué*; and she did not care much for appearances which are thought much of by other women. In her dress too she was an example of simplicity. A white muslin *Coadjoe*[1] with a blue *Cordelière*,—I believe they call this in Europe *peignoir*,—was her travelling costume. Round her neck she wore a thin silk cord, from which hung two little medallions, invisible, because they were concealed in the folds of her dress. Her hair *à la Chinoise*, with a garland of *melati*[2] in the *Kondek*,[3] —completed her toilette.

I said that she was not beautiful, and yet I should not like you to think her ugly. I hope that you will find her beautiful as soon as I have an opportunity to show her to you, burning with indignation at what she called the "disregard of genius" when her Max was concerned, or when she was animated with an idea in connexion with the welfare of her child.

---

[1] Dress.   [2] *Melati* = a beautiful and fragrant flower.
[3] *Kondek* = chignon.

It has too often already been said that the face is the
mirror of the soul, for us to speak well of an immovable
face that has nothing to reflect, because there is no soul
reflected in it.   Well, she had a noble soul, and certainly
he must be blind who did not think her face very beautiful, when that soul could be read in it.

Havelaar was a man of about thirty-five years. He was
slender and active in his movements; except his very
short and expressive upper lip, and his large pale blue
eyes—which, if he was in a calm humour, had something
dreamlike, but which flashed fire if he was animated with
a grand idea—there was nothing particular in his appearance.   His light hair hung flat round his temples, and I
can believe very well, that if you saw him for the first
time, you would not arrive at the conclusion, that there
was a person before you possessing rare qualities both of
head and heart.   He was full of contradictions: sharp as
a lancet, and tender-hearted as a girl, he always was the
first himself to feel the wound which his bitter words had
inflicted; and he suffered more than the wounded.   He
was quick of comprehension, grasped immediately the
highest and the most intricate matters, liked to amuse
himself with the solution of difficult questions, and to
such pursuits would devote all pains, study, and exertion.
Yet often he did not understand the most simple thing,
which a child could have explained to him.   Full of love
for truth and justice, he often neglected his most simple

and nearest obligations to remedy an injustice which lay
higher, or further, or deeper, and which allured him more
by the perhaps greater exertion of the struggle. He was
chivalrous and gallant, but often like that other Don
Quixote he wasted his valour on a windmill. He burned
with insatiable ambition, which made him look on all the
ordinary distinctions of social life as vanities, and yet
he considered his greatest happiness to consist in a calm,
domestic, secluded life. He was a poet in the highest
sense of the word; at the sight of a spark he dreamed of
solar systems; peopled them with creatures of his own
creation, felt himself to be lord of a world, which he had
animated, and yet could immediately thereupon have a
conversation on the price of rice, the rules of grammar, or
the economic advantages of the Egyptian system of artificial incubation. No science was entirely unknown to
him: he "guessed intuitively" what he did not know,
and possessed in a very high degree the gift of using the
little he knew (every one knows a little, and he, though
knowing more than some others, was no exception to
this rule) in a way that multiplied the measure of his
knowledge. He was punctual and orderly, besides being
exceedingly patient; but precisely because punctuality,
order, and patience were difficult to him,—his mind being
somewhat wild,—slow and circumspect in judging of
affairs; though this seemed not to be the case with those
who heard him reach his conclusions so quickly. His

impressions were too vivid to be thought durable, and yet he often proved that they were durable. All that was grand and sublime allured him, and at the same time he was simple and *naïf* as a child. He was honest, above all things where honesty became magnanimity, and would have left unpaid hundreds which he owed because he had given away thousands. He was witty and entertaining where he felt that his wit was understood, but otherwise blunt and reserved: cordial to his friends; a champion of sufferers; sensible to love and friendship; faithful to his given word; yielding in trifles, but firm as a rock where he thought it worth the trouble to show character; humble and benevolent to those who acknowledged his intellectual superiority, but troublesome to those who desired to oppose it; candid from pride, and sometimes reserved, where he feared that his straightforwardness might be mistaken for ignorance; equally susceptible to sensuous and spiritual enjoyment; timid and ineloquent where he thought he was not understood, but eloquent when he felt that his words fell on fertile soil; slow when he was not urged by an incitement that came forth from his own soul, but zealous, ardent, where this was the case; moreover, he was affable, polite in his manners, and blameless in behaviour,—such was within a little the character of Havelaar.

I say, "within a little," for if all definitions are difficult, this is particularly the case in the description of a person who differs much from the every-day cast of men.

That is also the reason, I think, why the poets of romance generally make their heroes either devils or angels. Black or white is easy to paint, but it is more difficult to produce the varieties between these two extremes, when truth must be respected, and neither side coloured too dark or too light. I feel that the sketch which I have tried to give of Havelaar is very imperfect. The materials before me are of so extensive a nature that they impede my judgment by excess of richness, and I shall perhaps again refer to this by way of supplement, while developing the events which I wish to communicate to you. This is certain,—he was an uncommon man, and surely worthy of careful study. I see even now, that I have neglected to give, as one of his chief characteristics, that he understood at the same time, and with the same quickness, the ridiculous and the serious side of things,—a peculiar quality, imparting unconsciously to his manner of speaking a sort of humour which made his listeners always doubt whether they were touched by the deep feeling that prevailed in his words, or had to laugh at the drollery that interrupted at once the earnestness of them.

It was very remarkable that his appearance, and even his emotions, gave so few traces of his past life. The boast of experience has become a ridiculous commonplace ; there

are people who have floated for fifty or sixty years in the
stream in which they think to swim, and who can tell of
that time little more than that they have removed from
A——— Square to B——— Street, and nothing is more common than to hear those very persons boast of experience,
who got their grey hairs so very easily. Other people
think that they may found their claims to experience on
external vicissitudes, without its appearing from anything
that they have been affected in their inner life. I can imagine that to witness, or even to take part in, important events, may have little or no influence on the souls
of some men. Who entertains a doubt of this, may ask
himself if experience may be ascribed to all the inhabitants of France who were forty or fifty years old in 1815 ?
And yet they were all persons who saw, not only the acting of the great drama which commenced in 1789, but
had even played a more or less important part in that
drama.

And, on the contrary, how many persons undergo a
series of emotions without the external circumstances
seeming to give occasion for it. Think of " Robinson
Crusoe," of Pellico's captivity ; of the charming " Picciola,"
of Saintine ; of the struggle in the breast of an old maid,
who cherished through her whole life but one love, without ever betraying by a single word what were the feelings of her heart ; of the emotions of the philanthropist,
who, without being externally involved in the current of

events, is ardently interested in the welfare of fellow-citizens or fellow-creatures, the more he alternately hopes and fears, the more he observes every change, kindles into enthusiasm for a beautiful idea, and burns with indignation if he sees it pushed away and trampled upon by those who, for some time at least, were stronger than beautiful ideas. Think of the philosopher, who from out his cell tries to teach the people what truth is, if he has to remark that his voice is overpowered by devout hypocrisy or adventurous quacks. Think of Socrates, not when he empties the poisoned cup—for I speak here of the experience of the mind, and not of that which owes its existence to external circumstances,—how intensely sad his soul must have been, when he, who loved what is right and true, heard himself called a corrupter of youth and a despiser of the gods. Or better still, think of CHRIST, gazing with such profound sadness on Jerusalem, and complaining that it " would not ! "

Such a cry of grief— above that of the poisoned cup, or cross—does not come from an untried heart. There must have been suffering——there is experience !

This outburst has escaped me,—it now stands, and may remain. Havelaar had experienced much. Will you have, for instance, something that counterbalances the removing from A—— Street ? He had suffered shipwreck more than once, he had experience of fire, insurrection, assassination, war, duels, luxury, poverty, hunger, cholera, love, and "loves." He had visited France, Germany, Belgium, Italy, Switzerland, England, Spain, Portugal, Russia, Egypt, Arabia, India, China, and America. As to his vicissitudes, he had many opportunities of experience, and that he had truly experienced much, that he had not gone through life without catching the impressions which it offered him so plentifully, was evidenced by the quickness of his mind and the susceptibility of his soul. What excited the wonder of all who knew or could conjecture how much he had experienced and suffered, was that you could see so little of that on his face. Certainly there was something like fatigue in his features, but this made you think rather of prematurely ripe youth than of approaching old age; yet approaching old age it ought to have been, for in India the man of thirty-five years is no longer young: His emotions too had remained young, as I said before. He could play with a child, and as a child, and often he complained that little Max was still too young to fly a kite, because he, "great Max," liked that so very much. With boys he played "leap-frog," and liked to draw a pattern for the girls' embroidery: he even often took the needle from them and amused himself with that work, though he always said that they could do something better than that "mechanical counting of stitches." With young men of eighteen he was a young student, liked to sing his *Patriam canimus* with them, or *Gaudeamus igitur,*— yes, I am not even quite certain, that not long ago, when he was in Amsterdam on leave, he pulled down a sign-board which did not please him, because a nigger was painted on it, chained to the feet of an European with a long pipe in his mouth, and under which was written, of course, " The smoking young merchant."

The 'baboe' whom he had helped out the coach resembled all 'baboes' in India when they are old. If you know that sort of servants, I *need* not tell you how she looked, and if you do not, I *cannot* tell you. This only distinguished her from other nurses in India, that she had little to do; for Madam Havelaar was an example of care for her child, and what there was to do for or with her little Max, she did herself, to the great astonishment of many other ladies, who did not think proper to act as " slaves to their children."

CHAPTER VII.

[CONTINUATION OF STERN'S COMPOSITION.]

THE Resident of Bantam introduced the Regent and the
Controller to the new Assistant Resident. Havelaar cour-
teously saluted both these functionaries; the Controller
(there is always something painful in meeting a new superior) he placed at once at his ease with a few friendly
words, as if he wished immediately to introduce a sort of
familiarity that would make intercourse easy. With the
Regent his meeting was as it ought to be with a person
entitled to a gold *payong*,[1] at the same time his younger
brother. With grave affability he rebuked his too great
civility, which had brought him, in such weather, to the
confines of his district, which, according to the rules of
etiquette, the Regent was not bound to do.

" Indeed, Mr. Adhipatti, I am angry with you for having given yourself so much trouble on my account.——I
thought I should see you first at *Rankas-Betong*."

[1] *Payong* = umbrella. A mark of distinction in the East,—a gold
one being the highest.

"I wished to see Mr. Assistant Resident as soon as possible," said the Adhipatti, "to make his acquaintance."

"Certainly, certainly, I am obliged; but I do not like to see a person of your rank and years exert himself too much——and on horseback too!"

"Yes, Mr. Assistant Resident! where duty calls me, I am even now always active and vigorous."

"That is too self-exacting——is it not, Mr. Resident?"

"Mr. Adhipatti——is——very——"

"Very well; but there is a limit * * "

"——zealous," drawled the Resident.

"Very well; but there is a limit," Havelaar had to say again, as if to swallow the former words. "If you agree to it, Resident, we will make room in the carriage. The 'baboe' can remain here; we will send her a *tandoo*[1] from Rankas-Betong. My wife will take Max on her lap—— won't you, Tine? there is room enough."

"It——is——very——"

"Verbrugge, we will make room for you too; I don't see——"

"——well," continued the Resident.

"I don't see why you should needlessly ride on horseback through the mud; there is room for all of us: we can then make acquaintance with each other——can't we, Tine?—we will arrange it. Here, Max—look here, Ver-

---

[1] Sedan-chair (palanquin).

brugge, is not this a pretty little fellow?—'tis my little boy, Max !"

The Resident had seated himself with the Adhipatti. Havelaar called Verbrugge to ask him who was the owner of that grey horse with red trappings; and when Verbrugge went to the entrance of the 'pendoppo' to see what horse he meant, he put his hand on his shoulder and asked—

" Is the Regent always so attentive ? "

" He is a strong man for his years, Mr. Havelaar, and you understand that he would like to make a good impression on you."

" Yes, I understand that. I have heard much good of him——he is an educated man ? "

" Oh, yes—— "

" And he has a large family ? "

Verbrugge looked at Havelaar, as if he did not understand the transition. This style often presented difficulties to those who did not know him. The quickness of his mind often made him omit in conversation some links in the reasoning; and although these links followed each other with regularity in *his* thoughts, he could not take it amiss on the part of one who was not so quick, or accustomed to his quickness, if he stared at him on such an occasion with the unuttered question on his lips—" Are you mad ?——or what is the matter ? "

Some such expression appeared in the face of Verbrugge;

and Havelaar had to repeat the question, before the Controller replied—

" Yes, he has a very large family."

" And do they build *Medjiets*[1] in the province ?" Havelaar continued, again in a tone which, quite in contradiction with the words, seemed to express his belief that there was some connexion between these mosques and the large family of the Regent.

Verbrugge answered that indeed much labour was bestowed on the mosques.

" Yes, yes, just as I thought," replied Havelaar. " And now tell me if they are much in arrear with their land-taxes ?"

" Yes, there is room for improvement——"

" Exactly so, and above all things in the district ' Parang-Koodjang,' "[2] added Havelaar, as if he thought it easier to reply himself.

" What does the taxation of this year amount to ?" he continued ; and Verbrugge hesitating a moment, as if to consider his reply, Havelaar anticipated him in the same breath—

" Very well, very well, I know it already—sixty-eight thousand and a few hundreds—fifteen thousand more than last year—but only six thousand more than in the year 1845—we have made since 1843 an augmentation of eight thousand—and the population too is very thin—yes, in

[1] Mosques.
[2] On Dutch maps of Java it is spelt " Parang-Koedjang."

twelve years we have had an increase of only eleven
per cent., and even this statement is questionable, for the
statistics were formerly very inexactly kept—and farther !
—from 1850 to 1851 there is even a diminution—and the
cattle market does not flourish—that is a bad omen
＊ ＊ ＊ What the deuce ! look how that horse jumps
and rears——come here, Max !"

Verbrugge saw that he would not have much to teach
the new Assistant Resident, and that there was no question of ascendency arising from " local acquaintance," an
advantage which the good fellow had not desired.

" But it is a matter of course," continued Havelaar, taking Max in his arms ; " in Tjikandi and Bolang they like
it—and so do the rebels in the Lampoons.[1] I recommend myself to your co-operation, Mr. Verbrugge ; the
Regent is a man old in years——his son-in-law is still
district-chief ? All things considered, I think him to be
a person who deserves indulgence——I mean the Regent——I am very glad that there is so much poverty
here——I hope to remain here a long time."

Thereupon he shook hands with Verbrugge, and the
latter returned with him to the table, where the Resident,
the Regent, and Madam Havelaar were seated, the Controller having perceived more than five minutes before
that " this Mr. Havelaar was not such a fool" as the

[1] On *Dutch* maps of Java, " Lampongs," but on the *English* maps of
Java, " Lampoons."

Commandant thought. Verbrugge was not at all ill furnished with intellect, and he who knew the province of Lebak almost as well as it is possible to know an extensive region, where nothing is printed, began to feel that there was surely some connexion between the apparently incoherent questions of Havelaar, and, at the same time, that the new Assistant Resident, though he had never been in the province, knew something of what happened there. Verbrugge did not understand, it is true, why he had rejoiced at the poverty of Lebak, but he supposed he had misunderstood that expression; and afterwards, when Havelaar often said the same, he understood how good and noble was that joy.

Havelaar and Verbrugge seated themselves at the table, and while drinking tea, and speaking of indifferent matters, we all waited, till Dongso came in to tell the Resident that fresh horses were put to the carriage. All took their places as well as they could in the carriage, and off it went. To speak was difficult, because of the jolting and bruising. Max was kept quiet with *pisang;*[1] his mother had him on her lap, and would not acknowledge that she was tired, when Havelaar proposed to relieve her of the heavy boy. During a compulsory rest in a mudhole, Verbrugge asked the Resident if he had yet mentioned Madam Slotering?

[1] Plantain. In the West Indies they are called bananas. Pisang is the fruit of the pisang or banana-tree.

"Mr. Havelaar——has——said——"

"Of course, Verbrugge, why not? that lady can stay with us: I should not like——"

"that——it——was——good," continued the Resident, with much difficulty.

"I should not like to forbid my house to a lady in such circumstances. That is a matter of course,—is it not, Tine?"

Tine, too, was of opinion that it was a matter of course.

"You have two houses at Rankas-Betong," Verbrugge said; "there is room enough for two families."

"But, even if this were not the case——"

"I——should——not——dare——"

"Well, Resident," said Madam Havelaar, "there is no doubt about it."

"to——promise——it,——for——it——is——"

"Were they ten of them, if they only liked to be with us——"

"a——great——deal——of——trouble——and—— she——is——"

"But to travel at such a time is an impossibility, Resident."

A heavy jolt of the carriage, just got out of the mud, put a point of exclamation after the declaration that to travel was an impossibility for Madam Slotering. Every one had said the usual "Oh!" which follows such a jolt; Max had recovered in his mother's lap the 'pisang' which he lost by the shock, and we were already pretty near to the next mud-hole before the Resident could resolve to finish his phrase, by adding—

" a——native——woman."

" Oh, that makes no difference," explained Madam Havelaar. The Resident nodded, as if he thought it good that the matter was thus arranged, and as it was so difficult to speak, we ended the conversation. This Madam Slotering was the widow of Havelaar's predecessor, who had died two months ago. Verbrugge, who had been charged *ad interim* with the duties of Assistant Resident, would have had a right to occupy, during that time, the large mansion which had been erected at Rankas-Betong, as in every district, for the head of the Government. Still he had not done so, partly because he feared that he should have to remove too soon, partly that this lady with her children might continue to occupy it. Yet there would have been room enough, for besides the large mansion for the Assistant Resident, there was near it, in the grounds, another house, that had served for the same purpose formerly, and though in a decayed condition, was still very inhabitable.

Madam Slotering had asked the Resident to intercede for her with the successor of her husband, and obtain permission for her to inhabit that old house till after her confinement, which she expected in a few months. This was the request which had been granted so readily by

Havelaar and his wife, for hospitable they were in the highest degree.

The Resident had said that Madam Slotering was a " native woman." This needs some explanation for readers who are not acquainted with India ; for otherwise they would be apt to come to the wrong conclusion—that she was a Javanese woman. European society in India is very sharply divided into two different parts, the Europeans proper, and those who, though lawfully belonging to the same jurisdiction, were not born in Europe, and have more or less Indian blood in their veins. In honour of the notions of humanity prevailing in the Indies, I hasten to add, that however clearly in social intercourse the difference between the two classes of persons, both having, in contradistinction to the native, the name of Europeans, may be marked, this separation has by no means the barbarous characteristic which predominates in America. I do not deny that there is still much injustice and exclusiveness in the relation of the parties, and that the word *liplap*[1] sounded often in my ears as a proof how removed the white man, not being a 'liplap,' often is from true civilisation. It is true that the 'liplap' is only by exception admitted into society ; that he is generally considered, if I may be allowed to make use of a very vulgar expression, "as not being *thoroughbred* ;" but such an

[1] The nickname in India for the child of a European and a native —an allusion to the protruding lips : *liplap* = *raglip*.

exclusion or slight is seldom defended as a principle. Every one is at liberty to choose his own companions, and one cannot take it amiss in the European proper, if he prefers the conversation of persons of his own nationality to that of persons who, not to speak of the greater or less esteem in which they are held in society, do not agree with his impressions or ideas, or—and this is perhaps the main point,—whose *prejudices have taken a different direction from his own.*

The 'liplap' has many good qualities, so has the European. Both have many bad qualities; in this way too they resemble each other. But the good and bad qualities which they have are too distinctive for intercourse between them to be, generally speaking, productive of mutual satisfaction. Moreover, and this is in a great measure the fault of the Government, the 'liplap' is often very badly educated. We are not now inquiring how the European would be if from youth he had been impeded in his mental development; but this is certain, that, generally speaking, the small mental development of the 'liplap' stands in the way of his equality with the European, and even where an individual 'liplap' is distinctly superior to a certain European, he is kept down on account of his origin. There is nothing new in this. It was a part of the policy of William the Conqueror to raise the most insignificant Normans above the most intelligent Saxons, and every Norman devoted himself to

furthering the ascendency of the Normans in general, for
the advantage of himself in particular, because he often
would have been most insignificant without the influence
of his countrymen as the prevailing party.

From anything of this kind arises *a priori* a constraint,
which can only be removed by philosophical liberal de-
signs on the part of the Government.

That the European who belongs to the dominant race
accommodates himself very easily to this artificial ascendency speaks for itself; but it is often curious to hear a
person who received his education in one of the lowest
streets of Rotterdam ridicule the 'liplap' because he makes
mistakes in pronunciation and grammar. A 'liplap' may
be polite, well educated, or learned—there are such——
as well as the European, who counterfeiting illness stayed
away from the ship in which he had dishes to wash, and
is now at the head of a commercial undertaking which
made prodigious profits on indigo in 18——, long before he
had the shop in which he sells hams and fowling-pieces
——as soon as this European perceives that the best
educated ' liplap ' has some difficulty not to confound the
h and *g*, he laughs at the stupidity of the man who does
not know what is the difference between a *" gek "* and
a *" hek "* (*fool* and *hedge*).

But to prevent him from laughing at that, he ought
to know that in the Arabic and Malay languages, the
cha and the *hha* are expressed by one and the same sign

—that *Hieronymus* becomes *Jerome*, viâ *Geronimo*, that we make *Guano* out of *Huano*, and that we say in Dutch for *Guild Heaume*—*Huillem* or *Willem* (William). This is rather too much to expect of a person who made his fortune in the indigo trade.

Yet such a European cannot converse with such a 'liplap.'

I understand how *Willem* (William) is derived from *Guillaume*, and must confess, that I have made acquaintance with many 'liplaps,' especially in the Moluccas or Spice Islands, who surprised me with the extent of their knowledge, and who gave me the idea that we Europeans, whatever advantages we possess, are often, and not comparatively speaking merely, much behind these poor pariahs, who have to struggle from their cradle upwards with an artificial, studied inferiority, and the prejudice against their colour.

But Madam Slotering was once for all guaranteed against faults in the Dutch language, because she spoke Malay. We shall see more of her afterwards when we are drinking tea with Havelaar, Tine, and little Max in the fore-gallery of the Assistant Resident's mansion at Rankas-Betong, where our travelling company arrived at last safe and sound after having had to endure much jolting and bruising.

The Resident, who had only come along with us to install the new Assistant Resident in his office, intimated

his wish to return that same day to Serang, " because——
he——"

Havelaar said he was likewise disposed to make all
possible speed.

"——had——still——so——much——to——do."

So it was arranged that we should all meet in half-an-
hour, in the Regent's large front portico. Verbrugge, who
was prepared for this, had many days ago summoned to
the capital[1] the heads of the districts, the *Patteh*,[2] the
Kliwon, the *Djaksa*, the tax-gatherer, some ' mantries '—in
a word, all the native officials who had to assist at the
ceremony.

The Adhipatti took his leave and drove home. Madam
Havelaar inspected her new house, and was much pleased
with it, above all things because the garden was so large :
which she liked so on account of Max, who required to
be much in the open air. The Resident and Havelaar
had retired to dress ; for at the solemnity which had to
take place, the official costume was indispensable. Hundreds of people were assembled around the house, who
had either followed the Resident's carriage on horseback,
or who had belonged to the retinue of the assembled
chiefs. The police and other officials were running to
and fro with much bustle ; in short, all indicated that the
monotony of that secluded spot was now broken.

[1] Where ' capital ' or ' metropolis ' is used, it means the chief town
of the district.

[2] The factotum of the Regent. *Kliwon, Djaksa*,—native officials.

Soon the handsome carriage of the Adhipatti drove up
the yard. The Resident and Havelaar, glittering with
gold and silver, but their movement somewhat impeded
by their own swords, entered it, and drove to the Regent's
mansion, where they were received with the music of
gongs, *gamlangs*, and all sorts of stringed instruments.
Verbrugge, too, who had put off his muddy costume, had
already arrived. The inferior chiefs, according to Oriental usage, were sitting in a great ring, on mats upon the
ground, and at the further end of the long gallery stood
a table, at which the Resident, the Adhipatti, the Assistant Resident, the Controller, and two native grandees
took their seats. Tea and pastry were served, and the
simple ceremony began.

The Resident stood up and read the decree of the
Governor-General, whereby Mr. Max Havelaar was appointed Assistant Resident of Bantam-Kidool (South
Bantam), as Lebak is called by the natives. He then
took the official paper, containing the oath which is
required of those entering upon employments in general,
providing, that " To be appointed or promoted to the
employment of ——, the candidate has neither promised
nor given anything to any one, and will not promise or
give anything ; that he will be loyal and faithful to his
Majesty the King of the Netherlands, obedient to his
Majesty's Representative in the Indies ; that he shall
punctually obey and cause to be obeyed the laws and

decrees that have been issued or shall be issued, and that
he shall behave himself in everything as becomes a good
——(here Assistant Resident)." This was of course concluded with the sacramental expression: "So truly help
me God Almighty." Havelaar repeated the words of the
oath as read to him. The promise to protect the native
population against oppression and extortion ought to be
considered as included in it, for after swearing that you
will maintain the existing laws and regulations, you have
only to do so, and you will consider a special oath superfluous. But it seems that the legislators have thought
that abundance of fair words would do no harm, for they
exact a special oath of the Assistant Residents, whereby
that obligation is once more expressly mentioned, and
Havelaar once more took God Almighty as a witness, that
he " would protect the native population against oppression, ill-treatment, and extortion."

To a nice observer, it would have been worth while to
remark the difference in tone and manner between the
Resident and Havelaar on this occasion. Both had often
attended such a solemnity; the difference which I refer
to was not, therefore, occasioned by their being more or
less affected by a novel and unwonted spectacle, but was
only a consequence of the very different characters of
the two persons. The Resident, it is true, spoke a little
quicker than he was used to do, because he only had to
read the decree and oaths, which saved him the trouble

of seeking for the last words of what he had to say ; but still all went on with a gravity and a seriousness which must have inspired the superficial spectator with a very high idea of the importance which he attached to this matter.

Havelaar, on the contrary, had something in expression of countenance, voice, and mien, when with uplifted finger he repeated the oath, as if he would say, " Of course, without ' any oath,' I should do that." Any one having a knowledge of men would have had more confidence in his freedom from constraint than in the sedateness of the Resident. Is it not ridiculous indeed to think that the man whose vocation it is to do justice, the man into whose hands is given the weal or woe of thousands, should think himself bound by a few uttered sounds, if his heart does not feel itself obliged even without those sounds to do so ?

We believe of Havelaar, that he would have protected the poor and oppressed wheresoever he might meet them, even if he had promised by " God Almighty" the reverse.

Thereupon followed a speech of the Resident, addressed to the chiefs, in which he introduced to them the Assistant Resident as lord-paramount of the district, and invited them to obey him, to perform punctually their duties, and other commonplaces. Then the chiefs were presented, every one in his turn, to Havelaar: he gave his hand to each of them, and the installation was at an end.

H

Dinner was served at the house of the Adhipatti, and the Commandant Duclari was among the guests. Immediately after it was finished, the Resident, wishing to be the same evening at Serang, " because——he——had—— so——much——business," entered again his travelling coach, and so Rankas-Betong was soon again as quiet as can be expected of a small town in Java, inhabited only by a few Europeans, and moreover far from the highway. Duclari and Havelaar soon became acquainted; the Adhipatti seemed to be well contented with his " elder brother ;" and Verbrugge said afterwards, that the Resident also, whom he had accompanied a part of his way to Serang, had spoken in very favourable terms of the family of Havelaar, who, on their journey to Lebak, had spent many days at his house; adding, that it was easy to foresee that Havelaar, who was in high esteem with the Government, would very probably be soon promoted to a higher office.

Max and " his Tine " had recently returned from a voyage to Europe, and were tired of what I once heard happily described as " the life of boxes." They esteemed themselves, therefore, very happy, to inhabit at last, after many changes, a spot where they were at home.

Before this voyage to Europe, Havelaar had been Assistant Resident at Amboyna, where he had to struggle with many difficulties, because the population of that island was in a state of excitement and revolt, in consequence of the many bad measures which had of late been taken; he had, with much energy, succeeded in repressing that spirit, but from vexation at the little assistance which the Government gave him in that affair, and from sorrow over the bad government which for many centuries has depopulated and corrupted the magnificent Moluccas (the reader should try if he can get to read what was written on that subject by the Baron Van der Capellen in 1825—the publications of this philanthropist are to be found in the Indian official papers of that year, and affairs have not since improved), from sorrow for all this he had become ill, and this had induced him to leave for Europe. Strictly considered, he had a right to a better choice than the poor unproductive district of Lebak, because his office at Amboyna was of more importance, and there, without an Assistant Resident as his superior, he had managed all the business himself. Moreover, long before he went to Amboyna, it was said that he would be appointed Resident, and, therefore, many were astonished that he got a district which gave him so little emolument, because many measure the importance of a function by the revenues it produces. Yet he himself did not complain about that. His ambition was not of the kind that he should ever play the beggar for a higher office or more money.

Yet the latter would have been useful to him, for in his voyages to Europe he had spent the little money which

he had saved in former years; he had even been obliged
to leave debts behind, and he was, in a word, poor. But
never had he considered his employment as a source of
emolument, and when appointed at Lebak, he intended
with contentment to pay up his arrears by economy; in
which intention his wife, who was also simple in tastes
and necessities, willingly seconded him.

But economy was a difficult thing to Havelaar. As
for himself, he could be content with the bare necessaries
of life; yea, even with less; but where others were in
want of assistance, to help, to give, was a strong passion
with him. He himself was aware of this foible; he considered with all the common-sense he had, how unjustly
he acted in succouring any one, when he himself had
a better claim to his own assistance, and felt this injustice the more when his Tine and Max, both of whom
he loved so dearly, suffered through the consequence of
his liberality. He often reproached himself for his good
nature as a foible, as vanity, as a desire to be considered
a prince in disguise: he promised amendment, and yet,
whenever any one presented himself to his notice as the
victim of adversity, he forgot all and helped him. Yet
he had some bitter experience of the consequences of this
too far-stretched virtue. A week before the birth of his
little Max he had not money enough to buy the iron
cradle wherein his darling was to rest; and a little before
he had sacrificed the few ornaments of his wife, to assist

somebody who was certainly in better circumstances than he.

But all this was far behind them when they arrived at Lebak. With a joyful calmness they had taken possession of the house, "where they hoped now to remain for some time." With peculiar satisfaction they had ordered the furniture at Batavia; they would make all so comfortable and snug. They showed each other the places where they should breakfast; where little Max should play; where the library should be; where he should read in the evening to her what he had written that day;—for he was always occupied in developing his ideas on paper— and when once these were printed, she thought that "people would see what her Max was——" But he had never given anything to the press, on account of scruples arising from modesty. He himself, at least, did not know how better to express that timidity, than by asking those who urged him to publicity, "Would you let your daughter walk the streets without a chemise?"

This was another saying which made his circle say "that Havelaar was a singular man," and I do not say the contrary; but if you took the trouble to interpret his uncommon manner of speaking, you would perhaps find in that strange question about a girl's dress the text for a treatise on intellectual modesty, which, shy of the glances of dull passers-by, retires behind the veil of maidenly timidity.

Yes, they should be happy at Rankas-Betong, Havelaar and his Tine! The only care that oppressed them
was the debts which they had left behind in Europe,
augmented by the still unpaid expenses of the voyage
back to the Indies, and of the furnishing of their house.
But they would live on half, even a third of his income
——perhaps he would soon be made Resident, and then
all would be arranged in a few years——

"Yet I should be sorry, Tine, to leave Lebak; for I
have many things to do here. You must be very economical, my dear, and perhaps we may pay off all even
without promotion——then I hope to remain here for a
long time."

Now she needed no incitement to economy. It was
not her fault that frugality had become necessary; but she
had so completely identified herself with her Max that
she did not consider this speech as a reproach, which, to
be sure, it was not; for Havelaar knew very well that
he alone had been wrong through excessive liberality,
and that her fault was this,—if fault there was on her
side,—that she, out of love for her Max, had always
approved of all that he did.

Yes, *she* had approved when he took those two poor
women from the Nieuwstraat (New Street), who had never
before left Amsterdam, and never had been out, to the
Haarlem fair, under the odd pretext that the King had
ordered him "to amuse little old women of respectable

character." *She* approved of his entertaining the orphans of all the asylums in Amsterdam with gingerbread and almond-milk, and loading them with playthings. *She* perfectly understood that he had paid the hotel-bill of that family of poor singers, who wanted to go back to their country, but did not like to leave the goods behind, including the harp, and the violin, and the violoncello, which they wanted for their poor profession. *She* could not disapprove his bringing to her the girl, who in the evening had accosted him in the street, giving her food and lodging, and not pronouncing the "Go and sin no more!" before he had placed it in her power not to sin. *She* approved of her Max causing the piano to be brought back to the parlour of the father of a family, whom she heard say " how sorry he was that by his bankruptcy the girls were deprived of their music." *She* quite understood that her Max had redeemed the family of slaves at Menado who were so intensely afflicted at having to mount upon the auctioneer's table. *She* thought it quite a matter of course that Max gave other horses in return for those that had been ridden to death by the officers of the *Bayonnaise*. *She* did not object to his lodging at Menado and at Amboyna all the survivors of the ship-wrecked American whalers, and thought himself far above sending in an innkeeper's bill to the American Government. *She* understood how it was that the officers of every man-of-war that arrived lodged for the most part with Max, and that his house was their favourite *pied-à-terre*. Was not he *her* Max?—Was it not too petty, too shabby, too absurd, to bind him, who had such princely notions, to the rules of frugality and economy applicable to other persons? And moreover, although there might sometimes be a disproportion between revenues and expenses, was not Max, "*her* Max," destined for a brilliant career?—Ought not he to be soon in a position which would allow a free course to his high-minded passions without exceeding his revenues? Was not her Max destined to become a Governor-General, or a King? Nay, was it not strange that he was not yet a King? If she had any fault at all, it was her deep affection for Havelaar; and here more than ever it should be: that much must be forgiven those who have loved much!

But there was nothing which she had to be forgiven. Without participating in the exaggerated ideas which she cherished about her Max, it appeared sufficiently evident that he had good prospects, and that, when these prospects were realized, the disagreeable consequences of his liberality would soon vanish. But yet another reason excused his apparent carelessness and hers. At an early age she had lost both parents, and had been educated by her father's relatives. At the time of her marriage, they told her that she had a small fortune, which was accordingly handed over to her; but Havelaar discovered, from some letters of earlier date, and from some loose notes

which she kept in a writing-desk that had belonged to
her mother, that her family had been very rich ; but he
could not make out where, or how, this wealth had been
lost. She, who had never herself taken any interest in
money matters, could give little or no information on this
subject. When Havelaar insisted upon some information
concerning the former possessions of her family, he found
that her grandfather, the Baron W., had emigrated with
William vi.[1] to England, and had been captain in the
army of the Duke of York. It seemed that he had led
a jolly life with the emigrant members of the Stadtholder's household, which was considered by many to
have occasioned the decline of his fortunes. He was
afterwards killed at Waterloo, in a combat among the
hussars of Boreel. The letters of her father, then a young
man of eighteen, were touching to read,—as lieutenant of
that corps, he had received in the same charge a sabre-cut
on the head, from the consequences of which he died
eight years afterwards in a state of madness,—letters
to his mother, in which he lamented how he had sought
in vain for his father's corpse.

She remembered that her grandfather on the mother's
side had lived in very high style, and it appeared from
some papers that he had been in possession of the post-

[1] Willem, Prince of Orange, Stadtholder of the United Provinces,
was obliged to leave his country in the year 1795, because of the
revolution ; he died at Fulda in 1806.

offices in Switzerland, in the same manner as till now, in
a great part of Germany and Italy, this branch of revenue
is an appanage of the princes of Tour and Taxis. Hence
a large fortune was to be expected; but from some entirely unknown causes, nothing, or very little at least, was
handed over to the second generation.

Havelaar did not learn the little that could be known
of this matter till after his marriage; and while investigating it, he was surprised that the said writing-desk,
with the contents, which she preserved from a feeling of
filial love, without knowing that it perhaps contained
papers of importance in a financial point of view, had
incomprehensibly disappeared. Disinterested as he was, he
built on this and many other circumstances the idea that
a *romantic story* was hidden in the background; and one
cannot be angry with him that he, who was in want of so
much for his style of living, desired that this romance
should have a happy end. However this may be, whether
there had been spoliation or not, it is certain that in
Havelaar's imagination something was produced which
one could call—*un rêve aux millions.*

It is again strange, that he who would have so carefully examined and so sharply defended the right of
another, though it might have been buried very deep
beneath dusky papers and thick-webbed chicanery, here,
where his own interest was at stake, carelessly neglected
the moment when he ought to have taken the matter up.

It seemed as if he was ashamed of it, because it concerned here his own interest, and I believe for certain, that had "his Tine" been married to another, and he been intrusted to break the cobweb in which her ancestral fortunes remained hanging, Havelaar would have succeeded in putting "the interesting orphan" in the possession of the fortune she was entitled to. But now this interesting orphan was his wife; her fortune was his: and he thought it something mean and degrading, something derogatory, to ask in her name, "Don't you owe me something more?"

Yet he could not shake off this dream of 'millions,' were it only to have an excuse at hand for the often repeated self-reproach that he spent too much money.

But a short time before returning to Java, when he had already suffered much under the pressure of impecuniosity, when he had to bow his proud head under the *furca caudina* of many a creditor, he succeeded in conquering his idleness or shyness, and set himself to work for the millions to which he still thought he had a right. And they sent him in reply a long-standing bill, an argument against which, as everybody knows, nothing can be said.

But they would be economical at Lebak. And why not? In such an uncivilized country you will not see girls in the streets who have a little honour to sell for a little food. There you will not meet persons who live on problematic employments. There it does not happen, that a family suddenly loses all through a change of fortune—— and of this kind were generally the rocks on which the good intentions of Havelaar had made shipwreck. The number of Europeans in this district was too small to be noticed; and the Javanese at Lebak were too poor to become interesting through any increase of poverty. Tine did not think of all this; for then she ought to have thought more than her love for Max permitted of the causes of their less favourable circumstances. There was something, however, in their new surroundings that breathed a calm, an absence of all cases of falsely romantic appearance, which had made Havelaar so often say in former days : " Is not this, Tine, a case from which I cannot withdraw ?" And the answer always was : "Certainly, Max, you cannot withdraw from it."

We shall see how the simple, apparently still life of Lebak, cost Havelaar more than all the former excesses of his heart taken together.

But that they did not know ! They expected the future with confidence, and were so happy in their love, and in the possession of their child.

" How full this garden is of roses !" said Tine, " and look at the *rampeh*, and *tjempaka*, and *melati*,[1] and beautiful lilies——."

And children as they were, they were delighted with

[1] Flowers.

their new house ; and when in the evening Duclari and Verbrugge, after a visit to Havelaar, returned to their common home, they made many remarks on the childlike joy of the newly arrived family.

Havelaar went to his office, and remained there till the next morning.

CHAPTER VIII.

HAVELAAR had requested the Controller to invite the chiefs who were at Rankas-Betong to stay there till the next day to be present at the *Sebah* (council) which he intended to convene. Such a council generally took place once a month; but either because he wished to spare some chiefs who lived very far from the capital the unnecessary journey to and fro, or because he wished to speak to them immediately impressively, and without waiting for the appointed day, he chose the next morning for the first Sebah.

To the left of his mansion, but in the same grounds, and opposite the house which Madam Slotering occupied, stood a building, part of which was used for the offices of the Assistant Resident, where was also the Treasury. This building contained a large open gallery, which made it a very good place for such a council. There the chiefs assembled betimes in the morning. Havelaar entered, saluted, and sat down. He received the written reports

on agriculture, police, and justice, and put them aside for
after examination.

Every one expected an address such as the Resident
had delivered the day before, and it was not quite certain
that Havelaar himself intended to say anything else to
the chiefs; but you ought to have seen him on such
occasions to conceive how he, at speeches like those, grew
excited, and, through his peculiar way of speaking, communicated a new colour to the most common things;
how he became taller, so to speak, how his glance shot
fire, how his voice passed from a flattering softness to a
lancet sharpness, how the metaphors flowed from his lips,
as if he was scattering some precious commodity round
about him, which, however, cost him nothing, and how,
when he ceased, every one looked at him with an open
mouth, as if asking, "Good God! who are you?"

It is true that he himself who spoke on such occasions
as an apostle, as a seer, afterwards did not exactly know
how he had spoken, and his eloquence was therefore
more powerful to astonish and to touch, than to convince by solid argument. He would have excited the
martial spirit of the Athenians to frenzy as soon as they
had decided to go to war with Philip; but he would
not have succeeded so well, if it had been his task to
incite them to this war through cogency of reasoning.
His harangue to the chiefs of Lebak was of course in
Malay,—a circumstance which added greatly to its effect,

because the simplicity of the Oriental tongues gives to
many expressions a force which has been lost in the
greater formality of the languages of the West; whilst,
on the other hand, it is difficult to render the sweetness
of the Malay in any other language. We must, moreover,
take into consideration, that the greater part of his listeners consisted of simple, but not at all stupid men, and
at the same time Orientals, whose impressions differ con-
siderably from our own.

Havelaar spoke almost as follows :—

"Mr. Radeen Adhipatti,[1] Regent of Bantam-Kidool,[2]
and you Radeens Demang, that are chiefs of the districts
of this province, and you Radeen Djaksa, administrator of
justice, and you too, Radeen Kliwon, governor of the chief
town, and you Radeens, Mantries, and all that are chiefs
in the district of Bantam-Kidool——I salute you.

"And I tell you that I feel joy in my heart when I see
you all assembled, and listening to the words of my mouth.

"I know that there are amongst you men who excel in
knowledge and goodness of heart: I hope to enlarge my
knowledge by contact with yours; for it is not so great
as I should wish; and I certainly love probity, but I perceive that there are often in my soul faults that over-
shadow the probity, and hinder the growth; for you know

---

[1] Titles—impossible to translate them into European languages.—
Radeen or *Radhen* almost = the French *Chevalier.*

[2] Bantam-Kidool = South Bantam = Lebak.

how the large tree pushes away and kills the little tree.
Therefore I shall look to those amongst you who excel in
virtue, to try to become better than I am.

"I heartily salute you all.

"When the Governor-General commanded me to come
to you as Assistant Resident in this district, my heart
rejoiced. You know that I had never set foot on Bantam-Kidool; therefore I have obtained information about
your district, and have seen that there is much good in
Bantam-Kidool. Your people possess rice-fields in the
valleys, and there are rice-fields on the mountains. And
you wish to live in peace, and you do not desire to
live in those districts that are inhabited by other persons. Yes, I know that there is much good in Bantam-
Kidool.

"But not on that account alone did my heart rejoice;
for elsewhere, also, I should have found much good.

"But I discovered that your population is poor, and
therefore I rejoiced with all my soul.

"For I know that Allah loves the poor, and that He
gives riches to whomsoever He will try; but to the poor
He sends all who speak His word, that they may rise in
the midst of their misery.

"Does not He give rain when the blade would otherwise wither, and a dewdrop in the cup of the thirsty
flower?

"And is it not sublime to be sent to seek them that

I

are weary, who have lingered behind after the work and have fallen down exhausted on the road, because their knees were not strong enough to carry them to the place where they should receive their wages? Should not I be glad to give a helping hand to him who tumbled into the ditch, and a staff to him who climbs the mountains?

"Should not my heart leap with joy when it sees that I have been selected amongst many to turn lamentation into prayer, weeping into thanksgiving?

"Yes, I am very glad to be in Bantam-Kidool.

"I said to the woman who shares my sorrows and increases my happiness:—

"'Rejoice, for I see that Allah gives a blessing on the head of our child! He has sent me to a place where work is to be done, and He thought me worthy to be there before harvest-time. For the joy is not in cutting *paddy*;[1] the joy is in cutting the paddy which one has planted. And the soul of man does not rejoice in wages, but in the labour that earns those wages.' And I said to her: 'Allah has given us a child; and there will come a time when he shall say: "Do you know that I am *his* son?" and then there will be those in the country who will greet him with love, who will put a hand on his head and say: "Sit down to our dinner, and live in our house, and take your portion of what we have; for we knew your father."'

[1] *Paddy* = rice in the field.

" For, chiefs of Lebak, there is much to be done in your district.

"Tell me, is not the labourer poor? Does not your paddy often ripen for those who did not plant it? Are there not many wrongs in your country? Is not the number of your children small?

" Is there no shame in your souls when the natives of Bolang, which lies over there in the East, visit your country, and ask, ' Where are the villages, and where the husbandmen, and why do not I hear the *gamlang*,[1] which speaks joy out of a mouth of brass, nor the stamping of paddy by your daughters?'

" Is there no bitterness in journeying from here to the South coast, in seeing the mountains that have no water on their sides, or the plains where the buffalo never drew the plough?

" Yes, yes, I tell you, that your soul and mine are sad because of these things; and, therefore, we are grateful to Allah, that He has given us the power to labour here.

" For we have in this country fields for many, though the inhabitants are few. And it is not the rain which fails, for the summits of the mountains suck the clouds of heaven to the earth. And not everywhere are rocks that refuse a place to the root; for in many places the ground is soft and fertile, and calls for the grain, which it is willing to return you in a bended blade. And there is

[1] *Gamlang* = musical instrument.

no war in the country, whereby the paddy is trodden down while yet green, nor is there sickness to paralyse the *patjol*.[1] Neither are the sunbeams more powerful than is necessary to ripen the grain, that has to be food for you and your children ; nor *banjers*,[2] that make you say, 'Show me the place where I have sown.'

"Where Allah sends inundations that wash away the fields ; where He hardens the ground as barren stones ; where He makes the sun burn even to scorching ; where He sends war to devastate the fields ; where He slays with diseases, that make the hands weak, or with dryness that kills the corn——there, chiefs of Lebak, we bend our heads, and say : 'His will be done !'

"But it is not so in Bantam-Kidool.

"I have been sent here to be your friend, your elder brother. Should not *you* warn your younger brother, if you saw a tiger in his way ?

"Chiefs of Lebak, we have often committed faults, and our country is poor, because we have committed so many faults.

"For in Tjikandi, Bolang, and Krawang, in the regions round about Batavia, there are many men who were born in our country, and who have left our country.

"Why do they seek labour far from the place where they buried their parents ? Why have they fled from the village where they were circumcised ? Why do they

---

[1] *Patjol* = spade.　　[2] *Banjers* = inundations.

prefer the coolness of the tree that grows *there*, to the shade of our woods?

"And even there to the North-West, over the sea, are many who ought to be our children, but who have left Lebak to wander in foreign countries with *Kris*,[1] and *Klewang*,[2] and gun! And there they die miserably; for the Government has power to beat the rebels.

"I ask you, chiefs of Lebak, why have many gone away, not to be buried where they were born? Why does the tree ask, 'Where is the man whom I saw playing at my foot when a child?'"

Havelaar waited here for a moment. To understand in some degree the impression which his words made, one ought to have heard and seen him. When he spoke of his child, there was a softness in his voice, something that was extremely touching, and which allured you to ask, "Where is the little one? I will at once kiss the child, that made his father speak so;" but when he soon afterwards passed with little order to the questions why Lebak was poor, and why so many inhabitants of these regions removed to other places, there was in his tone something which made you think of the noise that a drill makes when forcibly turned in hard wood. Yet he did not speak

---

[1] *Kris* = Indian weapon.

[2] *Klewang* = Indian weapon. "To wander in foreign countries with Kris, and Klewang, and gun," means here, that those persons go into other Residencies, where rebels are in arms against the Government.

very loud, neither did he put any stress on certain words; there was even something monotonous in his voice, but whether studied or natural, which by this very monotony made the impression of his words stronger on minds that were so particularly sensitive to such a language. His metaphors, which he always borrowed from the life that surrounded him, were to him as allies to make what he meant perfectly understood, and not, as often happens, troublesome appendages, which burden the phrases of orators, without adding any plainness to the conception of what is meant to be illustrated. We are now-a-days accustomed to the absurdity of the expression "Strong as a lion;" but he who first used this metaphor in Europe, showed that he had not drawn the comparison from the poetry of the soul, which furnishes figures of speech, and *cannot* speak otherwise, but that he had simply copied this from some book,—from the Bible, perhaps,—in which a lion was mentioned. For none of his hearers ever tried the strength of the lion, and it would therefore have been rather necessary to make them estimate that strength, by comparing the lion to some other creature whose strength was known to them, than otherwise.

You see, that Havelaar was truly a poet, that he, speaking of the rice-fields, that were on the mountains, directed his eyes thither through the open side of the hall, and that he really stood there; and in the imagination of

Havelaar's hearers he really looked about and asked for
the inhabitants of Lebak that had gone. He invented
nothing; he heard the tree speak, and only thought that
he repeated what he imagined to have heard so distinctly
in his poetical inspiration.

Should any one, perhaps, be inclined to make the
observation, that the originality of Havelaar's manner of
speaking is not so indisputable, as his language makes
you think of the style of the prophets of the Old Testament, I must remind him of what I said before, that in
moments of ecstasy he was indeed something of a seer,
and that he, fed by the impressions communicated to
him by living in forests and on mountains, and by the
poesy-breathing atmosphere of the East, would probably
not have spoken otherwise, even if he had never read
the sublime poems of the Old Testament.

Do we not find, in the verses written by him in *early
youth*, lines like the following, which were composed on
the Salak—one of the highest summits of the Preangan
Regencies,—in the exordium of which he displays the
softness of his emotions, and then suddenly passes to
the description of the thunder which he hears below
him :—

> " 'Tis sweeter here our Maker loud to praise :
> Prayer sounds more beautiful among the hills
> Than in the plains. Upon the mountain top
> The heart is nearer to its God, who makes

> Unto Himself an altar and a fane,
> Unsullied by the foot of human pride.
> 'Tis here He makes the rattling tempest heard—
> Summons His rolling thunder—Majesty!"

Do you not feel that he could not have written the last two lines if he had not really heard God's thunder, dictating to him in reverberating crashes along the mountain sides?

But he did not like to write poetry; it was, as he said, "like putting on a stiff corset," and when he was induced to read anything of what he had written, he took pleasure in abusing his own work, either by reading in a ridiculous tone, or by stopping short at a most solemn place, and throwing in a pun which shocked his hearers. This was nothing more than a satire upon the disproportion between his soul and *the corset* which confined it.

Havelaar had ordered by a sign the customary tea and sweetmeats; but few of the chiefs partook of the refreshments. It appears that he had paused with premeditation at the end of his speech; and there was a reason for it. What must the chiefs have thought of his knowing already that so many had left Lebak with bitterness in their hearts? of his knowing already how many families had emigrated to neighbouring countries to avoid the poverty that reigned here? and of his knowing the fact that there are so many Bantammers amongst the bands in revolt against the Dutch Government? What does he mean ? what is he aiming at ? who is concerned in his questions ?

And some of them looked at the district chief of Parang-Koodjang.   But most of them looked at the ground.

"Come here, Max," said Havelaar, who perceived his child playing before the house, and the Adhipatti took the boy on his knee; but he was too wild to remain there long; he jumped away and ran round the large circle amusing the chiefs with his talk, and playing with the hilts of their weapons.   When he came up to the *Djaksa*,[1] who excelled all the others in his uniform, and thereby attracted the child, the Djaksa showed something on little Max's head to the *Kliwon*,[2] who sat near him, and who seemed to assent to an observation about it.

"Go away now, Max," Havelaar said; "papa has something to say to these gentlemen," and the little boy ran away, kissing his hands to them.

"Chiefs of Lebak! we are all of us in the service of the King of Holland.   But he, who is just, and desires that we should perform our duty, is far from here.   Thirty times a thousand thousand souls, nay more, are under his rule, but he cannot be near all of those who are dependent on his will.

"The Governor-General at Buitenzorg[3] is just, and

---

[1] Administrator of Justice.
[2] Governor of the Capital, or chief town.
[3] The Residence of the Governor-General near Batavia.

desires that every one should do his duty; but powerful as he is, and commanding all authority in the cities, and the elders of the villages, and disposing of the army on land, and of the ships at sea, he likewise can no more than the King see where injustice has been done, for the injustice is far from *him*.

"And the Resident at Serang, who is lord of the Residency of Bantam, where live five times a hundred thousand men, desires that justice shall be done in his dominion, and that righteousness shall reign in those parts that obey him. But where injustice has been done he lives far from it, and whoever does wickedly, hides himself from his face because he fears punishment.

"And Mr. Adhipatti, who is Regent of South Bantam, wills that every one does good, and that there shall be no infamy in that country over which he is Regent.

"And I, who yesterday called God Almighty to witness that I would be just and merciful, that I would maintain justice without fear or hatred, that I would be 'a good Assistant Resident,' I wish to do my duty.

"Chiefs of Lebak! we all wish to do our duty.

"But if there should be amongst us any who neglect their duty for gain, who sell the Right for money, or who take away the buffalo from the poor, and bread from those who are hungry——who shall punish them?

"If any of you knew it, he would stop it, and the Regent would not suffer such an injustice to be done in his

Regency, and I myself should oppose it where I could, but if neither you, nor the Regent, nor I knew it——

"Chiefs of Lebak! who shall then do justice in Bantam-Kidool?

"Hear me, and I will tell you how justice would be done in such a case.

"There comes a time when our wives and children shall weep while preparing our shroud, and the passers-by shall say, 'A man has died there.' Then he who arrives in the villages shall bring the news of the death of him that has died, and the person who lodges him shall ask, 'Who was the man that died?'

"'He was good and just. He did justice, and drove not the suppliant from his door. He listened patiently to all who came to him, and returned that which had been taken away. And him who could not plough his land, because the buffalo had been taken out of his stables, he assisted to seek for the buffalo; and where the daughter had been carried off from the house of her mother, he sought the thief and brought the daughter back. And where work had been done, he did not withhold the wages, nor take away the fruit of him who planted the tree, nor the coat that was another's, nor eat the food that belonged to the poor.'

"Then it shall be said in the villages :—

"'Allah is great: Allah has taken him home. His will be done : a good man has died.'

"But again the passenger shall stand before a house and ask, 'What is this, that the gamlang is silent, and the song of the maidens is hushed?' And again it shall be said, 'A man has died.'

"And whosoever journeys to the villages, shall sit in the evening with the host, and round about him the sons and daughters of the house, and the children of those who live in the village, and he shall say:—

"'A man has died, who promised to be just; and he sold justice to every one who gave him money. He watered his field with the sweat of the labourer whom he had called away from his own labour. He did not pay the labourer his wages, but lived on the food of the poor. He became rich from the poverty of others. He had much gold and silver, and plenty of precious stones; but the labourer who lives in the neighbourhood did not know how to appease the hunger of his child. He smiled like a happy man; but there was gnashing of the teeth from the suppliant who sought justice. There was contentedness on his features; but there was no milk in the breasts of the mothers who would fain have given suck.'

"Then the people of the villages will say:—

"'Allah is great——we curse no one!'

"Chiefs of Lebak! there comes a time when all of us must die!

"What shall be said in the villages where we have

had power, and what by the bystanders who witness the funeral? and what shall we answer if, after death, a voice speaks to our soul, and asks, 'Why is there weeping in the fields, and how is it that the young men hide themselves? Who took the harvest out of the barn, and the buffalo that should have ploughed the fields out of the stall? What have you done with your brother whom I gave you to watch over? Why is the poor man sad? Why does he curse the fruitfulness of his wife?'"

Here Havelaar paused again for a few moments; and then continued, in the most simple tone possible, and as if nothing had been said to make an impression:—

"I wish to live on good terms with you, and therefore I beg you to regard me as your friend. Every one who has erred may reckon on a lenient sentence from me, for as I err so often myself, I shall not be severe; at least not in ordinary mistakes or negligences. Only where negligence becomes a custom, I will oppose it. Of faults of a more grave kind——of tyranny and extortion, I do not speak—such a thing shall not happen; is it not so, Regent?"

"Oh no, Mr. Assistant Resident, such a thing shall not happen in Lebak."

"Well then, gentlemen, chiefs of Bantam-Kidool! let us be glad that our province is so poor. We have a noble work before us. If Allah preserve us alive, we shall take care that prosperity comes. The ground is fertile enough, the population willing; if every one is suffered to remain in the enjoyment of the fruits of his labour, there is no doubt that within a short time the population will improve, as well both in the number of souls as in possessions and civilisation, for these things generally go hand in hand. I beg you again to regard me as a friend who will help you where he can, above all where injustice must be prevented. And now I commend myself to your co-operation.

" I will return to you the reports I have received on agriculture, cattle-breeding, police, and justice, with my orders.

" Chiefs of Lebak! I have said. You can return every one to his home. I cordially greet you all."

He bowed, offered his arm to the old Regent, and conducted him to his house, where Tine awaited him in the gallery.

" Come, Verbrugge, don't go home yet. Come, a glass of Madeira! And, yes, I *must* know that——Radeen Djaksa! stop a moment."

Havelaar said this whilst all the chiefs, bowing low, prepared to return to their homes. Verbrugge, too, was about to take his leave, but returned with the Djaksa.

" Tine, I'll take some Madeira; so will Verbrugge. I say, Djaksa! tell me what you said about Max to the Kliwon?

" *Minta ampong* (I beg your pardon), Mr. Assistant

Resident; I looked at his head, because you had spoken.

"What the deuce has his head to do with that? I have already forgotten what I said."

"Sir, I said to the Kliwon——" [Tine approached, they spoke about little Max.]

"I said to the Kliwon, that the Sinjo" (Portuguese, *Senko,* which here means *young* gentleman, on the same principle as *lucus a non lucendo*) "was made for a king."

Tine was glad to hear that——she thought so too!

"And the Adhipatti looked at the head of the little one, and to be sure! he too saw the *oeser-oeseran,*[1] according to Javanese superstition destined to wear a crown."

As etiquette did not permit the Djaksa a place in the presence of the Regent, he took his leave, and we were for some time together with the Regent without speaking of anything relative to the "service." But the Regent asked all of a sudden, "if the money which was to the tax-gatherer's credit could not be paid?"

"Certainly not," said Verbrugge, "Mr. Adhipatti knows that this cannot be done till his responsibility ceases."

Havelaar played with Max, but this did not prevent

---

[1] *Oeser-oeseran* = as the hairs are on the head. It means the place where the hairs of an animal meet (also said of the hair of the head). It is rather difficult to explain this peculiar hair vertebra—the *oeser-oeseran,* a peculiar one—a peculiar whirl in the hair. The Djaksa saw such a peculiar meeting of hairs on the head of little Max, just as some people in Europe look at the lines on your right hand.

him from reading in the Regent's face that Verbrugge's answer displeased him.

"Come, Verbrugge, don't let us be troublesome," said he, and he called for a clerk out of the office. "We will pray that his account will certainly be approved."

After the Adhipatti had taken his leave, Verbrugge, who was a confirmed *red-tapeist*, remonstrated—

"But, Mr. Havelaar, that must not be! The tax-gatherer's account is under examination at Serang.—— Suppose anything to be wanting?"

"Then I will make it good," Havelaar said.

Verbrugge did not understand this great consideration for the tax-gatherer.

The clerk soon returned with some papers; Havelaar signed his name, and ordered payment to be hastened.

"Verbrugge! I will tell you why I do this. The Regent has not a farthing in the house: his writer told me so——*he himself* wants this money, and the tax-gatherer will advance it to him. I would rather transgress, on my own responsibility, a form, than leave a man of his rank and years in perplexity. Moreover, Verbrugge! people at Lebak abuse their power in a fearful way——you *ought* to know it: *do* you know it?"

Verbrugge was silent.

"*I* know it!" Havelaar continued, "I do know it! Did not Mr. Slotering die in November? Well! *the day after his death*, the Regent forced the population to labour in his *rice-fields* without payment. *You ought* to have known it——*did* you know it?"

Verbrugge did *not* know it.

"You *ought* to have known it. *I* know it," continued Havelaar. "There you have the monthly reports of the districts,"—and he showed the parcel which he had received in the Council,—"look, I have opened nothing; there are statements of the number of labourers that have worked in the metropolis for the different chiefs.—— Well, are these statements correct?"

"I have not yet seen them——"

"Neither have I; still I ask you if they are correct? ——Were last month's statements correct?"

Verbrugge was silent.

"I will tell it you: They were false! For three times the number of labourers had to work for the Regent that the orders regulating such matters permit, and they did not dare put this in the reports——Is what I say true?"

Verbrugge was silent.

"The reports which I received to-day are likewise false," continued Havelaar; "the Regent is poor; the Regents of Bandong and Tjanjor are members of the family of which he is the head. He is an Adhipatti, and the Regent of Tjanjor is only a Tommongong, and because Lebak is not fit for coffee-culture, and therefore gives him no emolument, his revenues do not allow him to vie in magnificence and pomp with a simple *Demang* of the

K

Preangan Regencies, whose duty it would be to hold his nephews' horses——Is that true?"

"Yes, it is."

"He has nothing but his salary, and from that a deduction is made to pay off an advance which the Government gave him, when he——do you know?"

"Yes, I do."

"When he desired to build a new mosque, for which much money was required. Moreover, many members of his family——do you know?"

"Yes, I do."

"Many members of his family (who do not properly belong to Lebak, and are therefore not much esteemed) range themselves as a troop of plunderers round him, and extort money from him——is that true?"

"Yes," said Verbrugge.

"And when his purse is empty, which is often the case, they take, in his name, from the people what they like——is that so?"

"Yes, it is."

"I am also well informed——but more about that by and by. The Regent, who is old, has for some years been ruled by a desire to become meritorious through gifts to the priests; he spends much money for the travelling expenses of pilgrims to Mecca, who bring him back all sorts of old relics and talismans——Is it not so?

"Yes, that is true."

"Well, because of all this he is very poor. The Demang of Parang-Koodjang is his son-in-law. Where the Regent himself does not dare to take, out of shame for his rank, this Demang does it. But it is not the Demang alone—who courts the Regent by extorting money and goods from the poor population, and who carries the people away from their own rice-fields, by driving them to the Regent's rice-fields; and he——! I will believe, that he would willingly act otherwise, but necessity compels him to make use of such means—— Is not all this true, Verbrugge?"

"Yes, it is true," said Verbrugge, who perceived more and more that Havelaar's look was sharp.

"I knew," said Havelaar, "that he had no money in his house. You heard this morning, that it is my intention to do my duty. I will not suffer injustice; God help me, I will not suffer that!" And he jumped up, and there was something in his tone quite different from that of the day before, while taking his official oath.—"But I will do my duty with leniency. I do not care to know too exactly what has happened. But all that happens *henceforth* is on *my* responsibility; *I* shall, therefore, take care of that. I hope to remain here a long time. Do you know, Verbrugge, that our vocation is noble indeed? But, do you know, also, that I ought to have heard from *you* all that I have just told you? I know *you* quite well, as well as I know who are in revolt on the South coast: you are a good man, I know; but why did not you tell me of so much wrong going on here? You have been for two months temporary Assistant Resident, and moreover, you have been here a long time as Controller; you ought to know it."

"Mr. Havelaar, I never served under any one like you; —there's something very peculiar about you: don't be offended."

"Not at all; I know very well that I am not as all men——but what does that matter!"

"You communicate to others conceptions and ideas never heard of before."

"No! they had fallen asleep in that despicable official stillness, whose style is: '*I have the honour to be,*' and its feeling '*the perfect satisfaction of the Government.*' No, Verbrugge! do not trouble yourself about it. You need not learn anything from me.——For instance, this morning in the Council have I told you anything new?"

"No, no news——but you spoke quite differently from others."

"Yes, that is, because my education has been neglected. ——I speak at random. But you must tell me why you complied with all the wrong existing in Lebak?"

"I never before had such an impression at an initiation ——moreover, all this has always been so in these countries."

"Yes, yes; I know that very well——every one cannot

be a prophet or an apostle—wood would soon be too dear because of the crucifying. But certainly you will help me to make all right : you undoubtedly like to do your duty ?"

"To be sure! above all with you. But not every one would claim, or tax it so very severely, and then one gets so easily into the position of a man who fights windmills."

"No! those who love injustice because they live on it, say that there was no injustice to have the pleasure of railing at *you* as a Don Quixote, and keep *their* wind-mills turning at the same time. But, Verbrugge! you needed not to wait for me to do your duty. Mr. Slotering was a clever and honest man : he knew what happened ; he condemned it and opposed it. Look here!"—Havelaar took out of a writing-desk two sheets of paper, and show-ing them to Verbrugge, he asked—

" Whose handwriting is this?"

" That is the handwriting of Mr. Slotering——"

" Exactly so—well! Here are two rough copies, evi-dently containing subjects on which he wished to speak to the Resident. Look here:—1. 'On Rice Culture.' 2. 'On the Houses of the Village Chiefs.' 3. ' On the Gathering of the Land-taxes!!' etc. After the last are two points of exclamation——what did Mr. Slotering mean by that ?'

" I cannot tell," said Verbrugge.

" I can. That means that more taxes are paid than

flow into the exchequer of the country. But I will show you something which we both know, because it is written in words and not in signs. Look here :—

" ' 12. On the Abuses practised on the Population by the Regents and the Inferior Chiefs. On the keeping of different Houses at the Cost of the Population, etc.'

" Is that clear? You see that Mr. Slotering was certainly a man who knew how to take the initiative; you could have supported him. Listen :—

" ' 15. That many persons of the families and servants of the inland chiefs appear on the payment lists, who indeed take no part in the culture; whereby they have advantages to the prejudice of the real participants. They also get unlawfully into possession of rice-fields, ——which are only due to those persons who have a share in the culture.'

" Here I have another note written in pencil. Look here, too, we may read something that is very clear :—

" ' The emigration of the population at Parang-Koodjang can only be ascribed to the excess of abuses by which the people are victimized.'

" What do you say about that? You see I am not so eccentric as I appear to be, when I mean to do what is right, and that others shall do the same !"

" It is true," said Verbrugge; " Mr. Slotering often spoke to the Resident about all this."

" And what was the consequence ? "

"The Regent was summoned——and he had an inter-view with the Resident——"

"Exactly so! and what more?"

"The Regent generally denied all. Then witnesses were called for—nobody dared to bear witness against the Regent.——Mr. Havelaar, these things are very difficult!"

The reader, before he has finished the book, will know as well as Verbrugge why those things were so difficult.

"Mr. Slotering was much offended about this," continued the Controller; "he wrote sharp letters to the chiefs——"

"I read them last night," said Havelaar.

"And I often heard him say that, if there were no change, and if the Resident would not act with energy, he should apply direct to the Governor-General. This he also said at the last Council at which he presided."

"Then he would have done wrong, for the Resident was his superior, whom he ought not to pass over, and why should he? It is not, however, to be supposed that the Resident of Bantam approves of injustice and arbitrary power?"

"Approve——no; but one does not like to accuse a Regent——?"

"I do not like to accuse any one, whosoever it may be; but where it must be done, a Regent as well as anybody else. But accusing is still *out of* the question, God be praised! To-morrow I shall visit the Regent. I will

show him how bad it is to abuse one's power—above all,
where the possessions of poor people are concerned. But
in expectation that all will be restored, I will help him in
his critical circumstances as much as I can. You understand now why I made the tax-gatherer pay that money
immediately. I likewise intend to beg the Government
to acquit him of the advance. And to you, Verbrugge, I
propose that we perform our duty punctually, so long as
possible with leniency, but if *must* be so, fearlessly.
You are an honest man, I know, but you are timid. Say
henceforward resolutely how matters stand——*advienne que
pourra:* throw that vagueness away—and now stay to dinner with us: we have Dutch cauliflower—but all is quite
plain; for I must be very economical——Come, Max!"
And with Max on his shoulder, they entered the inner
gallery, where Tine waited for them at the table, which, as
Havelaar had said, was *very* simply provided. Duclari,
who came to ask Verbrugge if he meant to be home for
dinner, was likewise invited; and if you would like some
variation in my story, you must read the next chapter,
in which I shall tell you something of what was said at
this dinner.

CHAPTER IX.

READER, I would give anything to know exactly how long I could let a heroine float in the air, while *I* described a castle, without exhausting your patience, and causing you to look wearily aside, before the poor creature reached the earth? If my tale demanded such a caper, I should prudently choose a first storey for my *point de départ*, and a castle of which but little could be said. Once for all, however, I will make you easy on that head :—Havelaar's house had no storeys at all, and the heroine of my book,— the lovely, faithful, *anspruchlose* Tine, a heroine!—never jumped out of the window.

When I ended the foregoing chapter, with a reference to some variation in the next, it was rather a rhetorical artifice, and to make a good ending, than because I meant that the next chapter should only be valuable as a change. A writer is vain as a———man. Slander his mother, or ridicule the colour of his hair, say that he has an Amsterdam accent, such as no Amsterdammer ever had,—perhaps he will forgive you these things; but never say anything against him as an author——for this he will not forgive. If you don't think my book a good one, and you happen to meet me, just act as if we were strangers to each other.

No, even such a chapter "for a change" appears to me, through the magnifying-glass of my vanity as an author, to be most important and indispensable; and if you do not read it, and afterwards feel disappointed with my book, I shall not hesitate to tell you that your not reading it was the cause of your inability to appreciate my book, for the chapter you omitted was just the most essential of all——*I* therefore—for I am a man and an author —should hold every chapter to be essential which you had passed over with unpardonable readerlike levity. I imagine that your wife asks, "What do you think of that book?" And you say, for instance—[*horribile auditu* to me]—with the pomp of diction peculiar to married men—

"Humph! so-so.—I don't know yet."

Well then, barbarian! read on: what is most important is about to commence. And with trembling lips I look at you, and measure the thickness of the turned leaves—— and I look on your face for the reflection of that chapter "that is so important."——"No," I say, "he has not yet jumped up——embraced somebody in ecstasy——his wife perhaps——" But you read on. It appears to me that he has already had " the important chapter"——you have not jumped up at all, and have embraced nothing——

And fewer and fewer grow the leaves under your right thumb, and my hope for that embrace becomes fainter and fainter :

" Yes, truly, I reckoned on a tear !"

And you have finished the novel to " where they have met each other," and you say, yawning—[" that is another expression of true eloquence"]—

" Not much——it is such a book as is often written now-a-days !"

But don't you know, monster, tiger, European reader ! don't you know that you spent an hour in biting my soul as a tooth-pick; in gnawing and chewing the flesh and bone of your species ? Man-eater ! my soul was in that which you have ruminated on as once eaten grass. That was my heart that you swallowed there as a dainty bit, for I put my heart and my soul into that book: and so many tears fell on that manuscript, and my blood went back from the veins to the heart, as I wrote on, and I gave you all this; and you bought this for a few pence—and you say " Humph !"

The reader understands that I do not speak here about *my* book.

So that I will only say, that I quote the words of Abraham Blankaart [1]——

---

[1] One of the characters of a Dutch novel much in vogue some fifty years ago.

"Who is that Abraham Blankaart?" asked Louise Rose-meyer, and Fred told her, which gave me much pleasure; for this gave me an opportunity to get up and make an end of the reading—for this evening at least. You know that I am a coffee-broker—[No. 37 Laurier Canal]—and that I live for my profession; you will therefore be able to judge how little pleased I was with the work of Stern. I had hoped it would be about coffee, and he gave us—— yes, Heaven knows what! He has already had our attention during three parties, and, what is worse, the Rose-meyers like it. I make a remark, he appeals to Louise. Her approbation, he says, is dearer to him than all the coffee in the world, and moreover, when my heart burns, etc.—[look at that tirade, page so-and-so, or rather don't look for it at all.] There I am, and don't know what to do! That parcel of Shawlman's is a true Trojan horse; even Fred is corrupted by it. He helped Stern, as I per-ceive, for "Abraham Blankaart" is *too Dutch* for a German. Both are so very self-sufficient that I am truly perplexed with the matter. Worse still, I made an agreement with Gaafzuiger for the publishing of a book about the Coffee-Auctions. All Holland is waiting for it, and there Stern goes quite another way. Yesterday he said: " Be at your ease ; different roads lead to Rome : wait for the end of the introduction"—[is all this only "introduction ?"]—

"I promise you that all will come down to coffee,—coffee, coffee, and nothing but coffee." "Think of Horace," he continued; "has he not said, '*Omne tulit punctum qui miscuit*'——*Coffee with something else?* And do you not act in the same way, when you put sugar and milk in your cup?" And then I am forced to be silent; not because he is right, but because I and the firm Last and Co., have to take care that old Mr. Stern does not fall into the hands of Busselinck and Waterman, who would serve him very badly, because they are bunglers.

With your permission, reader! I give vent to my feelings, and in order that you, after reading what Stern has written—[have you really read it?]—should not pour out your wrath on an innocent head,—for what man will employ a broker who scolds him for a man-eater?—I take it for granted that you are convinced of my innocence. I cannot exclude young Stern from a share in my book, now that matters have gone so far. Louise Rosemeyer when she comes out of church—[the boys appear to wait for her]—asks if he will come early in the evening to read a good deal about Max Havelaar and Tine.

But as you bought or borrowed the book trusting in the respectable title, which promises something worth reading, I acknowledge your claims to something that is worth your money, and, therefore, I once more write a couple of chapters. You, reader, do not go to the parties of the Rosemeyers; and therefore you are more fortunate than I am, who have to hear all! You are at liberty to pass over the chapters that have a flavour of German excitement, and to read only what has been written by me, who am a respectable man and a coffee-broker.

With surprise I learnt from Stern's scribbling and Shawlman's parcel the fact that no coffee is planted in the district of Lebak. That is a great mistake, and I shall consider my pains largely rewarded, if the Government through my book perceives this fault.

From Shawlman's papers it would appear that the soil in these regions is not fit for coffee-culture; but that is no excuse; and I maintain that it is an unpardonable neglect of the interests of Holland generally, and of the coffee-brokers in particular; yes, of the Javanese, neither to make the ground fit for coffee—[the Javanese have nothing else to do]—or, if they think this impossible, to send the men who live there to other places where the ground is good for coffee.

I never say anything that I have not well considered, and I dare affirm that I here speak with a knowledge of business, because I have maturely considered this matter more than once since I heard Dominé[1] Wawelaar's sermon on the Fast-day[2] for the Conversion of the Heathen.

That was on Wednesday evening. You must know that I punctually fulfil my obligations as a father, and that I

[1] "Dominé,"—title of Dutch clergymen.
[2] Literally, "day of prayers."

take the moral education of my children very much to heart. As Fred has during the last few days assumed something in tone and manner which displeases me— [that confounded parcel is the cause of it all]—I have given him a good lecture, and said, " Fred, I am not satis- fied with you : I always set you a good example, and you forsake the right path; you are conceited and trouble- some; you make verses, and you have kissed Betsy Rose- meyer. The fear of the Lord is the source of all wisdom : therefore you must not kiss the Rosemeyers, and you must not be so conceited. Immorality leads to destruction : read the Scriptures, and mark that Shawlman. He left the ways of the Lord: now he is poor, and dwells in a little garret; that is the consequence of immorality and bad conduct; he wrote improper articles in the *Indépendance* and let the ' Aglaja ' fall: such are the consequences of being wise in one's own eyes. He does not now know what o'clock it is, and his little boy wears knee-breeches. Think that your body is a temple of God, and that your father has always had to work very hard for his bread— [it is the truth]. Raise your eyes upwards, and endeavour to become a respectable broker when I go to Driebergen.[1] And consider all those men, who will not listen to good counsel, who trample upon religion and morality, and see yourself in these men. Do not think yourself equal to Stern, whose father is so rich, and who will always have

[1] Driebergen,—a village of country-seats ; the *summum bonum* of a successful Amsterdam trader's aspirations.

money enough, even if he does not like to become a
broker.   Only think that wickedness is always punished :
look again at that Shawlman, who has no winter overcoat, and who looks like a clown.   Pay attention when
you are at church, and you must not fidget so much on
your bench, as if you were annoyed ; and do not wait for
girls when the service is over, for that destroys all chance
of edification.   Do not make Mary laugh when I am
reading the Bible at breakfast ; all this should not be in a
respectable household.

"You have also drawn caricatures on Bastianus' desk
when he was not at the office on account of the gout,
which continually plagues him,—this keeps them in the
office away from their work ; and you may read in the
Word of God that such follies end in ruin.   This Shawlman did the same when he was young : when a child he
beat a Greek on the Wester Market ; now he is idle, conceited, and sickly.   Do not always make fun with Stern ;
his father is rich ; and do as if you did not see it, when
he makes wry faces to the bookkeeper, and when he is
busy with verses outside the office.   Tell him that he had
better write to his father that he likes our Company very
much, and that he is so contented here, and that Mary
has embroidered slippers for him.   Ask him, if he thinks
that his father will go to Busselinck and Waterman, and
tell him that they are low fellows.   Do you see that you
will in this way bring him into the right path ? you owe

this to your fellow-creatures, and all that verse-making is nonsense. Be just and obedient, Fred, and do not pull the maid-servant's dress when she brings tea into the office; and do not make me ashamed that she spills it; and St. Paul says, that a son must never vex his father. These twenty years I have frequented the Exchange, and I may say, that I am esteemed there at my stall. Therefore listen to my exhortations, Fred; fetch your hat, put on your coat, and go with me to the prayer-meeting: that will do you all the good in the world."

So I have spoken, and I am convinced that I made some impression, above all because Dominé Wawelaar had for his subject :—The love of God evident in His wrath against unbelievers.--(Samuel's reproof of Saul : 1 Sam. xv. 33.)

I continually thought, while listening to his sermon, how great is the difference between human wisdom and divine. I have already told you, that in Shawlman's parcel, there is, amongst much rubbish, a great deal of what appeared to be sound common sense; but of how little significance is this, when compared with such language as that of Parson Wawelaar. And not from his own strength,—for I know Wawelaar, and consider him to be a man of middling capacity—his eloquence is given him by the power that comes from above. This difference was still more obvious, because he hinted at many things, about which Shawlman himself had written; for you have seen, that in his parcel, he speaks much about

L

Javanese and other Pagans—[Fred says that the Javanese are no Pagans; but I call every one who has a wrong
faith a Pagan]. From the Dominé's sermon I got my idea
of the unlawful revocation of the coffee-culture at Lebak,
about which I shall say more by and by; and because,
being an honest man, I am not willing that the reader
should receive nothing for his money, I will here communicate some extracts from the sermon, which I consider
particularly touching. He had proved in a few words
from the above-named text the love of God, and very soon
went on to the point in question, viz., the conversion of
Javanese, Malay, and other Pagan races, whatever may
be their names.

"Such, my beloved! was the vocation of Israel"—[he
meant the destruction of the inhabitants of Canaan]—
" and such is the vocation of Holland! No, it shall not
" be said that the light which beams upon us has been
" put aside under a bushel, nor that we grudgingly com-
" municate the bread of life. Glance at the islands of the
" Indian Ocean, inhabited by millions and millions of
" children of the accursed son—and of the rightly ac-
" cursed son—of the noble, God-serving Noah. There
" they creep in the disgusting snake-holes of Pagan ignor-
" ance, there they bow the black woolly head under the
" yoke of selfish priests. There they worship God, invok-
" ing a false prophet that is an abomination in the eyes
" of the Lord; and, beloved! as if it were not enough to

" obey a false prophet, there are even those among them
" who worship another God, or rather other gods; yes,
" gods of wood and stone, which they themselves have
" made in their own image—black, abominable, with flat
" noses, and devilish. Yes, beloved! tears almost arrest
" me; for deeper still is the depravity of the race of Ham.
" There are amongst them, that know no God under any
" name whatever; who think it sufficient to obey the laws
" of society; who consider a harvest-song, wherein they
" express their joy on the success of their labour, as a
" sufficient thanksgiving to the Supreme Being who made
" the harvest ripen.

" There are ignorant men, my beloved, who think that
" it is sufficient to love wife and child, and not to take
" from their fellow-beings what does not belong to them,
" and that they may then calmly lay down their heads
" and sleep! Do you not shiver with horror at this
" picture? does not your heart shrink when you think of
" what will be the fate of all those fools as soon as the
" trumpet shall sound which will summon the dead and
" separate the faithful from the unfaithful? Do you not
" hear? Yes, you *do* hear; for from the text you have
" perceived that your God is a mighty God, and a God
" who will inflict vengeance—yes, you hear the breaking
" bones, and the crackling of the flames in the eternal
" Gehenna, where there is weeping and gnashing of teeth :
" —there, there they burn and perish not, for the punish-

" ment is eternal :—there the flame licks with a never-
" satisfied tongue the screaming victims of unbelief :—
" there the worm dies not that gnaws their hearts through
" and through without destroying them, that there may
" always remain a heart to gnaw in the breast of the
" God-forsaken. Look how they strip off the black skin
" of that unbaptized child, that, scarcely born, was slung
" away from the breast of its mother into the abyss of
" eternal damnation——"[1]

[Now, at this moment a woman fainted away.]

" But, beloved," continued Dominé W., " God is a God
" of love. It is not His will that the sinner should
" perish, but that he should be saved by His mercy in
" Christ, *through* faith ! And therefore Holland has been
" selected to save as many as can be saved of these miser-
" able creatures. Therefore He has given power to a
" country small in extent, but great and strong by the
" knowledge of God,—power over the inhabitants of those
" regions, that they may be saved from the torments of hell
" by the holy, never sufficiently to be praised Gospel. The
" ships of Holland navigate the great waters, and bring
" civilisation, religion, Christianity, to the erring Javanese.
" No, our happy Holland does not desire salvation for
" itself alone ;—we wish to communicate it to the unfor-
" tunate creatures on far-off strands, that there lie bound

---

[1] Dominé Wawelaar and the *Holy Willie* of the Scottish poet Burns
appear to have been brought up in the same school of theology.

" in the fetters of unbelief, superstition, and immorality,
" —and the contemplation of the duties that rest on us
" shall be the seventh head of my sermon." For what
preceded was the sixth.

Amongst the obligations which we have to fulfil re-
specting these poor Pagans were named—

" 1. *The giving of large sums in money to the Missionary*
" *Societies.*

" 2. *The support of the Bible Societies, in order that they*
" *may be able to distribute Bibles in Java.*

" 3. *The erection of 'places for religious purposes at*
" *Harderwijk' for the use of the colonial recruiting depôt.*

" 4. *The writing of sermons and religious songs proper to be*
" *read and sung to the Javanese by the soldiers and sailors.*

" 5. *The formation of an association of influential men,*
" *whose duty it would be to supplicate our most worthy*
" *King——*

" (a.) *Only to appoint such governors, officers, and*
" *employés as can be regarded as steadfast in the true*
" *religion.*

" (b.) *To allow the Javanese to visit the barracks,*
" *the ships of war, and merchantmen, that by inter-*
" *course with Dutch soldiers and sailors they may be*
" *instructed in the kingdom of God.*

" (c.) *To prohibit the acceptance of Bibles or reli-*
" *gious treatises as payment in public-houses.*

" (d.) *To stipulate in the conditions of the opium*

" license[1] in Java, that in every opium-house a number
" of Bibles must be provided, in proportion to the ap-
" parent number of visitors of such a place ; and that
" the farmer binds himself not to sell any opium, unless
" the buyer takes a religious treatise at the same time.

  " (e.) To order that the Javanese be by labour
" educated to the kingdom of God.

" 6. *The giving of large sums of money to the Missionary*
" *Societies."*

I know that I have given the last statement under
No. 1 ; but he repeated it, and such a superfluity seems to
me to be very explicable in the enthusiasm of discourse.

But, reader, did you pay attention to No. 5 (*e.*) ? Now
then ; that was what put me so much in mind of the
Coffee-Auctions and the pretended sterility of the soil of
Lebak, that you will not be surprised, on my assuring
you, that this matter has not been for a moment out of
my thoughts since Wednesday evening. Dominé W. read
the reports of the missionaries ; nobody can dispute his
thorough knowledge of the business. Well then,—when
he, with these reports in his hands, and his eyes turned
to God, asserts that much labour will be favourable to
the conquest of Javanese souls to the kingdom of God,
then I may certainly assume that I am not so far from
the truth, when I say that Lebak will do very well for
coffee-culture ; and more still, that the Supreme Being

---

[1] The opium trade is a monopoly of the Dutch Government!!

perhaps made the ground unfit for coffee-culture, only in order that by the labour that is necessary to construct another soil there, the population of that province may be made fit for salvation.

I *do* hope that my book will fall under the King's eye, and that it may be very soon apparent in enlarged Auctions, how strong a relation there is between the knowledge of God and the well-known interest of all citizens. Look how the simple, humble Wawelaar, without wisdom of men—[the fellow never set foot in the Exchange]—but enlightened by the Gospel, which is a lamp to his path, suddenly gives me, a coffee-broker, a hint which is not only important to all Holland, but whereby I may be able to go perhaps five years earlier to Driebergen, if Fred behaves well—[he was very quiet during the sermon]. Yes, labour, labour, that is my maxim; labour for the Javanese, that is my principle, and my principles are sacred to me.

Is not the Gospel the *summum bonum?* Is there anything better than salvation? Is it not, therefore, our duty to make sure the salvation of these men? And when labour is necessary for that——I myself have frequented the Exchange for twenty years——can we then refuse labour to the Javanese, when it is necessary for his soul, in order that it may not be tormented hereafter? Selfishness! it would be abominable selfishness if we did not employ all possible efforts to save those poor erring men

from the terrible future which Dominé Wawelaar so
eloquently described. A lady fainted when he spoke
of that black child; perhaps she has a little boy of dark
features——such are women!

And should not I insist upon labour,—*I*, who think
from morning till evening only about business? Is not
even that book, which Stern makes me dislike so much,
a proof how good my intentions are for the welfare of the
country, and how I like to sacrifice all for that? And
when *I* have to labour so hard, *I* who was baptized (in
the Amstel Kirk), is it not lawful to exact of the Javanese, who has still to earn his salvation, that he should
employ his hands?

When that Society·—[I mean No. 5 (*e.*)]—is formed, I
will join it, and endeavour to engage the Rosemeyers to
join it too, because the sugar-refiners have also an interest
in it, though I do not believe that they are very particular
in their ideas,—I mean the Rosemeyers, for they have
a Roman Catholic servant. In any case, I shall do my
duty. *That* I promised myself while returning home with
Fred from the prayer-meeting. In *my* house the Lord
shall be served, I will take care of that; and with the
more zeal, the more I perceive how wisely all has been
settled, how good the ways are by which we are conducted to the hand of God, how He wills to preserve us
for eternal and temporal life——for that ground at Lebak
can be very well fitted for coffee-culture.

CHAPTER X.

THOUGH I spare nobody where principles are concerned, yet I have come to the conclusion that I must act otherwise with Stern than with Fred; and as I foresee that my name—[the firm is Last and Co., but my name is Drystubble—Batavus Drystubble]—will be connected with a book, wherein matters appear that are not in harmony with the respect which every honourable man and broker owes to himself, I conceive it to be my duty to communicate to you how I have endeavoured to bring this young man Stern back to the true path.

I did not speak to him of the Lord, because he is a Lutheran; but I worked on his mind and his honour. See how I did this, and observe how useful a knowledge of mankind is. I heard him say, "*auf Ehrenwort*," and asked him what he meant by that?

"Well," he said, "that I pledge my honour for the truth of what I say."

"That is much," I said. "Are you so sure of speaking the truth?"

"Yes," he replied, "I always speak the truth. When my breast glows * * *" The reader knows the rest.

"That is indeed very noble," said I, and I made as if I believed it.

But this was a part of the trap that I had prepared for him, to show the young fellow his right place, and to make him understand how great is the distance between a mere beginner—though his father may have a large business—and a broker who has frequented the Exchange for twenty years, but I said it in a manner not to run the risk of seeing old Mr. Stern fall into the hands of Busselinck and Waterman. I was acquainted with the fact that he knows all sorts of verses by heart; and as verses always contain lies, I was quite sure that I should very soon catch him telling lies. It was not long before I *did*. I sat in the back parlour, and he was in the *suite*[1]—for we have a suite; Mary was occupied with knitting, and he was going to tell her something. I listened very attentively, and when he had finished I asked him if he possessed the book containing the story which he had just narrated. He said Yes, and gave it me; it was a volume of one of the works of a certain fellow called Heine.

The following morning I handed to him—Stern, I mean —the following

---

[1] *Suite* is an Amsterdamism, and means a front room divided from a back parlour by folding-doors: to possess such a "suite" is considered in Amsterdam as the *ne plus ultra* of respectability.

" Contemplations on the love of truth of one who recites
   " the following nonsense of Heine to a young girl
   " occupied in knitting in the drawing-room—

' Auf Flügeln des Gesanges,
   Herzliebchen, trag' ich dich fort.'[1]

" *Herzliebchen*——? Mary your sweetheart? Do your
" parents and Louise Rosemeyer know that? Is it proper
" to say that to a child, who might, on account of it, very
" readily become disobedient to her mother, by thinking
" herself of age, because she is called *herzliebchen*. What
" is the meaning of that ' carrying away on your wings?'
" You have no wings, nor has your song. Try to fly over
" the Laurier Canal: it is not very wide. But if you had
" wings, could you propose such a thing to a girl who
" is not yet confirmed? what do you mean by that flying
" away together? For shame!

' Fort nach den Fluren des Ganges
   Da weisz ich den schönsten Ort.'[2]

" Then you may go there alone, and hire lodgings, but
" don't take with you a girl who has to help her mother
" at home. But you do not mean it; for you never saw
" the Ganges, and you cannot therefore know whether you
" will be comfortable there. Shall *I* tell you how matters

[1] "On song's exulting pinion
   I 'll bear thee, my sweetheart fair."
[2] " Where Ganges holds his dominion,—
   The sweetest of spots know I there."

" stand ?   You tell nothing but lies only, because you
" make yourself in the verses a slave of cadence and
" rhyme.   If the first line had ended in *cake*, you would
" have asked Mary whether she would go with you to a
" *lake*, and so on.   You see, therefore, that your proposed
" voyage was not meant, and that all depends on a tinkling
" of words without sense.   What if Mary should indeed
" like to undertake this journey ?   I do not speak now of
" the uncomfortable mode of conveyance which you pro-
" pose ; but she is, God be praised, too intelligent to long
" for a country of which you say :—

   ' Da liegt ein rothblühender Garten
    Im stillen Mondenschein ;
   Die Lotosblumen erwarten
    Ihr trautes Schwesterlein ;

   ' Die Veilchen kichern und kosen ;
    Und schau'n nach den Sternen empor ;
   Heimlich erzählen die Rosen
    Sich düftende Märchen in's Ohr !'[1]

" What do you intend to do with Mary in that garden
" in the moonshine ?   Is that moral, is that proper, is that

[1] " There a red blooming garden is lying
  In the moonlight silent and clear ;
 The lotos-flowers are sighing
  For their sister so pretty and dear.

" The violets prattle and titter,
  And gaze on the stars high above ;
 The roses mysteriously twitter
  Their fragrant stories of love."

" respectable, Stern ? Would you disgrace me to the level
" of Busselinck and Waterman, with whom no respectable
" commercial firm will have any dealings, because of the
" elopement of their daughter, and because they are
" bunglers. What should I have to say, when they
" asked me on the Exchange why my daughter remained
" so long in that garden ? For, you understand,—I hope
" that nobody would believe me if I said that she had to
" look after those *lotos* flowers, which, as you say, have
" been long waiting for her. And every intelligent man,
" too, would laugh at me if I was foolish enough to say,
" 'Mary is there in that red garden—[why red, and not
" yellow or purple ?]—to listen to the tattle and laughing
" of the violets, or to the tales which the roses tell each
" other in a clandestine manner.' Even though this might
" be the truth, of what use would it be to Mary if all
" happened so clandestinely that she did not understand a
" word ? But it's all lies, insipid lies, and ugly they are
" at the same time ; for take a pencil and draw a rose
" with an ear, and see how that looks. And what do you
" mean by saying, that those tales have a nice perfume ?
" Shall I tell you what it means in plain Dutch ? That
" means, that you can smell the lie——so it is !

> ' Da hüpfen herbei und lauschen
> Die frommen, klugen Gazellen ;
> Und in der Ferne rauschen
> Des heiligen Stromes Wellen,——

'Da wollen wir niedersinken
Unter den Palmenbaum
Und Ruhe und Liebe trinken
Und träumen seligen Traum.'[1]

"Cannot you go to the Zoological Gardens, if you wish
"to see foreign animals?   Must those animals be on the
"Ganges, which you never observe so well in the wilder-
"ness as in a nice enclosure of iron?   Why are those
"animals *pious* and *clever*?   I will not speak of the latter
"word (it serves to make foolish verses rhyme), but pious?
"What is the meaning of that?   Is not this an abuse of a
"holy word that should only be used of men who hold the
"true faith?   And then that holy stream?   These stories
"you tell to Mary might make her a Pagan, might make
"her faith waver as to the existence of any other holy
"water than that of baptism, and any holier river than
"the Jordan.   Is not that an undermining of morality,
"virtue, religion, Christianity, and respectability?

"Think about all this, Stern!   Your father is the head
"of a respectable firm, and I am quite sure that he

---

[1] "The gazelles so gentle (pious) and clever
    Skip lightly in frolicsome mood ;
    And in the distance roars ever
    The holy river's loud flood.

"And there, while joyously sinking
    Beneath the palm by the stream,
    And love and repose while drinking,
    Of blissful visions we'll dream."
            —From Bowring's *Heine's Poems.*   Lond. 1866.

" approves of my speaking thus in a straightforward way,
" and that he likes to do business with a person who de-
" fends virtue and religion.   Yes, principles are sacred to
" me, and I do not scruple to say plainly what I mean :
" therefore, make no secret of what I say ; you may write
" to your father that you are here in a respectable family,
" that shows you the right path, and ask yourself what
" would have become of you if you had gone to Bussel-
" inck and Waterman ?   There you would likewise have
" recited such verses, and nobody would have told you the
" folly of it, because they are bunglers.   You may write
" this to your father, for when principles are concerned I
" fear nobody.   *There* the girls would perhaps have gone
" with you to the Ganges, and then you would perhaps by
" this time be lying under that tree on the grass; whereas,
" because *I* warned you, you remain with us in a re-
" spectable house.   You may write all this to your father,
" and tell him that you are so grateful, that you came
" with us, and that I take such good care of you, and that
" the daughter of Busselinck and Waterman ran away ;
" make him my compliments, and say that I intend to
" drop $\frac{1}{16}$ per cent. of the brokerage, because I cannot
" suffer those low fellows, who steal the bread out of the
" mouth of a rival in trade by more favourable conditions.

   " And be so kind as to give us something more sub-
" stantial in your readings at the Rosemeyers'.   I have
" seen in Shawlman's parcel statements of the coffee-

" culture of the last twenty years, in all the Residencies
" in Java : read us something of that.   And you must not
" scold the girls and all of us, by saying that we are can-
" nibals, who have swallowed a part of you ; that is not
" respectable, my boy ; believe one who knows what goes
" on in the world.   I served your father before his birth
" —[I mean the firm, Last and Co., formerly it was Last
" and Meyer]—you understand, therefore, that I speak for
" your good.   And incite Fred to behave himself better,
" and do not teach him to make verses ; and make as if
" you did not see it when he makes wry faces at the
" bookkeeper, and suchlike things.   Show him a good
" example, because you are much older, and try to im-
" press him with steadiness and gravity, because he must
" become a broker.

          " I am your fatherly friend,

                    " BATAVUS DRYSTUBBLE,
                    (*Firm* LAST & Co., *Coffee-Brokers,*
                    No. 37 Laurier Canal.")

CHAPTER XI.

    *   *   *   *   *   *

So that I will only say, to speak with Abraham Blankaart, that I consider this chapter to be "essential," because it makes you, in my opinion, better acquainted with Havelaar, and he seems to be the hero of the history. "Tine, what sort of *Ketimon* (gherkin, cucumber) is this? Never, my dear, give such sour things with fruits; cucumbers with salt, pine-apples with salt, all that comes from the ground with salt. Vinegar with fish and meat . . . there is something about it in Liebig . . . ."

"Dear Max," Tine said, laughing, "how long have we been here? That Ketimon is from Madam Slotering."

And it seemed difficult for Havelaar to remember that he had arrived only the day before; and that Tine, with the best intentions, had not yet been able to regulate anything in kitchen or household. He had already been a long time at Rankas-Betong! Had not he spent the whole night in reading the archives, and had not too many things already passed through his soul in con-

M

nexion with Lebak, for him to know so soon that he
only arrived there the day before? Tine knew this very
well; she always understood.

"Oh yes, that is true," said he; "but still you may like
to read something from Liebig. Verbrugge, have you read
much of Liebig?"

"Who was he?" asked Verbrugge.

"An author who wrote much on the preserving of
gherkins; he also discovered how to change grass into
wool . . . . You understand?"

"No," said Verbrugge and Duclari together.

"Well, it had been known for a long time:—send a
sheep into the field, and you will see. But it was Liebig
who discovered the manner in which it happens. Others,
however, say that he knows but little about it: they are
now trying to discover the means of dispensing with the
sheep altogether . . . . Oh, those scholars! Molière knew
it very well . . . . I like Molière. If you like, we shall
have reading every evening; Tine will also be of the
party when Max is in bed."

Duclari and Verbrugge liked this. Havelaar said that
he had not many books, but amongst them he had Schiller,
Goethe, Heine, Lamartine, Thiers, Say, Malthus, Scialoja,
Smith, Shakespeare, Byron, Vondel . . . .

Verbrugge said that he was not acquainted with the
English language.

"What the deuce! You are more than thirty years of

age: what have you been about all this time? But it must have been very disagreeable for you at Padang, where English is so much spoken. Did you know Miss Matta-api (Fire-eye)?"

"No, I do not know the name."

"It was not her name; we gave her this nickname because her eyes were so brilliant. I think she must be married by this time; it was long ago. I never saw such eyes .... except at Arles .... you must go there. That is the prettiest place I ever visited in my travels. It seems to me that there is nothing that so well represents beauty in the abstract, as—a beautiful woman—a visible image of true immaterial purity——Believe me, go to Arles and Nîmes . . . ."

Duclari, Verbrugge, and Tine also, I must confess, could not suppress a loud laugh at the thought of stepping over so unexpectedly from the west of Java to Arles or Nîmes. Havelaar, who, perhaps, had stood on the tower[1] built by

---

[1] As Arles is renowned for its beautiful remains of Roman origin, the tower in question is probably also of Roman construction. True, the Saracens conquered this city in 730, yet soon afterwards they were beaten by Charles Martel, who took the city again. We are strengthened in our supposition by the communication of M. De Caumont, the celebrated French archæologist, that the Roman monuments are known by the French peasants of the different *départements* under the name of *Sarrazin.* Even M. Leroy de la Brière says that the workmen call the Roman coins *pièces de Mahomet.*—See *Annales de la Société Française d'archéologie pour la description et la conservation des monuments,* 1865 (*Congrès Archéologique de France, XXXI. session à Fontenoy* 1864) pag. 6 F.—TRANSLATOR.

the Saracens, near the old Roman amphitheatre at Arles,
had some difficulty in understanding the cause of this
augh, and then he continued :—

" Well, yes, I mean, when you are in that neighbourhood. I never saw such a thing. I was accustomed to
disappointments on seeing things that are generally so
loudly extolled. For instance ! look at the cataracts we
hear so much of ;—I felt little or nothing at Tondano,
Abaros, Schaffhausen, and Niagara. One requires to look
at his hand-book to know the exact measure of his admiration of the ' so many feet of fall,' and ' so many cubic
feet of water in a minute,' and when the figures are high,
he says, ' What !' I won't go to see any more cataracts,
at least not when I have to make a *détour* to get at them.
They do not tell me anything. Buildings speak louder to
me, above all when they are pages out of history ; but the
feeling which these inspire is quite different ; bringing up
the past, and making its shadows pass in review before us.
Amongst them are abominable ones, and therefore, however interesting they may be, one does not always find in
them what satisfies æsthetical tastes. And without reference to history, there is much beauty in some buildings ;
but this beauty is again corrupted by guides—either in
print, or of flesh and blood—who steal away your impression by their monotonous babble. ' This chapel was erected
by the Bishop of Munster in 1423 ; the pillars are sixty-
three feet high, and are supported by . . . .' I don't

know what. This is tiresome; for one feels it necessary to have exactly sixty-three feet of admiration at hand not to be taken for a Turk or a bagman. You will tell me now, perhaps, that you keep your guide, when a printed one, in your pocket, and in the other case, order him to hold his tongue, or stand outside; but sometimes to arrive at a correct judgment, information is wanted; yet even if that could be dispensed with, we might seek in vain in some building or other for anything to gratify for more than a moment our passion for the beautiful, because there is nothing to *move* us. This also holds good, in my opinion, of sculpture and paintings. Nature is *motion*. Growth, hunger, thought, feeling, all these are examples of motion . . . . Stagnancy is death. Without motion there is no grief, no enjoyment, no emotion. Sit there motionless for a while, and you will see how soon you will make a ghostly impression on every one else, and even on your own imagination. At a *tableaux vivants*, one soon wants a new figure, however impressive the sight may have been at the commencement. As our taste for beauty is not satisfied with one look at anything beautiful, but needs a good many successive looks to watch the motion of *the beautiful*, we are dissatisfied when contemplating works of art, and therefore I assert that a beautiful woman, provided her beauty is not too *still*, comes nearest to the ideal of the divinity.

"How great is the necessity for motion that I speak of,

you can partly realize from the loathing which a dancer
causes you, even if an Elssler or a Taglioni, when she
having just finished a dance, stands on her left foot, and
grins at the public."

" That is beside the question," Verbrugge said ; " for it
is absolutely ugly."

" That is just my opinion ; but she fancies it beautiful,
and as a *climax* to all the previous performance, in which
much beauty may have been displayed. She regards it
as the point of the epigram, as the ' *aux armes !* ' of the
Marseillaise which she sang with her feet ; or as the
murmuring of the willows on the grave of the love
represented in the dance. And that spectators, who
generally, like us, found their taste more or less on
custom and imitation, think that moment to be the
most striking is evident, because just then every one
explodes in applause, as if they said, ' All the former
was beautiful, but *now* we cannot refrain from giving
vent to our feelings of admiration.' You said that these
pauses were absolutely ugly, so do I ; but what is the
reason ? It is because motion was at an end, and with
that the *history* which the dancer told. Believe me, stag-
nation is death."

" But," interrupted Duclari, " you also rejected as an
exponent of beauty, the cataracts . . . yet *they* move . . ."

" Yes, but without a history. They move ; but do not
change their place. They move like a rocking-horse,

minus the 'to and fro.' They make a noise, but don't speak . . . They cry 'rroo . . . rroo . . . rroo !' . . . Try crying 'rroo, rroo' . . . for six thousand years, or more, and you will see how few persons will think you an amusing man."

" I shall not try it," said Duclari ; " but still I do not agree with you, that this *motion* is so strictly necessary. I give up the cataracts ;—but a good picture can express much, I should think."

" To be sure, but only for a moment. I will try to explain my meaning by an example. This is the 8th of February . . ."

" Certainly not," said Verbrugge, " we are still in January . . ."

" No, no; it is the 8th of February 1587, and you are shut up in the Castle of Fotheringay."

" *I ?*" asked Duclari, who thought that he had not quite understood the remark.

" Yes, *you.* You are weary, and try to get some variation. There in that wall is a hole ;—it is too high for you to look through, but still that is what you desire to do. You place your table under it, and upon this table a three-legged stool, one of the legs being decidedly weak. You have seen at a fair an acrobat, who piled seven chairs one above another, and then placed himself on the top with his head downwards. Self-love and weariness press you to do something of the kind. You climb on your chair, and reach the object. . . . You look for one moment through the hole. . . . 'Oh, dear!' You fall. . . . And don't you now know why?"

"I think that the weak leg of the stool broke down," said Verbrugge.

"Yes; that leg broke down,—but that is not the reason why you fell, the leg broke after your fall. Before every other hole, you could have stood a year on that chair, but now you would have fallen even if there had been thirteen legs to the stool. Yes, even had you been standing on the ground. . . ."

"I take it for granted," said Duclari. "I see that you intend to let me fall, *coûte que coûte*. I lie flat enough now, and at full length; but really I don't know why."

"Well; that is very simple . . . you saw there a woman, dressed in black, kneeling down before a block. She bowed her head, and white as silver was the neck, which appeared whiter from its contrast with the velvet . . . and there stood a man with a large sword;[1] and he held it high, and he looked at this white neck . . . and he considered the arc which his blade must describe, to be driven through just *there* . . . *there* between those joints with exactness and force——and then you fell, Duclari; you fell because you saw that, and, therefore, you cried: 'Oh, *dear!*' and not because your chair had only three legs.

[1] Headsman's axe.

"And long after you have been delivered from Fotheringay through the intercession of your cousin, or because
they have grown tired of feeding you there any longer
like a canary, long afterwards, yes, even now, your day-
dreams are of this woman; you are roused from sleep, and
fall down with a heavy shock on your bed, because you
want to arrest the arm of the executioner! . . . Is it
not so ?"

"I am willing to believe it, but I cannot say very
decidedly, because I have never looked through a hole in
the wall of Fotheringay."

"Granted! nor have *I*. But now I take a picture,
which represents the decapitation of Mary Stuart. Suppose the representation to be perfect: there it hangs in a
gilt frame, suspended by a red cord, if you like . . . I
know what you are about to say,—'Granted!' No! you
do not see the frame; you even forget that you left your
walking-stick at the entrance of the picture-gallery; you
forget your name, your child, the new model shako, not to
see a picture, but to behold in reality Mary Stuart, exactly
the same as at Fotheringay. The executioner stands
there exactly the same as he must have been standing in
reality; yes, I will even suppose that you extend your
arm to avert the blow, that you even cry, 'Let this woman
live, perhaps she will amend.' . . . You see, I give you fair
play as regards the *execution* of the picture."

"Yes, but what more ? Is the impression then not

exactly the same as when I saw the same in reality at Fotheringay ?"

" No, not in the least, because you did not climb on a chair with three legs. This time you take a chair,—with four legs, by preference an easy-chair,—you go and sit down before the picture, in order to enjoy it completely and for a long time—[We *do* enjoy ourselves in seeing anything dismal !]—and what is the impression which it makes on you ?"

" Well, dread, anguish, pity, trouble! . . . just the same as when I looked through the hole in the wall. You supposed the picture to be perfect, so I must have the same impression from it as from the reality."

" No, within two minutes you feel pain in your right arm out of sympathy with the executioner, who has to hold up so long that blade of steel . . ."

" *Sympathy* with the *executioner ?*"

" Yes; *an equal sense of pain and discomfort* . . . . and also with the woman who sits there so long in an uncomfortable position, and probably in an uncomfortable state of mind, before the block. You still sympathize with her; but this time not because she had to wait so long before being decapitated——and if you had anything to say or to cry,—suppose that you felt disposed to trouble yourself with the matter,—it would be nothing else than, ' Give the blow, man, she is waiting for it !' And if afterwards you look again at that picture, and look often at it, is your first impression that it is not yet done ? ' Is *he* still standing and she lying ?'"

" But what motion is there then in the beauty of the women at Arles ?" asked Verbrugge.

"Oh, that is quite different! In their features you may read a whole history.[1] Carthage flourishes, and builds ships : you hear Hannibal's oath against Rome . . . *here* they twist cords for their bows . . . . *there* the city burns . . ."

"Max! Max! I believe that you left your heart at Arles," said Tine.

"Yes, for a moment . . . . but I have got it back again : you shall hear it. Observe, I do not say I saw a woman there who was in this or that respect beautiful —no, they were all beautiful, and so it was impossible there to fall in love, because the next person always drove the preceding from your admiration, and really I thought of Caligula or Tiberius,—of which of them do they tell the story ?—who wished that all humankind had but one head . . . . now therefore involuntarily I wished that the women of Arles . . . ."

" Had but one head together ?"

" Yes."

" To knock it off ?"

" Certainly not . . . but to kiss it, I was going to say ;

---

[1] This appears to refer to the confident looks of the Carthaginians, who knew their own strength.

it is not that . . . No, to look at it, to dream of it, and
to . . . *be good !*"

Duclari and Verbrugge certainly thought this conclusion very strange.

But Max did not notice it, and continued :—

"For so noble were the features that one felt somewhat
ashamed to be only a man, and not a spark . . . . a beam
. . . . no, that would be substance . . . . a thought. . . . .
But——suddenly a brother or a father sat down beside
these women, ... goodness! I saw one blow her
nose!"

"I knew that you would draw a black stripe across it,"
said Tine.

"Is that my fault? I would rather have seen her fall
down dead ;——

"Ought such a girl so far to forget herself?"

"But, Mr. Havelaar," asked Verbrugge, "suppose she
had a bad cold?"

"Well, she ought not to have a bad cold with such a
nose. . . . ."

As if an evil spirit spoke, Tine suddenly sneezed . . .
and before she thought of it, she had blown her nose!

"Dear Max! don't be angry!" said she, with a suppressed laugh.

He did not reply; and however foolish it seems, or is,
—yes, he was angry. And what sounds strange too, Tine
was glad that he was angry, and that he required *her* to

be more than the women of Arles, even though she had no reason to be proud of her nose.

If Duclari still thought Havelaar a fool, one could not be surprised if he felt himself strengthened in this opinion, on perceiving the short anger that could be read in Havelaar's face, after that nose-blowing. But he had returned from Carthage, and he read on the faces of his guests, with the rapidity with which he *could* read, when his mind was not too far away from home, that they had made the two following theorems :—

" 1. Whoever will not let his wife blow her nose is a fool.

" 2. Whoever thinks that a beautiful nose may not be blown, is wrong to apply that idea to Madam Havelaar, whose nose is a little *en pomme de terre.*"

Havelaar would not speak of the first theorem, but the second one. . . . .—" Oh," he said, as if he had to reply, though his guests had been too polite to speak their thoughts, " I will explain that to you, Tine. . . . ."

" Dear Max !" she said entreatingly ; and she meant by these words to say, " Do not tell these gentlemen why I should be in your estimation elevated above a bad cold. . . ."

Havelaar appeared to understand what Tine meant; for he replied, " Very well, dear." But do you know, gentlemen, that one is often deceived in estimating the rights of men by material imperfections ? I am quite sure that his guests never heard of these rights.

" I knew a little girl in Sumatra," he continued, " the

daughter of a *datoo*[1] . . . well then, I am certain that she
had no claim to such imperfection; and yet I saw her
fall into the water in a shipwreck just like another. I, a
man, had to help her to land."

" But ought she to have flown like a sea-mew?"

" Certainly, . . . or, no . . . she ought not to have had
a body. Would you have me tell you how I became
acquainted with her? It was in '42, I was Controller at
Natal.[2] Have you been there, Verbrugge?"

" Yes."

" Now then, then you know that pepper is cultivated at
Natal. The pepper-grounds are situated at Taloh-Baleh,
north of Natal, near the coast. I had to inspect them,
and having no knowledge of pepper, I took with me in
the pirogue[3] (*prakoe*) a *datoo*—some one who knew more
about it than I. His daughter, then a child of thirteen
years, went with us. We sailed along the coast and found
it very wearisome."

" And then you were shipwrecked?"

" No, it was fine weather . . . the shipwreck happened
many years afterwards; otherwise I should not have been
weary. We sailed along the coast, and it was fearfully
hot. Such a pirogue gives little occasion for relaxation,
and, moreover, I was then in a very bad humour, to which

---

[1] *Datoo* = a petty chief in Sumatra.
[2] Natal in Sumatra—*not to be confounded* with Natal in Africa.
[3] *Pirogue* = *piragua*, a canoe formed of two trees united.

many causes had contributed. First of all, I had an un-
fortunate love,—that was in those days my daily bread;—
but, moreover, I found myself in a state between two
attacks of ambition. I had made myself a king, and been
dethroned, I had climbed up a tower, and had fallen down
again to the ground . . . . I shall now pass by the reason
of this. Enough, I was sitting there in that pirogue with
a sour face and a bad humour; I was, as the Germans
call it, *ungeniessbar*. I thought it derogatory to inspect
pepper-fields, and that I ought a long time ago to have
had the appointment of governor of a solar system. Moreover, I thought it moral murder to put a spirit like mine
in a pirogue with that stupid *datoo* and his child. I have
to tell you that generally speaking I liked the Malay
chiefs very much, and harmonized well with them. They
even possess qualities which make me prefer them to the
Javanese grandees. Yes, I know, Verbrugge, that you do
not agree with me in this matter, there are but few who
do . . . but I leave this question now. If I had performed
this voyage on another day, when less restless, I should
perhaps immediately have commenced a conversation
with this *datoo*, and perhaps have found that it was worth
my while. Perhaps the little girl would have spoken
too, and that would have entertained me; for a child has
generally something original,—though I was still myself
too much a child to take an interest in originality. Now
this is otherwise; now I see in every girl of thirteen

years old a manuscript, in which little or nothing has been effaced. They surprise the author *en négligé,* and that is often pretty.

"The child was stringing coral beads, and this seemed to absorb all her attention. Three red, one black . . . three red, one black . . . it was pretty !

"Her name was 'Si Oepi Keteh.' This means in Sumatra about the same as 'little miss.' . . . Yes, Verbrugge, you know it, but Duclari has always served in Java. Her name was 'Si Oepi Keteh,' but in my thoughts I called her 'poor creature,' because I was exalted in my own ideas so very much above her.

"It was afternoon . . . almost evening; the corals were laid aside. The land passed slowly by, and grew fainter and fainter behind us. To the left, far in the west, above the wide, wide ocean, which has no limit as far as Madagascar—the sun set over Africa, and his beams fell—more and more obliquely on the waves, and sought for coolness in the sea. What the dickens is it ?"

"What ? the sun ?"

"No, no . . . I used to make verses. . . .

"Thou askest why the ocean stream,
    That washes Natal's shore,
Elsewhere so gentle and serene,
    Is known to boil and roar.

"Thou askest the poor fisher's son,
    Who scarce can understand ;

And he points out th' horizon dun,
    Without a trace of land.

" He casts a glance of his dark eye
    Along the Western main ;
And he and you can nought descry
    But sea, and sea again.

" And here the Ocean tears the land,
    And beats the sandy shore,
Because from Madagascar's strand
    There 's sea and nothing more—

" A sea where shrieks of terror wild,
    To all the world unknown,
Unheard by friend, or wife, or child,
    Are heard by God alone !

" A hand with agonizing bound,
    Oft sprang above the wave ;
And snatched, and clutched, and swung around,
    For something that could save.

" But there was nought to give a hold :
    The waves that on him pressed,
Soon o'er his head for ever rolled——
    And—— * * * * "

" I don't know the rest !"

" You could ascertain it," said Verbrugge, " by writing to Krijgsman, who was your clerk at Natal ; he knows it."

" How did he get hold of it ?" asked Max.

" Perhaps out of your waste-basket. But certain it is

that he has it.   Does not then follow the story of the fall
of man, which made the island sink, that formerly protected Natal's coast . . . . the history of Djiwa and the
two brothers?"

"That is true.   This legend—was no legend at all, it
was a parable which I made, and which two hundred years
hence——will be a legend if Krijgsman often relates it.
Such has been the origin of all legends.   Djiwa is 'soul'
as you know. . . ."

"Max, what became of the little girl with the coral
beads?" asked Tine.

"*They* had been laid aside.   It was six o'clock, and
there under the equator—Natal being a few minutes
north of it [when I went on horseback to Ayer-Bangie,
I made my horse walk over the equator, or almost walk;
fearing I should fall over it]—it was six o'clock, a signal
for evening thoughts.   Now, I think that a man in the
evening is always a little better, or less vicious, than in
the morning—and that is natural.   A Controller wipes his
eyes, and dreads meeting an Assistant Resident, who
assumes a foolish ascendency because he has been a few
years more in the service; or has to measure fields that
day, and is in doubt between his honesty——you do not
know that, Duclari, because you are a military man; but
there are indeed honest Controllers——then he is in doubt
between that honesty and the fear that Radeen Demang
So-and-so will desire to have that grey horse that ambles

so well;—or, he has to say that day Yes or No in answer
to letter № ——. In a word, when you awake in the
morning, the world falls on your heart; and that is a
heavy burden for a heart, even when it is strong.

"But when it is evening you pause. There are ten
hours; thirty-six thousand seconds before you will see
your official coat again. That allures every one. That is
the moment when I hope to die . . . to arrive yonder
with an unofficial face. That is the moment when your
wife finds something once more in your face of what
caught her when she allowed you to keep that pocket-
handkerchief with an 'E' in the corner . . ."

"And before she had time to catch a bad cold."

"Ah, don't disturb me . . . I only mean to say, that
during the evening one is more susceptible (*gemüthlicher*).
So when the sun set, I became a better man, as the first
proof of my improvement may show, and said to the little
girl—

"'Now it will soon be cooler.'

"'Yes, sir,' she replied.

"But I lowered my dignity still further, and commenced
a conversation with this poor creature. My merits were
still greater, because she replied little. I was right in all
that I said; which is annoying, even in spite of one's
arrogance.

"'Should you like to go again to Taloh-Baleh?' I
asked.

" ' As you please, sir.'

" ' No, I ask *you* if *you* think such an excursion agreeable ? '

" ' If my father does,' she replied.—Was not this enough to anger me ? Well, then, I did not get angry, the sun had set, and I felt myself good (*gemüthlich*) enough not to be disheartened by so much stupidity; or rather, I believe, I began to enjoy hearing my own voice,—for few amongst us do not like to listen to their own voices,—and after my muteness during the whole day, I thought, now that I did speak, it merited something better than the silly replies of ' Si Oepi Keteh.'

" I will tell her something, I thought, then I shall hear it too, without wanting any replies. Now you know that, as at the unloading of a ship, the ' *Kranjang* ' (cask) of sugar last put on board is the first to be taken out, so we generally unload first that thought or tale that was acquired last. In the periodical paper, ' *Dutch India*,' I had read not long before a story by Jerome, ' *The Japanese Stone-Cutter*.' . . . This Jerome has written many beautiful things. Did you read his ' *Auction in the House of the Dead* ' ? And his ' *Tombs* ' ? And, above all, the ' *Pedatti* ' ? I will give you the last. I had just read ' *The Japanese Stone-Cutter*.' . . . . Now I suddenly remember that my anger that day was connected with the perilousness of the Natal roads . . . . You know, Verbrugge, that no man-of-war can approach these roads,

certainly not in July . . . Yes, Duclari, the rainy season
is there at its height in July, quite different from here . . .
now then, the perilousness of these roads was linked with
my mortified ambition. I had often proposed to the
Resident to construct at Natal a breakwater, or at least
an artificial harbour at the mouth of the river, with a
view to bring commerce into the district of Natal, which
unites the *battah* districts with the sea. One million and a
half of inhabitants in the interior do not know what to do
with their produce, because the Natal roads are so bad.
Now then, these proposals had not been approved by the
Resident, or at least he asserted that the Government
would not approve of them, and you know that the Residents never propose anything but what they know pretty
well beforehand will be agreeable to the Government.
The making of a harbour at Natal was in principle contradictory of the separate system ; and far from encouraging
ships there, it was even forbidden to admit ships with
yards on the roads, unless in case of superior force. Yet
when a ship came—they were mostly American whalers,
or French ships that had loaded pepper in the small independent countries on the north side—I always caused
a letter to be written by the captain, wherein he asked
permission to take in fresh water. My anger about the
miscarriage of my efforts to do something for the benefit
of Natal, or rather my offended vanity at being still of so
little consequence that I could not even have a harbour

made where I liked, and all this in connexion with my candidateship for the ruling of a solar system,—all this made me so peevish that day. When I recovered a little at sunset, for discontent is a sickness exactly,—this sickness reminded me of the Japanese stone-cutter, and perhaps I only thought this history aloud, in order to take the last drop of the medicine which I felt that I wanted, whilst I imposed upon myself by saying that I did it out of benevolence for the child. But she, the child, cured me, for some days at least, better than any tale.

"Oepi! There was a man who cut stones out of a rock. This labour was heavy, and he laboured much; but his wages were small, and he was not content. He sighed because his labour was heavy, and he cried, 'O that I were rich, in order to rest on a *baleh-baleh*[1] with *klamboo*.'[2]

"And there came an angel out of heaven, who said, 'Be it as you have said.'

"And he was rich. And he rested on a *baleh-baleh*, and the *klamboo* was of red silk.

"And the king of the country passed with horsemen before his carriage, and likewise behind the carriage there were horsemen, and the golden *pajong*[3] was held over the head of the king.

---

[1] *Baleh-baleh* = couch.   [2] *Klamboo* = curtains.
[3] *Pajong* = umbrella—distinctive of rank—a golden one being the highest.

" And as soon as the rich man heard this, he was sad, because they held no golden ' pajong' over *his* head, and he was not content. He sighed and cried, ' I should like to be a king.'

" And there came an angel out of heaven and said, ' Be it as you have said.'

" And he became a king. And before his carriage were many horsemen, and behind were also horsemen, and over his head they held the golden 'pajong.'

" And the sun shone with hot beams, and burned the earth in such a manner that the grass was dried up.

" And the king complained that the sun burned his face, and had more power than he ; and he was not satisfied.

" He sighed, and cried, ' I should like to be the sun.'

" And there came an angel out of heaven who said, ' Be it as you have said.'

" And he became the sun. And he sent up his beams on high, and down to the earth ; to the right and to the left——everywhere.

" And he burned up the grass on the earth, and the faces of the princes who were on the earth.

" And a cloud came between him and the earth, and the beams of the sun were turned back.

" And he was angry that his power was resisted ; and he complained that this cloud had more power than he ; and he was dissatisfied.

" He desired to be the cloud that was so mighty.

"And there came an angel from heaven who said, 'Be this as you have said.'

"And he became a cloud, and placed himself between the sun and the earth, and intercepted the beams, so that the grass became green.

"And the cloud rained in large drops on the earth, and made the rivers swell, and the 'banjers' carried away the herds.

"And the cloud devastated the field with much water.

"And it fell on a rock which did not move, and rattled in large streams, but the rock did not yield.

"And the cloud was angry because the rock would not yield; and because the strength of its streams was vain. And it was not contented.

"It cried, 'This rock has more power than I have. I wish to be this rock.'

"And there came an angel out of heaven who said, 'Be this as you have said.'

"And it became a rock, and moved neither when the sun shone nor when it rained.

"And there came a man with pickaxe and sharp chisel, and heavy hammer, who cut stones out of the rock.

"And the rock said, 'What is this, that the man has power over me, and cuts stones out of my bosom?' And it was discontented.

"It cried, 'I am weaker than he, I should like to be that man.'

" And there came an angel out of heaven who said, ' Be this as you have said.'

" And he became a stone-cutter. And he cut stones out of the rock with heavy labour, and he laboured hard for small wages, and *was* contented."

" Very nice," said Duclari, " but now you still owe us the proof that this little ' Oepi' ought to have been imponderable."

" No, I did not promise to prove that. I only desired to tell you how I got acquainted with her. When I had done with my story, I asked : ' And you, " Oepi," what would you choose, if an angel from heaven came to ask you what you desired ?'"

" Sir, I should pray him to take me with him to heaven."

" Is not that beautiful ?" said Tine to her guests, who perhaps thought it very foolish.

Havelaar stood upon his legs, and wiped away something from his forehead.

CHAPTER XII.

" DEAR MAX," said Tine, " our dessert is so scanty——
would you not——you remember Madam Geoffrin—— ?"

" Talk to us of something else than pastry ? What the
deuce ! I am hoarse ; it is Verbrugge's turn."

" Yes, Mr. Verbrugge! Please relieve Max," said
Madam Havelaar. Verbrugge hesitated for a moment ;
and began :

" Once upon a time there was a man, who stole a
turkey."

" Oh you rogue," cried Havelaar, " that is from PADANG !
And how does it go on ?"

" It is finished. Do you know the end of this story ?"

" To be sure, I ate the turkey in company with . . . .
somebody. Do you know why I was suspended at
Padang ?"

" People said that there was a deficit in your cash at
Natal," replied Verbrugge.

" That is not altogether untrue, but neither is it true.
From many causes I had been very careless in my pecu-

niary responsibilities at Natal, on which many observations were made. But this happened in those days very often : matters in Northern Sumatra were, soon after the pacification of Baros, Tapos, and Singkel,[1] so confused, all was so turbulent, that fault could not be found with a young man who was more inclined to be on horseback than at the desk, or in keeping cash-books in order. It could not be expected that everything would be in such strict order as if an Amsterdam bookkeeper had been in charge with nothing else to do. The *Battah*-countries were in revolt, and you know, Verbrugge, how all that happens there reacts on Natal. I slept every night in my clothes, to be ready for anything : which was often necessary. Moreover there was danger,—a few days before my arrival a plot had been discovered to revolt and murder my predecessor, and danger has something attractive, above all to a man of twenty-two, and this attractiveness makes him the more incapable for office-work, or the stiff accuracy which is wanted for the proper management of money matters. Moreover, I had all sorts of nonsense in my head. . . . ."

" It is not necessary," said Madam Havelaar in reply to a man-servant.

---

[1] Three Dutch settlements on the west coast of North Sumatra. Singkel is the most northern of the Dutch possessions in that island, and is separated by a river of the same name from the still independent little states of Troomon and Analaboo. Still further north commences the Sultanat of Atchin. The whole coast from Ayer-Bangie to the northern point is known to sailors by name of Pepper Coast.

" What is not necessary ?"

" I had told them to make something ready in the kitchen——an omelet—or some such thing."

" Ah ! . . . . and that is not necessary, because I have begun my story—that is naughty, Tine. Very well, as far as I am concerned ; but these gentlemen have also a voice in the matter. Verbrugge ! what do you like ?—your share of the omelet or the story ?"

" That is a difficult choice for a polite man," said Verbrugge.

" Nor should I like to choose," added Duclari, " for it would be a verdict between man and wife; and——"

" *Entre l'écorce et le bois, il ne faut pas mettre le doigt.*"

" I will help you, gentlemen, the omelet is . . ."

" Madam," said the courteous Duclari, " the omelet will certainly be worth as much . . . ."

" As the story? Certainly, if it is worth anything ; but there is a difficulty . . . ."

" I wager that there is no sugar in the house," said Verbrugge ; " pray fetch from mine whatever you want."

" There *is* sugar, from Madam Slotering ; no, it is not that. If the omelet were good, that would not matter. . . ."

" What then, Madam ; has it fallen into the fire ?"

" I wish it had. No, it cannot fall into the fire; it is . . . ."

" But, Tine," said Havelaar, " what is it then ?"

" It is imponderable, Max ! as your women at Arles

.... ought to have been. I have no omelet——I have nothing more."

"Then, for heaven's sake, the story," said Duclari in droll despair.

"But we *have* coffee," cried Tine.

"Good! Then we shall drink coffee in the fore-gallery,[1] and let us invite Madam Slotering and the girls," said Havelaar, whereupon the small company moved.

"I suppose that she will not come, Max; you know that she prefers not to dine with us, and in this I cannot say that she is wrong."

"She may have heard that I tell stories," said Havelaar, "and that must have frightened her."

"You are wrong there, Max! This would not harm her —she doesn't understand Dutch. No, she told me that she wished to have her own household; and I understand that very well. You know how you translated my name —'E. H. v. W.'"

"Eigen Haard veel Waard."[2]

"Just so: she is quite right; she seems, moreover, a little unsociable. Only fancy, she makes the servants drive away all strangers that come near the house. . . ."

"I beg for the story or the omelet," said Duclari.

---

[1] Such a fore-gallery is open on *three* sides and supported by pillars. The reader will find a description of an Indian house *infra*, p. 231.

[2] *Eigen Haurd veel Waard* = "One's own hearth is worth much." (There's no place like home.) The lady's name was Everdine Huberte van Wÿnbergen.

"So do I," cried Verbrugge; "evasions *are not* accepted. We are entitled to a complete dinner, and therefore I ask for the history of the turkey."

"I have told you that already," said Havelaar: "I stole the turkey from General van Damme, and ate it with *somebody*."

"Before something went to heaven," said Tine playfully.

"No, that's an evasion," cried Duclari, "we want to know why you stole that turkey."

"Well, because I was hungry, and that was the fault of General van Damme, who had suspended me."

"If you don't tell me more than that, I will bring an omelet next time myself," complained Verbrugge.

"Believe me, it was nothing more than that. He had many turkeys, and I had none. These birds were driven before my door; I took one, and said to the man who imagined that he watched them, 'Tell the General that I, Max Havelaar, take this turkey, because I want to eat it.'"

"And what about that epigram?"

"Did Verbrugge speak to you about it?"

"Yes."

"That has nothing to do with the turkey. That was because he had suspended so many functionaries: there were at Padang seven or eight of them whom he had suspended, with more or less justice, from their functions. Many amongst them deserved it less than I. The Assistant Resident of Padang himself had been suspended, and for a reason which, as I believe, was quite a different one from that given in the decision. I must tell you, however, that I cannot assure you that I know all about it, and that I say only what was thought to be true at Padang, and what may have been true, when taking into consideration above all the peculiarities of the General.

" He married his wife to gain a wager of an anker of wine. He often went out in the evening, and went everywhere. Mr. Valkenaar on one occasion so respected his incognito, that in a small street near the girls' orphanhouse, he gave him a thrashing, as a common disturber of the public peace. Not far from that place lived Miss ——. There was a rumour that this Miss —— had given birth to a child, that had disappeared. The Assistant Resident was about to examine into the matter, and seems to have expressed his intention at a whist-party at the General's. The next day he received an order to go to a certain district, whose Controller had been suspended from his functions because of true or supposed dishonesty, there to examine and report upon these affairs. The Assistant Resident certainly wondered that he was charged with a thing that had no connexion whatever with his district; but as he could, strictly speaking, consider this charge as an honourable distinction, and as he was on very good terms with the General, so that he had no cause to think of a snare, he acquiesced in the mission, and went to —— I don't know where, to execute his orders. After some

time he returns and makes a report, that was not unfavourable to the Controller. But lo! the public (that is, 'nobody and every one') at Padang had now discovered that
the Controller had only been suspended to afford an
opportunity for the removal of the Assistant Resident from
the place, in order to prevent his intended investigation
of the disappearance of that child, or at least to delay it
till it would be more difficult to clear up the mystery. I
now repeat that I do not know whether that was true,
but since my better acquaintance with General van
Damme, it appears to me very credible; and at Padang
likewise there was nobody who did not think him capable
of such a thing, considering how very bad his morals were.
Most people only gave him credit for one quality, intre-
pidity in danger; and if I, who have seen him in danger,
stuck to the opinion that he was, after all, a courageous
man, that alone would induce me to withhold this story.
It is true that he, in Sumatra, had caused many 'to be
sabred down,' but that ought to have been seen more
closely, to form a correct estimate of his valour; and,
however strange it may appear, I believed that he owed
his military glory in a great measure to the spirit of *contradiction* which animates us all more or less. One readily
admits, it is true, that Peter or Paul is *this*, or *that*; but
what he is, *that* one must leave him, and never can you
be so sure to be praised as when you have a great, a very
apparent fault. You, Verbrugge, are drunk every day . . ."

"I?" asked Verbrugge, who was a pattern of temperance.

"Yes, *I* make you drunk every day. You forget yourself so far that Duclari tumbles over you in the fore-gallery. That he will find unpleasant, but he will immediately remember to have seen something good in you, which he did not remark before. And when I come, and I find you thus *horizontal*, then he will put his hand on my arm and say, 'Oh, believe me, he is otherwise such a good, honest, nice fellow!'"

"I say that of Verbrugge, even when he is *vertical*," said Duclari.

"Not with the same fire and persuasion. Think of it, how often one hears people say, 'Oh, if this man would be attentive to his business, he would be somebody, but ——' and then comes the story, how that he is *not* attentive to business, and is, therefore, nobody. I believe that I know the reason of this. Of those that are dead we always hear good qualities which we never before perceived. This is because they are in nobody's *way*. All men are more or less concurrents; we should like to place everybody else completely under us, and to have *all things under us*. Politeness, even self-interest, prevents the confession of this, for very soon nobody would believe us, even if we asserted something true. A subterfuge is sought for, and look how we do it. When you, Duclari, say, 'Lieutenant Slobkous is a good soldier, to be sure he is a good soldier,

o

I cannot sufficiently express what a good soldier Lieutenant Slobkous is, ... but he is no theorist . . . .' did you not say so, Duclari ? "

" I never knew or saw a Lieutenant Slobkous."

" Very well, make one, and say that of him."

" Well, I make him, and say it."

" Do you know what you have now said ? You have said that *you*, Duclari, are thoroughly acquainted with theory. I am not a bit better. Believe me, we are wrong to be so angry with one who is very bad, for the good ones amongst us are very near the bad. Suppose we call perfection 0, and take 100 degrees to be bad, how very wrong we are then, who fluctuate between 98 and 99, to call shame on a person who stands at 101. And still I believe that many do not attain the 100th degree for want of good qualities, courage, for instance, to be quite what 1 is."

" At what degree do *I* stand, Max ?"

" I want a magnifying-glass for the subdivisions, Tine."

" I object," cried Verbrugge,—" no, Madam ! considering your proximity to the 0,—no, functionaries are suspended, a child is lost, a General is accused. . . ."

" But where's the story ?"

" Tine, take care that next time there is something in the house. No, Verbrugge, you will not get ' the story ' until I have been a little time longer on my hobby-horse, on the spirit of contradiction. I said every man sees in his fellow-creature a sort of rival. One must not always blame what is but too obvious, therefore, we like to exalt a good quality excessively, to make the bad quality (which is properly the only thing we want to reveal) the more obvious, without displaying the appearance of partiality. If any one comes to me complaining that I have called him a thief, when I have also called his daughter a lovely girl, then I reply : 'How can you be so angry since I have called your daughter a lovely girl ?' Do you see, I win both ways. Each of us is a grocer; I take away *his* customers, who will not buy raisins of a *thief*,—and at the same time, it is said that *I* am a good man, because I praise the daughter of a rival in business."

"No, it is not so bad," said Duclari; "that is going much too far."

"You think so, because I made the comparison a little short and blunt. You must mitigate it a little. But if we must indeed acknowledge that somebody is in the possession of a quality which merits esteem, respect, or credit, then we are pleased to discover, near this quality, something which releases us in part or altogether of this tribute.

"To such a poet we should bow, but . . . . he beats his wife. You see, then, we like to use the *black and blue* of this wife as a motive to keep our backs straight; and in the end we are pleased that he beats the poor creature, —a practice which in any other case we should condemn. If we must acknowledge that somebody possesses qualities

that allow him the honour of a statue, if we can no
longer deny his claims thereto without being thought
ignorant, insensible, or jealous, then we say, 'Well: set
him up!' But already, while mounting him upon the
pedestal, and while he himself still thinks that we are
full of admiration of his excellence, we have already made
the noose in the *lasso*, that is intended, on the first favourable opportunity, to pull him down. The greater the
changes among the occupiers of pedestals to have a turn
too, and this so true, that we from habit, and for exercise,
like a sportsman who shoots crows which he does not bag,
like to pull down even these statues, whose foot-piece
never can be mounted by *us*. If *Kappelman* lives on
sauerkraut and hard beer, he likes to say: 'Alexander
was not great .... he was intemperate,' whilst there
exists for Kappelman not the least chance of rivalry with
Alexander in conquering the world. How this may be,
I am sure that many never would have the idea that
General Van Damme was so very brave, if his bravery
could not have served as a vehicle for the always added:
'but ... his morality!' And at the same time, that
this immorality would not have been much thought of by
many, who were not themselves so very invulnerable in
this respect, if it had not been wanted to counterbalance
his renown for prowess, which disturbed the slumbers of
some. One quality he possessed in a very high degree
—energy. What he intended to happen did generally

happen.   You see, however, I have immediately an anti-thesis ready—but in the choice of the means he was very free, and, as Van der Palm[1] has said, as I believe unjustly, of Napoleon, 'Obstacles of morality never arrested him,' and then it is certainly easier to attain your aim than when you think yourself bound by such rule.

" The Assistant Resident of Padang had made a report that sounded favourably for his suspended Controller, whose suspension got in this way a colour of injustice. The Padang scandal continued: people always were talking about the disappearance of the child; the Assistant Resident was again obliged to notice the matter; but before he could clear up the mystery, he received an order, whereby he was suspended by the Governor of Western Sumatra 'because of negligence.'   He had, as it was said, out of friendship or pity, and while he knew better, represented the matter of the Controller in a false light.   I did not read the documents concerning this affair; but I know that the Assistant Resident was not in the least connected with this Controller, which is already evident from his having been chosen to examine the matter.   I know, moreover, that he was an estimable person, and the Government thought so too, which appears from the annulling of the suspension after the affair had been

1 Johannes Henricus Van der Palm, a celebrated Dutch author and orator, born 1763, died 1840 ; best known by his Bible for children and his Bible translations.

examined elsewhere than on the west coast of Sumatra. This Controller also was afterwards restored to his honour. It was their suspension which inspired me with the epigram that I caused to be put down on the General's breakfast-table by somebody who was then in his service, and had been formerly in mine—

'Suspension on legs, the suspension that rules—
 Old Jack the Suspender, the bogie of fools—
 Would surely his Conscience itself have suspended,
 Were 't not that it long ago finally ended !' "[1]

" Such a thing was not proper," said Duclari.

" I quite agree ; . . . but I was bound to do something. Only fancy : I had no money, received nothing : that I feared every day starvation, which in reality I was very near, I had few or no relations at Padang, and, moreover, I told the General that *he* was responsible if I perished from hunger, and that I should accept aid of nobody. In the interior there were persons who, on hearing what had happened, invited me to come to their homes; but the General prohibited the issue of my passport thither. Neither was I allowed to go to Java. Anywhere else I could have managed it, and perhaps there too, if people had not been so afraid of the mighty General. It ap-

[1] "Het wand'lend schorsbesluit, dat schorsend ons regeert,
   Jan Schorsäl, Gouverneur, de weerwolf onzer dagen,
      Had zijn geweten zelf met vreugd gesuspendeerd,—
   Als 't niet voor langen tijd finaal reeds ware ontslagen."

peared to be his intention to let me starve. Such a state of things lasted nine months!"

"And how did you live all that time? had the General plenty of turkeys?"

"No, I did that only once . . . I made verses, and wrote comedies . . . . and so on."

"And was that enough to buy rice at Padang?"

"No, but I did not ask that for it, . . . I would rather not say how I lived."

Tine pressed his hand; *she* knew it.

"I have read a few lines which you wrote at that time on the back of a receipt," said Verbrugge.

"I know what you mean; the lines give you an idea of my position. There was at that time a periodical paper, the '*Copyist*,' to which I subscribed. As it was under the protection of the Government, the editor being an official under the General Secretary, the subscribers' money went into the Exchequer. They offered me a receipt for twenty guilders. As this money had to be booked at the Governor's office, and the receipt, if the money was not paid, had to pass these offices to be sent back to Batavia, I made use of this opportunity, and protested against my poverty on the back of the paper.

'*Vingt florins . . . quel trésor! Adieu littérature.*
Adieu, Copiste, adieu! Trop malheureux destin.
Je meurs de faim, de froid, de soif, et de chagrin . . .
Vingt florins font pour moi deux mois de nourriture.

Si j'avais vingt florins . . . je serais mieux botté,
Mieux nourri, mieux logé, j'en ferais bonne chère.
Il faut vivre avant tout, soit vie de misère.
Le crime fait la honte, et non la pauvreté.'

But when, afterwards, I went to the publishers of the
'*Copyist*,' to give them my twenty guilders, I was told
that I owed nothing. It appears that the General had
himself paid the money for me, to prevent this illustrated
receipt being sent back to Batavia. But——what did he
do, after the taking away of that turkey——?

"It was a theft; and after that epigram?"

"He punished me terribly. If he had accused me as
being guilty of want of respect for the Governor of Western
Sumatra, which could have been explained in those days
with a little ingenuity, as an endeavour to undermine, to
revolt, 'or as theft on the public road,' he would have
showed himself to be a right-minded man. But no, he
punished me better! He ordered the man who had to
watch the turkeys to choose henceforth another road;
and as to my epigram . . . that is still worse—he said
nothing, and did *nothing*. You see that was cruel! He
did not grant me the smallest claim to be a martyr . . . I
did not become interesting by persecution, and was not
allowed to be unhappy through excess of wit . . . it
was enough to disgust me once for all with epigrams and
turkeys. So little encouragement extinguishes the flame
of genius to the last spark! I never did it again!"

CHAPTER XIII.

[COMPOSED BY STERN.]

"And may we now hear why you were suspended?" asked Duclari.

"Oh yes; for as I can assure you of, and even prove, the truth of all that I say on the subject, you will see that I did not act rashly, when I, in telling the story about that lost child, did not quite disregard the scandal of Padang; because you will think it very credible, as soon as I shall have made you acquainted with this General in affairs that concern *myself*.

"There were in my accounts at Natal inaccuracies and omissions. You know how every inaccuracy ends in loss: inaccuracy never increases money. It is pretended that I was short of thousands. But, observe, they did not tell me *that* so long as I was at Natal. Quite unexpectedly I received an appointment in the highlands of Padang. You know, Verbrugge, that in Sumatra an appointment to the Padang highlands is considered as more profitable and more agreeable than one in the Northern Residency. As

the Governor had visited me a short time before—by and
by you will know why, and how—and things had happened
in my house, in which I thought I had acted as a man;
I accepted this appointment as a distinction, and set out
from Natal for Padang. I made the passage on board
a French ship, the 'Baobab,' of Marseilles, which had
loaded pepper at· Atchin, and, of course, on arriving at
Natal was in want of fresh water. As soon as I arrived
at Padang, with the intention to depart from there to the
interior, I wished, as in duty bound, to visit the Governor,
but he sent word that he could not receive me; and, at
the same time, that I must delay my setting out for my
new situation till further orders. You may believe that
I was very much surprised at that,—the more so because
he left me at Natal in a humour which made me think
that he entertained a high opinion of me. I had but few
acquaintances at Padang, but from the few I had, I heard,
or rather perceived, that the General was very angry with
me. I say that I perceived it, because, at a country place
such as Padang was then, the goodwill of many can serve
as a thermometer of the favour in which one stands in
the eye of the Governor. I felt that a storm was near,
without knowing from which point of the compass the
wind would come. As I was in want of money, I asked
one and another of my friends to lend me some, and was
quite astonished that I was met everywhere by a refusal.
At Padang, as everywhere else in the Indies, there is

great liberality in this respect. In every other case, a few hundred guilders would have been lent with pleasure to a Controller who had been detained on his journey contrary to his expectations. But *I* was refused every assistance. I pressed some to tell me the cause of this distrust; and by little and little I got to know at last that in my money matters at Natal faults and oversights had been discovered, which now caused me to be suspected of dishonest administration. That there were faults in my administration I was not surprised to hear; the contrary would have surprised me; but I wondered that the Governor, who had himself witnessed how I had always to struggle far from my office with a discontented population, ready to revolt at any moment;—that he, who had himself given me credit for what he called 'manliness,' could accuse me of dishonesty, as he knew better than any one that there could be no other question than that of '*force majeure.*' And though this *force majeure* was denied, though they wanted to make me responsible for faults that had happened at moments when I, often in danger of my life, far away from the cash or anything connected with it, had to intrust others with the administration of it,—even if it was expected that I, while doing one thing, ought not to have neglected the other, even *then* my only fault would have been a carelessness that had nothing in common with dishonesty. Moreover in those days there were many instances in which the Government took into

consideration this difficult position of their functionaries
in Sumatra; and it seemed to be accepted as a principle
on such occasions that some allowance should be made.
It only required that these functionaries should make
good the deficiency, and the word 'dishonest' was never
pronounced without very clear proofs. This was so much
a custom that I myself told the Governor at Natal, that I
feared I should have to pay a good deal, after my account
had been examined at the offices at Padang, whereupon he
replied, shrugging his shoulders: 'Ah! . . . those money
matters . . . ' as if he himself felt that matters of smaller
importance ought to give place to those of greater.

"I readily admit that money affairs are important; but,
however important in themselves, they were in this case
subordinate to other branches of duty and business. If
through carelessness or oversight some thousands[1] failed
in my administration, I call this no trifle; but if these
thousands failed in consequence of my successful efforts
to prevent a revolt, that would have devastated the district of Mandhéling with fire and sword, and that would
have brought back the Atchinese to the haunts from where
we had just driven them, with great sacrifice of blood and
treasure, then the magnitude of the short-coming disap-
pears, and it seems even a little unjust to make him re-
fund who has saved infinitely more important interests.

---

[1] 1000 guilders = £83, 6s. 8d. The English reader will bear in
mind that when 'thousands' are spoken of, guilders are referred to.

Yet I thought such a repayment right; for the non-exaction of it would lay one open to a charge of dishonesty.

" After waiting for many days, you may conceive with what feelings I received at last from the Governor's Secretary a letter, in which I was given to understand that I was suspected of dishonesty, and I was ordered to reply to a number of charges that had been made against my administration. Some of them I could explain immediately, for others I wanted to look at documents, and, above all, it was most important for me to look into these matters at Natal. I could have examined clerks and other *employés*, to ascertain the causes of the mistakes, and very likely I should have succeeded in my endeavours to clear up all. The neglect, for instance, to book money that had been sent to Mandhéling—[you know, Verbrugge, that the troops in the interior are paid out of the Natal exchequer]—or something like that, which I should, perhaps, have seen immediately, if I could have examined into it on the spot, as having been the cause of these sad faults. But the General refused to let me go to Natal. This refusal caused me to pay still more attention to the strange manner in which this accusation of dishonesty had been brought forward against me. Why had I been suddenly transferred from Natal, and under colour of good intentions to me, if I was really suspected of dishonesty ? Why did they communicate to me that disgraceful suspicion only for the first time, when I was far from the place

where I should have had an opportunity to clear myself?
And above all, why had these affairs been brought against
me in the most unfavourable light, contrary to the usual
custom, and to justice?

" Before I had replied to all these observations as well as I
could without written or verbal information, I learned that
the reason why the General was so angry with me was—

" ' Because I had opposed him so much at Natal,' in
which, as was added, ' I had done wrong.'

" Now, then, I saw it all. Yes, I had opposed him;
but with the innocent idea that he would esteem me because I had opposed him; but after his departure nothing
made me suppose that he was angry with me on that
account; stupid as I was, I had accepted the favourable
transfer to Padang as a proof that he had thought my
opposition very noble. You will see how little I knew
him then. But when I heard that this was the cause of
the severity with which my money administration was
condemned, I was at peace with myself. I answered
every point as well as I could, and ended my letter, of
which I still have a copy, with the words, ' I have answered the observations made on my administration as
well as is possible without consulting documents or having
recourse to local investigation. I beg your honour, on all
benevolent considerations, to excuse me. I am young and
insignificant in comparison with the power of the dominant ideas, which my principles compel me to oppose; but

I remain, nevertheless, proud of my moral independence, proud of my honour.'

"The following day I was suspended on the plea of dishonest administration. The officer of justice was ordered to fulfil my office and duty; and such was my position at Padang, when scarcely twenty-three years of age. I contemplated the future that must bring me infamy. People advised me to appeal on the score of my youth; for I was still under age when the pretended mistake occurred. But I would not do that. Had not I thought, suffered, and I daresay laboured too much already, to advance the plea of youth? You may see from the end of the letter above named, that I would not be treated as a child, I who had done my duty at Natal against the Governor, and like a man; and at the same time, you may perceive from this letter, how unfounded the accusation was which they brought to bear against me; for a guilty man writes in another style. I was not, however, taken into custody; though this ought to have been done, if this accusation had been well founded. Perhaps this apparent neglect was not without foundation, for a prisoner must be housed and fed. As I could not leave Padang, I was in reality still a prisoner, but a prisoner without shelter and without bread. I had often written, but without success, to the. General, requesting that he would not prevent my departure from Padang, for, even supposing me to be guilty, no crime was punishable with starvation.

" After the Council of Justice, which was at a loss how
to deal with the affair, had found a way out of the difficulty by declaring itself unable to decide, because a prose-
cution for crime in the service of the country could not be
held without the authorization of the Government at Batavia, the General kept me, as I said, nine months at Padang.

" At last he himself received instructions from head-
quarters to let me set out for Batavia.

" A few years afterwards, when I had some money——
dear Tine, you had given it me——I paid some thousand
guilders to clear the Natal accounts of 1841 and 1842,
and then a person, who may be considered to represent
the Government of the Dutch Indies, said, ' I would not
have done that in your place . . . I should have drawn
a bill of exchange on eternity.'

" *Ainsi va le monde !* "

Havelaar was about to recommence the narrative, which
his guests expected from him, and wherein he was to explain in what and why he had so opposed General van
Damme at Natal, when Madam Slotering appeared in her
fore-gallery, beckoning to the policeman who sat on a
bench near Havelaar's house. The policeman went over
to her, and then said something to a man who had just
entered the grounds, probably intending to go to the
kitchen that was behind the house. Our company would
probably have paid no attention to this, if Madam Havelaar had not said that afternoon at dinner that Madam

Slotering was so shy, and appeared to exercise a sort of control over every one that came into the grounds. We saw the man, who had been called by the policeman, go to her, and she questioned him, apparently much to his dissatisfaction. At least he retraced his steps, and was soon outside. " I am very sorry for that," said Tine; " perhaps it was a man selling fowls, or vegetables; I have nothing yet in the house."

"Then send some one after him," replied Havelaar; "you know that native ladies like to exercise power. Her husband was formerly the first man in the place, and however small an Assistant Resident may be as an individual, he is in his own district a petty king: she is not yet accustomed to dethronement. We must not grudge this small pleasure to the poor woman; act as if you did not perceive it."

This was not difficult for Tine; she had no desire for power.

A digression is necessary here, and I even intend to digress about digressions. It is not easy for an author to sail exactly between the two rocks of the *too much* or *too little*, and this difficulty is enhanced if one describes situations that have to remove the reader to unknown countries. There exists too nice a connexion between the places and the events for us to be able to abstain entirely from describing the former; and to avoid the two rocks, already mentioned, becomes doubly difficult for him who

P

has chosen the Indies for the scene of his narrative.   For whereas the author who deals with European situations may suppose many affairs to be known, on the other hand he whose story refers to the Indies has continually to ask himself whether the non-Indian will rightly understand this or that.   If the European reader thinks of Madam Sloter- ing as lodging with the Havelaars, as would be the case in Europe, it must appear incomprehensible that she was not present with the company that took coffee in the fore- gallery.   I have certainly already observed that she lived in a separate house; but to understand this aright, and also events to be described, it is indeed necessary to make you acquainted with Havelaar's house and grounds.   The accusation often made against the great artist who wrote *Waverley,* that he often abuses the patience of his readers by devoting too many pages to topography, seems to me to be unfounded, and I believe that in order to judge of the appropriateness of such descriptions, one has only to consider—Was this topography required ex- actly to convey the impression which the author wanted to communicate to you?   If so, do not be offended be- cause he expects you to take the trouble to read what he had taken the trouble to write.   But, if it was *not* re- quired, then throw the book aside; for the author who is empty-headed enough unnecessarily to give topography for ideas, will be very seldom worth reading, even when at last his topography is at an end.   But the judgment of the reader about the necessity of a deviation is often false, because he cannot know before the catastrophe what is necessary, and what not, to the systematic development of the situation; and when after the catastrophe he reads the book again—of books which one reads but once I do not speak—and even then thinks that this or that digression could have been omitted without marring the impression of the whole, the question remains whether he would have had the same impression of the whole if the author had not conducted him thither in a more or less artificial manner, just by means of the digressions which seem to him to be superfluous.

Do you think that the death of Amy Robsart would have touched you, if you had been a stranger in the halls of Kenilworth? And do you think that there is no connexion—connexion through contrast—between the rich dress wherein the unworthy Leicester showed himself to her, and the blackness of his soul? Do you not understand that Leicester—every one knows this who is acquainted with him from other sources than the novel only—was infinitely worse than he was painted in *Kenilworth*? But the great novelist, who liked better to charm by an artistic arrangement of colours than by coarseness of colour, thought it beneath him to dip his brush in all the mud and all the blood that clung to the unworthy favourite of Elizabeth. He wished to point out only one spot in the mud-pool; but he knew how to present such spots vividly to the eye, by means of what he put in juxtaposition, in his immortal writings. He who thinks that all this juxtaposition may be rejected as superfluous, quite forgets that in so doing in order to bring about effects, one would be obliged to go over to the school which, since 1830, has flourished so long in France; though I must say to the honour of that country, that the authors who in this respect have offended the most against good taste have been valued most in foreign countries, and not in France itself. The authors,—I believe that this school is now no more,— thought it easy to dip their hands in pools of blood and throw it in great spots on the picture, in order to be able to see them from a distance. To be sure they are easier to paint, those rough lines of red and black, than the beautiful lines in the calyx of a lily. Therefore that school generally chose kings for the heroes of narratives by preference, from the time when the nations were still in their infancy. You see, the affliction of the king is represented on paper by cries of the people: *his* anger gives the author an opportunity to kill thousands on the field of battle: *his* errors give room to paint famine and plague— suchlike things give work to rough pencils. If you are not touched at the sight of the corpse that lies *there*, there is room in my narrative for another man, convulsed with pain, and still shrieking. Did you not weep for the mother, who sought in vain for her child?—Well, I will show you another mother, who sees the quartering of her child. Did you remain unmoved at the martyrdom of that man?—I increase the number a hundredfold by torturing ninety-nine at his side. Are you hardened enough not to shudder when seeing this soldier, who, in the besieged fortification, devours his left arm because of hunger . . . . ?—

Epicure! I propose you give order, "Right and left wheel, form circle, left files eat left arms of right files . . . march!"

Yes, in this manner, artificial horrors become folly . . . which *en passant* I would fain prove.

And yet we would be reduced to this if we condemned too soon an author who wished to prepare you for his catastrophe without having recourse to these *screaming*[1] colours. But the danger of the other extreme is still greater. You despise the efforts of coarse literature, which thinks it must take your feelings by storm with such rough weapons; but if the author falls into the other extreme, if he sins by *too much* deviation from the principal matter, by *too much* pencilling, then your anger is still greater, and quite right; for then he has bored you, and that is unpardonable.

If we walk together and you stray every moment from the road, and call me into the underwood only with the intention to prolong the walk, I think this disagree-

---

[1] This is a literal rendering of the word used by the author.

able, and intend to walk alone for the future.   But if you can show me there a plant which I did not know before, or in which I may see something that I overlooked, if you show me from time to time a flower, which I like to pluck and carry in my button-hole, then I forgive your deviation from the road; yes, I am grateful for it.

And even without flower or plant, when you call me aside to show me through the trees the path that we shall walk upon by and by, but which now is still far from us in the depth, and which winds itself as a scarcely perceptible line through the field there below, then likewise I do not take this deviation amiss.   For when at last we have arrived thus far, I shall know how our road has wound—— through the mountain, how it is that the sun, that was a few minutes ago *there*, is now on our left; why that hill is now behind us, whose summit was just now before us . . . . then through that deviation you have made it easy for me to comprehend my walk——*and to comprehend is to enjoy.*

Reader, I have often in my narrative left you on the broad way, though it has cost me much not to take you with me into the underwood.   I was afraid that the walk would weary you, as I did not know if you would be pleased with the flowers and plants which I would show you; but as I believe that you will afterwards be pleased to have seen the path we shall walk upon presently, I am obliged to tell you something about Havelaar's house.

You would be very wrong to form your ideas of a house in the Indies according to European notions, and to think of a heap of stones, small rooms piled upon large rooms, with the street before it, neighbours right and left, whose household gods lean against yours, and a little garden with three gooseberry-bushes behind. With a few exceptions, the houses in the Indies have but one storey. The European reader will think this very strange, for it is a peculiarity of civilisation, or what passes for it, to consider strange all that is natural. The Indian houses are quite different from ours, but *they* are not strange; *our* houses are strange. He who was the first to allow himself the luxury of not sleeping in the same room with his cows, put the second room of his house not *upon*, but *next* to the first, for to build them all on the ground is both more simple and more comfortable. Our high houses owe their origin to want of space: we seek high in the air what we miss on the ground; and so every maid-servant, who in the evening shuts the window of her bed-room under the eaves, is a protest against this crowding, even when she is thinking, what I can readily believe, of something else.

In those countries, also, where civilisation and over-crowding of the population have *not yet* pushed mankind high up, because of the pressure below, the houses are of one storey, and Havelaar's did not belong to the few exceptions to this rule. On entering, ... but no, I will give a proof that I abandon all claims to ·the picturesque. "Given," an oblong: divide it into twenty-one parts, three in breadth, seven in depth. You give each of these partitions a number, beginning with the upper corner on the left-hand side, from there to the right, so that *four* comes under *one*, and so on.

1	2	3
4	5	6
7	8	9
10	11	12
13	14	15
16	17	18
19	20	21

The first three numbers together form the fore-gallery, which is often open on three sides, and whose roof is supported in the front by pillars. From there, one enters by two folding doors, the inner gallery which is represented by the three following numbers. The partitions 7, 9, 10, 12, 13, 15, 16, and 18, are rooms, most of them being connected by doors with each other. The three last numbers form the open gallery behind, and what I have not mentioned is a sort of closed inner gallery or passage. I am very proud of this description.[1]

I do not know what expression is used in Holland to give the idea conveyed in the Indies by the word "estate." "Estate" is there neither garden, nor park, nor field, nor wood, but either something, or that, or altogether, or none of these. It is the 'ground' that belongs to the house, in

[1] Nos. 7 and 10, 10 and 13, 13 and 16, are connected by doors with each other; 9 and 12, 12 and 15, 15 and 18 are connected by doors with each other. Between 5 and 8 a door; between 17 and 20 a door; between 7 and 8, 10 and 11, 13 and 14, 16 and 17 doors; between 8 and 9, 11 and 12, 14 and 15, 17 and 18 doors.

so far as it is not covered by the house; thus, in India, the expression, "garden *and* estate" would be a pleonasm. There are no houses, or very few, without such ground. Some estates contain wood, and garden, and field, and make you think of a park; others are flower-gardens; elsewhere, again, the whole estate is one large grass-field; and lastly, there are some very simple ones reduced to a macadamised square, which is perhaps less agreeable to the eye, but which promotes cleanliness in the houses, because many insects are harboured by grass or trees.

Havelaar's "estate" was very large; yes, however strange it may sound, it might be called on one side boundless, as it was bordered by a ravine that extended to the shores of the Tji-Udjung, the river that surrounded Rankas-Betong with one of its many windings. It would be difficult to say where the ground of the Assistant Resident's house ended, and where the common commenced, as the great ebb-tides and floods of the Tji-Udjung, which at this time had drawn back its shores as far as the horizon, and which at another time filled the ravine up to very near Havelaar's house, changed its limits every moment. This ravine had always been a thorn in the eye of Madam Slotering,—that was very clear. The vegetable growth, everywhere so rapid in India, was always particularly luxuriant, on account of the mud that was left behind, to such an extent that, though the rising and falling of the water happened with a force that rooted up and carried

away the underwood, a little time was sufficient to cover
the ground with a shagginess which rendered the clearing
of the grounds, even near the house, very difficult. And
this would have been no little grief even to one who was
not a mother. For not to speak of all sorts of insects that
generally flew during the evening round the lamp in such
a multitude that to read and write became impossible,
which is very tiresome in many parts of the Indies,
there were a number of snakes and other animals in the
underwood, not only in the ravine, but even found every
moment in the garden, near and behind the house, or in
the grass of the square in front.

Standing in the fore-gallery with the face to this square,
one's back was to the house; on the left was the building
with the offices, the counting-house, and the place for
meetings, where Havelaar had spoken that morning to the
chiefs, and behind that was the ravine which extended to
the Tji-Udjung. Exactly opposite the offices was the old
mansion of the Assistant Residents, which was now tem-
porarily inhabited by Madam Slotering; and as one could
reach the estate by two ways that were approached on both
sides by the grass-fields, of course every one who came on
the estate to go to the kitchen or stalls that were behind
the principal building, had either to pass the offices or
Madam Slotering's house. On one side of the principal
building, and behind it, was the very large garden, which
had excited the joy of Tine, because of the many flowers

which she found there, and above all, because there little
Max could so often play.

Havelaar had made his excuses to Madam Slotering for
not having yet paid her a visit; he would go there next
morning, but Tine had been there and made acquaintance
with her. I have already said that this lady was a *so-
called* "native," who spoke no other language than Malay.
She had intimated her desire to keep her own household,
to which Tine readily agreed. And she did not comply
for want of hospitality, but chiefly out of fear that she,
just arrived at Lebak, could not receive Madam Slotering
so well as she considered she ought under the peculiar
circumstances in which she was placed. True, this lady,
who understood no Dutch, need not have apprehended any
harm from the narratives of Max, as Tine had said; but
she understood that more was required than not to *harm*
the Slotering family, and the scanty kitchen, in connexion
with the intended economy, made her consider the intention of Madam Slotering very wise. It is also doubtful
whether, had the circumstances been otherwise, the intercourse with a person who spoke only one language, wherein
nothing is printed that civilizes the mind, would have
conduced to mutual pleasure. Tine would have kept her
company as much as possible, and would have spoken
much with her about the "kitchen" and "puddings," but
this would always have been a sacrifice, and it was therefore thought much better that matters had been arranged

through Madam Slotering's voluntary retirement in such a manner as left every one in perfect liberty. Yet it was curious that this lady had not only refused to take part in social dinners, but that she even made no use of the offer to have her food prepared in the kitchen of Havelaar's house, and this reserve went a little too far, as Tine said, for the kitchen was large enough.

CHAPTER XIV.

"You know," began Havelaar, "that the Dutch possessions on the west coast of Sumatra are bounded on the North by independent districts, of which Atchin is the most important. It is said that a secret article in the treaty of 1824 restrains us from extending our frontier in that direction beyond the river Singkel. General van Damme, who with a *faux air Napoléon* wanted to extend his government as far as possible, here, therefore, stopped short at the insurmountable obstacle. I must believe in the existence of that secret article, because otherwise it would surprise me that the *Rajahs*[1] of Troomon and Analaboo, whose provinces are not without importance on account of their active trade in pepper, have not long ere now been brought under the Dutch power. You know how easy it is to find a pretext for war with such petty sovereigns, and for the annexation of their territory. To steal a province will always be easier than to steal a

[1] Independent petty princes.

mill.[1] I believe that General van Damme would even
have taken a mill, if he had pleased, and do not understand, therefore, how he could have abstained from those
provinces in the North if there had not existed more
substantial reasons for so doing than right and justice.
However this may be, he extended his conquests, not
north but east. The provinces Mandhéling and Ankola
—[the latter was the name of the Assistant-Residency
formed out of the hardly tranquillized Battah countries]
—were not yet quite freed from Atchinese influence (for
when once fanaticism has taken firm root in a country,
extirpation of it is difficult), although the Atchinese were
no longer there; but this was not enough for the Governor.
He extended his power to the east coast; and Dutch
functionaries and Dutch garrisons were sent to Bila and
Pertibea, which places were, as you know, afterwards eva-
cuated, when at last a Government Commissioner came to
Sumatra, who thought this extension purposeless, and therefore disapproved of it, above all because it was contrary to
the principles of economy, on which the mother country so
much insisted. General van Damme asserted that this extension would not add to the budget; for that the new
garrisons consisted of troops for whom money had already
been voted, and that he had thus brought a very large
province under the Dutch Government without incurring

---

[1] Allusion to *Le Meunier de Sans-souci*, by *Andriena*, in which he
says of Frederick the Great of Prussia, "*On respecte un moulin, on vole
une province.*"

any additional expenses. And as for diminishing the garrisons of other places, above all in Mandhéling, he believed that he could place sufficient confidence in the fidelity and alliance of Jang di Pertoean, the most influential chief in the Battah district. The Government Commissioner reluctantly concurred, upon the reiterated assurance of the General, that he would be personally responsible for the fidelity of Jang di Pertoean.[1]

"Now the Controller, who was my predecessor in the province of Natal, was the son-in-law of the Assistant Resident of the Battah countries, who was at enmity with Jang di Pertoean. I afterwards heard many complaints brought against this Assistant Resident, but received them with caution, as coming from Jang di Pertoean, who had himself been recently accused of other offences, and on that account perhaps tried to make good his own defence by exposing the faults of his accuser. However this may be, the Controller of Natal took his father-in-law's part against Jang di Pertoean; and the more readily because this Controller was very intimate with a certain Soetan Salim, a chief of Natal, who also bore the Battah chief a grudge. There was a feud between the families of these two chiefs; the rejection of marriage proposals, jealousy of each other's influence, pride on the part of Jang di Pertoean, who was of better family, and many more causes contributed to keep Natal and Mandhéling at enmity with each other.

[1] Literally : He who reigns—the highest title in Sumatra.

"Suddenly a report was circulated that a conspiracy had been discovered in Mandhéling, in which Jang di Pertoean was concerned, and which had for its object to display the holy banner of revolt, and murder all the Europeans. The first discovery of this was of course made at Natal, as one is always better instructed in neighbouring provinces how matters stand, than on the spot, because many who at home, from fear of compromising a chief, are careful not to mention a circumstance known to them, lay aside that fear as soon as they enter a territory where such a chief has no influence. This is also the reason, Verbrugge, why I am no stranger to the affairs of Lebak. I knew much of what happened there, before I ever thought I should be appointed here. I was in 1846 in the Krawang districts, and made many excursions in the Preangan, where, as early as 1842, I met with many landed proprietors in the neighbourhood of Buitenzorg[1] and Batavia, and I know how those landlords have always rejoiced at the miserable condition of the Lebak district, whose refugees flock to cultivate *their* estates. . . .

"Now, then, the conspiracy at Mandhéling, which, if real, would have branded Jang di Pertoean as a traitor, must have been discovered in the same manner at Natal.

"According to the evidence of witnesses examined by the Controller of Natal, that chief, together with his brother, Soetan Adam, would have summoned Battah

---

[1] The residence of the Governor-General.

chiefs to assemble in a sacred grove, where they were to swear not to rest before the power of the Christian dogs in Mandhéling was destroyed. Of course, he had received an inspiration from heaven to this effect : you know this qualification is never wanting on such occasions.

"Whether such was the intention of Jang di Pertoean, I cannot say for certain; I read the evidence; but you will see why implicit reliance was not to be placed on it. It is certain that he, with his Islam fanaticism, was quite capable of such a project.

"He, with the whole population of Battah, had recently been converted by the *paderies*[1] to the true faith; and new converts are generally fanatical.

"The consequences of this true or supposed discovery was, that Jang di Pertoean was apprehended and conveyed to Natal, where the Controller shut him up in the fortress and sent him by sea, on the first opportunity, to the Governor of the west coast of Sumatra at Padang, to whom were submitted the documents, in which the heavy accusations had been set forth that justified the severity of the measures already taken. Jang di Pertoean had thus left Mandhéling as a prisoner; at Natal he was kept in confinement on board the man-of-war that had transported him thither; he expected, therefore,—innocent or not, because he had been accused in legal form of high treason —to arrive at Padang as a prisoner; and he must certainly

---

[1] Mohammedan Priests.

Q

have been astonished to learn, on landing, not only that
he was free, but that the General, whose carriage awaited
him on shore, would consider it as an honour to receive
him into his house and lodge him.   Certainly never was a
person accused of high treason more agreeably surprised.
A short time afterwards, the Assistant Resident of Mandhéling was suspended from his office because of all sorts
of deficiencies, about which I do not care to express an
opinion.   Now Jang di Pertoean, who, after having been
for some time at Padang in the General's house, and
treated by him with the utmost distinction, returned
through Natal to Mandhéling, not with the self-esteem of
one found innocent, but with the arrogance of a person
who stands so high that he needs no declaration of innocence.   Indeed, the matter had not been examined; and,
suppose that the accusations brought against him were
thought to be false, why, this very suspicion ought to have
required an examination, to punish the false witnesses, and
those who had induced them to tell such falsehoods.   It
appears that the General found reasons why this examination should not take place.   The accusation against Jang
di Pertoean was considered as "*non-avenue*," and I am
sure that the documents relating to the matter have
never been submitted to the eyes of the Government of
Batavia.

"A few days after the return of Jang di Pertoean,
I arrived at Natal, to take in hand the government of that

district. My predecessor told me, of course, what had just happened in Mandhéling, and gave me the necessary information as to the political condition of that province in relation to my department. It could not be taken amiss, that he complained much of the (in his eyes) unjust treatment which his father-in-law had had to undergo, and of the incomprehensible protection which Jang di Pertoean appeared to receive from the General. Neither he nor I was acquainted at that time with the fact that the sending of Jang di Pertoean to Batavia was a blow aimed at the General's face, and that he had good reasons, whatever they might be, to guarantee that chief against a charge of high treason. This was of so much the more importance to the General, because the Government Commissioner, mentioned above, had become in the meanwhile Governor - General, and probably would have recalled him from his government, from displeasure at the unfounded confidence in Jang di Pertoean, and the obstinacy founded upon that,—with which the General had opposed the evacuation of the East coast.

"'But,' said my predecessor, 'whatever may move the General to admit all the accusations against my father-in-law, and yet not to think worth an examination the much heavier accusations against Jang di Pertoean——this matter is not yet ended! And if at Padang, as I suppose, the sworn evidence has been destroyed, I have here something else that *cannot* be destroyed.'

And he showed me a sentence of the Court of Justice

at Natal, of which he was president, containing the condemnation of a certain Si Pamaga to the penalty of flogging, branding, and, I believe, twenty years' hard labour, for attempting to murder the Toeankoe[1] (an Indian functionary) of Natal.

" 'Read the *procès-verbal* of the session,' said my predecessor, ' and then you may judge whether my father-in-law will be believed at Batavia, when he there accuses Jang di Pertoean of high treason!'

"I read the documents. According to declarations of witnesses, *and the confession of the defendant*, he had been bribed by Si Pamaga to murder at Natal the Toeankoe, his guardian Soetan, and the governing Controller. In order to execute this design, he had gone to the house of the Toeankoe, and had there commenced a conversation about a *Sewah*,[2] with the servants who sat on the staircase of the inner-gallery, intending thereby to prolong his stay till he perceived the Toeankoe, who actually made his appearance very soon, surrounded by a number of relations and servants. Pamaga had fallen upon the Toeankoe with his ' sewah,' but, from unknown circumstances, had not been able to execute his criminal design. The Toeankoe, much frightened, jumped out of the window, and Pamaga fled ; he hid himself in the wood, and was a few days afterwards taken by the Natal police.

[1] *Toeankoe*—title of rank *only* used in Sumatra.
[2] *Sewah* == Indian weapon.

" When the accused was asked what had moved him to
this assault, and the intended murder of Soetan Salim and
the Controller of Natal, he replied ' that he had been
bribed to that by Soetan Adam, in the name of his brother
Jang di Pertoean of Mandhéling.'

" ' Is that clear or not ?' asked my predecessor. The
Resident's sentence '*fiat* execution' was carried out, as
regards the flagellation and branding, and Si Pamaga is
now on his way through Padang, to be sent to Java, there
to undergo his hard labour. At the same time with him
the documents of the *procès-verbal* arrive at Batavia, to
show who the man was upon whose accusation my father-
in-law was suspended. That sentence the General cannot
annul, even if he would.

" I undertook the Government of the Natal district, and
my predecessor left. After some time they acquainted me
that the General would come in a war-steamer to visit
the North, and also Natal. He arrived with a large retinue at my house, and asked to see the original documents concerning that poor man who had been so
extremely ill-treated."

" ' The accusers themselves,' added he, ' deserved to be
flogged and branded.' "

" I did not understand it at all. For the causes of this
contest about Jang di Pertoean were then still unknown to
me, and I could therefore not conceive, either that my

predecessor had wilfully and knowingly condemned an innocent person to such heavy punishment, or that the General wished to protect a criminal from a just sentence. I was charged to have Soetan Salim and the Toeankoe taken prisoners. As the young Toeankoe was very much beloved by the population, and as we had but a small garrison in the fortress, I begged to be allowed to leave him at large, which was granted me; but for Soetan Salim, the enemy of Jang di Pertoean, there was no pardon. The population was in great excitement. The Natallers took it into their heads that the General was debasing himself to be a tool of Mandhéling hatred, and it was under these circumstances that I could do from time to time something which he deemed a brave action, above all because he did not give me for escort the small force that could be spared out of the fortress, and the detachment of mariners which he had brought from the ship, when I went on horseback to the places where there were seditious assemblies. I observed, on this occasion, that the General van Damme took good care of his own safety, and, therefore, I do not subscribe to his military renown.

" He formed a council which I might call ' *ad hoc.*' The members were a few adjutants, other officers, the Magistrate, whom he had taken from Padang, and myself. This council was to investigate how under my predecessor the *procès* had been conducted against Si Pamaga. I had to summon a number of witnesses, whose declarations were necessary for the purpose. The General, who of course presided, interrogated, and the evidence was written down by the Magistrate. As the latter understood but little Malay, and nothing at all of the Malay spoken in North Sumatra, it was often necessary to translate to him the replies of the witnesses, which the General, for the most part, did himself. From the sessions of this Council resulted documents that show very clearly that Si Pamaga never had the intention to murder any person whatever; that he had never seen or known Soetan Adam or Jang di Pertoean; that he had *not* assaulted the Toeankoe of Natal, who did *not* jump out of the window, and so on. Further, that the sentence against the unhappy Si Pamaga had been pronounced under the pressure of the President, my predecessor, and of Soetan Salim, a member of the Council, the persons who had invented the pretended crime of Si Pamaga, to give to the suspended Assistant Resident of Mandhéling a weapon for his defence, and to give vent to their hatred against Jang di Pertoean.

" The mode of investigation by the General reminded one of a certain whist-party of one of the Sultans of Morocco, who said to his partner :[1] ' Play hearts, or I will cut your throat.' The translations also, as he caused the officer of justice to write them down, left much to be desired.

" Whether my predecessor and Soetan Salim had exercised pressure on the Court of Justice to declare Si Pamaga

[1] The French Ambassador.

guilty, I do not know; but this I know, that General van
Damme did exercise pressure on the evidence assigned to
prove his innocence. Without as yet knowing the tendency of these proceedings, I opposed them, and went so
far that I was obliged to refuse to sign some documents,
and in this it was I so offended the General. You understand now the drift of the words, with which I ended the
reply to the observations that had been made on my
pecuniary administration, and in which I begged to be
excused on all benevolent considerations."

" It was very brave for one of your years," said Duclari.

" I thought it a matter of course, but it is certain that
General van Damme was not accustomed to anything of
the kind. I have suffered much from the consequences
of this affair. Oh no, Verbrugge, I see what you
mean to say, I *never* regretted it. I must even add,
that I should not have contented myself with simply pro-
testing against the manner in which the General examined
the witnesses, and refusing my signature to the documents,
if I could have guessed at that time, what I learned only
afterwards, that all this arose from a determination fixed
beforehand to accuse my predecessor in question. I
thought that the General, convinced of the innocence of
Si Pamaga, allowed himself to be carried away by a praise-
worthy desire to save an innocent victim from the consequence of any error in justice, as far as was possible, after
the flagellation and the brand. Though this opinion made

me oppose falsehood, yet for that reason I did not become so indignant as I should have been if I had known that all this was not to save an innocent man, but that this falsehood was designed to annul the proofs that stood in the General's way, at the expense of the honour and the welfare of my predecessor."

" And what became of your predecessor ?" asked Verbrugge.

" Happily for him, he had already gone to Java before the General returned to Padang. It seems that he has been able to account for his conduct to the Government at Batavia; at least he has remained in the service. The Resident of Ayer-Bangie, who had issued the '*fiat* execution' was . . ."

" Suspended ?"

" Of course. You see that I was not so very wrong, when I said in my epigram that the Governor ' reigned over us as a suspender.' "

"And what became of all these suspended functionaries?"

" Oh, there were still many more. All of them have been, one after another, re-established in their functions. Some of them have afterwards been invested with very considerable employments."

" And Soetan Salim ? "

" The General took him as a prisoner to Padang, and from thence he was exiled to Java. He is now at Tji-andjoor, in the Preangan Regencies. In 1846 I was there, and paid him a visit. . . . . Do you now remember, Tine. why I came to Tji-andjoor?"

"No, Max, I have quite forgotten that."

"Well, who can remember everything? . . . . I was married there, gentlemen!"

"But," asked Duclari, "as you have told us several things, is it true that you fought so many duels at Padang?"

"Yes, I fought very often. There were many reasons for that. I told you already, .that the favour of the Governor in such an out-of-the-way place is the rule with which many measure their friendliness. Most of them were very ill-disposed towards me, and this often showed itself in rudeness. I, on the other hand, was very sensitive. A salutation not acknowledged, a taunt on the 'folly of one who would take up the cudgels with the General,' an allusion to my poverty, my state of starvation, the poor food, that seemed to be the reward of moral independence—all this, you conceive, made me bitter. Many, above all amongst the officers, knew that the General liked to see people duelling, and, above all, with one so much in disgrace as I was. Perhaps, therefore, my sensitiveness was intentionally excited——likewise I sometimes fought for somebody else, whom I considered to be wronged.——However this may be, duelling was the order of the day, and it often happened that I had two meetings in one morning;——there is something very attractive in duelling, particularly with the sabre. Yet you understand that I would not do such a thing now, even if there were as much reason for it as in those days.——Come here, Max!——no—don't catch that little insect—come here. I say you must never catch butterflies. That little creature at first crept for a long time as a caterpillar on a tree,—that was no happy life. Now it has just got wings and likes to flutter in the air and enjoy itself, seeking food in the flowers and hurting nobody:—look, is it not prettier to see it fluttering there?"

So the conversation went on from duelling to butterflies, from the compassion of the merciful man to his cattle to cruelty to animals, from the "*loi Grammont*"[1] to the French Parliament at Paris where that law was accepted from the republic, to many other things.——At last Havelaar got up. He excused himself to his guests, because he had business to attend to.

When the Controller visited him the following morning at his office, he did not know that the new Assistant Resident had ridden out the day before to Parang-Koedjang after the conversation in the fore-gallery, and had only just returned.

I beg the reader to believe that Havelaar was too courteous to speak so much at his own table as I have represented in the last chapters, by which I make him appear to monopolize the conversation, and neglect

[1] The General de Grammont was the proposer of this law. It was accepted in the *Corps Législatif* in the year 1850.

those duties of a host which prescribe that guests should take or decline the opportunity "of showing what they are." I have selected a few of the many materials that were before me, and I could have prolonged the table-talk for a longer time with less difficulty than the breaking it off has cost me. I hope that what I have communicated will be sufficient to justify in part the description which I gave of Havelaar's character and mind, and that the reader will observe with some interest the adventures that are in store for him and his family at Rankas-Betong. The small family lived on in peace. Havelaar went out very often during the day, and spent half the nights in his office. The intercourse between him and the commandant of the garrison was most agreeable, and also in his familiar conversation with the Controller no trace could be discovered of difference in rank, which often makes social intercourse in the Indies so stiff and disagreeable; whilst the inclination of Havelaar to lend assistance where he could, was often to the advantage of the Regent, who also was very fond of "his elder brother;" and finally, the amiability of Madam Havelaar contributed much to the agreeable intercourse between the few Europeans and the native chiefs. The correspondence about the service with the Resident of Serang showed a mutual cordiality: the orders of the Resident were given with courtesy, and very punctually followed.

The household of Tine was soon in good order. After

we had waited for it a long time, the furniture arrived from Batavia. Ketimons (gherkins) were pickled; and in future when Max related anything at table, it was not for want of eggs for the omelet, though the manner in which the little family lived showed very clearly that the intended economy was strictly adhered to.

Madam Slotering seldom left her house, and only now and then joined the Havelaar family at tea in the front veranda. She spoke little, and always kept a vigilant eye upon every one who approached her own or Havelaar's house; people got accustomed to what they called her monomania, and soon paid no more attention to it.

All seemed to breathe peace; for Max and Tine it was comparatively a trifle to submit to the privations which are inevitable at a place in the interior with but little communication. As no bread was baked in the neighbourhood, they had no bread. We could have had it brought from Serang, but the expenses of transport were too high. Max knew as well as others, that there were many means of having bread brought to Rankas-Betong without payment; but UNPAID LABOUR, that Indian cancer, was horrible in his eyes. So there was much at Lebak that could be got for nothing, through power, but could not be bought for a reasonable price, and in such cases Havelaar and his wife willingly endured privation. To be sure, they had undergone other privations. Had not the poor woman lived for months on board of an Arab vessel, without other bed than the deck, without other shelter from the heat of the sun and the showers of the rainy season, than a small table, between the legs of which she had to squeeze herself? Had not she been obliged to satisfy herself in that vessel with a small allowance of dry rice and dirty water? And had not she in these and many other circumstances always been contented if she could only be with her Max?

One circumstance, however, at Lebak caused her pain: —little Max could not play in the garden, because there were so many snakes. When she perceived this and complained of it to Havelaar, he promised the servants a reward for every snake they could catch, but on the first day he paid so many premiums that he was obliged to withdraw his promise for the future; for even in ordinary circumstances, and without the economy so necessary for him, this payment would soon have exceeded his means. It was resolved that little Max should henceforward leave the house no more, and that when he wished to take an airing, he would have to content himself with playing in the fore-gallery. Notwithstanding this precaution Tine was always anxious; and above all in the evening, as it is known that snakes often creep into the houses, and, seeking warmth, hide themselves in the bed-rooms. Snakes and suchlike vermin are to be found everywhere in the Indies; but in the chief towns, where the population live closer together, they are of

course more rare than in wilder places such as Rankas-
Betong. If Havelaar could have decided to have his
estate cleared of weeds, as far as the border of the ravine,
the snakes would still from time to time have showed
themselves in the garden, but not in such large numbers
as was now the case. The nature of these reptiles makes
them prefer darkness and lurking-holes to the open daylight, so that, if Havelaar's grounds had been kept clean,
the snakes would not then, as it were, unwillingly have
lost their way, and left the weeds of the ravine. But
Havelaar's grounds were not cleared, and I wish to explain the reason of it, as it gives another opportunity of a
view of the abuses that reign almost everywhere in the
Dutch Indian possessions.

The houses of the persons intrusted with power in the
interior are built on common lands, if one may speak of
such as existing in a country where the Government
appropriates all.

Enough, these grounds do not belong to the official
inhabitant. For he would take care not to buy or to hire
grounds the maintenance of which was too much for him.
Now, when the grounds of the house assigned to him are
too large to be maintained in good order, they degenerate
in a few weeks (so luxuriant is the growth of plants)
into a wilderness. And yet, such grounds are seldom if
ever to be seen in a bad condition——yes, the traveller is
often astonished at the beautiful park that surrounds a

Resident's house. No functionary in the interior has a sufficient income to get this labour done for fair wages, and as a respectable appearance of the administrator's house is necessary, in order that the population, attaching so much importance to externals, may find nothing in it to excite contempt, the question is, how has this result been obtained ?

In most places the administrators have at their disposal persons condemned elsewhere, but not, however, kept at Bantam, on account of political reasons. But even in places where such are located, their number, considering the other kinds of labour required of them, is seldom in proportion to the work that would be required to keep large grounds in good order. Other means must be found, and the summoning of labourers to perform feudal tasks is had recourse to. The Regent or Demang who receives such a summons makes haste to obey it, for he knows very well that it will be very difficult for the administrator who abuses his power, afterwards to punish a native chief for a similar fault, and so the error of the one becomes the passport of the other.

Yet it seems to me, that such a fault on the part of an administrator must not, in some cases, be judged of with too much severity, and, above all, not according to European notions. The population itself would think it strange, perhaps because so unwonted, if he always and in every case held too strictly to the stipulations that prescribed the number of those destined for feudal labour, as circumstances may occur which were not foreseen when these stipulations were made.

But as soon as the limit of what is strictly lawful has been exceeded, it is difficult to fix the point where such an excess would become criminal; above all, great circumspection is wanted, when it is known that the chiefs only wait for a bad example to imitate it in still greater excess. The story of that king who ordered that every grain of salt which he had used at his simple dinner, when he travelled through the country at the head of his army, should be paid for, because otherwise, as he said, this would be a beginning of an injustice that would at last destroy his kingdom——his name may have been Tamerlane, Noer-eddien, or Genghis Khan—certainly either this fable, or if it is no fable, the occurrence itself, is of Asiatic origin; and just as looking at sea-dikes makes you think of the possibility of high water, so it must be admitted that there exists an inclination to *such* abuses, in a country where *such* lessons are given.

The persons whom Havelaar had lawfully at his disposal could only keep clear a very small part of his grounds, in the immediate neighbourhood of his house, from weeds and underwood. The rest was in a few weeks a wilderness. Havelaar wrote to the Resident about the means of remedying this, either by paid labour, or by proposing to the Government to cause persons under

sentence of hard labour, to work in the Residency of
Bantam, as elsewhere. Thereupon he received a refusal,
with the observation that he had a right to put to work
on his grounds the persons who had been condemned by
him, as a magistrate, to "labour on the public roads."
Havelaar knew this very well ; but he had never made
use of this right, neither at Rankas-Betong, nor at
Amboina, nor at Menado, nor at Natal. It shocked him
to have his garden kept in good order as a fine for small
errors, and he had often asked himself how the Government
could permit stipulations to remain, of a nature to tempt
the functionary to punish small excusable offences, not in
proportion to the offences themselves, but in proportion
to the condition or the extension of his estate. The very
idea, that he who was punished, even justly, might think
that self-interest was hidden under the sentence pronounced, made him, where he was obliged to punish, always
give preference to the system, otherwise very objection-
able, of confinement.

And it was from this cause that little Max could not
play in the garden, and that Tine had not so much pleasure
from the flowers as she had anticipated on the day of her
arrival at Rankas-Betong. Of course, this and suchlike
small misfortunes had no influence on the minds of a family
that possessed so much material to procure itself a happy
domestic life ; and it was not to be ascribed to these trifles
when Havelaar sometimes entered with a clouded brow,

after his return from an excursion, or after having listened
to some one who had asked to speak to him. We have
heard from his speech to the chiefs that he would do his
duty, that he would oppose injustice ; and at the same time,
I hope that the reader may have seen from the conversations which I have communicated, that he certainly was a
person capable of discovering and bringing to light what
was hidden from others, or but dimly seen. It might
therefore be supposed that not much of what happened in
Lebak escaped his observation. We have also seen that
many years before he had paid attention to this province
in such a manner that, from the very first day when he
met Verbrugge in the 'pendoppo,' where my history begins,
he showed that he was no stranger in his new sphere of
duty. By investigation on the spot, he had discovered
much that was confirmatory of what he had previously
suspected ; and, above all, the official records had made
him acquainted with the exceedingly miserable condition in
which this country was. From the letters and notes of his
predecessor, he observed that the latter had made the same
observations. The letters to the chiefs contained reproach
upon reproach, menace upon menace, and showed very
clearly how this functionary would at last have said, that
he intended to apply direct to the Government if this state
of affairs continued.

When Verbrugge communicated this to Havelaar, the
latter had replied that his predecessor would in that case

have acted very wrongly, as the Assistant Resident of Lebak ought in no case to pass over the Resident of Bantam; and he had added, that this could in no case be justified, as it was not likely that that high functionary would side with extortion and tyranny.

Such countenance of injustice was not to be supposed, in the way that Havelaar meant, namely, that the Resident would derive any advantage or gain from these crimes; but still there was a cause which made him unwilling to do justice to the complaints of Havelaar's predecessor. We have seen how this predecessor had often spoken to the Resident about the prevailing abuses, and of how little use this had been. It is therefore not quite without interest to examine why he who, as the head of the whole Residency, was obliged to take care as much as the Assistant Resident, yes, even more than he, that justice was done, chose rather continually to oppose it.

When Havelaar was staying at the Resident's house at Serang, he had already spoken to him about the Lebak abuses, and had received for answer,--"that this was everywhere the case in a greater or less degree."

Now Havelaar could not deny this. Who could pretend to have seen a country where nothing wrong happened? But he thought that this was no motive to tolerate abuses where they were found; above all, not when one is appointed to oppose them; and, moreover, that after all that he knew of Lebak, the question was not of abuses "*more or less,*" but of abuses on a *very large scale,* whereupon the Resident replied, " that it was still worse in Tjiringien" (likewise belonging to Bantam).

If it is now taken for granted, as it may be, that a Resident has no direct advantage in extortion, and the tyrannical disposal of the population, the question presents itself, what then induces many to tolerate such abuses, without acquainting the Government with them, and that contrary to their oath and duty ? And he who thinks about this, must think it very strange indeed, that the existence of these abuses is so coolly acknowledged, as if it were a question of something out of reach or competence. I will try to explain the causes of this.

To bring bad news is generally disagreeable, and it seems as if something of this unfavourable impression sticks to him whose lot it is to communicate them. Now, when this alone is a reason with some for denying, while they know better, the existence of something unfavourable, how much more this becomes the case, if one runs the risk, not only of falling into the disgrace, which seems to be the fate of the bringer of bad tidings, but, at the same time, of being regarded as the *cause* of them.

The Government of Dutch India likes to write home to its masters in the mother country that all goes on satisfactorily. The Residents like to announce this to the Government. The Assistant Residents, who receive themselves from their Controllers nothing but favourable accounts, send again, in their turn, no disagreeable tidings to the Residents.   From all this arises in the official written accounts of these matters, an artificial optimism, contradictory not only to the truth, but also to the real opinions of these optimists themselves, as soon as they treat these same matters by word of mouth, or, what is still more curious, even in contradiction to their own written reports.   I can cite many examples of reports that rate very high the prosperous condition of a Residency, but at the same time give themselves the lie, especially when accompanied by figures.   These examples would,—if the matter were not too serious on account of the final consequences,—give occasion for laughter and satire, and the *naïveté* is really astonishing, with which, in such cases, the grossest untruths are maintained; though the writer exposes himself, a few sentences further on, to the weapons with which these untruths can be rebutted.   I will quote a single example, to which I could add many more. Among the documents which I have before me I find the yearly account of a Residency.   The Resident praises the flourishing state of trade, and asserts that everywhere the greatest prosperity and activity are to be seen.   A little further on, he speaks of the scanty means which he has in his power to prevent smuggling; but to take away the disagreeable impression which would be produced on the Government at the thought that in his Residency many import duties are evaded, "No," he immediately adds, "there is no fear of that; little or nothing is smuggled into my Residency, for ... so little business is done here, that nobody would venture his capital in the trade."

I have read a Report that commenced with the words, " During the past year, in this Residency, *tranquillity has remained tranquil. . . . .*"[1] Such phrases certainly testify to a very *tranquil tranquillity* founded on the indulgence of the Government to every one who spares it disagreeable tidings, or, as the saying goes, "does not bother it with sad reports!"

Where the population does not increase, it is ascribed to inexactness in the census of former years. Where the taxes do not rise, this circumstance must be attributed to the necessity for a low taxation, in order to encourage agriculture, which will eventually—that is to say, when the writer of the Report shall have retired from office,— be sure to produce inestimable treasures. Where disturbances have taken place, that *could not* be concealed, they were occasioned by a few malefactors, and need be no more feared for the future, as there exists a *general* contentment. Where poverty or famine has thinned the population, this was the consequence of scarcity, drought, rain, or something else,——NEVER OF MISGOVERNMENT.

The memorandum of Havelaar's predecessor, wherein he ascribed the emigration of the people from the district of Parang-Koodjang to " *excessive abuses,*" lies before me.

---

[1] " Tranquillity has remained tranquil,"—this is a literal rendering of the phrase used by many Residents.

This notice was *un*official, and contained matters about which this functionary had to *speak* to the Resident of Bantam. But in vain Havelaar sought in the archives for a proof that his predecessor had described plainly what he meant by its true name in *a public official* missive.

In short, the official reports of the functionaries to the Government, and likewise the reports founded thereupon which are sent to the Government in the mother country, *are for the greater and more important part* UNTRUE.[1] I know that this accusation is serious; yet I maintain it, and feel myself capable of proving it. Whosoever is angry because of this undisguised utterance of my opinion, let him consider how many millions of money, how many human lives might have been spared to England, if the eyes of the Nation had been opened in time to the true condition of affairs in British India. Let him consider what a large debt of gratitude would have been due to the man that had had the courage to be the Job's comforter before it was too late to repair the wrong without bloodshed.[2]

I said that I could prove the charge. I will show, where it is necessary, that famine often reigned in regions that had been held up as models of prosperity; and where it was said that the population was tranquil and contented, I assert that it was often on the verge of a furious

---

[1] "Max Havelaar" has never been refuted. The laws and regulations are good. They even look so philanthropic *on paper!*

[2] The English reader will bear in mind that this was written subsequent to the great Indian mutiny of 1857.

outbreak. It is not my intention to give these proofs in *this* book; yet I trust that it will not be laid aside, without the readers believing that these proofs exist.

For the present I confine myself to another and unique example of the ridiculous optimism of which I have spoken, an example that will be understood by every one, whether acquainted or not with Indian affairs.

Every Resident sends in a monthly statement of the rice that has been imported into his province or exported elsewhere. These statements show how much of this rice is exported or imported. On comparing the quantity of rice which, according to the returns, is transported *from* Residencies in Java *to* Residencies in Java, we shall see that this quantity amounts to many thousand more *picols* (Javanese weight) than the rice that, according to the same returns, is imported *into* Residencies in Java *from* Residencies in Java.[1]

I will not speak now of what may be thought of the intelligence of the Government that receives and publishes such returns, and will only show the reader the tendency of this cheat.

The reward per cent.[2] to European and native function-

---

[1] A sends more to B than B receives from A; B sends more to C than C receives from B, etc.

[2] The European and native functionaries are paid a certain percentage on products raised by the Dutch Government for the European marts. The Dutch government has its coffee-plantations, sugar-fields, etc. The European and native officials have to encourage labour in those government gardens, or fields, or plantations.

aries for products that must be sold in Europe, had caused such a neglect of the rice-culture, that in some parts a famine has reigned that could not be juggled away from before the eyes of the nation.

　I have already said that orders were then given not to let things go so far as that again.　To the many results of *these* orders belonged the statements referred to of the quantity of exported and imported rice, that the Government might be able to keep an eye on the ebb and flow of that produce.　*Exportation* from a Residency represents prosperity, *importation* scarcity.

　On comparing and examining these statements, it appears from them that the rice is everywhere so abundant that ALL THE RESIDENCIES TOGETHER EXPORT MORE RICE THAN IS IMPORTED INTO ALL THE RESIDENCIES TOGETHER, I repeat, that the tables alluded to only refer to rice grown on the island.　Thus the conclusion of the matter is the absurd theorem : *that there is more rice in Java than there is rice in Java.*[1] . . . .

　That is what I call prosperity !!

　I have already said that the desire to communicate no other than good news to the Government would be ridiculous, if the consequences of all this were not very sad. What amendment is to be hoped for much that is wrong, if there exists a preconcerted intention to bend and dis-

---

　[1] *Max Havelaar* was published in 1860.　Since 1860 the Dutch Chambers have done nothing, but declare themselves horror-struck.

tort all in the reports to the Government ? What, for
instance, is to be expected of a population that, from its
nature mild and submissive, has complained, year after
year, of tyranny, when it sees the departure of one Resident after another, on furlough or on half-pay, or called to
another office, without anything ever being done towards
the redress of the grievances under which it bows ? Will
not the bent bow rebound ? Will not the long suppressed
discontent—suppressed in order to be able to deny it—be
turned at last into fury, despair, frenzy ? Cannot you
see the Jacquerie at the end of all this ?

And where will the functionaries then be that succeeded
each other for years, without ever having had the idea
that there existed anything higher than the " favour of
the Government," anything higher than the " satisfaction
of the Governor General ?" Where will they be then,
those insipid report-writers, that blindfold the eyes of
the Government by their untruths ? Shall those who before lacked the courage to put a manly word on paper, fly
to arms and preserve for Holland the Dutch possessions ?
Will they give back to Holland the treasures that will be
required to stamp out revolt, to prevent revolution ? And
finally, will they give back life to the thousands that have
fallen *through their fault ?*

And those functionaries, those Controllers and Residents,
are not the most guilty.   It is the Government itself which,
as it were, struck with incomprehensible blindness, invites,

encourages, and rewards the sending in of favourable reports, and above all this is the case where the question is that of the oppression of the population by native chiefs.

Many persons ascribe this protection of the chiefs to the ignoble calculation, that as they have to exhibit pomp and magnificence to preserve that influence on the population which the Government requires, they ought to enjoy a much higher salary than they do now, if they were not to be at liberty to supply what was still wanting by unlawfully disposing of the possessions and the labour of the people. However this may be, the Government consents but very unwillingly to the application of the regulations ostensibly for the protection of the Javanese against extortion and plunder. For the most part it is easy to find, in political reasons not to be called in question, but often fictitious, a cause why *this* Regent or *that* chief should be spared, and the idea is therefore generally spread throughout the Indies that the Government would rather dismiss ten Residents than one Regent. These pretended political reasons—if they are founded on anything—are generally supported by false reports, because it is the interest of every Resident to extol the influence of his Regents on the population, so that, if afterwards there arose a question of excessive indulgence towards the chiefs, he might shelter himself behind them.

I will not speak now of the horrible hypocrisy of the humane-sounding stipulations, and of the oaths that protect the Javanese against tyranny, and beg the reader to remember how Havelaar, when repeating these oaths, had something of a disdainful look;—and will only now point out the difficult situation of the man who thought himself bound to his duty quite independently of the repeated oaths.

And for him this difficulty was greater still than it would have been for many others, because his heart was soft, and in contrast with his mind, which, the reader may have perceived by this time, was quite the opposite. So he had not only to contend with the fear of man, and the cares of office or advancement, but also with the duties which he had to fulfil as a husband and a father: he had to conquer an enemy in his own heart. He could not see suffering without suffering himself, and it would lead me too far, if I quoted examples, of how he always took even where he was injured and offended, the part of an adversary against himself. He had told Duclari and Verbrugge how in his youth he had found something attractive in duelling with the sabre, which was true; but he did not add, how he, after having wounded his adversary, generally wept, and cherished his late enemy as a loved sister, till he was quite recovered. I could relate how he, at Natal, had spoken in a friendly manner to the man condemned to hard labour who had shot at him, how he caused him to be fed, and gave him more liberty than others, because he thought he had discovered that the exasperation of this condemned man was the consequence of a too severe sentence pronounced elsewhere. Generally, the mildness of his disposition was either denied or thought ridiculous——denied by those who confounded his heart with his mind—thought ridiculous by those who could not understand how an intelligent man gave himself pains to save a fly that had stuck fast in a spider's web——denied again by every one—except Tine—who afterwards heard him scoff at those "stupid animals," and at "stupid Nature" that created such animals.

But there was still another means of pulling him down from the pedestal whereupon his acquaintances—*nolens volens*—were compelled to place him. "Yes, he is witty . . . . but there is inconsiderateness in his wit. He is intelligent . . . . but he makes no good use of his intelligence. Yes, he is good-natured, but . . . . he plays the coquette with it!"

For his mind and his intelligence I do not stand up, ... but his heart? Poor insects, which he saved when he was quite alone, will *you* defend his heart against the accusation of coquetry?

But you fled away, and did not care about Havelaar— you, that could not know that he would once need your testimony.

Was it coquetry of Havelaar, when at Natal he jumped into the estuary after a dog (the animal's name was Sappho), because he feared that the young creature could not swim well enough to escape the sharks that are so numerous there? I find such a coquetting with good-nature more difficult to believe than good-nature itself.

I call you to witness that have known Havelaar—if you are not stiffened by the cold of winter, and dead or dried up and withered by the heat yonder, under the Equator!—I summon you to testify of his heart, all of you who have known him! Now, above all, I summon you with confidence, because you need no more seek for the spot where the cord must be hooked in to pull him down ever so little.

Yet, however inopportunely it may appear, I will here insert a few lines from his pen, which will, perhaps, make such witnesses superfluous. Max was once far from wife and child. He had to leave her behind in the Indies, and was in Germany. With the quickness which I ascribe to him, but which I won't defend if attacked, he mastered the language of the country where he had been for a few months. Here are the lines which picture his love for his household :—

"' Mein Kind, da schlägt die neunte Stunde, hör!
Der Nachtwind säuselt, und die Luft wird kühl,
Zu kühl für dich vielleicht, dein Stirnchen glüht:
Du hast den ganzen Tag so wild gespielt
Du bist wohl müde, komm, dein *Tikar*[1] harret.'
    ' Ach Mutter, lasz mich noch ein Augenblick;
Es ist so sanft zu ruhen hier . . . und dort,
Da drin auf meiner Matte schlaf' ich gleich,

---

[1] *Tikar*, a straw-mat.

Und weisz nicht einmal was ich träume, . . . hier
Kann ich doch gleich dir sagen was ich träume,
Und fragen was mein Traum bedeutet . . . hör,
Was war das?'

           ''s War ein *Klapper*[1] der da fiel.'
'Thut das dem Klapper weh?'

             'Ich glaube nicht,
Man sagt die Frucht, der Stein hat kein Gefühl.'
'Doch eine Blume, fühlt, die auch nicht?'

             'Nein
Man sagt sie fühle nicht.'

         'Warum denn Mutter,
Als gestern ich die *Pukul ampat*[2] brach
Hast du gesagt : es thut der Blume weh?'

      'Mein Kind, die Pukul ampat war so schön,
Du zogst die zarten Blättchen roh entzwei,
Das that mir für die arme Blume leid,
Wenn gleich die Blume selbst es nicht gefühlt
Ich fühlt' es für die Blume, weil sie schön war.'
      'Doch Mutter, bist du auch schön?'

           'Nein mein Kind,
Ich glaube nicht.'

        'Allein *du* hast Gefühl?'
      'Ja, Menschen haben's, . . . doch nicht alle gleich.'
      'Und kann *dir* etwas weh thun? thut dir's weh,
Wenn dir im Schoos so schwer mein Köpfchen ruht?'
      'Nein, *das* thut mir nicht weh !'

          'Und, Mutter ich,
Hab *ich* Gefühl?'

        'Gewisz, erinn're dich
Wie du gestrauchelt einst,—an einem Stein
Dein Händchen hast verwundet, und geweint.
Auch weintest du als *Saoedien*[3] dir erzählte
Dasz auf den Hügeln dort ein Schäflein tief
In eine Schlucht hinunter fiel und starb ;

---

[1] *Klapper* (Malay, *Klappa*)—cocoa-nut.
[2] *Pukul ampat*—literally, four o'clock ; also, a flower which opens
at four o'clock in the afternoon.
[3] *Saoedien*—the child's guardian ; *pron.* Sudin.

Da hast du lang geweint,—das war Gefühl.'
  ' Doch Mutter, ist Gefühl denn Schmerz ?'
                                          ' Ja oft,
Doch immer nicht, . . . bisweilen nicht ! Du weisst
Wenn's Schwesterlein dir in die Haare greift,
Und krähend dir's Gesichtchen nahe drückt,
Dann lachst du freudig, das ist auch Gefühl.'
  ' Und dann mein Schwesterlein . . . es weint so oft,
Ist das vor Schmerz . . . hat sie denn auch Gefühl ?'
  ' Vielleicht, mein Kind, wir wissen's aber nicht,
Weil sie so klein es noch nicht sagen kann.'
  ' Doch Mutter . . . höre, was war das ?'
                                     ' Ein Hirsch

Der sich verspätet im Gebüsch, und jetzt
Mit Eile heimwärts kehrt und Ruhe sucht
Bei andren Hirschen die ihm lieb sind '—
                                ' Mutter,
Hat solch ein Hirsch ein Schwesterlein wie ich,
Und eine Mutter auch ?'
                       ' Ich weisz nicht, Kind.'
  ' Das würde traurig sein wenn's nicht so wäre !
Doch, Mutter sieh . . . was schimmert dort im Strauch,
Sieh wie es hüpft und tanzt . . . ist das ein Funk ?'
  ' 's Ist eine Feuerfliege.'
                    ' Darf ich 's fangen ?'
  ' Du darfst es, doch das Flieglein ist so zart,
Du wirst gewisz es weh thun und sobald
Du 's mit den Fingern all zu roh berührst,
Ist 's Thierchen krank, und stirbt und glänzt nicht mehr.'
  ' Das würde Schade sein . . . ich fang 'es nicht, . . .
Sieh da verschwand es, . . . nein, es kommt hierher, . . .
Ich fang 'es doch nicht . . . wieder fliegt es fort,
Und freut sich dasz ich's nicht gefangen habe, . . .
Da fliegt es . . . hoch . . . da oben . . . was ist *das*,
Sind das auch Feuerflieglein dort ?'
                              ' Das sind
Die Sterne.'
            ' Ein', und zwei und zehn und tausend !
Wieviel sind denn wohl da ?'
                         ' Ich weiss es nicht ;

Der Sterne Zahl hat Niemand noch gezählt !'
   'Sag' Mutter, zählt auch *Er* die Sterne nicht ?'
   'Nein liebes Kind, auch *Er* nicht.'
                      'Ist das weit
Dort oben wo die Sterne sind?'
                  'Sehr weit.'
   'Doch haben diese Sterne auch Gefühl ?
Und würden sie, wenn ich sie mit der Hand
Berührte, gleich erkranken, und den Glanz
Verlieren wie das Flieglein? . . . Sieh noch schwebt es . . .
Sag, würd' es auch den Sternen weh thun ?'
                  'Nein
Weh thut's den Sternen nicht, . . . doch 's ist zu weit
Für deine kleine Hand, du reichst so hoch nicht.'
   'Kann *Er* die Sterne fangen mit der Hand?'
   'Auch *Er* nicht, das kann Niemand.'
                   'Das ist Schade,
Ich gäb so gern dir einen . . . . wenn ich grosz bin,
Dann will *ich so dich lieben dasz ich 's kann.*'

Das Kind schlief ein und träumte von Gefühl,
Von Sternen die es faszte mit der Hand. . . . .
Die Mutter schlief noch lange nicht !
                 Doch träumte
Auch sie, und dacht an den der fern war . . . . .
" CASSEL, *Januar* 1859."

Yes, at the risk of becoming tedious, I have inserted
the above lines. I wish to lose no opportunity of making
known the man who plays the principal part in my
narrative, in order to inspire the reader with interest, as
black clouds afterwards gather over our hero's head.

CHAPTER XV.

[COMPOSED BY STERN.]

HAVELAAR'S predecessor had good intentions, but seemed to have been in some measure afraid of the displeasure of his superiors——had many children and no fortune—— had thus preferred *speaking* to the Resident, about what he called *excessive* abuses, than describing them plainly in an official report. He knew that a Resident does not like to receive a written report, which remains in his archives, and which may be afterwards a proof that he had been made acquainted in time with this or that wrong, whilst a verbal communication leaves him, without danger, the choice of paying attention to a complaint or not. Such verbal communications generally brought about a conversation with the Regent, who, of course, denied all, and asked for proof. Then the men were summoned who had the boldness to complain, and creeping before the feet of the Regent, they begged pardon. "No, that buffalo had not been taken away from them without payment; they certainly believed that double its value would be paid for it. No, they had not been summoned from their fields to labour without payment in the Regent's 'sawahs;'

they knew very well that the Regent would pay them afterwards handsomely for their labour. They had complained in a moment of groundless malice—they had been mad, and begged that they should be punished for such excessive disrespect." . . .

Then the Resident knew very well that he had to think about this revocation of the complaint, but it gave him nevertheless a nice opportunity to maintain the Regent in office and honour, and spared himself the disagreeable task of troubling the Government with an unfavourable report. The rash accusers were punished by caning, the Regent triumphed, and the Resident returned to the capital with the agreeable consciousness of having again managed so nicely.

But what was the Assistant Resident now to do, when the next day other complainers announced themselves? Or—and this often happened—when the same plaintiffs returned and revoked their revocation? Must he again insert this affair in his memoranda, to speak to the Resident about it a second time, to see the same comedy played again, to run the same risk as before, to pass at last for a person who, stupid and malicious, was continually producing complaints that were to be rejected every time as unfounded. And what would become of the relation so necessary between the first Native chief and the first European functionary, when the latter seemed to give ear continually to false complaints against his younger brother?

And, above all, what became of those poor plaintiffs, after they had returned to their village, under the power of the district or village chief, whom they had accused as the instrument of the Regent's arbitrariness,—what became of these poor men? He who could fly, fled.

Therefore were there many Bantam people in the neighbouring provinces. Therefore were there so many inhabitants of Lebak among the rebels in the Lampong district. Therefore had Havelaar asked in his speech to the chiefs: —"Why is it that so many houses are empty in the villages; and why do many prefer the shadow of the wood elsewhere to the coolness of the forests of Lebak?'

But not every one *could* fly. The man whose corpse floats down the river in the morning, after having asked the foregoing evening—secretly, hesitatingly, and anxiously —for an audience of the Assistant Resident, *he* needs flight no more. Perhaps it may be deemed philanthropy to spare him a further life, by consigning him to an immediate death. The torture was spared him that awaited him on his return to the village, and the stripes which are the punishment of every one who could for a moment think himself above the brute, and no inanimate piece of wood or stone,—the punishment for him who in a moment of folly had thought that there was justice in the country, and that the Assistant Resident had the will and the power to maintain that justice.

Was it not indeed better to prevent that man from

returning the next day to that Assistant Resident, as he had given notice in the evening ; and to smother his complaint in the yellow water of the Tji-berang, that would carry him away softly to its mouth, accustomed as that river was to be bearer of the brotherly presents of salutation from the sharks in the interior to the sharks in the sea ?

And Havelaar was acquainted with all this ! Does the reader understand what went on in his mind, when he considered that his vocation was to do justice, that he was responsible for that to a HIGHER POWER than the power of a Government, that to be sure stipulated for this justice in its laws, but did not always like to see the application of it ? Do you understand how he was perplexed with doubt, not of *what* he had to do ; but of *how* he ought to act ? He had commenced with moderation, he had spoken to the Regent as to an elder brother, and he who thinks that I, captivated with the hero of my history, try to extol too much the manner of his speaking, may hear how once after such an interview the Regent sent his *Patteh*[1] to him, to thank him for the benevolence of his words, and how again long afterwards this Patteh, speaking to the Controller Verbrugge, after Havelaar had ceased to be Assistant Resident of Lebak, when nobody had anything more to hope of or fear from him, how the Patteh at the remembrance of these words had been touched, and cried, " Never as yet any gentleman spoke like him."

[1] A person in service of the Regent.

Yet he would save, restore—not destroy. He had sympathy with the Regent; he who knew how want of money oppresses, above all where it leads to humiliation and scorn, sought for reasons to avoid the unpleasant duty. The Regent was old, and the head of a family that lived magnificently in neighbouring provinces, where much coffee was reaped,[1] and where many emoluments were enjoyed. Was it not grievous for him to be so far behind his younger relatives in style of living?

Moreover he was fanatical, and thought whilst his years advanced to be able to purchase the welfare of his soul by paying for pilgrimages to Mecca, and by giving alms to prayer-singing idlers.

The functionaries who had preceded Havelaar in Lebak had not always shown a good example, and finally, the extensiveness of the Lebak family of the Regent, that lived entirely at his expense, made it very difficult for him to return to the right path.

Therefore Havelaar sought for reasons to delay all severity, and to try once more, and still once more, what could be done by gentle means.

And he went further still than kindness. With a generosity which reminded him of the faults that had made him

[1] The Dutch Government has its coffee-gardens. If a Regent encourages labour in those gardens, or better still, compels men and women to work for nothing in the government gardens,—these government gardens will produce much coffee, and the Regent receives a certain percentage, so much for every pical.

so poor, he continually advanced money to the Regent,
and that on his own responsibility, in order that necessity should not urge too strongly to rapine, and, as was
ordinarily the case, he forgot himself so far as to offer
to retrench in his own family to what was strictly necessary, that he might assist the Regent with the little that
he could still spare of his income.

Were it still necessary to prove the gentleness with
which Havelaar fulfilled his difficult duty, that proof could
be found in the verbal message which he intrusted to the
Controller, when Verbrugge was going for a few days to
Serang. "Tell the Resident that he, on hearing of the
abuses that take place here, must not believe that I am
indifferent on the subject, of which I do not immediately
make an official report, because I would spare the Regent,
for whom I feel pity, from too great severity, so I will try
first to bring him to a sense of duty by gentleness."

Havelaar was often out for many days together. When
he was at home, he was for the most part to be found in
the room which we represented in our plan as No. 7.
There he was generally occupied in writing, and received
the persons who asked an audience. He had chosen this
spot, because there he was near his Tine, who was
generally in the next room;—for so cordially were they
bound together, that Max, even when he was occupied
with work that needed attention and exertion, continually
wanted to see and hear her. It was often comical how he

suddenly spoke to her about what came up in his thoughts
about the subjects that occupied him, and how quickly
she, without understanding of what he treated, knew how
to seize the sense of his meaning, which he did not generally explain, as if it was a matter of course, that she
knew what he meant. Often when he was discontented
with his own labour, or bad news just received, he would
jump up and say something unkind to her, who was not
to blame for his discontent. But she liked to hear this,
because it was another proof how Max confounded her
with himself. And, therefore, there was never a question
of repentance of such apparent unkindness, or of pardon
on the other side. This would have appeared to them as
if somebody had asked his own pardon, because he in ill
humour had beaten his own forehead.

She knew him so well, that she could tell exactly when
she had to be there to procure him a moment's relaxation
—exactly when he needed her advice, and not less exactly
she knew when she had to leave him alone.

In this room Havelaar was seated on a certain morning,
when the Controller entered with a letter in his hand just
received.

"This is a difficult matter," he said, entering; "very
difficult."

When I state that this letter imposed on him the duty
of stating to Havelaar why there was a change in the
prices of joiners' work and labourers' wages, the reader

will think that the Controller Verbrugge saw difficulties rather too readily. I make haste, therefore, to add, that many others would have thought the answer of this simple question very difficult.

A few years ago a prison had been built at Rankas-Betong. Now it is generally known that the functionaries in the interior of Java understand the art of erecting buildings that are worth thousands, without spending more than so many hundreds for them. This gains them the reputation for capacity, and zeal for the service of the country. The difference between the money expended and the value of what they get for it IS SUPPLIED BY UNPAID LABOUR. For a few years regulations have existed which forbid this. It is not the question here whether these regulations are observed, nor if the Government itself wishes them to be fulfilled with an exactness that would be burdensome on the budget of the building-department. It is with this as with other regulations that look so philanthropic on paper.

Now many buildings had to be erected at Rankas-Betong, and the engineers who were instructed to prepare plans of these had of course asked for information regarding the local rates of wages and the price of materials. Havelaar had charged the Controller to prepare an exact estimate of these matters, and had recommended him to give the true prices, without looking back to what had happened before, and Verbrugge had fulfilled this duty. But these prices did not agree with the statements made a few years back. The reason of this difference was asked, and that was what Verbrugge deemed so very difficult. Havelaar, who knew very well what was concealed behind this apparently simple business, replied that he would communicate his ideas about this difficulty in writing; and I find amongst the documents before me a copy of the letter, which seems to be the consequence of this promise.

If the reader should perhaps complain of this detention with a correspondence on the price of joiners' work, with which he has apparently nothing to do, I must beg him to observe that the question here is properly about quite another matter, viz., the condition of the official Indian economy, and that the letter which I communicate does not only throw another ray of light on the artificial optimism of which I have spoken, but paints at the same time the difficulty with which a man like Havelaar had to struggle, who would go on straightforward.

" No. 114.

" RANKAS-BETONG, *March* 15, 1856.

" *To the Controller of Lebak.*

" When I sent you the letter of the Director of " Public Works, dated the 16th ultimo, No. 271/354, I " begged you to answer the questions which that letter " contained, after having consulted the Regent and duly

" considered what I wrote in my missive of the 5th inst.,
" No. 97.

" This missive contained some hints about what may
" be considered right and just with regard to the fixing of
" the prices of materials to be supplied by the people, to
" and at the charge of the Government.

" This you have done in your letter of the 8th inst.,
" No. 6, and as I believe to the best of your knowledge, so
" that I, confiding in your local information and that of
" the Regent, have submitted these accounts, as prepared
" by you, to the Resident.

" This was followed by a missive from that chief func-
" tionary, dated the 11th inst., No. 326, whereby informa-
" tion was required about the cause of the difference
" between the prices given by me and those that had been
" sent in in 1854 and 1855 (the two preceding years) for
" the building of a prison.

" I, of course, put this letter into your hands, and
" verbally required you now to justify your statements,
" which ought to be less difficult for you, as it enabled
" you to appeal to the instructions given you in my letter
" of the 5th inst., and of which we spoke at length more
" than once. Up to this point all is very plain and simple.
" But yesterday, you entered my office with the Resident's
" letter in your hands, and began to speak of the difficulty
" of clearing up the questions put therein. I perceived
" again some reluctance to give certain things their true

" names, which I have told you of before, and lately in
" the presence of the Resident, something which I call for
" shortness' sake *halfness*, and against which I often
" warned you in a friendly way. *Halfness* leads to nothing.
" Half is no good. Half true is *untrue*. For full pay-
" ment, for a full rank, after a distinct *complete* oath, *full*
" duty must be done. If courage is sometimes necessary
" to fulfil that duty, one must possess that courage. For
" myself, I should not have the courage to lack that
" courage. For apart from the discontentedness with one's-
" self, which is a consequence of neglect of duty or luke-
" warmness, the seeking for easier byeways, the desire
" always and everywhere to escape collisions, to settle,
" produces indeed more care, more danger than is to be
" met with in a straight policy.

" During the course of a very important affair, which is
" now under the consideration of the Government, and in
" which you ought to be concerned in an official way, I
" left you tacitly, as it were, neutral, and alluded laugh-
" ingly from time to time to the circumstance. When,
" for instance, I lately received your report about the
" causes of poverty and starvation among the population,
" and replied thereto :—' All this may be the truth ; it is
" not the whole truth, nor the cardinal truth ; the prin-
" cipal or main cause lies deeper '—you freely assented to
" this, and I made no use of my right to exact that you
" should make known that cardinal truth. For this in-

" dulgence I had many reasons, and, amongst others, this,
" that I thought it unjust to exact suddenly from you
" what many others in your place would have readily
" afforded ; to force you to say farewell in such a hurry to
" a course of reserve and timorousness that is not your
" fault, but that of the training which you have received.
" Finally, I wished to give you first an example how much
" simpler and easier it is to do one's duty *fully* than only
" *by halves*. But now that I have had the honour of seeing
" you so long under my orders, and after having continu-
" ally given you occasion to make yourself acquainted
" with principles, which, unless I err, will triumph at
" last, I should wish that you accepted them, that you
" would make your own the power which is not wanting,
" but merely in disuse, to tell me to the best of your
" knowledge what you have to say, and that you would
" bid adieu at once and for ever to that unmanly fear of
" telling the plain truth.

" I expect, therefore, a simple but complete report of
" what seems to you to be the cause of the difference in
" price between 1854 and 1856. I sincerely hope that
" you will not consider any phrase of this letter meant to
" hurt you. I trust that you understand me well enough,
" to know that I say neither more nor less than I mean,
" and, moreover, I give you the assurance that my obser-
" vations refer less to you than to the school in which you
" were trained for an Indian functionary. Yet this ' *cir-*

" *constance atténuante*' would disappear if you, continuing
" longer with me, and serving the Government under my
" orders, should go on to follow the course against which
" I set myself.

" You may have observed that I have omitted the title
" ' Right Honourable,'[1]—it annoyed me. Do the same to
" me, and let our honourableness, where it is necessary,
" come forward in another manner than by this annoying
" style, spoiling the use of titles.—The Assistant Resident
" of Lebak,

(Signed) " MAX HAVELAAR."

The reply to this letter was an accusation against some
of Havelaar's predecessors, and proved that he was not
very wrong in quoting the bad examples of former times
amongst the reasons that pleaded as an excuse for the
Regent.

In communicating this letter I have departed from the
order of time, to make it at once obvious how little help
Havelaar could expect from the Controller, as soon as
quite different and more important transactions were to
be called by their right names, when the latter, who was
without doubt a good man, had to be addressed in this
way about telling the truth, when the question was only to

---

[1] Right Honourable is by no means a good translation of the Dutch
" *WelEdelGestrenge.*" It is impossible to translate this into English,
just as " Right Worshipful " could hardly be translated into Dutch
without becoming ridiculous.

give information about the prices of wood, stone, lime, and
wages, and how Havelàar had not only to struggle with
the power of those who reaped advantage from crime, but
likewise with the timorousness of those who, though condemning that crime as much as he, did not mean coura-
geously to combat it.   Perhaps the reader, after having
perused this letter, will think no more with such disdain
of the servile submission of the Javanese, who in presence
of his chief revokes like a coward an accusation however
well founded it may be.   For if you consider that there
was so much cause for fear, even for the European functionary, who certainly may be deemed to be somewhat
less exposed to vengeance, what then awaited the poor
husbandman who, in a village far from the capital, fell
entirely into the power of his accused oppressors?   Is it
surprising that these poor men, afraid of the consequences
of their boldness, endeavoured to escape or to soften those
consequences by humble submission?   And it was not
only the Controller Verbrugge who did his duty with a
shyness characteristic of neglect of duty.   The Djaksa
likewise, the native chief, who fills in the council of the
country the office of public prosecutor, preferred entering
in the evening, unseen and without attendants, the house
of Havelaar.   He whose duty it was to prevent theft, he
whose vocation it was to catch the sneaking thief, sneaked
softly in at the back door, as if he were himself a thief,
fearing to be seized, after having firstly convinced himself

that there was no company which could have afterwards betrayed him *as guilty of performing his duty*. Was it to be wondered at that the soul of Havelaar was very sad, and that Tine had to go more than ever to his room to console him, when she saw him sitting there with his head resting on his hand?

And yet his greatest difficulty was not in the shyness of those who were near him, nor in the accessory cowardice of those who had invoked his help. No! quite alone, if necessary, he would do justice, without or with the help of others; yes, against all, even were it against the will of those who were in want of that justice. For he knew the influence he had over the people, and how, if once the poor oppressed were summoned to repeat loudly, and before the tribunal, what they had whispered to him during the evening and the night in solitude,—he knew how he had the power to work upon their minds, and how the force of his words would be stronger than the fear of the revenge of district chief or Regent. The fear that his *protégés* would forsake their own cause did not restrain him.

It cost him so much to accuse this old Regent—that was the reason of his internal struggle; but, on the other hand, he ought not to yield to this reluctance, because the whole population, besides their good right, had as much claim to pity. Fear for himself had no part in his doubts. For though he knew the unwillingness with which the Government generally entertains the accusation of a

T

Regent, and how much easier it is to take away the bread of the European functionary than to punish a Native chief, he had a special reason to believe that exactly at this moment other than the ordinary principles would predominate in the decision of such an affair.

It is true that he would have done his duty as faithfully even without this opinion ; with more pleasure if he had deemed the danger for himself and his household greater than ever. We have already said how difficulty enticed him, how he thirsted for sacrifice ; but he thought that the charm of a self-sacrifice did not exist here, and he feared that when at last he should have to commence a more serious struggle against injustice, he should come short of the chivalrous pleasure of having commenced this struggle as the weakest party.

Yes, *that* was what he *feared*. He thought that at the head of the Government was a Governor-General who would be his ally, and it was another peculiarity of his character, that this opinion restrained him from severe measures, and would do so longer than anything else, because it prevented his attacking injustice at a moment that he thought justice stronger than ever.

I have already said, in my attempt to describe his character, that with all his sharpness he was ingenuous (*naïf*).

I will endeavour to explain how Havelaar arrived at this opinion.

Few European readers can form an exact idea of the

height on which a Governor-General must stand as an individual, not to be beneath the dignity of his office; and it is therefore not too severe a judgment, if I maintain that very few, perhaps none, have been able to respond to so heavy a claim. Not to speak of the qualities of head and heart that are required, only cast an eye on the giddy height on which so suddenly the man is placed, who—— yesterday only a citizen——to-day has power over millions of subjects. He who a short time ago was still hidden among his acquaintances without being more than they in rank or power, feels himself suddenly, for the most part unexpectedly, elevated above a multitude infinitely greater than the small circle in which he had been before but imperfectly known, and I believe that I was not wrong in calling this height giddy; which, indeed, puts us in mind of the giddiness of one who sees suddenly a precipice before him, or which makes you think of the blindness that strikes us, if we come suddenly from a deep darkness into bright light. Against such transitions, the nerves of vision and the brain are no match, even where they are of extraordinary strength.

When also the nomination to the rank of Governor-General bears in itself causes of corruption, which will affect even one remarkable for excellent understanding and thorough conscientiousness, what may be expected of persons who already before their nomination had many faults?

And if we suppose that the King is always well informed before he signs his august name at the foot of the document, in which he says he is convinced of " the good faith, the zeal, and the capacity " of the newly appointed Governor, even if we suppose that the new Viceroy *is* zealous, faithful, and able, then the question still remains, whether this zeal, and above all, this capacity, exist with him in a *measure* high enough elevated above *mediocrity* to satisfy the claims of his vocation.

For the question cannot be whether the man, who for the first time leaves the King's cabinet at the Hague as Governor-General, possesses at that moment the capacity necessary for his new office,—that is impossible. By the declaration of confidence in his capacity can only be meant the belief, that he, in a quite different situation, on a given moment, shall know, as it were by intuition, what he could not have learnt at the Hague,—in other words, that he is a genius, a genius which suddenly must know and understand what before it neither knew nor understood. Such geniuses are rare, even among persons who are in favour with kings.

As I speak of geniuses, the reader will understand that I wish to omit what could be said of many a Governor. It would likewise disgust me to insert in my book pages that should expose the serious design of this work to the suspicion of hunting after scandal. I omit, therefore, the peculiarities that can only reach certain persons, but as a

general history of the malady of the situation of the
Governors-General, I believe that I can give:—*First
period*—DIZZINESS, INCENSE-DRUNKENNESS, SELF-CONCEIT,
IMMODERATE SELF-CONFIDENCE, DISDAIN OF OTHERS, above
all of persons who have been long in India. *Second
period*—FATIGUE, FEAR, DEJECTION, INCLINATION TO SLEEP
AND REST, IMMODERATE CONFIDENCE IN THE COUNCIL OF
INDIA, HOME-SICKNESS AND DESIRE FOR A DUTCH COUNTRY-
SEAT.

Between these two periods, and as a sort of transition,
perhaps as cause of this transition, there is DYSENTERY.

I trust that many persons in India will thank me for
this *diagnosis.*

The application is very useful, for it may be accepted
as very certain, that the patient, who through over-exer-
tion in the first period, would choke at a gnat, would
later, after the *dysentery,* swallow without difficulty a
camel;—or, to speak more plainly, that a functionary
who " accepts presents, not with the intention of enriching
himself,"—for instance a bundle of *pisang* worth a few
pence,—would, in the *first* period of the malady, be driven
away with scorn and disgrace; but if that official has
patience enough to wait for the *second* period, he may seize
very calmly, and without any fear of punishment, the garden
where the *pisang* grew, with the adjoining gardens, and
the houses round, and what there may be in those houses,
and other things . . . . *ad libitum.*

Every one may take advantage of this pathological philosophical observation, and keep secret my advice to prevent too much competition. . . .

A curse on it, that indignation and grief are so often clothed in the rags of satire! A curse on it, that a tear, to be understood, must be accompanied with a sneer!

Or is it the fault of my inexperience, that I seek in vain for words to name the depth of the wound that cankers in our Indian Government, without borrowing the style of *Figaro* or *Punch?* Style, . . . Yes! There are documents before me, in which there is style; style that showed that there was a *man* in the neighbourhood; a man, to whom it would have been worth the trouble to give a helping hand! And of what use was this style to poor Havelaar? He did not translate his tears into grins, he did not scoff, he did not endeavour to touch by a medley of colours or insipid farces; . . . . of what use was it to him?

If I could write like him, I should write otherwise than he.

Style? . . . Did you hear how he spoke to the chiefs? And of what use was it to him?

If I could speak like him, I should speak otherwise than he.

Away with conscientious language, away with considerateness, straightforwardness, plainness, simplicity, feeling; away with all that puts you in remembrance of Horace's

"*Justum et tenacem;*" trumpets here, and the sharp
rattle of kettledrums, whizzing of rockets, screeching of
tuneless strings, here and there a true word sneaking in
as contraband, under cover of so much drumming and so
much trumpeting! Style? . . . He had style! *He* had
too much soul to drown his thoughts in, "I have the
honour to be," and the "Right Honourable," and the
"respectfully giving in considerations," that was the
luxury of the small world in which he moved. When he
wrote, something impressed you in the reading of it, which
made you understand that there were clouds accompanying this thunderstorm, and that you did not hear the
rattling of tin thunderstorm as in a theatre. When he
struck fire from ideas, the heat of his fire was felt by all
but born clerks, or Governor-Generals, or the writer of
that most disgusting report about "*tranquil tranquillity.*"

And what was the use of it to him? . . . If I want to
be heard, and, above all, understood—must I then write
otherwise than he? But how, then?

Do you see, reader! I look for an answer to this "*how,*"
and therefore my book is such a medley: it is a pattern-
card, make your choice; afterwards I will give you yellow
or blue or red, as you please.

Havelaar had already so often observed the Governor's
malady in so many sufferers, and often *in anima vili*,
for there are analogical Residents', Controllers', Clerks'
maladies, that are in proportion to the first as the measles

to the small-pox, and finally, he himself had suffered from this malady; he had already so often observed this, that he knew the symptoms very well. He had remarked that the present Governor-General[1] had been less dizzy at the commencement of the malady than most others, and he concluded from this that the rest of the malady would likewise take another course. Therefore he feared to be the strongest, if at last he should have to come forward as the champion of the rights of the inhabitants of Lebak.[2]

[1] Duymaer van Twist.
[2] He would BEGIN the campaign as the weakest, and yet *at last* be the strongest.

CHAPTER XVI.

[COMPOSED BY STERN.]

HAVELAAR received a letter from the Regent of Tjanjor, wherein the latter communicated to him that he wished to pay a visit to his uncle the Regent of Lebak. This was very disagreeable news for him. He knew how the chiefs in the Preangan Regencies were accustomed to display much magnificence, and how the Regent of Tjanjor could not undertake such a journey without a train of many hundreds, all of whom must be lodged and fed, as also their horses. He would gladly have prevented this visit; but he thought in vain of the means of doing so, without offending the Regent of Rankas-Betong; as the latter was very proud and would have felt deeply offended if his comparative poverty had been mentioned as a motive for not visiting him. And if this visit could *not* be avoided, it would inevitably give occasion to aggravate the oppression of the people.

It is to be doubted if Havelaar's speech had made a lasting impression on the chiefs; with many this was certainly not the case; but it is certain that, in all the villages, the report had spread, that the gentleman who had power at Rankas-Betong would do justice, and if his words were powerless to prevent crime, they had at least given the victims the courage to complain, however hesitatingly and secretly.

In the evening they crept through the ravine, and when Tine was sitting in her room, she was frightened by an unexpected noise, and saw before the open windows dark forms that sneaked along with a shy step. But very soon she started no more, for she knew what it meant when these forms wandered like so many spectres round the house, and asked protection of her Max. Then she beckoned him, and he got up to call in the complainants. Most of them came from the district of Parang-Koodjang, where one of the chiefs was a son-in-law of the Regent; and though this chief did not omit to take his part of the extortion, yet it was no secret that he generally robbed in name of the Regent, and for his benefit. It was affecting to see how these poor men relied upon the chivalry of Havelaar, that he would not summon them to repeat the following day openly what they told him in his room. This would have caused the ill-treatment of them all, and the death of many. Havelaar made notes of what they said, and after that ordered the plaintiffs to return to their village. He promised that justice should be done, provided they made no opposition, and did not emigrate, as was

the intention of many. Generally, he was shortly afterwards at the place where the injustice happened, yes,
he had often been there already, and had for the most part
examined into the affair before the plaintiff himself had
returned to his dwelling. In this manner he visited in
this extensive department, villages that were eighty miles
distant from Rankas-Betong, without the Regent or even
the Controller Verbrugge knowing that he was absent
from the capital. His object in so doing was to shield
the complainants from the danger of revenge, and at the
same time to spare the Regent the shame of a public inquiry, which with Havelaar would not have ended in a
revocation of the complaint. He still **hoped that** the
chiefs would turn back on the dangerous road which they
had already walked so long; and he would in that case
have been contented merely to claim indemnification for
the poor sufferers.

But on every occasion of his speaking to the Regent,
it was evident to him that all promises of amendment
were vain; and he was deeply pained at the ill-success of
his endeavours.

We shall now leave him for a time in his disappoint-
ment and the difficult work he had undertaken, to relate
to the reader the history of the Javanese Saïdjah in the
dessah Badoer. I extract from Havelaar's notes the name
of this village and that of the Javanese concerned. It is a

case of extortion and plunder; and lest my history should
be thought fictitious, I give the assurance that I can furnish the names of the thirty-two persons in the district of
Parang-Koodjang *alone*, from whom in the course of *one*
month thirty-six buffaloes had been stolen for the use of
the Regent; or, still better, I can give the names of
thirty-two persons in that district, who in *one* month
dared to complain, and whose complaints, having been
examined by Havelaar, were found to be true.[1]

There are five such districts in the Residency of Lebak.
Now if one chooses to believe that the number of stolen
buffaloes was less in those parts that had not the honour
of being governed by the son-in-law of the Regent, I will
grant that; though the question still remains, whether the
rapacity of other chiefs was not founded on as sure
ground as that of near relationship? For instance, the
district chief of Tjilangkahan on the south coast could in
default of a father-in law, of whom one was much afraid,
rely upon the difficulty with which the poor in their
complaints had to contend, that, namely, of walking forty
or sixty miles before hiding themselves during the evening in the ravine near Havelaar's house. And if we observe the fact that many started never to reach that house,
that many did not even leave their village, frightened as
they were by their own experience or by the sight of the

---

[1] This statement the author published in 1861 at Amsterdam.
(*Minnebrieven*, by Multatuli.)

fate which overtook other plaintiffs, then I believe that we should be wrong in thinking that the multiplication by five of the number of buffaloes stolen out of one district would be too high an estimate of the number of cattle stolen every month in the five districts, to provide for the wants of the Regent of Lebak's court.

And it was not buffaloes alone; nor was buffalo-robbing the main thing. A somewhat less degree of shamelessness is required—above all in India, where statute-labour is still lawful—to summon the people unlawfully for unpaid labour, than is necessary to take away property. It is easier to make the population believe that the Government wants labour without wishing to pay for it, than that it should claim the poor man's buffalo for nothing; and even if the timorous Javanese dared to investigate whether the statute-labour required of him agreed with the regulations on the subject, even then it would be impossible to succeed, as the one has nothing to do with the other, and he cannot therefore calculate whether the fixed number of persons has not been exceeded ten or fifty times. Where also the most dangerous, the most easily discovered abuse, is executed with such boldness, what may not then be thought of the abuses that are much easier of execution, and less liable to discovery ? I said that I was going to relate the history of the Javanese Saïdjah; yet I am compelled first to make one of those digressions which are so difficult to avoid when describing situations that are quite strange

to the reader. I will state at the same time the causes
that make it so difficult for those who have not been in
India to judge of Indian affairs.

I have repeatedly spoken of the people as Javanese, and
however natural this nomenclature may appear to the
European reader, it must have sounded wrong to the ears
of any one acquainted with Java. The Western Residencies of Bantam, Batavia, Preangan, Krawand, and a
part of Cheribon,—all together called Soondah-countries,[1]
—are not considered as belonging to Java proper; and not
to speak now of the foreigners that came from over the
sea into these regions, the aboriginal population is quite
different from that of the middle of Java, or that of the
so-called east corner. Language, character of the people,
manners, dress, change so much as you go eastward, that,
indeed, there is more difference between the Soondanese
and the Javanese proper, than between the English and
the Dutch. Such differences are often the cause of dis-
putes in judging of Indian affairs. If we observe that
Java alone is so sharply divided into two distinct parts,
without marking the many subdivisions of these, we may
calculate how great the difference must be between populations that live further from each other, and are separated
by the sea. He whose knowledge of Dutch India is
confined to Java, can no more form a just idea of the
Malay, the Amboynese, the Battah, the Alfoer, the

[1] Soondah or Sundah.

Timorese, the Dayak, or the native of Macassar, than he
who never left Europe; and for a person who has had
the opportunity of observing the difference between these
populations, it is indeed often amusing to hear the conversations, and afflicting to hear the speeches, of persons
who get their knowledge of Indian affairs at Batavia or
at Buitenzorg. I have often wondered at the courage
with which, for instance, a late Governor-General endeavoured, in the Representative Chambers, to give weight
to his words, by a pretended claim to local knowledge
and experience. I esteem very highly the knowledge
acquired by profound study in the library, and have often
been astonished at the extent of the knowledge of Indian
affairs which some have displayed without having ever
trod Indian ground, and when a late Governor-General
gives proofs of having acquired such knowledge in this
manner, we feel for him the respect which is the legi-
timate reward of the conscientious and fruitful labour of
many years. This respect would be still greater for him,
than for the scholar who had fewer difficulties to conquer,
because he at a far distance, without inspections, ran a
less risk of falling into the errors which are the consequence of a *defective* view, as was the lot of the late
Governor-General.[1]

[1] Because usually the Governors-General have never before been in
India. The late Governor-General, for instance, when he was appointed by the king, had never been in India, or connected in anything with Indian matters.

I said that I was surprised at the confidence which
some have shown in the treatment of Indian affairs. For
they know that their words are heard by others than
those who think it enough to have passed a few years at
Buitenzorg, to know India ; that these words are likewise
read by those persons in India itself, who were the
witnesses of *their* inexperience, and who, as much as I,
are astonished at the boldness with which a man, who,
only a short time ago, tried to hide this incapacity behind
the high rank which the King had given him, speaks now
all at once as if he really possessed a knowledge of the
affairs of which he treats.

Again and again, therefore, you hear complaints of
incompetent interference, again and again this or that
system is opposed in the Representative Chambers by
denying the competency of him who represents such a
system, and it would perhaps not be inopportune to make
an exact inquiry into the qualities which make a person
competent to judge of competency. Generally, the touch-
stone of an important question is not the matter of which
it treats, but the value which is ascribed to the opinion of
the person who speaks of it ; and as he is often one who
is considered to be qualified above all others, one who
had, in India, such " a high position," the consequence of
it is, that the results of the voting bear generally the
colour of the errors that seem to stick to " these important
positions." If this is the case where the influence of such

a person is only exercised by a member of the Representative Chambers, how great then will be the inclination to judge wrongly if such influence is accompanied by the confidence of the King, who placed this functionary at the head of the ministry of the colonies? It is a peculiar phenomenon (perhaps owing its origin to a sort of dulness, which shuns the trouble of judging for ourselves), how easily one gives his confidence to persons who know how to give themselves the appearance of more knowledge, when this knowledge has been drawn from a foreign source. The reason perhaps is, that self-love is less hurt by the acknowledgment of such an ascendency, than would be the case if one could have recourse to the same expedients when anything like emulation should arise. It is easy for the representative of the people to give up his opinion, as soon as it is combated by a person who may be deemed to pass a more accurate judgment than he, and this accuracy need not be ascribed to personal superiority, confession of which would be more difficult, but only to the particular circumstances wherein such an opponent has been. And not to speak of those who have filled high offices in India, it is indeed strange how often value is ascribed to the opinion of persons who really possess nothing to justify the credit given them, than the remembrance of a residence of so many years in those regions, and this is so much the more strange, because they, who attach importance to such a source of information, would

U

not readily believe all that would be told them, for instance, about political economy in Holland, by a person who could show that he had lived forty or fifty years in Holland. There are persons who have lived more than thirty years in Dutch India without ever coming in contact with either the population or the native chiefs; and it is sad that the Council of India is often totally, or for a great part, composed of such persons,—that the means have even been found to make the King sign the appointment, as Governor-General, of a person who belonged to this class.

When I said that this supposed capacity of a newly appointed Governor-General might be considered as implying that he was held to be a genius, I did not mean to recommend the appointment of geniuses. Besides the difficulty of having this important employment continually vacant, another reason pleads against this. A genius would not be able to work under a Minister of the colonies, and would therefore be useless, as geniuses generally are.

It would, perhaps, be desirable that the main faults given by me in the form of a diagnosis should get the attention of those who are called upon to the choice of a new Governor. Taking it for granted that all the persons considered eligible are conscientious, and in the possession of a faculty of comprehension sufficient to enable them to learn a little of what they will have to know, I think it a main thing that the avoidance may be expected of them of that presumptuous self-conceit in the beginning, and, above all, of that apathetic sluggishness in the last years of their administration. I have already said that Havelaar, in his difficult duty, thought he could rely upon the help of the Governor-General; and I added that this opinion was *naïf*. That Governor-General was expecting his successor . . . . his rest in Holland was near. We shall see what this sluggishness brought upon Havelaar, and upon the Javanese Saïdjah, whose monotonous history—one amongst many—I am now about to relate.

Yes, "monotonous" it will be! Monotonous as the history of the activity of the ant, which had to carry up its contribution for the winter store over the clod—the mountain—which blocks up the way to the storehouse. Again and again it falls back with its burden, to try again to put its feet on that little stone high there on the rock at the top of the mountain. But between it and this top there is an abyss, a depth which a thousand ants could not fill——this must be passed. Therefore the ant, that has scarcely the strength to drag its burden on even ground— a burden many times heavier than its own body—that can hardly lift it up and balance itself on an unsteady footing, has to preserve its equilibrium—when it climbs with its burden between the fore-legs, it has to sling it round to the side to make it come down on the point which stretches out on the rock,—it staggers, totters, is frightened, sinks down, endeavours to take hold of the half rooted-up trunk of a tree—of a blade of grass—which, with its top, points to the depth—it loses the fulcrum which it sought for, the tree gives way, the blade of grass yields under its weight, and the ant falls back into the depth with its burden. Then it is still for a moment, which is long in the life of an ant. It is stunned by the pain of its fall—or does it yield to grief that so much exertion was in vain? No, its courage does not forsake it. Again it seizes the burden, and again drags it aloft, again soon to fall into the depth. So monotonous is my tale. But I shall not speak of ants, whose joy or sorrow escapes our observation through the dulness of our organs; I shall speak of men who move in the way same as we do. It is true he who shuns emotion, and would fain avoid compassion, will say that those men are yellow or brown —many call them black,—and for them the difference of colour is reason enough for turning the eye from their misery, or at least for looking down on it without emotion. My narrative is therefore only addressed to those who are capable of the difficult faith, that hearts throb under that dark epidermis, and that he who is blessed with a white skin, and the civilisation thereunto belonging—generosity, mercantile knowledge, and religion, virtue, etc.—might use these qualities of the white man better than has yet been experienced by those less blessed in colour and mental capacity.

Yet my confidence in your sympathy with the Javanese

does not go so far as to make me imagine when I tell you how the last buffalo has been carried off from the enclosure, in broad daylight, without fear, under protection of Dutch power, when I cause the stolen cattle to be followed by the owner and his weeping children, and make him sit down upon the steps of the robber's house, speechless and senseless, absorbed in sorrow, to be chased away with out-rage and disdain, menaced with stripes and prison. . . . .

See! I neither claim nor expect that you will be moved by this in the same manner as you would be if I sketched the destiny of a Dutch peasant whose cow had been taken away. I ask no tear for the tears that flow on such dark faces, nor noble indignation when I shall speak of the despair of the sufferer. Neither do I expect that you will rise and go with my book in your hand to the King, say-ing: "Look here, O King, that happens in *your* empire, in your beautiful empire of Insulinde!" . . . .

No, no; all this I do not expect. The excess of misery at home overmasters your feeling of sympathy for what is far off. Was there not yesterday but little business going on at the Exchange, and does not the glutting of the coffee-market threaten a reduction in price?

"Don't write such nonsense to your papa, Stern," I said, and perhaps a little passionately, for I can't bear untruth; that has always been a fixed principle with me.

I wrote that evening to old Mr. Stern, telling him to beware of false reports.

The reader understands what I have again suffered in listening to the last chapters. Was I not right when I said that Shawlman had made them all mad with his parcel? Would you recognise in this writing business of Stern——and Fred too helps, that is certain——young men that were educated in a respectable house?

What foolish sallies are these against a sickness which reveals itself in a desire for a country seat? Is that aimed at me? Am not I allowed to go to Driebergen as soon as Fred is a broker? And who speaks of dysentery in the company of mothers and daughters? It is a fixed principle with me always to remain quiet, for I think it useful in business; but I must confess, that it has often cost me a great deal to listen to all the nonsense that Stern reads. What does he mean? What must be the end of all this? When shall we hear anything substantial? Of what interest is it for me whether Havelaar keeps his garden clean or not, and whether those people enter in front of the house or at the back? At Busselinck and Waterman's one has to go through a small entrance, near an oil warehouse, where it is always abominably dirty.——And then those tiresome buffaloes. Why do they want buffaloes, those black fellows? . . . . *I* never had a buffalo, and yet I am contented;—there are men who are always complaining. And as regards that scoffing at forced labour, I perceive that he had not heard that sermon of Dominé Wawelaar's, otherwise he would know how useful labour is in the extension of the kingdom of God. It is true, he is a Lutheran. . . . .

To be sure, if I could have known how he would write the book, which was to be so important to all coffee-brokers—and others—I would rather have done it myself. But he is supported by the Rosemeyers, who trade in sugar, and this makes him so bold. I said plainly, for I am honest in those things, that we can dispense with the history of that man Saïdjah; but just then, all at once, Louise Rosemeyer began to cry. It appears that Stern had told her that there would be something about love in it, and girls are mad after that. Yet this would not have made me yield, if the Rosemeyers had not told me that they would like to be acquainted with Stern's father. Of course, through the father they will arrive at the uncle, who trades in sugar. If I am now too much for common-sense, and against Stern junior, I get the appearance as if I would keep them away from him, and that is not at all the case, *for* they trade in sugar.

I don't understand what Stern means by what he writes. There are always discontented people, and does it become him who enjoys so much good in Holland——only this week my wife gave him camomile tea——to scoff at the Government? Does he mean to excite public discontent? Does *he* want to become Governor-General? He is self-conceited enough for that. I told him the other day that he spoke very bad Dutch. "Oh, that is nothing," said he, "it seems that a Governor is very seldom sent over who understands the language of the country."

What shall I do with such a self-conceited fellow? He has not the least respect for my experience. When I told him this week that I had been a broker for seventeen years, he cited Busselinck and Waterman, who have been brokers for eighteen years, "and," said he, "they have one year's more experience." Thus he caught me, for I must confess, because I like truth, that Busselinck and Waterman have little knowledge of business, and that they are old women and sneaks. Mary too is led astray. Only this week——it was her turn to read at breakfast, we were about to have the history of Lot——when she suddenly stopped, and refused to proceed. My wife, who likes religion as much as I do, tried gently to persuade her to obedience, because it does not become a modest girl to be so obstinate. All in vain. Thereupon I, as a father, was obliged to scold her with much severity, because she spoiled, by her obstinacy, the comfort of the breakfast, which always has a bad influence on the whole day. But nothing would help, and she went so far as to say, that she would rather be beaten till she was dead than proceed with reading. I have punished her with three days' confinement to her room on coffee and bread; I hope that it will do her good. To make this punishment severe, at the same time a moral lesson, I have ordered her to copy the chapter which she would not read ten times, and I have treated her with this severity above all, because I have perceived that she has, during the last few days—whether from Stern or not I do not know—taken up ideas which appear to me to be dangerous to morality, to which my wife and I are so much attached. I heard her sing, for instance, a French song—by Béranger, I believe—in which the poet pities a poor old beggar, who in her youth sung at a theatre, and yesterday at breakfast she had no stays on——Mary, I mean —that was really not respectable.

I have likewise to confess that Fred brought home little good from the prayer-meeting. I had been much pleased with his sitting so quietly in church. He did not move, and always looked at the pulpit, but afterwards I heard that Betsy Rosemeyer was sitting near it. I said nothing about it, for one must not be too severe towards young people, and the Rosemeyers are a respectable firm. They have given their eldest daughter, who married Bruggeman the druggist, something very nice, and therefore I believe that this will keep Fred away from the Wester Market, which is very gratifying to me, because I am so attached to morality.

But I am grieved to see that this does not prevent Fred from hardening his heart, like Pharaoh, who was less guilty, because he had no father to show him continually the right path, for the Scriptures do not speak of old Pharaoh. Dominé Wawelaar complains of his conceit—— I mean Fred's——at catechism, and he seems—again from Shawlman's parcel,—to have derived this self-conceit, which drives the conscientious Wawelaar almost mad. It is touching how the worthy man, who often lunches with us, endeavours to work on Fred's feelings, and how the scamp is always ready with new questions, which show the perversity of his heart. It all comes from that accursed book of Shawlman's. With tears of emotion on his cheeks, the zealous servant of the Gospel endeavours to move him to turn away the eyes from the wisdom of men, to be introduced into the mysteries of the wisdom of God. With gentleness and meekness he prays him not to throw away the bread of eternal life, and to fall while acting thus into the clutches of Satan, who, with his angels, inhabits the fire prepared for him to all eternity. " Oh," said he yesterday——Wawelaar, I mean——"O my young friend, open now eyes and ears, and hear and see what the Lord gives you to see and hear by my mouth. Pay attention to the evidences of the saints who have died for the true faith. Look at Stephen, sinking down under the stones that crush him, see how he still looks to heaven, and how he ceases not to sing psalms . . . ."

" I would rather have thrown stones in return," said Fred in reply.——Reader ! what shall I do with this fellow ?

A moment afterwards Wawelaar commenced again ; for

he is an ardent servant, and sticks to his work. "Oh,"
said he, "young friend . . . . (the preamble was as above),
can you remain insensible when you think of what shall
become of you when once you are counted amongst the
goats on the left hand . . . ."

Thereupon the rogue burst out laughing——I mean
Fred——and Mary laughed too. I even thought that I
perceived something like a laugh on my wife's face. But
then I helped Wawelaar: I punished Fred with a fine out
of his money-box to the missionary society.

But all this touches me deeply. And could any one
take pleasure in hearing stories about buffaloes and the
Javanese with such grievances of his own? What is a
buffalo to the salvation of Fred? What do I care about
the affairs of those people away there, when I have to fear
that Fred will spoil my business by his unbelief, and that
he will never become a good broker? For W. himself
has said, that God so directs all things that orthodoxy
leads to wealth! "Look only," he said, "is there not
much wealth in Holland? That is because of the Faith.
Is there not in France every day murder and homicide?
That is because there are Roman Catholics there. Are
not the Javanese poor? They are Pagans. The more the
Dutch have to do with the Javanese, the more wealth will
be here, and the more poverty there."

I am astonished at Wawelaar's penetration. For it is
the truth, that I, who am exact in religion, see that my

business increases every year, and Busselinck and Waterman, who do not care about God or the Commandments,
will remain bunglers as long as they live. The Rosemeyers, too, who trade in sugar, and have a Roman Catholic
maid-servant, had a short time ago to accept 27 per cent.
out of the estate of a Jew who became bankrupt. The
more I reflect, the further I advance in tracing the un-
searchable ways of God. Lately it appeared that thirty
millions had been gained on the sale of products furnished
by the Pagans, and in this is not included what I have
gained thereby, and others who live by this business. Is
not that as if the Lord said—"Here you have thirty
millions as a reward for your faith?" Is not that the
finger of God, who causes the wicked one to labour to
preserve the righteous one? Is not that a hint for us to
go on in the right way, and to cause those far away to
produce much, and to stand fast here to the True Religion?
Is it not therefore—"Pray and labour," that we should
pray, and have the work done by those who do not know
the Lord's Prayer?

Oh, how truly Wawelaar speaks, when he calls the yoke
of God light! How easy the burden is to every one who
believes. I am only a few years past forty, and can retire
when I please to Driebergen, and see how it ends with
others who forsake the Lord. Yesterday I saw Shawlman
with his wife and their little boy: they looked like
ghosts. He is pale as death, his eyes protrude, and his

cheeks look hollow. His attitude is bent, though he is younger than I am. She too was dressed very poorly, and she seemed to have been weeping again : I perceived immediately that she is of a discontented temper ; I need only see a person once to form an opinion——that comes from my experience. She had on a thin cloak of black silk, and yet it was very cold. There was no trace of a crinoline; her thin dress hung loose round the knees, and a fringe hung from the edge. He had not even his shawl, and looked as if it was summer. Yet he seems to possess a kind of pride, for he gave something to a poor woman sitting on a bridge. He who has himself so little sins if he gives anything to another. Moreover, I never give in the streets, that is a principle of mine, for I always say, when I see such poor people, Perhaps it is their own fault, and I must not encourage them in their wickedness. Every Sunday I give twice: once for the poor, and once for the church. So it is right. I do not know if Shawl-man saw me, but I passed rapidly and looked upwards, and thought of the justice of God, who would not have allowed him to walk along without an overcoat if he had behaved better, and if he were not idle, self-conceited, and sickly.

As regards my book, I must indeed beg pardon of the reader on account of the unpardonable manner in which Stern abuses our contract. I must confess that I look forward without pleasure to our next party, and the love-story of this Saïdjah. The reader knows already the sound notions which I have about love ;—think only of my criticism of that excursion to the Ganges. That young ladies take pleasure in such things I understand, but that men of years hear such nonsense without disgust is inexplicable to me. I will endeavour to hear nothing of this Saïdjah, and hope that the fellow will marry soon, if he is to be the hero of a love-story. It was very good of Stern to warn us that it will be a monotonous story. When he afterwards commences with something else, I will listen again. But I am tired almost as much of his always condemning the Government as of his love-stories. It may be seen from everything that Stern is young, and has little experience. To judge rightly of affairs one must see them clearly. When I married I went to the Hague, and visited the Museum with my wife: I there came in contact with persons in all sorts of positions in society ; for I saw the Minister of Finance pass by ; and we bought flannel together in Veene Street——I and my wife I mean ——and nowhere did I perceive the slightest evidence of discontent against the Government. The young woman in the shop looked healthy and contented; and when in 1856 some tried to deceive us by saying that at the Hague all was not as it ought to be, I said at the party what I thought about the discontent, and I was believed; for every one knew that I spoke from experience. When returning from my journey, the conductor of the diligence played a gay popular melody, and he would not have done that if there had been so much wrong. So having paid attention to all, I knew immediately what to think of all that grumbling in 1856.

Opposite to us there lived a young woman whose cousin has a *Toko* in the East Indies, as they call a shop there. If all was so very bad as Stern represents, she would likewise know something about it, and yet it seems that she is very contented, for I never hear her complain. On the contrary, she says that her cousin lives there at a country seat, and that he is member of the consistory, and that he has sent her a cigar-case ornamented with peacocks'- feathers, which he had himself made of bamboo. All this shows distinctly how unfounded all these complaints about misgovernment are. Likewise it is clear that for a person who will behave properly, there is still something to gain in that country, and that when this Shawlman was there, he was idle, conceited, and sickly, otherwise he would not have come home so very poor; to walk about here without a greatcoat. And the cousin of the young woman who lives opposite us is not the only one who has made his fortune in the East Indies. In the club I see so many persons who have been there, and who are very nicely dressed. But it is plain one must pay attention to one's business yonder as well as here. In Java pigeons will not fly into anybody's mouth ready roasted; there must be work, and whoever will not work is poor, and remains so as a matter of course.

CHAPTER XVII.

[CONTINUATION OF STERN'S COMPOSITION.]

SAÏDJAH'S father had a buffalo, with which he ploughed his field. When this buffalo was taken away from him by the district chief at Parang-Koodjang he was very dejected, and did not speak a word for many a day. For the time for ploughing was come, and he had to fear that if the *sawah*[1] was not worked in time, the opportunity to sow would be lost, and lastly, that there would be no paddy to cut, none to keep in the *lombong* (store-room) of the house. I have here to tell readers who know Java, but not Bantam, that in that Residency there is personal landed property, which is not the case elsewhere. Saïdjah's father, then, was very uneasy. He feared that his wife would have no rice, nor Saïdjah himself, who was still a child, nor his little brothers and sisters. And the district chief too would accuse him to the Assistant Resident if he was behind-hand in the payment of his land-taxes, for this is

[1] Rice-field.

punished by the law. Saïdjah's father then took a *kris*,[1] which was *poosaka*[2] from his father. The *kris* was not very handsome, but there were silver bands round the sheath, and at the end there was a silver plate. He sold this *kris* to a Chinaman who dwelt in the capital, and came home with twenty-four guilders, for which money he bought another buffalo.

Saïdjah, who was then about seven years old, soon made friends with the new buffalo. It is not without meaning that I say " made friends," for it is indeed touching to see how the *Karbo*[3] is attached to the little boy who watches over and feeds him. Of this attachment I shall very soon give an example. The large, strong animal bends its heavy head to the right, to the left, or downwards, just as the pressure of the child's finger, which he knows and understands, directs.

Such a friendship little Saïdjah had soon been able to make with the new-comer, and it seemed as if the encouraging voice of the child gave still more strength to the heavy shoulders of the strong animal, when it tore open the stiff clay and traced its way in deep sharp furrows.

The buffalo turned willingly, on reaching the end of the field, and did not lose an inch of ground when ploughing backwards the new furrow, which was ever near the old,

[1] *Kris* = poniard.
[2] *Poosaka* = inheritance—such a poosaka is kept as a holy keepsake (family heirloom).
[3] *Karbo* = buffalo.

as if the 'sawah' was a garden ground raked by a giant.
Quite near were the 'sawahs' of the father of Adinda
(the father of the child that was to marry Saïdjah); and
when the little brothers of Adinda came to the limit of
their fields just at the same time that the father of Saïdjah
was there with his plough, then the children called out
merrily to each other, and each praised the strength and the
docility of his buffalo.   But I believe that the buffalo of
Saïdjah was the best of all; perhaps because its master
knew better than any one else how to speak to the animal,
and buffaloes are very sensible to kind words.   Saïdjah
was nine and Adinda six, when this buffalo was taken
from the father of Saïdjah by the chief of the district of
Parang-Koodjang.   Saïdjah's father, who was very poor,
thereupon sold to a Chinaman two silver *klamboo*[1] hooks
—'poosaka' from the parents of his wife—for eighteen
guilders, and for that money bought a new buffalo.   But
Saïdjah was very dejected.   For he knew from Adinda's
little brothers that the other buffalo had been driven to
the capital, and he had asked his father if he had not seen
the animal when he was there to sell the hooks of the
'klamboo.'   To this question Saïdjah's father refused to give
an answer.   Therefore he feared that his buffalo had been
slaughtered, as the other buffaloes which the district chief
had taken from the people.   And Saïdjah wept much
when he thought of this poor buffalo, which he had known

[1] *Klamboo* = curtain.

for such a long time, and he could not eat for many days, for his throat was too narrow when he swallowed. It must be taken into consideration that Saïdjah was a child.

The new buffalo soon got acquainted with Saïdjah, and very soon obtained in the heart of Saïdjah the same place as his predecessor,—alas! too soon; for the wax impressions of the heart are very soon smoothed to make room for other writing . . . . However this may be, the new buffalo was not so strong as the former: true, the old yoke was too large for his neck, but the poor animal was willing, like his predecessor, which had been slaughtered; and though Saïdjah could boast no more of the strength of his buffalo when he met Adinda's brothers at the boundaries, yet he maintained that no other surpassed his in willingness; and if the furrow was not so straight as before, or if lumps of earth had been turned, but not cut, he willingly made this right as much as he could with his *patjol*.[1] Moreover, no buffalo had an *oeser-oeseran*[2] like his. The *Penghooloo*[3] himself had said that there was *ontong*[4] in the course of the hair-whirls on its shoulders. Once when they were in the field, Saïdjah called in vain to his buffalo to make haste. The animal did not move. Saïdjah grew angry at this unusual refractoriness, and could not refrain from scolding. He said "a——

---

[1] *Patjol* = spade.
[2] *Oeser-oeseran*, see p. 143.
[3] *Penghooloo* = village priest.
[4] *Ontong* = gain, good luck.

s——." Every one who has been in India will understand
me, and he who does not understand me gains by it if I
spare him the explanation of a coarse expression.

Yet Saïdjah did not mean anything bad.   He only said
it because he had often heard it said by others when they
were dissatisfied with their buffaloes.   But it was useless;
his buffalo did not move an inch.   He shook his head, as
if to throw off the yoke, the breath appeared out of his
nostrils, he blew, trembled, there was anguish in his blue
eye, and the upper lip was curled upwards, so that the
gums were bare . . . .

"Fly! Fly!" Adinda's brothers cried, "fly, Saïdjah!
there is a tiger!"

And they all unyoked the buffaloes, and throwing themselves on their broad backs, galloped away through
sawahs, *galangans*,[1] mud, brushwood, forest, and *allang-
allang*,[2] along fields and roads, and when they tore pant-
ing and dripping with perspiration into the village of
Badoer, Saïdjah was not with them.

For when he had freed his buffalo from the yoke, and had
mounted him as the others had done to fly, an unexpected
jump made him lose his seat and fall to the earth.   The
tiger was very near . . . . Saïdjah's buffalo, driven on by
his own speed, jumped a few paces past the spot where his
little master awaited death.   But through his speed alone,

[1] *Galangan* = a trench for irrigating the rice-fields.
[2] *Allang-allang* = jungle.

and not of his own will, the animal had gone further than
Saïdjah, for scarcely had it conquered the momentum
which rules all matter even after the cause has ceased,
when it returned, and placing its big body, supported by
its big feet, like a roof over the child, turned its horned
head towards the tiger, which bounded forward . . . .
but for the last time. The buffalo caught him on his
horns, and only lost some flesh, which the tiger took out
of his neck. The tiger lay there with his belly torn open,
and Saïdjah was saved. Certainly there had been 'ontong' in the 'oeser-oeseran' of the buffalo.

When this buffalo had also been taken away from
Saïdjah's father and slaughtered . . . . . .

I told you, reader, that my story is monotonous.

When this buffalo was slaughtered, Saïdjah was just
twelve, and Adinda was wearing 'sarongs,' and making
figures on them.[1] She had already learned to express
thoughts in melancholy drawings on her tissue, for she
had seen Saïdjah very sad. And Saïdjah's father was
also sad, but his mother still more so ; for she had cured
the wound in the neck of the faithful animal which had
brought her child home unhurt, after having thought,
by the news of Adinda's brothers, that it had been taken
away by the tiger. As often as she saw this wound, she
thought how far the claws of the tiger, which had entered

[1] Adinda had already learned to express thoughts on her tissue ; *she
drew sad pictures on her tissue.* (See page 77.)

so deeply into the coarse flesh of the buffalo, would have penetrated into the tender body of her child; and every time she put fresh dressings on the wound, she caressed the buffalo, and spoke kindly to him, that the good faithful animal might know how grateful a mother is.

Afterwards she hoped that the buffalo understood her, for then he must have understood why she wept when he was taken away to be slaughtered, and he would have known that it was not the mother of Saïdjah who caused him to be slaughtered. Some days afterwards Saïdjah's father fled out of the country; for he was much afraid of being punished for not paying his land-taxes, and he had not another heirloom to sell, that he might buy a new buffalo, because his parents had always lived in Parang-Koodjang, and had therefore left him but few things. The parents of his wife too lived in the same district. However, he went on for some years after the loss of his last buffalo, by working with hired animals for ploughing; but that is a very ungrateful labour, and moreover, sad for a person who has had buffaloes of his own.

Saïdjah's mother died of grief, and then it was that his father, in a moment of dejection, fled from Bantam, in order to endeavour to get labour in the Buitenzorg districts.

But he was punished with stripes, because he had left Lebak without a passport, and was brought back by the police to Badoer. There he was put in prison, because he was supposed to be mad, which I can readily believe, and because it was feared that he would run *amuck* [1] in a moment of *mata-glap*. [2] But he was not long in prison, for he died soon afterwards. What became of the brothers and sisters of Saïdjah I do not know. The house in which they lived at Badoer was empty for some time, and soon fell down; for it was only built of bamboo, and covered with *atap*. [3] A little dust and dirt covered the place where there had been much suffering. There are many such places in Lebak. Saïdjah was already fifteen years of age, when his father set out for Buitenzorg; and he did not accompany him thither, because he had *other* plans in view. He had been told that there were at Batavia many gentlemen, who drove in *bendies*, [4] and that it would be easy for him to get a post as *bendie-boy*, for which generally a young person is chosen, so as not to disturb the equilibrium of the two-wheeled carriage by too much weight behind. He would, they told him, gain much in that way if he behaved well,—perhaps he would be able to spare in three years money enough to buy two buffaloes. This was a smiling prospect for him. With the proud step of one who has conceived a grand idea, he,

[1] *Run amuck.*—A man who runs *amuck* kills everybody whom he meets, till he is at last killed himself like a mad dog.

[2] *Mata-glap*—literally = darkened eye—darkness, frenzy. This is the name one gives to the peculiar state wherein a Javanese is, when, because of jealousy, or oppression, he soon becomes so mad as to run amuck.

[3] A sort of cane.   [4] A sort of carriage.

after his father's flight, entered Adinda's house, and communicated to her his plan.

"Think of it," said he, "when I come back we shall be old enough to marry, and shall possess two buffaloes!"

"Very well, Saïdjah, I will gladly marry you when you return. I will spin and weave *sarongs*[1] and *slendangs*,[2] and be very diligent all the time."

"Oh, I believe you, Adinda, but . . . if I find you married?'

"Saïdjah, you know very well that I shall marry nobody but you; my father promised me to your father."

"And you yourself?"

"I shall marry you, you may be sure of that."

"When I come back, I will call from afar off."

"Who shall hear it, if we are stamping rice in the village?"

"That is true, . . . but, Adinda, . . . oh yes, this is better, wait for me under the *djati*[3] wood, under the *ketapan*[4] where you gave me the *melatti*."[5]

"But, Saïdjah, how can I know when I am to go to the *ketapan?*"

[1] *Sarong*, see page 77.

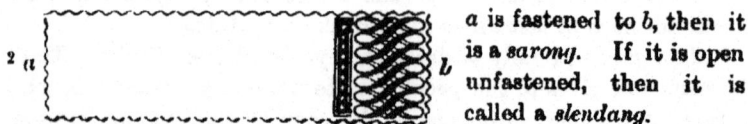

[2] *a* ... *b*   *a* is fastened to *b*, then it is a *sarong*. If it is open unfastened, then it is called a *slendang*.

[3] *Djati* = *Quercus indicus*, Indian Oak.

[4] *Ketapan*—An Indian tree.   [5] *Melatti* – A beautiful flower.

Saïdjah considered and said :—

" Count the moons ; I shall stay away three times twelve moons, . . . this moon not included. . . . See, Adinda, at every new moon, cut a notch in your rice-block. When you have cut three times twelve lines, I will be under the Ketapan the next day, . . . do you promise to be there ?"

" Yes, Saïdjah, I will be there under the ketapan, near the djati-wood, when you come back.

Hereupon Saïdjah tore a piece off his blue turban, which was very much worn, and gave the piece of linen to Adinda to keep it as a pledge; and then he left her and Badoer. He walked many days. He passed Rankas-Betong, which was not then the capital of Lebak, and Warong-Goonoong, where was the house of the Assistant Resident, and the following day saw Pamarangang, which lies as in a garden. The next day he arrived at Serang, and was astonished at the magnificence and size of the place, and the number of stone houses covered with red tiles. Saïdjah had never before seen such a thing. He remained there a day, because he was tired ; but, during the night, in the coolness, he went further, and the following day, before the shadow had descended to his lips, though he wore the large *toodoong*[1] which his father had left him, he arrived at Tangerang.

At Tangerang he bathed in the river near the passage, and rested in the house of an acquaintance of his father's,

[1] See p. 83.

who showed him how to make straw-hats like those that
come from Manilla.   He stayed there a day to learn that,
because he thought to be able to get something by that
afterwards, if he should perhaps not succeed at Batavia.
The following day towards the evening when it was cool
he thanked his host very much, and went on.   As soon as
it was quite dark, when nobody could see it, he brought
forth the leaf in which he kept the ' melatti' which
Adinda had given him under the ' Ketapan' tree, for he
was sad because he should not see her for so long a time.
The first day, and the second day likewise, he had not felt
so much how lonely he was, because his soul was quite
captivated by the grand idea of gaining money enough to
buy two buffaloes, and his father had never possessed more
than one; and his thoughts were too much concentrated
in the hope of seeing Adinda again, to make room for
much grief at his leave-taking.   He took that leave in
anxious hope, and mingled the memory of it in his
thoughts, with the prospect of again seeing Adinda at
last under the ketapan.   For this prospect so occupied his
heart that he, on leaving Badoer, and passing that tree,
felt something like joy, as if the thirty-six moons were
already past that separated him from that moment.   It
had appeared to him as if he had only to turn round, as if
on his return from the journey, to see Adinda waiting for
him under the tree.   But the further he went away from
Badoer, the more attention he paid to the duration of one

day, the longer he thought the period of the thirty-six moons before him. There was something in his soul which made him walk less quickly—he felt affliction in his knees, and though it was not dejection that overcame him, yet it was mournfulness, which is not far from it. He thought of returning ;—but what would Adinda think of so little heart ?

Therefore he walked on, though less rapidly than the first day. He had the 'melatti' in his hand, and often pressed it to his breast. He had become much older during the last three days, and he no longer understood how he had lived so calmly before, when Adinda was so near him, and he could see her as often as he liked. But now he could not be calm, when he expected that he should see her again by and by. Nor did he understand why he after having taken leave had not returned once more to look at her again. And he even remembered how a short time ago he had quarrelled with her about the cord which she had made for the *lalayang*[1] of her brother, and which had broken because there was a defect in her work by which a wager had been lost against the children of Tjipoeroet. "How was it possible," he thought, " to have been angry about that with Adinda ? For if there was a defect in the cord, and if the wager of Badoer against

---

[1] *Lalayang* = kite,—a game wherein they try to cut each other's cord. Often matches take place between different villages. This is a national game in Java, like cricket in England.

Tjipoeroet had been lost in consequence, and not by the
piece of glass which little Djamien had thrown while hiding himself behind the *pagger*,[1] ought I then to have
been so rough to her, and called her by unseemly names?
What if I die at Batavia without having asked her pardon
for such harshness? Will it not make me appear as if I
were a bad man, who scolds a girl? And when it is heard
that I have died in a foreign country, will not every one
at Badoer say, 'It is good that Saïdjah died; for he had
an insolent mouth against Adinda?'"

Thus his thoughts took a course which differed much
from their former buoyancy, and involuntarily were
uttered, first in half words and softly, soon in a monologue,
and at last in the melancholy song, of which a translation
follows. My first intention was to have recourse to measure and rhyme in this translation; but, like Havelaar,
I thought it better to leave it without the corset.

> " I do not know where I shall die.
> I saw the great sea on the south-coast,
> > when I was there with my father making salt;[2]
> If I die at sea, and my body is thrown into the
> > deep water, then sharks will come:
> They will swim round my corpse, and ask, 'Which of
> > us shall devour the body, that goes down into the water?'
> > > I shall *not* hear it!

---

[1] *Pagger*,—an enclosure constructed of bamboo canes.

[2] Making salt. This means to do something against the law. Salt
is a monopoly of the Government. The Javanese is obliged to buy
from the magazines of the Government. Saïdjah in his simplicity is
saying something—which the police ought not to hear!

"I do not know where I shall die.
I saw in a blaze the house of Pa-ansoe, which he
   himself has set on fire because he was *mata-glup* ;
If I die in a burning house, glowing embers
   will fall on my corpse ;
And outside the house there will be many cries of
   men throwing water on the fire to kill it ;—
      I shall *not* hear it !

"I do not know where I shall die.
I saw the little Si-Oenah fall out of a klappa-tree,
   when he plucked a *klappa*[1] for his mother ;
If I fall out of a klappa-tree I shall lie dead
   below, in the shrubs, like Si-Oenah.
Then my mother will not weep, for she is dead. But
   others will say with a loud voice : 'See, there lies Saïdjah.'
      I shall *not* hear it !

"I do not know where I shall die.
I have seen the corpse of Pa-lisoe, who died of
   old age ; for his hairs were white :
If I die of old age, with white hairs,
   hired women will stand weeping near my corpse ;
And they will make lamentation, as did the mourners over
   Pa-lisoe's corpse ; and the grandchildren will weep, very loud ;
      I shall *not* hear it !

"I do not know where I shall die.
I have seen at Badoer many that were dead. They
   were dressed in white shrouds, and were buried in the earth ;
If I die at Badoer, and I am buried beyond the dessah,[2]
   eastward against the hill, where the grass is high ;
Then will Adinda pass by there, and the border of
   her sarong will sweep softly along the grass, . . .
      I SHALL hear it."

Saïdjah arrived at Batavia. He begged a gentleman
to take him into his service, which this gentleman did,

---

[1] *Klappa* = cocoa-nut.
[2] *Dessah* = Javanese village.

because he did not understand Saïdjah's language;[1] for they like to have servants at Batavia who do not speak Malay, and are, therefore, not so corrupted as others, who have been longer in connexion with Europeans. Saïdjah soon learned Malay, but behaved well; for he always thought of the two buffaloes which he should buy, and of Adinda. He became tall and strong, because he ate every day, what could not always be had at Badoer. He was liked in the stable, and would certainly not have been rejected, if he had asked the hand of the coachman's daughter. His master even liked Saïdjah so much that he soon promoted him to be an indoor servant, increased his wages, and continually made him presents, to show that he was well pleased with his services. Saïdjah's mistress had read Sue's novel,[2] which for a short time was so popular: she always thought of Prince Djalma when she saw Saïdjah, and the young girls, too, understood better than before how the Javanese painter, Radeen Saleh, had met with such great success at Paris.

But they thought Saïdjah ungrateful, when he, after almost three years of service, asked for his dismissal, and a certificate that he had always behaved well. This could not be refused, and Saïdjah went on his journey with a joyful heart.

He passed Pisang, where Havelaar once lived many years ago. But Saïdjah did not know this, . . . and even

---

[1] Soondanese.   [2] *Le Juif Errant.*

if he had known it, he had something else in his soul
which occupied him. . . . He counted the treasures which
he was carrying home. In a roll of bamboo he had his
passport and a certificate of good conduct. In a case,
which was fastened to a leathern girdle, something heavy
seemed to sling continually against his shoulder, but he
liked to feel that. . . . And no wonder ! . . . this contained thirty piastres,[1] enough to buy three buffaloes !
What would Adinda say ? And this was not all. On his
back could be seen the silver-covered sheath of the *kris*,[2]
which he wore in the girdle. The hilt was certainly very
fine, for he had wound it round with a silk wrapper.
And he had still more treasures ! In the folds of the
kahin[3] round his loins, he kept a belt of silver links, with
gold *ikat-pendieng*.[4] It is true that the belt was short, but
she was so slender. . . . Adinda !

And suspended by a cord round his neck, under his
baadjoe,[5] he wore a small silk bag, in which were some
withered leaves of the ' melatti.'

Was it a wonder that he stopped no longer at San-
gerang than was necessary to visit the acquaintances of his
father who made such fine straw hats ? Was it a wonder

---

[1] 54 guilders.

[2] The Javanese is never without his poniard; it belongs to his
dress.

[3] *Kahin* = a piece of linen.

[4] *Ikat-pendieng*—pendieng is a girdle of small plates of silver or
gold, and ikat-pendieng—the clasp of it (*agrafe*).

[5] *Baadjoe* = clothes.

that he said little to the girls on his road, who asked
him where he came from, and *where* he was going—the
common saluation in those regions?   Was it a wonder
that he no longer thought Serang so beautiful, he who
had learnt to know Batavia?   That he hid himself no
more behind the 'pagger' as he did three years ago,
when he saw the Resident riding out; for he had seen
the much grander lord, who lives at Buitenzorg, and
who is the grandfather of the *Soosoohoonan* (Emperor) of
Solo?[1] Was it a wonder that he did not pay much attention to the tales of those who went a part of the way with
him, and spoke of the news in Bantam-Kidool; how the
coffee culture had been quite suspended after much un-
rewarded labour; how the district chief of Parang-Koodjang had been condemned to fourteen days' arrest at the
house of his father-in-law for highway robbery; how the
capital had been removed to Rankas-Betong; how a new
Assistant Resident was there, because the other had died
some months ago; how this new functionary had spoken
at the first *Sebah* meeting; how for some time nobody had
been punished for complaining; how the people hoped
that all that had been stolen would be returned or paid
for?

   No, he had sublime visions before his mind's eye.   He
sought for the 'Ketapan' tree in the clouds, as he was still
too far off to seek it at Badoer.   He caught at the air

---

[1] A superstition of the Javanese.

which surrounded him, as if he would embrace the form
which was to meet him under that tree.   He pictured to
himself the face of Adinda, her head, her shoulders; he
saw the heavy *kondeh* (chignon), so black and glossy, confined in a net, hanging down her neck; he saw her large
eye glistening in dark reflection; the nostrils which she
raised so proudly as a child, when he——how was it possible ?——vexed her, and the corner of her lips, where she
preserved a smile; he saw her breast, which would now
swell under the *kabaai*;[1] he saw how well the *sarong* of
her own making fitted her hips, and descending along the
thighs in a curve, fell in graceful folds on the small foot.

No; he heard little of what was told him.   He heard
quite different tones; he heard how Adinda would say
"Welcome, Saïdjah! I have thought of you in spinning
and weaving, and stamping the rice on the floor, which
bears three times twelve lines made by my hand.   Here I
am under the 'Ketapan' the first day of the new moon.
Welcome, Saïdjah, I will be your wife."

That was the music which resounded in his ears, and
prevented him from listening to all the news that was told
him on the road.

At last he saw the 'Ketapan,' or rather he saw a large
dark spot, which many stars covered, before his eye.
That must be the wood of Djati, near the tree where he
should see again Adinda, next morning after sunrise.   He

[1] Indian dress.

sought in the dark, and felt many trunks—soon found the
well-known roughness on the south side of a tree, and
thrust his finger into a hole which Si-Panteh had cut
with his *parang*[1] to exorcise the *pontianak*[2] who was
the cause of his mother's toothache, a short time before
the birth of Panteh's little brother.   That was the *Ketapan* he looked for.

Yes, this was indeed the spot where he had looked upon
Adinda for the first time with quite a different eye from
his other companions in play, because she had for the first
time refused to take part in a game which she had played
with other children—boys and girls—only a short time
before.   There she had given him the 'melatti.'   He sat
down at the foot of the tree, and looked at the stars; and
when he saw a shooting-star he accepted it as a welcome
of his return to Badoer, and he thought whether Adinda
would now be asleep, and whether she had rightly cut the
moons on her rice floor.   It would be such a grief to him
if she had omitted a moon, as if thirty-six were not
enough! . . .   And he wondered whether she had made nice
'sarongs' and 'slendangs?'   And he asked himself, too, who
would now be dwelling in her father's house?   And he
thought of his youth, and of his mother; and how that
buffalo had saved him from the tiger, and he thought of
what would have become of Adinda if that buffalo had

[1] An implement used by farmers in cutting grass and wood.
[2] Evil spirit.

been less faithful! He paid much attention to the sinking
of the stars in the west, and as each star disappeared in
the horizon, he calculated how much nearer the sun was
to his rising in the east, and how much nearer he himself
was to seeing Adinda. For she would certainly come at
the first beam——yes, at daybreak she would be there, ...
Ah! Why had not she already come the day before?

It pained him, that she had not anticipated the supreme
moment which had lighted up his soul for three years
with inexpressible brightness; and, unjust as he was in
the selfishness of his love, it appeared to him that Adinda
ought to have been there waiting for him, who complained before the time appointed, that he had to wait
for *her*.

And he complained unjustly, for neither had the sun
risen, nor had the eye of day cast a glance on the plain.
The stars, it is true, were growing pale up there! ashamed
as they were of the approaching end of their rule; strange
colours were flowing over the tops of the mountains,
which appeared darker as they contrasted sharply with
places more brightly illuminated; here and there flowed
something glowing in the east—arrows of gold and of
fire that were shot hither and thither, parallel to the
horizon;—but they disappeared again, and seemed to fall
down behind the impenetrable curtain, which hid the
day from the eyes of Saïdjah. Yet it grew lighter and
lighter around him—he now saw the landscape, and could

already distinguish a part of the Klappa-wood behind which Badoer lay :—there Adinda slept.

No! surely she did not sleep; how could she sleep? . . Did she not know that Saïdjah would be awaiting her? She had not slept the whole night certainly; the night police of the village had knocked at her door to ask, why the *pelitat* (Javanese lamp) continued burning in her cottage; and with a sweet laugh she had said, that a vow kept her awake to weave the 'slendang,' in which she was occupied, and which must be ready before the first day of the new moon.

Or she had passed the night in darkness, sitting on the rice floor and counting with her eager finger, that indeed thirty-six deep lines were cut near each other. And she had amused herself with an imaginary fright as to whether she had miscalculated, perhaps had counted one less, to enjoy again and again, and every time, the delicious assurance, that without fail three times twelve moons had passed since Saïdjah saw her for the last time.

And now that it was becoming light, *she* too would be exerting herself with useless trouble, to bend her looks over the horizon to meet the sun, the lazy sun, that stayed away . . . . stayed away. . . .

There came a line of bluish-red, which touched the clouds and made the edges light and glowing ;—and it began to lighten, and again arrows of fire shot through the atmosphere; but this time they did not disappear, they seized upon the dark ground, and communicated their blaze in larger and larger circles, meeting, crossing, unrolling, turning, wandering, and uniting in patches of fire and lightnings of golden lustre on the azure ground . . . there was red, and blue, and silver, and purple, and yellow, and gold, in all this . . . oh God! that was the daybreak, that was seeing Adinda again!

Saïdjah had not learnt to pray, and it would have been a pity to teach him; for a more holy prayer, more fervent thanksgiving than was in the mute rapture of his soul, could not be conceived in human language. He would not go to Badoer—to see Adinda in reality seeming to him less pleasurable than the expectation of seeing her again. He sat down at the foot of the 'Ketapan,' and his eyes wandered over the scenery. Nature smiled at him, and seemed to welcome him as a mother welcoming the return of her child, and as she pictures her joy by voluntary remembrance of past grief, when showing what she has preserved as a keepsake during his absence. So Saïdjah was delighted to see again so many spots that were witnesses of his short life. But his eyes or his thoughts might wander as they pleased, yet his looks and longings always reverted to the path which leads from Badoer to the Ketapan tree. All that his senses could observe was called Adinda. . . . He saw the abyss to the left, where the earth is so yellow, where once a young buffalo sank down into the depth,—they had descended with strong

rattan cords, and Adinda's father had been the bravest.
Oh, how she clapped her hands, Adinda! And there,
further on, on the other side, where the wood of cocoa-
trees waved over the cottages of the village, there somewhere, Si-Oenah had fallen out of a tree and died. How
his mother cried, "because Si-Oenah was still such a little
one," she lamented, . . . as if she would have been less
grieved if Si-Oenah had been taller. But he was small,
that is true, for he was smaller and more fragile than
Adinda. . . . Nobody walked upon the little road which
leads from Badoer to the tree. By and by she would
come . . . it was yet very early.

Saïdjah saw a *badjing* (squirrel) spring with playful
nimbleness up the trunk of a cocoa-tree. The graceful
animal—the terror of the proprietor of the tree, but still
lovely in form and movement—ran untiringly up and
down. Saïdjah saw it, and forced himself to stay and look
at it, because this calmed his thoughts after their heavy
labour since sunrise—rest after the fatiguing expectancy.
Soon he uttered his impressions in words, and sang what
his soul dictated him. I would rather *read* you his lay
in Malay, that Italian language of the East :—

"See, how the 'badjing' looks for his means of living
On the Klappa-tree. He ascends, descends, wantons right and left,
He turns (round the tree), springs, falls, climbs, and falls again.
He has no wings, and yet he is as quick as a bird.
    Much happiness, my 'badjing,'—I give you hail!
You will surely find the means of living which you seek;
But I am sitting alone near the wood of Djati-trees

> Waiting for the food of my heart.
> Long has the small appetite of my badjing been sated ;
> Long has he returned to his little nest ;
> But still my soul
> And my heart are very sad . . . Adinda !"

Still there was nobody on the path leading from Badoer to the *Ketapan.* . . .

Saïdjah caught sight of a butterfly which seemed to enjoy itself in the increasing warmth . . . .

> "See how the butterfly flutters everywhere :
> His wings glisten like a flower of many colours ;
> His heart is in love with the blossoms of the *kenari,*[1]
> Certainly he looks for his fragrant sweetheart.
> Much joy, my butterfly,—I give you hail !
> You will surely find what you seek ;
> But I am sitting alone near the Djati-wood,
> Waiting for what my heart loves :
> Long since has the butterfly kissed
> The *kenari* blossom which it loves so well ;
> But still my soul
> And my heart are very sad . . . . Adinda !"

And still there was no one on the path leading from Badoer to the *Ketapan.*

The sun began to rise high,—there was warmth in the air.

> " See how the sun glitters on high,
> High above the *waringi*[2]—hill !
> He feels too warm and wishes to descend,
> To sleep in the sea as in the arms of a spouse.

---

[1] *Kenari,* a beautiful tree. The kenari produces a nut, of which very good oil is made.

[2] *Waringi,* one of the most beautiful trees in Java.

Much joy, O sun,—I give you hail !
What you seek you will surely find ;
But I sit alone by the Djati-wood
Waiting for rest for my heart.
    Long the sun will have set
And will sleep in the sea, when all is dark ;
And still my soul
And my heart will be very sad . . . Adinda !"

And there was nobody on the road leading from Badoer
to the *Ketapan*.

"When no longer butterflies shall flutter about,
    When the stars shall no longer glitter,
    When the *melatti* shall no longer yields its perfume,
    When there shall be no longer sad hearts,
    Nor wild animals in the wood,
    When the sun shall go wrong
    And the moon forget the east and the west,
    If Adinda has not yet arrived,
    Then an angel with shining wings
    Will descend on earth, to look for what remained behind :
    Then my corpse shall be here under the ketapan—
    My soul is very sad, ... Adinda ! "

There was nobody on the path leading from Badoer to
the *Ketapan*.

"Then my corpse will be seen by the angel,
    He will point it out with his finger to his brethren—
    ' See, a dead man has been forgotten,
    His. rigid mouth kisses a *melatti* flower :
    Come, let us take him up to heaven,
    Him who has waited for Adinda, till he died,
    Surely, he may not stay behind alone,
    Whose heart had the strength to love so much,'
    Then my rigid mouth shall open once more.
    To call Adinda whom my heart loves,
    I will kiss the *melatti* once more,
    Which *she* gave me . . . . Adinda ! . . . . Adinda !"

And still there was nobody on the path leading from Badoer to the *Ketapan*.

Oh! she must have fallen asleep towards morning, tired of watching during the night, of watching for many nights :—she had not slept for weeks : so it was !

Should he rise and go to Badoer!—No, that would be doubting her arrival. Should he call that man who was driving his buffalo to the field ? . . . . That man was too far off, and moreover, Saïdjah would speak to no one about Adinda, would ask no one after Adinda . . . . He would see her again, he would see her alone, he would see her first. Oh, surely, surely she would soon come !

He would wait, wait . . . .

But if she were ill, or . . . . dead ?

Like a wounded stag Saïdjah flew along the path leading from the 'Ketapan' to the village where Adinda lived. He saw nothing and heard nothing; and yet he *could* have heard something, for there were men standing in the road at the entrance of the village, who cried—"Saïdjah, Saïdjah !"

But, ... was it his hurry, his eagerness, that prevented him from finding Adinda's house ? He had already rushed to the end of the road, through the village, and like one mad, he returned and beat his head, because he must have passed her house without seeing it. But again he was at the entrance of the village, and, ... Oh God, was it a dream ? . . .

Again he had not found the house of Adinda. Again he flew back and suddenly stood still, seized his head with both his hands to press away the madness that overcame him, and cried aloud—

"Drunk, drunk; I am drunk!"

And the women of Badoer came out of their houses, and saw with sorrow poor Saïdjah standing there, for they knew him, and understood that he was looking for the house of Adinda, and they knew that there was no house of Adinda in the village of Badoer.

For, when the district chief of Parang-Koodjang had taken away Adinda's father's buffaloes. . . .

I told you, reader! that my narrative was monotonous.

. . . . Adinda's mother died of grief, and her baby sister died because she had no mother, and had no one to suckle her. And Adinda's father, who feared to be punished for not paying his land-taxes. . . .

I know, I know that my tale is monotonous.

. . . . had fled out of the country; he had taken Adinda and her brothers with him. But he had heard how the father of Saïdjah had been punished at Buitenzorg with stripes for leaving Badoer without a passport. And, therefore, Adinda's father had not gone to Buitenzorg, nor to the Preangan, nor to Bantam. He had gone to Tjilang-kahan, the quarter of Lebak bordering on the sea. There he had concealed himself in the woods, and waited for the arrival of Pa Ento, Pa Lontah, Si Oeniah, Pa Ansive,

Abdoel Isma, and some others that had been robbed of their buffaloes by the district chief of Parang-Koodjang, and all of whom feared punishment for not paying their land-taxes.

There they had at night taken possession of a fishing-boat, and had gone to sea. They had steered towards the west, and kept the country to the right of them as far as Java Head: then they had steered northwards till they came in sight of Prince's Island, and sailed round the east coast of that island, and from there to the Lampoons.

Such at least was the way that people told each other in whispers in Lebak, when there was a question of buffalo robbery and unpaid land-taxes.

But Saïdjah did not well understand what they said to him; he did not even quite understand the news of his father's death. There was a buzzing in his ears, as if a gong had been sounded in his head: he felt the blood throbbing convulsively through the veins of his temples, that threatened to yield under the pressure of such severe distension. He spoke not: and looked about as one stupefied, without seeing what was round and about him; and at last he began to laugh horribly.

An old woman led him to her cottage, and took care of the poor fool.

Soon he laughed less horribly, but still did not speak. But during the night the inhabitants of the hut were frightened at his voice, when he sang monotonously: " I do not know where I shall die," and some inhabitants of Badoer put money together, to bring a sacrifice to the *bojajas*[1] of the Tji-Udjung for the cure of Saïdjah, whom they thought insane.   But he was not insane.

For upon a certain night when the moon was very clear, he rose from the *baleh-baleh*,[2] softly left the house, and sought the place where Adinda had lived.   This was not easy, because so many houses had fallen down; but he seemed to recognise the place by the width of the angle which some rays of light formed through the trees, at their meeting in his eye, as the sailor measures by light-houses and the tops of mountains.

Yes, there it ought to be :—there Adinda had lived !

Stumbling over half-rotten bamboo and pieces of the fallen roof, he made his way to the sanctuary which he sought.   And, indeed, he found something of the still standing *pagger*,[3] near to which the *baleh-baleh* of Adinda had stood, and even the pin of bamboo was still with its point in that *pagger*, the pin on which she hung her dress when she went to bed. . . . .

But the *baleh-baleh* had fallen down like the house, and

---

[1] *Bojajas* = crocodiles.   " To bring a sacrifice to the crocodiles." Such sacrifices are much in vogue.   Some fruits and some pastry, or a few hen's eggs, are placed on a saucer of bamboo, one or more burning wax-lights are added, all this is placed on the river, and the floating down of many such sacrifices is a beautiful sight.

[2] *Baleh-baleh* = couch.   [3] Enclosure.

was almost turned to dust. He took a handful of it, pressed it to his opened lips, and breathed very hard. . . .

The following day he asked the old woman, who had taken care of him, where the rice-floor was which stood in the grounds of Adinda's house. The woman rejoiced to hear him speak, and ran through the village to seek the floor. When she could point out the new proprietor to Saïdjah, he followed her silently, and being brought to the rice-floor, he counted thereupon thirty-two lines. . . .

Then he gave the woman as many piastres as were required to buy a buffalo, and left Badoer. At Tjilang-kahan, he bought a fishing-boat, and, after having sailed two days, arrived in the Lampoons, where the insurgents were in insurrection against the Dutch rule. He joined a troop of Badoer men, not so much to fight as to seek Adinda; for he had a tender heart, and was more disposed to sorrow than to bitterness.

One day that the insurgents had been beaten, he wandered through a village that had just been taken by the Dutch army, and was *therefore*[1] in flames. Saïdjah knew that the troop that had been destroyed there consisted for the most part of Badoer men. He wandered like a ghost among the houses, which were not yet burned down, and found the corpse of Adinda's father with a

[1] Read the address of the Lieutenant-General Van Swieten to his soldiers. See *Ideen* (Ideas) of Multatuli, first bundle, and the speech of Mr. Douwes Dekker in the *Annales* of the International Congress for the Promotion of Social Science (Amsterdam, 1864).

bayonet-wound in the breast. Near him Saïdjah saw the
three murdered brothers of Adinda, still boys—children,
—and a little further lay the corpse of Adinda, naked, and
horribly mutilated. . . .

A small piece of blue linen had penetrated into the
gaping wound in the breast, which seemed to have made
an end to a long struggle. . . .

Then Saïdjah went to meet some soldiers who were
driving, at the point of the bayonet, the surviving insurgents into the fire of the burning houses; he embraced the
broad bayonets, pressed forward with all his might, and
still repulsed the soldiers, with a last exertion, until their
weapons were buried to the sockets in his breast.

A little time afterwards there was much rejoicing at
Batavia for the new victory, which so added to the laurels
of the Dutch-Indian army. And the Governor wrote that
tranquillity had been restored in the Lampoons; the King
of Holland, enlightened by his statesmen, again rewarded
so much heroism with many orders of knighthood.

And probably thanksgivings mounted to heaven from
the hearts of the saints in churches and tabernacles, at the
news that "the Lord of hosts" had again fought under
the banner of Holland. . . .

> "But God, moved with so much woe,
> Did not accept the sacrifices of that day!"[1]

---

[1] "But God in high displeasure turned away,
And honoured not the offerings of that day."

I have made the end of the history of Saïdjah shorter than I could have done if I had felt inclined to paint something dreary. The reader will have observed how I lingered over the description of the waiting under the Ketapan, as if I was afraid of the sad catastrophe, and how I glided over that with aversion. And yet that was not my intention, when I began to speak about Saïdjah. For I feared that stronger colours were requisite to move when describing such strange circumstances. Yet while writing I felt that it would be an insult to the reader to believe that I ought to have put more blood in my picture——

I could have done it, for I have documents before me . . . but no !—rather a confession.

Yes ! a confession. I do not know whether Saïdjah loved Adinda : I know not whether he went to Badoer, nor whether he died in the Lampoons by Dutch bayonets. I do not know whether his father died by being beaten with rods, because he left Badoer without a passport, I do not know whether Adinda counted the moons by lines in her rice-floor.

All this I do not know.

But I know *more* than all this. I know, *and I can prove it*, that there were *many* Adindas and *many* Saïdjahs, and that *what was fiction in one case, becomes truth generally speaking*. I have already said that I can give the names of persons who, like the parents of Saïdjah and Adinda, were driven away by oppression from their country. It is not my intention to publish in this book communications such as would be suitable for a tribunal that had to decide on the manner in which the Dutch power is exercised in India,——communications that would have the power to convince him only who had patience enough to read them all, which cannot be expected of the public that looks for recreation in its reading. Therefore instead of barren names of persons and places with the dates, instead of a copy OF THE LIST OF THEFTS AND EXTORTIONS WHICH LIES BEFORE ME, I have tried to give a sketch of what *can* take place in the hearts of the poor people who are robbed of their means of *subsistence*; or even, I have only made you guess this, as I feared to be mistaken in painting emotions which I never experienced.

But as regards the main point . . . O that I were summoned to prove what I wrote! O that it were said, "You invented that Saïdjah: he never sang that lay; there never lived an Adinda in Badoer!" O that it were said with the power and the will to do justice as soon as I have proved myself to have been no slanderer!

Is there untruth in the parable of the Good Samaritan, because perhaps a plundered traveller was never taken to the Samaritan's house? Is there untruth in the parable of the Sower, because it is clear that no husbandman will throw his seed on a rock? or, to descend to more conformity with my book, can the main thing——truth——be

denied to "Uncle Tom's Cabin," because there never existed
an Evangeline ?   Shall people say to the author of that
immortal protest——immortal, not because of art or
talent, but because of tendency and impression——shall
they say to her, "You have lied : the slaves are not ill-
treated ; for there is untruth in your book—it is a novel ? "
Had not she to give a tale, instead of an enumeration of
barren facts, a tale which surrounded those facts, to introduce them into our hearts ?   Would her book have been
read if she had given it the form of a law-suit ?   Is it her
fault or mine, that *truth*, to find entrance, has so often to
borrow the DRESS of a *lie ?*

And to some who will pretend that I have too much
idealized Saïdjah and his love, I ask how they can know
this ; as only very few Europeans have given themselves
the trouble to stoop to observe the emotions of the coffee
and sugar machines, called " Natives."   But even if this
observation were well founded, whosoever quotes this as a
proof against the cardinal tendency of my book, *gives me a
complete triumph*.   For that observation when translated
is as follows :—" The evil which you combat does not
exist, or not in such a high degree, because the native is
not like your Saïdjah : there is not in the ill-treatment of
the Javanese so much evil as there would be if you had
rightly drawn your Saïdjah.   The Soondanese do not sing
such songs, do not love so, do not feel thus. . . ."

No, Colonial Ministers ! no, Governors-General in retirement! you have not to prove that. *You have to prove that the population is not ill-treated, whether there are sentimental Saïdjahs amongst this population or not; or should you dare to pretend that you may steal buffaloes of men who do not love, who do not sing melancholy songs, who are not sentimental?*

On an attack upon literary performances I should defend the exactness of the picture of Saïdjah, but on political grounds I admit immediately all observations on this exactness, *to prevent the great question from being removed to a wrong basis.* It is quite indifferent to me whether I am thought to be an incapable painter, if it is only admitted that the ill-treatment of the native is EXCESSIVE; that is the word on the notice of Havelaar's predecessor which he showed to the Controller Verbrugge : ——a notice which lies before me.

But *I have* other proofs, and that is fortunate. For this predecessor of Havelaar could also have been mistaken.

Alas, if *he* was mistaken, he has been very severely punished for his mistake!

CHAPTER XVIII.

[CONTINUATION OF STERN'S COMPOSITION.]

IT was afternoon. Havelaar, coming out of his room, found Tine in the fore-gallery, waiting for him at the tea-table. Madam Slotering had just left her house, and seemed to have the intention of going to Havelaar's, but suddenly she went to the gate, and there, with very violent gestures, sent back a man who had just entered. She remained standing still till she felt sure that he had gone away, and then returned along the grass-field to Havelaar's.

"I will know at last what this means," said Havelaar; and when the salutation was over he asked, jokingly, that she might not think he grudged her influence in grounds which formerly were hers:

"Now, Madam, do tell me why you always send back the men who come into the grounds. What if that man, for instance, had fowls to sell, or any other kitchen requisite?"

There was in the face of Madam Slotering a painful expression, which did not escape Havelaar's observation.

" Ah," she said, " there are so many bad men."

" Certainly, that is the case everywhere ; but if you are so particular, the good ones will stay away too.——Come now, Madam, tell me why you keep such a sharp look-out over the grounds ?"

Havelaar looked at her, and endeavoured in vain to read the reply in her watery eyes. He again pressed for an explanation, and the widow burst into tears, saying that her husband had been poisoned at Parang-Koodjang, in the house of the district chief.

" He would do justice, Mr. Havelaar !" continued the poor woman ; " he wished to put an end to the oppression of the people. He exhorted and threatened the chiefs in councils and in writing ; you must have found his letters in the archives . . ."

That was the case : Havelaar had read those letters, of which I have copies before me.

" He spoke repeatedly to the Resident," continued the widow, " but always in vain ; for as it was generally known that the extortion was for and under the protection of the Regent, whom the Resident would not complain of to the Government, all these conversations had no other effect than the ill treatment of the complainants. Therefore my poor husband had said that if no alteration should be made before the end of the year, he would apply direct to the Governor-General. That was in November. A few days later he made a journey of inspection, took his dinner at the house of the Demang of Parang-Koodjang, and soon afterwards was brought home in a pitiable condition. He cried, while pointing to his stomach, ' Fire, fire,' and in a few hours he was dead; he who had always been remarkable for good health."

" Did you send for the Serang doctor ?" asked Havelaar.

" Yes, but my husband died soon after his arrival. I did not dare to tell the doctor my suspicion, because I foresaw that I should not be able soon to leave this place, and I feared revenge. I have heard that you, like my husband, oppose the abuses which reign here, and therefore I have not a moment's peace. I would have concealed all this from you to avoid frightening you and Madam Havelaar, and so I only watched the grounds to prevent strangers from entering the kitchen."

Now it was clear to Tine why Madam Slotering had kept her own household, and would not even make use of the kitchen, which was so large. Havelaar sent for the Controller. Meanwhile he sent a request to the physician at Serang, to make a statement of the symptoms attending the death of Slotering. The reply which he received the next day to that request, was not in accordance with the widow's suspicions. According to the doctor, Slotering had died of " an abscess in the liver." I do not know whether such a disease can manifest itself suddenly, and cause death in a few hours. I think I must bear in mind the evidence 'of Madam Slotering, that her husband had

formerly been always healthy; but if no value is attached
to such evidence, because the notion of what is called
health varies with different persons, particularly in the
eyes of non-medical individuals, yet the important question remains, whether a person who dies to-day of an
" abscess in the liver," could ride on horseback yesterday,
with the intention of inspecting a mountainous country,
which is in some directions eighty miles in extent ?

The doctor who treated Slotering may have been a
skilful physician, and yet have been mistaken in his
judgment of the symptoms of the disease, unprepared as
he was to suspect crime.   However this may be, I cannot
prove that Havelaar's predecessor was poisoned, because
Havelaar was not allowed time to clear up the matter;
but I can prove that every one believed in the poisoning,
and that this was suspected on account of his desire to
oppose injustice.

The Controller Verbrugge entered Havelaar's room;
the latter asked abruptly—

" What did Mr. Slotering die of ?"

" I don't know."

" Was he poisoned ?"

" I don't know; . . . . but——"

" Speak plainly, Verbrugge."

" But he endeavoured to oppose the abuses, as you do
. . . . and he would certainly have been poisoned if he
had remained here longer."

" Write that down !"

Verbrugge wrote it . . . . it lies before me.

" To proceed, Is it *true*, or untrue, that much extortion is committed in Lebak ?"

Verbrugge made no reply.

" Answer me, Verbrugge !"

" I dare not."

" Write down that you dare not."

Verbrugge wrote it down . . . . it lies before me.

" Well, to proceed, you dare not answer the last question. You told me lately, when there was a question about *poisoning*, that you were the only support of your sisters at Batavia,—is that the reason of your fear, of what I always called your *halfness ?*"

" Yes."

Verbrugge wrote it down . . . . his declaration *lies before me.*

" That will do," said Havelaar, " I know enough." And Verbrugge left. Havelaar went out and played with little Max, whom he kissed very fervently. When Madam Slotering was gone, he sent away the child, and called in Tine.

" Dear Tine ! I have a favour to ask you. I should like you and Max to go to Batavia :—to-day I accuse the Regent."

She fell on his neck, for the first time opposed to his wishes, and cried, sobbing—

"No, Max; no, Max, I will not go . . . I will not go; we eat and drink together."

Was Havelaar wrong when he made out that she had as little right to blow her nose as the women at Arles?

He wrote and despatched the letter of which I here present a copy. After I have given a slight sketch of the circumstances under which that letter was written, I believe that it is not necessary for me to show the circumspection which he observed, while not uttering a syllable of the discovery just made, not to weaken his positive accusation by the uncertainty of a very important but as yet unproved accusation. His intention was to exhume the corpse of his predecessor, and to have it scientifically examined as soon as the Regent should have been removed, and his party made harmless; but as I have already said, he was not allowed the opportunity of doing this.

In the copies of official documents—copies which strictly conform with the originals—I think I may use single pronouns instead of the foolish titles. I expect that the good taste of my readers will approve of this change.

"No. 88. $\left\{ \begin{array}{l} \textit{Private.} \\ \textit{Immediate.} \end{array} \right.$

"RANKAS-BETONG, 24th February 1856.

" *To the Resident of Bantam.*

"Since returning a month ago to my duties here, I have
" occupied myself principally in examining how the chiefs

" discharge their obligations towards the population as
" regards statute-labour, poondootan,[1] and suchlike.

" I very soon discovered that the Regent, on his own
" responsibility, and for his advantage, summoned the
" population to work for him, far above the legally autho-
" rized number of pantjens or kemits.[2]

" I hesitated between the choice of sending at once an
" official report and the desire to make this native func-
" tionary change his policy by gentle means, or even
" afterwards by threats, in order to attain the double pur-
" pose of putting an end to abuse, and at the same time
" not acting too severely against this old servant of the
" Government, particularly considering the bad examples
" which, I believe, have often been set before him; and in
" connexion with the peculiar circumstance that he ex-
" pected a visit from two relations (the Regents of Bombang
" and Tjandoer, at least of the latter, who, as I hear, is
" already coming with a large train), and he being thus
" more than usually in temptation—and with regard to
" the critical embarrassment of his pecuniary circum-
" stances, as it were obliged—to provide by unlawful
" means the necessary preparations for that visit.

[1] Poondootan is the obtaining of provisions and goods under the pretext of Government service.   In the journeys of important personages
invited by the Regent or district chiefs, all necessaries are supplied by
the population, and that as often as required.

[2] Followers and serving-people summoned to increase the pomp, and
attend upon the chief or other personage.

" All this made me incline to moderation, with regard to
" what *had* already happened, but not at all to indulgence
" for the future.

" I insisted upon the immediate cessation of every un-
" lawful act.

" I made you acquainted with that previous experiment
" to induce the Regent by moderation to do his duty.

" Yet it is evident to me that he casts all to the winds
" with rude insolence; and I feel bound to communicate
" to you *in virtue of my official oath;*

" That I *accuse* the Regent of Lebak, Radeen Adhipatti,
" Karta Natta Negara, of abuse of power, by disposing
" unlawfully of the labour of his subordinates, and *suspect*
" him of extortion while exacting productions *in naturâ,*
" without payment, or for prices arbitrarily fixed :

" That I suspect, moreover, the Demang of Parang-
" Koodjang (the Regent's son-in-law) of complicity in the
" above-mentioned abuses.

" In order conclusively to prove both these charges I
" take the liberty of proposing to you to order me—

" 1. To send the Regent of Lebak with the utmost speed
" to Serang, and to take care that he shall not have occa-
" sion, either before his departure or during the journey,
" to influence by corruption, or in any other way, the
" witnesses. I require,

" 2. Previously to take the Demang of Parang-Koodjang
" into custody.

" 3. To apply the same measure to such persons of

" inferior rank as, belonging to the family of the Regent,
" may be expected to mar the impartiality of the examina-
" tion to be instituted.

" 4. To order that examination to take place im-
" mediately, and to report circumstantially on the issue.
" I take the liberty of submitting to your. consideration
" the advisability of countermanding the visit of the
" Regent of Tjanjar.

" Finally, I have the honour to give you, as one who
" knows the district of Lebak better than it is as yet
" possible for me to know it, the assurance that, from a
" *political* point of view, the strictly just treatment of this
" affair has no difficulty at all, and that I should be rather
" apprehensive if it was *not* cleared up, for I am informed
" that the poor man is, as a witness told me, '*poessing*'
" (tired, sick, disgusted) of all the vexation he has suffered,
" and that he has long sought relief.

" I have partly derived the strength to fulfil *my difficult*
" *duty* in writing this letter, from the hope that I may be
" allowed in due time to bring forward one or two excuses
" for the old Regent, for whose position, though caused by
" his own fault, I nevertheless feel great compassion.—
" The Assistant Resident at Lebak,

(Signed) " MAX HAVELAAR."

The next day the Resident of Bantam replied ? . . . .
no, but " Mr. Slymering " did so, in a private letter.

That reply is a precious contribution to the knowledge

of how the Government is carried on in Dutch India. Mr.
Slymering complained "that Havelaar had not first communicated verbally to him the affair mentioned in the
letter No. 88,"—of course because then there would have
been more chance of "*arranging*" matters ; adding, moreover, that Havelaar "*disturbed him in pressing business !*"

The man was surely busy in writing the yearly report
on TRANQUIL TRANQUILLITY . . . . I have that letter before
me, and do not trust my eyes.   I read once more the letter
of the Assistant Resident of Lebak . . . . I compare
Havelaar and Slymering. *   *   *   *   *   *

————————

This Shawlman is a low beggar.   You must know,
reader, that Bastianus is again very often absent from the
office, because he has gout.   Now, as I cannot reconcile it
with my conscience to throw away the funds of the firm
(Last and Co.)—for where principles are concerned, I am
immoveable.   I thought the day before yesterday that
Shawlman wrote a good hand, and, as he looked so very
poor, that he could therefore certainly be got for small
wages.   I therefore thought that it was my duty to provide in the cheapest manner for the removal of Bastianus.
I went accordingly to Shawlman's house in the Lange
Leidsche Dwarsstraat.[1]   The woman of the shop was at
the door, but she seemed not to recognise me, though I

————

[1] Long Leiden Cross-street.

had lately told her that I was Mr. Drystubble, coffee-broker, of the Laurier Canal. There is always a sort of insult in such a non-recognition; but as it was now not so cold, and as I wore last time I was there my coat trimmed with fur, I ascribed it to that, and think nothing of it—I mean the insult. I said therefore again that I was Mr. Drystubble, of the Laurier Canal, coffee-broker, and begged her to go and see if Shawlman was in, because I did not wish, as on the last occasion, to have to speak to his wife, who is always discontented. But the woman refused to go up-stairs. "She could not walk up and down stairs the whole day for that beggarly family," said she, "but I could go and look for myself." And then followed again a description of the staircase and doors, which I had no need of; for I always know a place where I have been once, because I pay such attention to every-thing. I have got accustomed to that in my business. So I went up-stairs, and knocked at the well-known door, which opened. I entered, and as I saw nobody in the room, I looked round. There was not much to be seen. A child's trousers with an embroidered stripe hung over a chair—why need such people wear embroidered trousers?

In a corner stood a not very heavy travelling box, which I lifted up by the hinge, and on the mantel-piece there were some books, which I looked at. A curious collection! A couple of volumes of Byron, Horace, Bastiat, Béranger, and, . . . do guess! . . . a Bible, a complete Bible, with the Apocrypha. This I had not expected of Shawlman. It appeared also to have been read, for I found many notes on loose pieces of paper relating to the Scriptures, all written in the same handwriting as the pieces in that unwelcome parcel. Above all he seemed to have studied carefully the Book of Job, for there the leaves bore the marks of it. I think that he begins to feel the chastisement of the Lord, and will therefore reconcile himself to God by reading the Holy Scriptures, and I am not opposed to that. But while waiting, my eye caught sight of a lady's work-box which stood on the table. Without thinking about it, I looked at it : there were in it a pair of half-finished child's stockings, a lot of foolish verses, and a letter addressed to Shawlman's wife, as could be seen by the inscription. The letter was open, and it seemed as if it had been rumpled with some anger. Now it is a firm principle with me never to read anything that is not addressed to me, because I do not think it respectable. I never do such a thing when I have no interest in it ;—but now I got an inspiration that it was my duty to read this letter, because the contents would perhaps further me in the humane intentions that made me go to Shawlman. I thought about it, how the Lord is always near to those who believe in Him, as He gave me here quite unexpectedly an opportunity to know a little more about this man, and protected me too from the danger of performing an act of charity to an immoral person.

I pay much attention to such directions of the Lord :—
this has done me a great deal of good in business. With
much surprise I saw that the wife of Shawlman belongs to
a respectable family ; the letter at least was signed by a
relation whose name in Holland is respected, and I was
indeed in ecstasies with the beautiful contents of those
lines. It appeared to be from a person who laboured
zealously for the Lord ; for he wrote that the wife of
Shawlman ought to be divorced from such a wretch, who
made her suffer poverty,—who could not earn his livelihood, who was, moreover, a rascal, because he had debts.
That the writer of the letter pitied her condition, though
that condition was her own fault, because she had for-
saken the Lord, and stuck to Shawlman ;—that she ought
to return to the Lord, and that in that case her family
would all of them assist her, and furnish her with needle-
work, but before all things she ought to put away this
Shawlman, who was a disgrace to the family.

In a word, you could not get in church itself more piety
than was to be found in this letter.

I knew enough, and was grateful to have been warned
in such a miraculous way. Without this warning I should
certainly have become a victim of my own good heart. I
resolved, therefore, again to keep Bastianus till I could
find a fitter person to take his place ; for I do not like to
turn any one to the streets.

 ˙ The reader will be curious to know how I got on at the

Rosemeyers' last party.   I was not there, ... wonderful things have happened!   I had gone to Driebergen with my wife and Mary.   My father-in-law, old Mr. Last, the son of the first Last (the Meyers were then still in the firm, but they have left it long ago), said some years ago that he should like to see my wife and Mary.   Now, it was very fine weather, and my fear of the love-history with which Stern had menaced us, made me think all at once of this invitation.   I spoke of it to our bookkeeper, who is a man of experience, and who, after mature deliberation, recommended me to sleep a night on it.   This I intended immediately to carry out, for I am quick in the execution of my decisions.   The following day I perceived already how wise this advice was, for during the night I got the idea that I could not do better than delay my decision till Friday.   In a word, after having carefully considered all things,—there was much in favour of the plan, but also much against it,—we went on Saturday afternoon, and came back on Monday morning.   I would not tell you all this, if it was not in connexion with my book.

First of all I think it necessary that you should know why I do not protest against the nonsense which Stern certainly brought out last Sunday.   (What nonsense is that about a person who would hear when he was dead? Mary mentioned it to me: she had heard it from the Rosemeyers—who trade in sugar;) secondly, because I am now again convinced that all those stories about misery and trouble in the East Indies are downright lies. Thus it may be seen how travelling gives a person the opportunity to penetrate deeply into affairs.

Saturday evening, for instance, my father-in-law had accepted an invitation from a gentleman, who had been formerly a Resident in the East Indies, and who lives now at a large country-seat. We went there, and, indeed, I cannot sufficiently praise the excellent reception we met with. Our host sent his carriage to fetch us, and the coachman had on a red waistcoat. Now it was certainly a little too cold to inspect the country-seat, which must be magnificent in the summer, but in the house itself there was nothing to desire; for it was replete with luxury: a billiard-room, a library, a covered iron and glass conservatory, and a cockatoo on a silver perch. I never saw such a thing. I made the observation, how good conduct is always rewarded; that that man had been attentive to his business was evident, for he had more than three orders of knighthood. He had a beautiful country-seat, and, moreover, a house in Amsterdam. At the supper all was *truffé*, and even the servants who waited at table wore red waistcoats, like the coachman.

As I take great interest in Indian affairs, because of the coffee, I began a conversation on the subject, and perceived very soon what I had to think about it. This Resident told me that he was always very well off in the East Indies, and that there was, therefore, not a word of truth in those stories of discontent among the population. I turned the conversation upon Shawlman. He knew him, and that unfavourably. He said that the Government had done well in dismissing him, for that this Shawlman was a very discontented person, who made remarks about everything, and there was, moreover, much to disapprove in his own conduct. For instance, he was always running away with girls, and bringing them home openly before his wife; he did not pay his debts, a thing which is very unseemly. As I knew so exactly from the letter I had read how well-founded this accusation was, I was very well pleased to find that I had judged of all so correctly, and was quite satisfied with myself. I am also known for this at the Exchange—I mean for always possessing a sound judgment.

This Resident and his wife were agreeable and kind. They told us much of their manner of life in the Indies: it must be very pleasant there. They said that their country-seat near Driebergen was not half so large as what they called their "grounds," in the interior of Java, and that a hundred men were required to keep it in order. But—and this is a proof how they were liked—all this was done for nothing, and out of pure attachment. They told us also, that when they went away the sale of their furniture had produced a large profit, as it fetched ten times its value; for that the native chiefs were all of them so fond of buying a keepsake of a Resident. I told this afterwards to Stern, who maintained that this was done by coercion, and that he could prove it out of Shawlman's parcel; but I told him that this Shawlman was a slanderer,—that he had run away with girls, like that young German at Busselinck and Waterman's,—that I did not attach the least value to his judgment, for that I had now learnt from a Resident himself how matters stood, and had therefore nothing to learn from Shawlman.

There were still more persons from the Indies, amongst others a very rich gentleman, who had gained much money on tea, which the Javanese made him for little money, and which the Government bought from him for a high price, to encourage the activity of the Javanese. This gentleman was also very angry with all those discontented persons, who are always speaking and writing against the Government. He could not say enough in praise of the government of the Colonies; for he said that he had the conviction that it lost a great deal in tea, which it bought from him, and that was therefore very generous in invariably paying such a high price for an article, intrinsically of little value, which he himself did not like, for he always drank Chinese tea. He said also, that the Governor-General, who had prolonged the so-called tea-contracts, notwithstanding the calculation that the nation lost so much on this, such a clever, good man was he, and, above all, a good friend of those who had known him formerly; for that this Governor-General had not paid the least attention to the talk about losses on the tea, and had done him therefore a great deal of good by not cancelling those tea-contracts. "Yes," he went on, "my heart bleeds, when I perceive that such noble persons are slandered: if he had not been there, I should have to walk with my wife and children." Thereupon he ordered his carriage, and it looked so magnificent, and the horses were so beautiful and so fat, that I can understand why he is full of gratitude to such a Governor-General. It does one's heart good to behold such charming emotions, above all when comparing them with that accursed grumbling and complaining of persons like that Shawl-man.

The following day, the Resident and that gentleman for whom the Javanese make tea, returned our visit.

Both of them at once asked us by what train we thought of going to Amsterdam. We did not know what this meant, but afterwards it was clear to us, for when we arrived there on Monday morning, there were two servants at the station, one with a red waistcoat, and one with a yellow one, who both at the same time told us that he had received an order by telegram, to fetch us in a carriage. My wife was confused, and I thought what would Busselinck and Waterman have said if they had seen that,——I mean that there were two carriages for us. But it was not easy to make a choice, for I could not resolve to hurt one of the parties by refusing such a nice offer. Good advice was dear ; but I came victorious out of this great difficulty. I put my wife and Mary in the red carriage, the red waistcoat I mean——and I went in the yellow one,——I mean the carriage.

How those horses tore along ! on the Weesper Street where it is always so dirty, the mud flew as high as the houses, and there I saw the miserable Shawlman, his back bent, his head bowed down——and I saw how he tried to wipe the mud off his pale face with the sleeve of his threadbare coat.

CHAPTER XIX.

In the private letter which Mr. Slymering sent to Havelaar, he communicated to him, that he, notwithstanding his pressing business, would come the next day to Rankas-Betong, to deliberate on what ought to be done. Havelaar, who knew what such a deliberation meant—his predecessor had so often deliberated with the Resident of Bantam——wrote the following letter, which he sent to meet the Resident, and be read by him before his arrival at Lebak :—

" No. 91. $\left\{\begin{array}{l} \textit{Private.} \\ \textit{Immediate.} \end{array}\right.$

" Rankas Betong,
" 25th Feb. 1856, 11 p.m.

" Yesterday at 12 o'clock, I had the honour to send " you my missive (*Immediate*, No. 88) containing in " substance—

"That I, after a long investigation, and after having ' tried in vain to bring back by moderation the party con-

" cerned from his perversity, felt myself obliged by my
" official oath to *accuse* the Regent of Lebak of abuse of
" power, and to add that I *suspected* him of extortion. I
" have taken the liberty to propose to you in that letter,
" to summon that native chief to Serang, in order to ex-
" amine after his departure, and after the corrupting
" influence of his extensive family had been neutralized,
" whether my accusation and suspicion were well founded.

" Long, or to speak more accurately, much have I re-
" flected before determining upon this.

" I took care to let you know that I have endeavoured,
" by exhortation and threats, to save the old Regent from
" misfortune and shame, and myself from the deep regret
" of having been the immediate cause of his troubles.

" But on the other hand, I saw the (*for many years*)
" *plundered and much oppressed* population. I thought of
" the necessity of an example—for *I shall have to* report
" to you *many more vexations,*—if, at least *this* affair, by
" its reaction makes no end of them,—and, I repeat it,
" *after mature consideration,* I did what I thought to be
" my duty.

" I have just received your kind and esteemed private
" letter communicating that you will come here to-morrow,
" and at the same time a hint that I ought to have treated
" this affair privately at first. To-morrow I shall therefore
" have the honour to see you, and it is exactly on that
" account that I have taken the liberty to send you this

" letter, to add, before our meeting, the following consi-
" derations :—

" All my investigations about the Regent were quite
" secret ; only *he* and the Patteh (Adjutant of the Regent)
" knew it, for I myself had frankly warned him. Even the
" Controller knows only a part of my investigations. This
" secrecy had a double aim. At first when I still hoped to
" bring back the Regent to the right way, it was my object
" if I succeeded not to compromise him. The Patteh
" thanked me in the name of the Regent for this discretion.
" (It was on the 12th inst.)   But afterwards when I began
" to despair of the success of my endeavours,—or rather,
" when the measure of my indignation overflowed on hear-
" ing of a recent occurrence ;—when a longer silence would
" have become *participation* as an accomplice—then that
" secrecy would have been to *my* advantage ; for I too have
" to fulfil duties towards my household and myself.

" For after writing my letter of yesterday, I should be
" unworthy to serve the Government, if what I wrote down
" then was vain, unfounded, or invented. And would or
" will it be possible to me to prove that I have done *what*
" *a good Assistant Resident ought to do*—to prove that I am
" not unworthy the functions which I have received ;—to
" prove that I do not risk *thoughtlessly and rashly* my seven-
" teen hard years in the service of the Government, and,
" what is of more importance still, the interest of wife and
" child—will it be possible for me to prove all this, unless

" deep secrecy does not hide my investigations, and pre-
" vent the criminal from concealing himself?

" At the least suspicion the Regent would send an ex-
" press to his nephew, who is coming here, and whose
" interest it is to maintain him, at any sacrifice, and to
" distribute money with a profuse hand to every one
" whom he had recently swindled, the consequence
" would be (I need not say *will* be) that *I* have passed a
" rash judgment, and am an unserviceable functionary,
" not to say worse.

" To prevent that result I write this letter. I have the
" highest esteem for you; but I know the spirit of East
" Indian functionaries, and I do *not* possess that spirit.

" Your hint that it would have been better to have
" treated the affair privately at first, makes me apprehen-
" sive of such a course. What I said in my missive of
" yesterday is *true;* but perhaps it would *seem* untrue if
" the affair was treated in such a manner as would reveal
" my accusation and suspicion *before* the removal of the
" Regent. I may not conceal from you that even your
" unexpected arrival in connexion with the express sent
" by me yesterday to Serang, gives me reason to fear that
" the accused, who would not listen to my exhortations,
" will now awake too soon, and endeavour, if possible, *tant*
" *soit peu* to exculpate himself.

" I have the honour to say that I still refer literally to
" my missive of yesterday; but I take the liberty to

" observe that this missive contained a proposal to remove
" the Regent before the investigation, and previously to
" make his adherents harmless ; and at the same time that
" I believe myself to be no further responsible for what I
" advanced,.than so far as you may be pleased to agree to
" my proposition as regards the manner of investigation—
" that it should be impartial, open, and above all, *free*.

" This liberty cannot exist before the removal of the
" Regent ; and according to my humble opinion, there is
" nothing dangerous in that ; as he can be told that *I*
" accuse him and suspect him, that *I* am in danger, and
" not *he*, in the event of his innocence being established :—
" for I myself am of opinion that I ought to be dismissed, if
" it shall appear that *I* have acted precipitately or rashly.

" Precipitately ! . . . After *years and years* of abuses !

" Rashly ! . . . as if an honest man could sleep, and live,
" and enjoy, while *they*, over whose welfare he is called
" upon to watch, who are in the highest sense his *neigh-*
" *bours*, suffer extortion and injustice !

" I have been here, it is true, but a short time.   I hope,
" however, that the question will for once be, what has
" been done, if anything has been well done, and not
" whether it has been done in too short a time.   For me,
" every moment is too long, when characterized by extor-
" tion and oppression, and every second weighs heavy on
" me that is passed in misery by *my* negligence, by *my*
" ' spirit of arranging.'

" I regret the days which I allowed to pass away before
" reporting to you officially, and I apologize for that
" neglect.

" I have taken the liberty to request you to give me the
" opportunity to justify my letter of yesterday, and to
" guarantee me against the miscarriage of my endeavours
" to free the province of Lebak from the worms which
" have gnawed, since the memory of man, at its welfare.

" It is therefore that I have again taken the liberty of
" asking you to approve my action, which consists only of
" *investigating, reporting, and proposing* to remove the Re-
" gent of Lebak, without *direct or indirect* notice before-
" hand; and moreover to order an investigation to take
" place of what I communicated in my letter of yesterday,
" No. 88.—The Assistant Resident of Lebak,

(Signed)   " MAX HAVELAAR."

This request, not to take the criminals under his protection, the Resident received on the way. An hour after
his arrival at Rankas-Betong, he paid a visit to the Regent,
and asked him whether he could " say anything to the
prejudice of the Assistant Resident," and whether he, the
Regent, " wanted money." To the first question the Regent replied, " I have nothing against him! I can solemnly
swear to that!" The second question he answered in the
affirmative, whereupon the Resident gave him a couple of
bank-notes.

It may be understood that Havelaar knew nothing of this. We shall see by and by how he became acquainted with so shameful a transaction.

When the Resident Slymering entered Havelaar's house, he was paler than usual, and the intervals between his words were longer than ever. It was indeed no small thing for a person who so excelled in arranging and making out the yearly reports of " tranquillity," to receive so unexpectedly letters in which there was no trace either of optimism or of artificial colouring, or of fear of the disapprobation of the Government.

The Resident of Bantam was in a fright; and if I may be forgiven the ignoble comparison for the sake of exactness, I feel inclined to liken him to a little street-boy who complains of the violation of old customs, because he has been beaten without previous abusive language.

He began by asking the Controller why the latter had not endeavoured to restrain Havelaar from his accusation? Poor Verbrugge, who was entirely unacquainted with the circumstances, said so, but was not believed. Mr. Slymering could not believe that any person without assistance could do his duty in such a manner. As Verbrugge, however, maintained his ignorance, the Resident began to read Havelaar's letters.

What Verbrugge suffered in listening is indescribable. He was an honest man, and would not have lied if Havelaar had appealed to him to confirm the truth of the contents of these letters. But even without that honesty, he had not always been able to avoid the truth in many written reports, even where it was dangerous to tell it. How would it be if Havelaar made use of those reports?

After having read these letters, the Resident said that, if Havelaar chose to recall these documents, it would be agreeable to *him* to consider them as not written, which Havelaar firmly but politely refused.

Having in vain tried to move him to this, the Resident said that he must investigate the charges, and that he had therefore to request Havelaar to summon the witnesses in support of the accusation he had brought against the Regent.

Ye poor creatures, whose sides had been wounded by the thorns in the ravine, how anxiously would your hearts have beaten if you could have heard this request!

And you, poor Verbrugge, you first witness, chief witness, *ex officio* witness, a witness in virtue of office and oath, a witness who had already borne witness on paper, which lay there on the table under Havelaar's hand! . . . .

Havelaar replied :—

"Mr. Resident,—I am Assistant Resident of Lebak; I have promised to protect the population from extortion and tyranny; I accuse the Regent and his son-in-law ot Parang-Koodjang; I will prove my accusation as soon as that opportunity is given me, which I proposed in my letters. *I* am guilty of slander if this accusation is false!"

How freely Verbrugge breathed again !

And how strange the Resident thought Havelaar's words.

The conversation lasted long. With politeness,—for Slymering was polite and well-bred,—he urged Havelaar to turn aside from such wrong principles; but with as much politeness the latter remained immoveable. The result was, that the Resident had to yield, in saying as a threat, what was to Havelaar a victory, that he should be compelled to bring the matter under the notice of the Government.

The meeting was ended. The Resident paid the visit to the Regent, to put to him the questions already mentioned, and then dined at the scanty board of the Havelaars, after which he returned in great haste to Serang, " because——he——had——still——so——much——to——do."

The next day Havelaar received a letter from the Resident of Bantam, the contents of which may be understood from the reply, of which I here give a copy :—

" No. 93.—*Private.*

     " RANKAS-BETONG, 28*th February* 1856.

" I have had the honour to receive your missive of the " 26th inst. (La. O, private), containing mainly the fol- " lowing :—

"That you had reasons for not accepting the proposals
"made in both my official letters of the 24th and 25th
"inst., Nos. 88 and 91 ;

"That you had desired a previous confidential commu-
"nication ;

"That you do *not* approve of my transactions described
"in both those letters ;

"And lastly, some orders.

"I have now the honour again to assert, as I did ver-
"bally in the meeting of the day before yesterday :—

"That I fully respect the legality of your power as re-
"gards deciding whether to accept my proposition or
"not :—

"That the *orders* received shall with exactness be
"obeyed—with self-sacrifice, if need be, as if you were
"present to witness all I do or say, or, more properly, all
"I do *not* do or do *not* say.

"I know that you place confidence in my good faith in
"this matter.

"But I take the liberty solemnly to protest against the
"least semblance of disapprobation of any action, any
"word, any phrase, done, spoken, or written by me in this
"matter. I am convinced that I have done my *duty* :—
"in my object and in the manner of executing it quite my
"*duty ;—nothing but my duty*, without the least deviation.

"I have long pondered before acting (that is : before
"*examining, reporting,* and *proposing*), and if I have been

" to a certain extent mistaken in anything,—my fault was
" not precipitancy.

" In the same circumstances I should do again——yet
" a little quicker——exactly, exactly the same.

" Even if it happened that a higher power than yours
" disapproved anything which I did,—(except perhaps the
" peculiarity of my style, which is a part of myself, a de-
" fect for which I am as little responsible as a stammerer
" for *his* defect;)—even if that happened . . . . but no,
" that cannot be, even if it were so, ... I have done
" my DUTY.

" Certainly I am sorry—yet without being astonished,
" —that you judge differently of this; and as far as re-
" gards myself, I should rely upon what appears to me to
" be a slight——but there is a question about *a principle,*
" and I have conscientious reasons which require that it
" shall be decided which opinion is correct, *yours* or *mine.*

" Serve otherwise than I served at Lebak, I cannot.

" If the Government desires to be served otherwise, then
" I shall be obliged as an honest man to ask the Government
" to discharge me;—then I must endeavour, at the age of
" thirty-six years, to commence a new career;—then I,
" after seventeen years, after seventeen heavy difficult
" years of service as a functionary, after having devoted
" the best of my lifetime to what I considered to be my
" duty, then I must again ask society for bread, if it will
" give me bread, for my wife and child—bread in exchange

" for thoughts—bread perhaps in exchange for labour with
" spade or wheelbarrow, if the strength of my arm is ap-
" proved more than that of my soul.

" But I cannot and will not believe that your opinion is
" shared by his Excellency the Governor-General, and I
" am therefore compelled, before I pass to the bitter ex-
" treme of what I wrote in the last paragraph, to beg you
" respectfully to propose to the Government:

" To order the Resident of Bantam to approve so far the
" transactions of the Assistant Resident of Lebak, including
" his letters of the 24th and 25th inst., Nos. 88 and 91;—

" Or:

" To call the above-mentioned Assistant Resident to
" account on the points of disapprobation to be given by
" the Resident of Bantam.

" I have, finally, the honour to give you the grateful
" assurance that if *anything* could bring me back from my
" long calculated, and calm but fervently adhered to prin-
" ciples in this,—it would have been indeed the polite,
" engaging manner in which you, at the meeting of the
" day before yesterday, opposed those principles.—The
" Assistant Resident of Lebak,

(Signed)   "MAX HAVELAAR."

Without deciding as to the correctness of the suspicions
of Slotering's widow, concerning the cause which made
her children orphans, and only accepting what may be

2 B

proved, that there was a strong connexion in Lebak
between fulfilment of duty and poison—even if that
connexion existed only in public opinion—yet it may be
conceived, that Max and Tine passed sorrowful days after
the visit of the Resident. I believe that I need not paint
the anguish of a mother, who, when offering food to her
child, has continually to ask whether she is not perhaps
murdering her darling?

And certainly little Max was an "adored child," who
had stayed away seven years after the marriage, as if the
rogue knew that it was no advantage to come into the
world as the son of such parents.

Twenty-nine long days had Havelaar to wait before the
Governor-General communicated with him, ...

But we are not yet so far.

A short time after the vain endeavour to move Havelaar
to withdraw his letters, or to betray the poor people who
had confided in his magnanimity, Verbrugge entered
Havelaar's house. The good man was deadly pale, and
had some difficulty in speaking.

"I have been with the Regent," he said; "it is scandalous, . . . but do not betray me!"

"What? What must I not betray?"

"Do you pledge me your word to make no use of what
I shall tell you?"

"More *halfness*," said Havelaar; "but well! I pledge
my word."

And then Verbrugge told Havelaar what the reader knows already,—that the Resident had asked the Regent, if the latter could say anything against the Assistant Resident, and had quite unexpectedly given him money. At the same time Verbrugge knew it from the Regent himself, who had asked him what reasons the Resident could have had for this.

Havelaar was indignant, but he had pledged his word.

The next day Verbrugge returned and said that Duclari had told him how ignoble it was to leave Havelaar, who had to fight *such* opponents, so completely alone, whereupon Verbrugge released him from his pledge.

" Very well," said Havelaar, " write it down."

Verbrugge wrote it down. This declaration is likewise before me.

The reader will have long understood why I renounced so cheaply any pretensions to authenticity in the history of Saïdjah.

It was touching to observe how Verbrugge—timorous before he was awakened by the reproaches of Duclari—dared to trust Havelaar's pledged word, in a matter which so induced violation of it !

And another thing. Years have passed since the events which I relate. Havelaar has suffered much during this time, he has seen the suffering of his household—the documents which lie before me bear witness of this, and it

seems that he has waited. . . . I give the following note
from his hand :—" I read in the newspapers that Mr.
" Slymering has been made Knight of the Order of the
" Dutch Lion. He appears to be now Resident of Djocjo-
" carta. I can therefore now speak of the affairs of Lebak
" without danger to Verbrugge."

CHAPTER XX.

[COMPOSED BY STERN.]

IT was evening. Tine was reading in the inner gallery; and Havelaar was drawing an embroidery pattern; little Max was putting together a puzzle picture, and was getting angry because he could not find that red lady's body.

"Will it be right so, Tine?" asked Havelaar. "See, I have made this palm a little larger . . . it is exactly Hogarth's line of beauty."

"Yes, Max! but these lace-holes are too near each other."

"Are they? And the others?"

"Max! do let me see your trousers, . . . have you that stripe?"

"Ah! I remember where you embroidered that, Tine!"

"Not I—where then?"

"It was at the Hague, when Max was ill, and we were so frightened because the physician said that he had such an uncommonly shaped head, and that so much care was required to prevent congestion of the brain . . . then you were busy with that stripe."

Tine went and kissed the little one.

"I have found her stomach, I have found her stomach!" cried the little boy gaily; and the red lady was complete.

"Whose bedtime is it?" asked the mother.

"Mine; but I have not yet supped," said little Max.

"You shall have some supper first of course."

And she rose up, and gave him his simple supper, which she seemed to have fetched out of a well-secured cupboard in her room; for the noise of many locks had been heard.

"What are you giving him?" asked Havelaar.

"Oh, don't be uneasy! It is biscuit out of the tin box from Batavia, and the sugar too has been kept under lock and key."

Havelaar's thoughts turned again to the point where they had been interrupted.

"Do you know," he continued, "that we have not yet paid that doctor's bill? . . ."

"Oh! that is very hard!"

"Dear Max, we live so economically here, we shall soon be able to pay all: moreover, you will certainly soon be appointed Resident, and then all will be arranged in a little time."

"That is exactly the thing that makes me sad," said Havelaar. "I should be so unwilling to leave Lebak. . . .

I will explain that to you. Don't you believe that we loved our Max more after his illness? Now, it appears to me that I shall love poor Lebak still more, after it has recovered from the cancer from which it has suffered for so many years. The thought of promotion frightens me, and yet on the other side, when I think again that we have debts. . . ."

"All will be right, Max! even if you had to go from here, then you could help Lebak afterwards on being made Governor-General."

Then came wild lines in Havelaar's pattern——there was anger in those flowers, . . . those strips were sharp, angular, crossing each other. . . . Tine understood that she had said something wrong.

" Dear Max !" she began kindly.

"A curse on it! . . . Will you have them starve so long? . . . . Can *you* live on *sand?*"

" Dear Max! . . ."

But he jumped up from his chair, and there was no more drawing that evening.

He went up and down in the inner gallery, and at last he spoke in a tone which would have sounded rough and hard to every stranger, but which was thought of quite differently by Tine.

" A curse on this indifference, this shameful indifference! Here I have waited a month for justice, and meanwhile the poor people are suffering terribly. The Regent seems

to calculate upon nobody daring to take it up against him
—look . . . ."

He went into his office, and came back with a letter in
his han   a letter which lies before me, reader !

" Look, in this letter, he dares to make me proposals
about the kind of labour which he intends to have done
by men whom he has summoned unlawfully . . . . is not
that shamelessness going too far ?   And do you know who
these persons are ?   They are women with little children,
with sucklings ; women who are pregnant, who have been
driven from Parang-Koodjang to the capital, to work for
him——there are no more men !   And they have nothing
to eat, and they sleep on the road, and eat sand . . . . Can
you eat sand ?   Must they eat sand till I am Governor-
General ?

" Curse it ! . . . ."

Tine knew very well with whom alone Max was angry,
when he spoke thus to her whom he loved.

" And," continued Havelaar, " that is all on *my* responsibility.   If at this moment some of these poor creatures
are wandering there outside, and seeing the light of our
lamps, will say : ' There lives the wretch who ought to
protect us ; there he sits quietly with wife and child, and
draws embroidery patterns, while we lie here like dogs on
the road, and starve with our children !'   Yes, I hear it,
I hear it ; that cry for vengeance upon my head ! . . . .
here, Max, here ! . . . ."

And he kissed the child with a wildness which frightened it.

"My child, if they tell you that I am a wretch, who had no courage to do justice, that so many mothers have died by my fault; if they tell you that the neglect of your father stole away the bliss of your life . . . . Max, bear witness how I suffered!"

And he burst into tears, which Tine kissed away. Then she put little Max to bed—a mat of straw—and when she returned found Havelaar in conversation with Verbrugge and Duclari, who had just come in. The conversation was about the expected decision of the Government.

"I understand very well that the Resident is in a difficult position," said Duclari. "He cannot advise the Government to accept your proposals, for then too much would be brought to light. I have been long in Bantam, and know much about it,—more than you, Mr. Havelaar! I was here as sub-lieutenant, and in that position one hears things that the native does not dare to tell the functionaries. But if now, after an open investigation, all this comes to light, the Governor-General will summon the Resident to account for it, and ask him how it is that he has not discovered in two years what was obvious to you immediately? He must, therefore, prevent that investigation.

"I have considered that," replied Havelaar, "and put on my guard by his endeavours to move the Regent to

say something against me, which seems to show that he
will try to remove the question, for instance, by accusing
me of . . . . I know not what; I have covered myself
against that by sending copies of my letters direct to the
Government. In one of these letters, I beg to be called
to account, if perhaps it should be pretended that I had
done something wrong. If, now, the Resident of Bantam
attacks *me*, no decision can be made, according to justice,
before I have been heard—that is allowed even to a
criminal—and I have done nothing wrong. . . . ."

"There is the post!" said Verbrugge.

Yes, it was the post!—the post that brought the following letter from the Governor-General of the Dutch Indies
to Havelaar, *late* Assistant Resident of Lebak :—

"*Official.*—No. 54.   "BUITENZORG, 23d *March* 1856.

"The manner in which you have acted on the discovery
"or supposition of wrong-doing on the part of the chiefs
"in the district of Lebak, and your attitude towards your
"superior, the Resident of Bantam, have excited, in a high
"degree, my displeasure. In your acts there is not only
"a want of the deliberate judgment, caution, and prudence
"so indispensable to a functionary intrusted with power
"in the interior of Java (*sic*), but also notions of insubor-
"dination to your immediate superior. Only a few days
"after your appointment to your present office, you made
"the head of the native Government of Lebak the subject

" of irritating examinations, without first consulting (*sic*) the
" Resident. In these examinations you found cause, with-
" out substantiating your accusations against that chief
" by facts (*sic*), much less by proofs, to make proposals
" which tended to subject a native functionary of the rank
" of the Regent of Lebak (a man of sixty years, but still
" a zealous servant, related to neighbouring influential
" Regents, and of whom favourable testimony has always
" been given) to a morally quite annihilating treatment.
" Moreover, you have, when the Resident did not feel
" inclined to give his consent to your proposals, refused to
" satisfy the just desire of your superior, that you should
" say openly what you knew of the actions of the native
" Government of Lebak.

" Such conduct merits all disapprobation, and sanctions
" belief in your incapacity to bear office in the interior
" Government of Java. I am therefore obliged to dismiss
" you from your employment as Assistant Resident of
" Lebak.

" Yet, in consideration of the favourable reports received
" formerly of you, I have not found cause to deprive you
" of the prospect of again getting a situation in the
" Government of the interior. I have therefore given
" you the temporary appointment of Assistant Resident
" of Ngawie. On your behaviour in this office, it will
" entirely depend whether you remain a functionary in
" the service of the Government."

And beneath that stood the name of the man on whose " *zeal, capacity, and good faith,*" the King said that he could rely, when he signed his appointment as Governor-General of the Dutch Indies.

" We go from here, dear Tine," said Havelaar; and he gave the letter to Verbrugge, who read the document with Duclari.

Verbrugge had tears in his eyes, but did not speak. Duclari, a very polite and well-bred man, burst out with a wild curse.

" G——, I have seen rogues and thieves in the Government here, . . . they have gone from here with honours, and to *you* they write such a letter!"

" It is nothing," said Havelaar; " the Governor-General is an honest man, . . . he must be deceived; though he could have guarded himself against that deceit, by first hearing me. But I will go to him, and show him how matters stand here . . . he will do justice, I am certain of it."

" But if you go to Ngawie . . . ."

" I know this for certain. The Regent of Ngawie is related to the Regent of Bantam. I should have to do the same at Ngawie that I have done here : that would be a useless journey.

" Moreover, it was impossible for me to serve the trial as if I had behaved ill . . . . and, finally, I see that to put an end to all this deceit, I can no longer be a functionary.

As functionary, there are too many persons between me
and the Government who have an interest in denying the
misery of the population. There are other reasons that
prevent me from going to Ngawie. There was no vacancy
there; there has been one made for me——Look here!"

And he showed in the Javanese newspaper, which had
come by the same post, that indeed, in the same decree of
the Government whereby he was appointed Assistant
Resident of Ngawie, the Assistant Resident of that place
was appointed to another district where there was a
vacancy.

"Do you know why I have to go to Ngawie, and not to
the district where there was a vacancy?

"I will tell you——the Resident of Madioen, to which
Ngawie belongs, is the *brother-in-law of the late Resident of
Bantam.* I have said that such scandalous things went on
here,——that the Regent had had such bad examples . . ."

"Ah," cried Verbrugge and Duclari at the same time.
They understood why Havelaar was transferred to Ngawie
in particular, to be tried if he would perhaps correct himself.

"And there is still another reason why I cannot go
there," said he. "The present Governor-General will
soon resign,——I do not know his successor, nor what I
may expect of him.[1] In order to do something in time for

[1] In the original MS. the author wrote : " I *know* his successor, I
know what I may expect of him." This was changed against the will

those poor people, I must speak to the present Governor before his departure, and if I went now to Ngawie, that would be impossible . . . . Tine!"

"Dear Max!"

"You have courage, have you not?"

"Max! you know I have courage when I am with you."

"Good!"

He went and wrote the following, in his own opinion an example of eloquence :—

"RANKAS-BETONG, 29th *March* 1856.

"*To the Governor-General of the Dutch Indies.*

"I have had the honour to receive the official letter of "your Excellency of the 23d inst., No. 54. In reply to "that document, I feel constrained to beg your Excellency "to grant me an honourable discharge from the service of "the Government.

(Signed)   "MAX HAVELAAR."

It needed not so long a time at Buitenzorg to grant the asked-for discharge, as was needed to decide how Havelaar's accusation could be turned away. For the latter a month was required, and the news of the discharge arrived in a few days at Lebak.

and without the knowledge of the author. We give this note with the authorization of the author.

"God be praised," said Tine, "that you can be your own self at last."

Havelaar received no instructions to surrender the Government to Verbrugge; he therefore awaited his successor. The latter was a long time in coming, because he had to travel from a remote corner of Java. After waiting three weeks, the *ex-officio* Assistant Resident of Lebak, who had, however, still acted as such, wrote the following letter to the Controller Verbrugge :—

" No. 153.

"RANKAS-BETONG, 15th *April* 1856.

" *To the Controller of Lebak.*

"You know that I have received at my own request an " honourable discharge from the service of the Government " by decree of 4th inst., No. 4. Perhaps I should have " acted rightly, if, on the receipt of this decree, I had re- " signed my office of Assistant Resident immediately; as " it seems to be an anomaly to fulfil a function without " being a functionary.

"Yet I received no instructions to surrender my office, " and partly from the idea of the obligation not to leave " my post without being duly relieved, partly from causes " of subordinate interest, I waited for the arrival of my " successor, thinking that that functionary would arrive " soon, at least this month.

"Now I hear from you that my successor may not be

" expected so soon——you have, as I think, heard this
" news at Serang,—and at the same time that the Resident
" was astonished that I, in the very peculiar position in
" which I am, have not yet asked to be allowed to transfer
" the Government to you.   Nothing could be more agree-
" able to me than this news, for I need not assure you,
" that I, who have declared myself unable to serve other-
" wise than I have done, who have been punished for this
" way of serving with censure,[1] with a ruinous and dis-
" creditable transfer, with an order to betray the poor
" men who confided in my good faith, with the choice also
" between dishonour and starvation . . . . that I had to
" consider with pains and care, everything if it was in
" harmony with my duty, and that the most simple matter
" was difficult for *me*, placed as I was between my con-
" science and the principles of the Government, to which
" I owe fidelity as long as I am not freed from my func-
" tions.   This difficulty showed itself principally in the
" reply which I had to give to *plaintiffs*.

     " I had once promised to betray nobody to the rancour
" of his chiefs ;—once I had, imprudently enough, given
" my word for the justice of the Government.

     " The poor population could not know that this promise
" and this bail had been denied, and that I, poor and impot-
" ent, stood alone with my desire for justice and humanity.

     " And people went on complaining. It was painful,

---

[1] Literally—" For the manner in which I served."

" after the receipt of the missive of 23d March, to sit there
" as a supposed refuge, as a powerless protector.

" It was heart-rending to hear the complaints of ill-
" treatment, extortion, poverty, hunger, whilst I myself
" had, with a wife and child, to meet hunger and poverty !

" Neither could I betray the Government. I might not
" say to these poor people : ' Go and suffer, for it is the
" *will* of the Government that you should suffer extortion.'
" I might not avow my impotence, one as it was with the
" shame and unconscionableness of the Governor-General's
" counsellors.

" Here is what I replied :

" ' I cannot help you immediately, but I will go to
" Batavia ; I will speak to the Governor about your
" misery. He is just, and he will assist you. Go now
" quietly to your home ; do not oppose, do not remove—
" wait patiently : I think, ... I hope that justice will
" be done !'

" So I thought, ashamed as I was of the violation of my
" promise of help, to bring my ideas in harmony with my
" duty to the Government, which *pays me still this month*,
" and I would have continued thus till the arrival of my
" successor, if a particular occurrence had not obliged me
" to-day to put an end to this equivocal position. Seven
" persons had complained. I gave them the above-men-
" tioned reply. They returned to their homes. The dis-
" trict chief met them on the way. He must have for-

" bidden them to leave their village again, and taken away
" (as I am told) their clothes, to oblige them to remain at
" home. One of them escaped, came to me *again* and
" declared '*that he did not dare to return to his village.*'

" What I ought to reply to *this* man, I did not know.

" I could *not* protect him;——I *might* not avow my im-
" potence; I *would* not prosecute the accused chief, because
" this would have appeared as if the matter had been
" picked up by me, *pour le besoin de ma cause* I did not
" know what to do. . . . .

" I charge you, until further instructions from the Resi-
" dent of Bantam, with the Government of the district of
" Lebak, from to-morrow morning.—The Assistant Resi-
" dent of Lebak,

(Signed)   " Max Havelaar."

Then Havelaar departed with wife and child from
Rankas-Betong. He refused all escort. Duclari and Verbrugge were deeply touched at the leave-taking. Max was
likewise moved; above all, when he found at the first
stage a great number of persons who had gone secretly
from Rankas-Betong to bid him a last farewell.

At Serang, the family was received into the house of
Mr. Slymering, with the ordinary Indian hospitality.

In the evening many visitors came to the Resident.
They said they had come to say farewell to Havelaar, and
Havelaar received many an eloquent shake of the hand . . .

But he had to go to Batavia to speak to the Governor-General.

When they arrived there, he sought for an audience. This was refused him, because his Excellency had a pain in his foot.

Havelaar waited till the foot was cured. Then he again sought an audience.

His Excellency " had so much to do that he had been obliged to refuse an audience even to the Director-General of Finance, and could not see Havelaar."

Havelaar waited till his Excellency should have struggled through all this ; meanwhile he felt something like jealousy for the persons who had to help his Excellency in his labour, for he liked to work quickly and hard, and generally so much business disappeared under his hand. This was, however, out of the question. Havelaar's labour was heavier than labour. . . . He waited.

He waited. At last he again sought an audience. He received an answer that his Excellency could not see him, as he had too much to do, being on the point of departure.

Max sought the favour of his Excellency to be heard for half-an-hour as soon as there should be some space between two " businesses."

At last he heard that his Excellency would depart the next day ! That was a thunderbolt for him. Still he believed with spasmodic energy that the resigning Governor

was an honest man, and had been deceived. A quarter of
an hour would have sufficed to prove the justice of his
cause, and it appeared that this quarter of an hour would
not be granted him.

I find among Havelaar's papers the copy of a letter
which he seems to have written to the retiring Governor-
General, on the last evening before his departure to the
mother country. In the corner I find the words written
in pencil "*not exact,*" which gives me to understand that
some phrases were changed in copying. I make this
observation in order that no doubt may arise regarding
the *authenticity* of the *other official documents* which I have
communicated, and which have all been signed by another
hand for exact copy; I mention this, because of the want
of literal conformity with this document. Perhaps he
to whom this letter was addressed may feel inclined to
make public the exact text; then one may see how far
Havelaar deviated from this copy.

" BATAVIA, 23*d May* 1856.

" YOUR EXCELLENCY,---My official request, by missive
" of 28th February, to be heard on the affairs of Lebak,
" has remained unanswered.

" Neither has your Excellency thought fit to grant my
" repeated request for an audience.

" A functionary, who was ' favourably known to the
" Government ' (I quote your Excellency's own words),

" —one who has served his country in these regions for
" seventeen years,—one who not only never neglected his
" duty, but who conceived what was good with unexampled
" self-sacrifice, and who chose to sacrifice all for honour
" and duty,—such a one your Excellency has placed be-
" neath the criminal, for the criminal is at least *heard.*

" That they have deceived your Excellency with regard
" to me, I understand,—but that your Excellency did not
" catch the opportunity to escape from this deceit, I do
" not understand.   To-morrow your Excellency goes from
" here, and I may not let you depart without having said
" once more that I did my duty,—only my duty,—with
" judgment, with calmness, with humanity, with modera-
" tion, and with courage.

" The grounds on which is based the censure contained
" in your Excellency's missive of 23d March are *entirely*
" *invented and false.*   I can prove this, and it would have
" been proved already, if your Excellency had granted me
" half-an-hour's interview, if your Excellency could have
" found half-an-hour *to do justice.*

" This you could not; and an honest family has been
" ruined.

" Yet I do not complain of this.

" But your Excellency HAS SANCTIFIED THE SYSTEM OF
" ABUSE OF POWER, OF PLUNDER AND MURDER, BY WHICH
" THE POOR JAVANESE SUFFER, and I complain of that.

" That is what I complain of !

" Your Excellency, blood cleaves to the money saved
" out of the Indian salary thus earned !   Once more I beg
" for a moment's interview, be it this night, be it early to-
" morrow !   And again I do not ask this for myself, but
" for the cause which I defend, the cause of justice and
" humanity, which is, at the same time, the cause of good
" policy.

" If your Excellency can reconcile it with your con-
" science, to depart from here without hearing me, mine
" will be quiet in the persuasion that I have endeavoured
" all that I could to prevent the sad bloody events, which
" will soon be the consequence of the self-willed ignorance
" in which the Government is left as regards the popu-
" lation. . . . .

(Signed)   " MAX HAVELAAR."

Havelaar waited that evening. He waited the whole
night. He had hoped that perhaps anger at the tone of
his letter would bring about what he had tried in vain to
obtain by moderation and patience.

His hope was vain. The Governor-General departed
without having heard Havelaar . . . .

Another Excellency had retired to the mother country
to rest !

Havelaar wandered about poor and neglected. He
sought *   *   *   *   *   *

Enough, my good Stern! *I*, Multatuli, take up the pen. You are not called upon to write Havelaar's biography. I created you: I brought you over from Hamburg: I taught you good Dutch in a very short time: I made you kiss Louise Rosemeyer, of the Rosemeyers, who trade in sugar . . . . it is enough,——Stern! you may go.

"This Shawlman and his wife . . . ."

Stop!! miserable spawn of dirty covetousness and blasphemous hypocrisy! I created you :——you have grown into a monster under my pen :——I am disgusted with my own creation . . . . choke yourself with coffee and begone!

Yes, I, MULTATULI, "who have suffered much,"——I take the pen. I do not make any excuses for the form of my book,——that form was thought proper to obtain my object. That object has a double end——

In the first place, I would bring forward something which may be preserved as a holy *poosaka* by "little Max" and his sister, when their parents have died of sheer want.——I would give to these children a testimonial from my own hand.

And in the second place, *I will be read!*   Yes, I will be read!   I will be read by statesmen, who are obliged to pay attention to the signs of the times; by men of letters, who must also peep into the book of which so many bad things are said; by merchants, who have an interest in the coffee-auctions; by lady's-maids, who read me for a few farthings; by Governors-General in retirement; by Ministers who have something to do; by the lackeys of these Excellencies; by mutes, who, "*more majorum,*" will say that I attack God Almighty, where I attack only the god which they made according to their own image; by the members of the Representative Chambers, who must know what happens in the extensive possessions over the sea, which belong to Holland. . . . .

Ay, I *shall* be read!

When I obtain this I shall be content.   For I did not intend to write well. . . . . I wished to write so as to be heard, and, as one who cries " Stop thief!" does not care about the style of his *impromptu* address to the public, I too am indifferent to criticism of the manner in which I cried *my* " Stop thief!"——

" The book is a medley; there is no order, nothing but a desire to make a sensation.   The style is bad; the author is inexperienced; no talent, no method." . . . .

Good! good! . . . . . all very well! . . . . . *but the Javanese are ill-treated!*

For, the merit of my book is this :—that *refutation* of its main features is *impossible*. And the greater the disapprobation of my book, the better I shall be pleased, for the chance of being *heard* will be so much the greater ;— and that is what I desire.

But you, whom I dare to interrupt in your business, or in your retirement, ye Ministers and Governors-General—do not calculate too much upon the inexperience of my pen. I could exercise it, and perhaps, by dint of some exertions, attain to that skill which would make the truth heard by the people. Then I should ask of that people a place in the Representative Chambers, were it only to protest against the certificates which are given *vice versa* by Indian functionaries.

To protest against the endless expeditions sent, and heroic deeds performed against poor, miserable creatures, whose ill-treatment has driven them to revolt.

To protest against the cowardice of general orders, that brand the honour of the nation, by invoking public charity on behalf of the victims of inveterate piracy.

It is true those rebels were reduced by starvation to skeletons, while those pirates could defend themselves.

And if that place were refused me, ... if I were still disbelieved . . . .

Then I should translate my book into the few languages that I know, and the many that I yet can learn, to put that question to Europe, which I have in vain put to Holland.

And in every capital such a refrain as this would be heard: "There is a band of robbers between Germany and the Scheldt!"

And if this were of no avail ? . . . .

Then I should translate my book into *Malay, Javanese, Soondanese, Alfoer, Boegi,* and *Battah.*

And I should sharpen *Klewangs,* the scimitars and the sabres, by rousing with warlike songs the minds of those martyrs whom *I* have promised to help——*I Multatuli* would do this!

Yes! delivery and help, *lawfully if possible;—lawfully with violence,* if need be.

And that would be very pernicious to the COFFEE AUCTIONS OF THE DUTCH TRADING COMPANY!

For I am no fly-rescuing poet, no soft dreamer, like the down-trodden Havelaar, who did his duty with the courage of a lion, and endured starvation with the patience of a marmot in winter.

This book is an introduction . . . .

I shall increase in strength and sharpness of weapons, according as it may be necessary.

Heaven grant that it may not be necessary ! . . . .

No, it *will* not be necessary ! For it is to thee I dedicate my book : WILLIAM THE THIRD, King, Grand Duke, Prince, . . . more than Prince, Grand Duke and King,

. . . . EMPEROR of the magnificent empire of INSULIND, which winds about the equator like a garland of emeralds ! . . . .

I ask THEE if it be thine IMPERIAL will that the Havelaars should be bespattered with the mud of Slymerings and Drystubbles; and that thy *more* than *thirty millions* of SUBJECTS far away should be *ill-treated and should suffer extortion* in THY name ?

EDINBURGH : T. CONSTABLE,
PRINTER TO THE QUEEN, AND TO THE UNIVERSITY

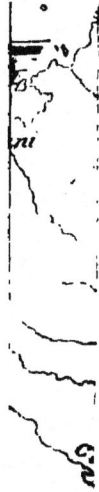

E

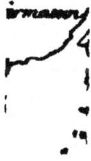

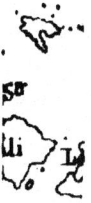

EDMONSTON & DOUGLAS'
LIST OF WORKS

————oOo————

Wanderings of a Naturalist in India,

The Western Himalayas, and Cashmere. By DR. A. L. ADAMS, of the 22d Regiment. 1 vol. 8vo, with illustrations, price 10s. 6d.

A Short American Tramp in the fall of 1864.

By the Editor of 'Life in Normandy.' 8vo, price 12s.

Memoir of Lieutenant-General Sir Ralph Abercromby, K.B.,

1793-1801. By his Son JAMES LORD DUNFERMLINE. 8vo, price 10s. 6d.

Essays and Tracts:

The Culture and Discipline of the Mind, and other Essays. By JOHN ABERCROMBIE, M.D., Late First Physician to the Queen for Scotland. New Edition. Fcap. 8vo, cloth, 3s. 6d.

The Malformations, Diseases, and Injuries of the Fingers

and Toes, and their Surgical Treatment. By THOMAS ANNANDALE, F.R.C.S., Assistant Surgeon, Royal Infirmary, Edinburgh. The Jacksonian Prize for the Year 1864. 1 vol. 8vo, with Illustrations, price 10s. 6d.

Odal Rights and Feudal Wrongs.

A Memorial for Orkney. By DAVID BALFOUR of Balfour and Trenaby. 8vo, price 6s.

Basil St. John.

An Autumn Tale. 1 vol. 8vo, price 12s.

By the Loch and River Side.

Forty Graphic Illustrations by a New Hand. Oblong folio, handsomely bound, 21s

Aunt Ailie.

Second Edition. By CATHARINE D. BELL, Author of 'Cousin Kate's Story,' 'Margaret Cecil,' etc. Fcap. 8vo, cloth, 3s. 6d.

Charlie and Ernest; or, Play and Work.

A Story of Hazlehurst School, with Four Illustrations by J. D. By M. BETHAM EDWARDS. Royal 16mo, 3s. 6d.

Homer and the Iliad.

In three Parts. By JOHN STUART BLACKIE, Professor of Greek in the University of Edinburgh. In 4 vols. demy 8vo, price 42s.

> PART   I.—HOMERIC DISSERTATIONS.
> II.—THE ILIAD IN ENGLISH VERSE.
> III.—COMMENTARY, PHILOLOGICAL AND ARCHÆOLOGICAL.

By the same Author.

On Democracy.

A Lecture delivered to the Working Men's Institute, Edinburgh. Sixth Edition, price 1s.

On Beauty.

Crown 8vo, cloth, 8s. 6d.

Lyrical Poems.

Crown 8vo, cloth, 7s. 6d.

On Greek Pronunciation.

Demy 8vo, 3s. 6d.

Memoirs of the Life, Writings, and Discoveries of Sir Isaac

Newton. By SIR DAVID BREWSTER, K.H., A.M., LL.D., D.C.L., F.R.S., etc., etc. With Portraits. New and Cheaper Edition, 2 vols. fcap. 8vo, cloth, 12s.

Works by Margaret Maria Gordon (nee Brewster).

LADY ELINOR MORDAUNT; or, Sunbeams in the Castle. Crown 8vo, cloth, 9s.

LETTERS FROM CANNES AND NICE. Illustrated by a Lady. 8vo, cloth, 12s.

WORK; or, Plenty to do and How to do it. Thirty-fourth thousand. Fcap. 8vo, cloth, 2s. 6d.

LITTLE MILLIE AND HER FOUR PLACES. Cheap Edition. Fiftieth thousand. Limp cloth, 1s.

SUNBEAMS IN THE COTTAGE; or, What Women may do. A narrative chiefly addressed to the Working Classes. Cheap Edition. Forty-first thousand. Limp cloth, 1s.

PREVENTION; or, An Appeal to Economy and Common-Sense. 8vo, 6d.

Works by Margaret Maria Gordon—*Continued.*

THE WORD AND THE WORLD. Price 2d.

LEAVES OF HEALING FOR THE SICK AND SORROWFUL. Fcap. 4to, cloth, 3s. 6d. Cheap Edition, limp cloth, 2s.

THE MOTHERLESS BOY; with an Illustration by J. NOEL PATON, R.S.A. Cheap Edition, limp cloth, 1s.

France under Richelieu and Colbert.

By J. H. BRIDGES, M.B., late Fellow of Oriel College, Oxford. In 1 vol. small 8vo, price 8s. 6d.

Memoirs of John Brown, D.D.

By the Rev. J. CAIRNS, D.D., Berwick, with Supplementary Chapter by his Son, JOHN BROWN, M.D. Fcap. 8vo, cloth, 9s. 6d.

Works by John Brown, M.D., F.R.S.E.

LOCKE AND SYDENHAM, with other Professional Papers. By JOHN BROWN, M.D. A New Edition in 1 vol. extra fcap. 8vo, price 7s. 6d.

HORÆ SUBSECIVÆ. Sixth Edition, in 1 vol. extra fcap. 8vo, price 7s. 6d.

LETTER TO THE REV. JOHN CAIRNS, D.D. Second Edition, crown 8vo, sewed, 2s.

ARTHUR H. HALLAM; Extracted from 'Horæ Subsecivæ.' Fcap. sewed, 2s.; cloth, 2s. 6d.

RAB AND HIS FRIENDS; Extracted from 'Horæ Subsecivæ.' Thirty-fifth thousand. Fcap. sewed, 6d.

MARJORIE FLEMING: A Sketch. Fifteenth thousand. Fcap. sewed, 6d.

OUR DOGS; Extracted from 'Horæ Subsecivæ.' Nineteenth thousand. Fcap. sewed, 6d.

RAB AND HIS FRIENDS. With Illustrations by George Harvey, R.S.A., J. Noel Paton, R.S.A., and J. B. New Edition, small quarto, cloth, price 3s. 6d.

"WITH BRAINS, SIR;" Extracted from 'Horæ Subsecivæ.' Fcap. sewed, 6d.

MINCHMOOR. Fcap. sewed, 6d.

JEEMS THE DOORKEEPER: A Lay Sermon. Price 6d.

THE ENTERKIN. Price 6d.

Lectures on the Atomic Theory, and Essays,

Scientific and Literary. By SAMUEL BROWN. 2 vols., crown 8vo, cloth, 15s.

The Biography of Samson

Illustrated and Applied. By the Rev. JOHN BRUCE, D.D., Minister of Free St. Andrew's Church, Edinburgh. Second Edition. 18mo, cloth, 2s.

My Indian Journal,

Containing descriptions of the principal Field Sports of India, with Notes on the Natural History and Habits of the Wild Animals of the Country—a visit to the Neilgherry Hills, and the Andaman and Nicobar Islands. By COLONEL WALTER CAMPBELL, author of 'The Old Forest Ranger.' 8vo, with Illustrations, price 16s.

Popular Tales of the West Highlands,

Orally Collected, with a translation by J. F. CAMPBELL. 4 vols., extra fcap., cloth, 32s.

Inaugural Address at Edinburgh,

April 2, 1866, by THOMAS CARLYLE, on being Installed as Rector of the University there. Price 1s.

Book-keeping,

Adapted to Commercial and Judicial Accounting, giving Systems of Book-keeping for Lawyers, Factors and Curators, Wholesale and Retail Traders, Newspapers, Insurance Offices, and Private House-keeping, etc. By F. H. CARTER, C.A. 8vo, cloth, price 10s.

Characteristics of Old Church Architecture, etc.,

In the Mainland and Western Islands of Scotland. 4to, with Illustrations, price 25s.

Ballads from Scottish History.

By NORVAL CLYNE. Fcap. 8vo, price 6s.

Life and Works of Rev. Thomas Chalmers, D.D., LL.D.

MEMOIRS OF THE REV. THOMAS CHALMERS. By Rev. W. Hanna, D.D., LL.D. 4 vols., 8vo, cloth, £2 : 2s.

—— Cheap Edition, 2 vols., crown 8vo, cloth, 12s.

POSTHUMOUS WORKS, 9 vols., 8vo—

Daily Scripture Readings, 3 vols., £1 : 11 : 6. Sabbath Scripture Readings, 2 vols., £1 : 1s. Sermons, 1 vol., 10s. 6d. Institutes of Theology, 2 vols., £1 : 1s. Prelections on Butler's Analogy, etc., 1 vol., 10s. 6d.

Sabbath Scripture Readings. Cheap Edition, 2 vols., crown 8vo, 10s.
Daily Scripture Readings. Cheap Edition, 2 vols., crown 8vo, 10s.

ASTRONOMICAL DISCOURSES, 1s. COMMERCIAL DISCOURSES, 1s.

SELECT WORKS, in 12 vols., crown 8vo, cloth, per vol., 6s.

Lectures on the Romans, 2 vols. Sermons, 2 vols. Natural Theology, Lectures on Butler's Analogy, etc., 1 vol. Christian Evidences, Lectures on Paley's Evidences, etc., 1 vol. Institutes of Theology, 2 vols. Political Economy; with Cognate Essays, 1 vol. Polity of a Nation, 1 vol. Church and College Establishments, 1 vol. Moral Philosophy, Introductory Essays, Index, etc., 1 vol.

'Christopher North;'

A Memoir of John Wilson, late Professor of Moral Philosophy in the University of Edinburgh. Compiled from Family Papers and other sources, by his daughter, MRS. GORDON. Third Thousand. In 2 vols. crown 8vo, price 24s., with Portrait, and graphic Illustrations.

Chronicle of Gudrun;

A Story of the North Sea. From the mediæval German. By EMMA LETHERBROW. With frontispiece by J. NOEL PATON, R.S.A. New Edition for Young People, price 5s.

Of the Light of Nature,

A Discourse by NATHANIEL CULVERWELL, M.A. Edited by JOHN BROWN, D.D., with a critical Essay on the Discourse by John Cairns, D.D. 8vo, cloth, 12s.

Dainty Dishes.

Receipts collected by LADY HARRIET ST. CLAIR. Sixth edition, with many new Receipts. 1 vol. crown 8vo. Price 7s. 6d.

"Well worth buying, especially by that class of persons who, though their incomes are small, enjoy out-of-the-way and recherché delicacies."—*Times.*

The Annals of the University of Edinburgh.

By ANDREW DALZEL, formerly Professor of Greek in the University of Edinburgh; with a Memoir of the Compiler, and Portrait after Raeburn. In 2 vols. demy 8vo, price 21s.

Gisli the Outlaw.

From the Icelandic. By G. W. DASENT, D.C.L. 1 vol. small 4to, with Illustrations, price 7s. 6d.

The Story of Burnt Njal;

Or, Life in Iceland at the end of the Tenth Century. From the Icelandic of the Njals Saga. By GEORGE WEBBE DASENT, D.C.L. In 2 vols. 8vo, with Map and Plans, price 28s.

Popular Tales from the Norse,

With an Introductory Essay on the origin and diffusion of Popular Tales. Second Edition, enlarged. By GEORGE WEBBE DASENT, D.C.L. Crown 8vo, 10s. 6d.

Select Popular Tales from the Norse.

For the use of Young People. By G. W. DASENT, D.C.L. New Edition, with Illustrations. Crown 8vo, 6s.

On the Application of Sulphurous Acid Gas

to the Prevention, Limitation, and Cure of Contagious Diseases. By JAMES DEWAR, M.D. Eighth edition, price 1s.

The Fifty Years' Struggle of the Scottish Covenanters,

1638-88. By JAMES DODDS. Third Edition, fcap., cloth, 5s.

The Last Years of Mary of Lorraine,

1557 to 1560. By JAMES DODDS, author of 'The Fifty Years' Struggle of the Scottish Covenanters.'

Memoir of Thomas Drummond, R.A., F.R.A.S.,

Under-Secretary to the Lord-Lieutenant of Ireland, 1835 to 1840. By JOHN F. M'LENNAN, M.A. 1 vol. demy 8vo, price 15s.

Studies in European Politics.

By M. E. GRANT DUFF, Member for the Elgin District of Burghs. 1 vol. 8vo. Price 10s. 6d.

"We have no hesitation in saying that there is no work in the English Language which has anything like the same value to persons who wish to understand the recent history and present position of the countries described."—*Saturday Review.*

Inaugural Address

Delivered to the University of Aberdeen, on his Installation as Rector, March 22, 1867, by MOUNTSTUART E. GRANT DUFF, Member for the Elgin District of Burghs. Price 1s.

Notes on Scotch Bankruptcy Law and Practice.

By GEORGE AULDJO ESSON, Accountant in Bankruptcy in Scotland. Second edition, price 2s. 6d.

Karl's Legacy.

By the Rev. J. W. EBSWORTH. 2 vols. ex. fcap. 8vo. Price 6s. 6d.

Social Life in Former Days;

Chiefly in the Province of Moray. Illustrated by letters and family papers. By E. DUNBAR DUNBAR, late Captain 21st Fusiliers. 2 vols. demy 8vo., price 19s. 6d.

Veterinary Medicines; their Actions and Uses.

By FINLAY DUN. Third Edition, revised and enlarged. 8vo, price 12s.

The Story of Waldemar Krone's Youth.

A Novel. By H. F. EWALD. 2 vols. crown 8vo, price 16s.

The Secret of Happiness.

A Novel. By ERNEST FEYDEAU. 2 vols. fcap. 8vo, price 7s.

Forest Sketches.

Deer-stalking and other Sports in the Highlands fifty years ago. 8vo, with Illustrations by Gourlay Steell, price 15s.

L'Histoire d'Angleterre. Par M. LAMÉ FLEURY. 18mo, cloth, 2s. 6d.

L'Histoire de France. Par M. LAMÉ FLEURY. 18mo, cloth, 2s. 6d.

Christianity viewed in some of its Leading Aspects.

By Rev. A. L. R. FOOTE, Author of 'Incidents in the Life of our Saviour.' Fcap., cloth, 3s.

Frost and Fire;

Natural Engines, Tool-Marks, and Chips, with Sketches drawn at Home and Abroad by a Traveller. Re-issue, containing an additional Chapter. In 2 vols. 8vo, with Maps and numerous Illustrations on Wood, price 21s.

"A very Turner among books, in the originality and delicious freshness of its style, and the truth and delicacy of the descriptive portions. For some four-and-twenty years he has traversed half our northern hemisphere by the least frequented paths; and everywhere, with artistic and philosophic eye, has found something to describe—here in tiny trout-stream or fleecy cloud, there in lava-flow or ocean current, or in the works of nature's giant sculptor—ice."—*Reader*.

Clinical Medicine.

Observations recorded at the Bedside, with Commentaries. By W. T. GAIRDNER, M.D., Professor of the Practice of Physic in the University of Glasgow. 8vo, 742 pp., with numerous Engravings on wood, 12s. 6d.

By the same Author.

Medicine and Medical Education. 12mo, cloth, price 2s. 6d.

Clinical and Pathological Notes on Pericarditis. 8vo, sewed, price 1s.

A Girl's Romance.

1 vol. ex. fcap. cloth, price 6s.

Camille.

By MADAME DE GASPARIN, Author of 'The Near and Heavenly Horizons.' 1 vol. fcap. 8vo, price 3s. 6d.

By the Seaside.

By MADAME DE GASPARIN, Author of 'The Near and Heavenly Horizons.' 1 vol. fcap. 8vo, price 3s. 6d.

Great Harefield.

A new Novel by a new Writer. 1 vol. small 8vo, price 12s.

"A book with a great deal of cleverness in it. Nearly all the satirical touches—and they sparkle everywhere—are keen, truthful, and brilliant."—*Star*.

An Ecclesiastical History of Scotland,

From the Introduction of Christianity to the Present Time. By GEORGE GRUB, A.M. In 4 vols. 8vo, 42s. Fine Paper Copies, 52s. 6d.

The Earlier Years of our Lord's Life on Earth.

By the Rev. WILLIAM HANNA, D.D., LL.D. Extra fcap. 8vo, price 5s.

The Ministry in Galilee.

By the Rev. WILLIAM HANNA, D.D., LL.D.   1 vol. ex. fcap. 8vo.

The Last Day of our Lord's Passion.

By the Rev. WILLIAM HANNA, D.D., LL.D   46th thousand, extra fcap. 8vo, price 5s.

The Forty Days after our Lord's Resurrection.

By the Rev. WILLIAM HANNA, D.D., LL.D.   Extra fcap. 8vo, price 5s.

The Passion Week.

By the Rev. WILLIAM HANNA, D.D., LL.D.   Extra fcap. 8vo, price 5s.

The Healing Art, the Right Hand of the Church;

Or, Practical Medicine an Essential Element in the Christian System.   Crown 8vo cloth, price 5s.

Hidden Depths.

2 vols. crown 8vo, price 21s.

"This book is not a work of fiction, in the ordinary acceptation of the term : if it were, it would be worse than useless, for the hidden depths, of which it reveals a glimpse, are not fit subjects for a romance."—*Preface.*

Notes of a Cruise of H.M.S. 'Fawn'

In the Western Pacific in the year 1862. By T. H. HOOD. Demy 8vo, with numerous Illustrations from Photographs, price 15s.

Homely Hints from the Fireside.

By the author of 'Little Things.'   Cheap Edition, limp cloth, 1s.

Herminius.

A Romance.   By I. E. S.   In 1 vol. fcap. 8vo, price 6s.

Sketches of Early Scotch History.

By COSMO INNES, F.S.A., Professor of History in the University of Edinburgh. 1. The Church ; its Old Organisation, Parochial and Monastic. 2. Universities. 3. Family History. 8vo, price 16s.

Concerning some Scotch Surnames.

By COSMO INNES, F.S.A., Professor of History in the University of Edinburgh. 1 vol. small 4to, cloth antique, 5s.

Death Scenes of Scottish Martyrs.

By HENRY INGLIS. Square 12mo, cloth, price 6s.

The New Picture Book.

Pictorial Lessons on Form, Comparison, and Number, for Children under Seven Years of Age. With Explanations by NICHOLAS BOHNY. 36 oblong folio coloured Illustrations. Price 7s. 6d.

Instructive Picture Books.

Folio, 7s. 6d. each.

"These Volumes are among the most instructive Picture-books we have seen, and we know of none better calculated to excite and gratify the appetite of the young for the knowledge of nature."—*Times*.

I.

The Instructive Picture Book. A few Attractive Lessons from the Natural History of Animals. By ADAM WHITE, late Assistant, Zoological Department, British Museum. With 58 folio coloured Plates. Seventh Edition, containing many new Illustrations by Mrs. BLACKBURN, J. STEWART, GOURLAY STEELL, and others.

II.

The Instructive Picture Book. Lessons from the Vegetable World. By the Author of 'The Heir of Redclyffe,' 'The Herb of the Field,' etc. Arranged by ROBERT M. STARK, Edinburgh. New Edition, with many New Plates.

III.

Instructive Picture Book. The Geographical Distribution of Animals, in a Series of Pictures for the use of Schools and Families. By the late Dr. GREVILLE. With descriptive letterpress by ADAM WHITE, late Assistant, Zoological Department, British Museum.

The History of Scottish Poetry,

From the Middle Ages to the Close of the Seventeenth Century. By the late DAVID IRVING, LL.D. Edited by JOHN AITKEN CARLYLE, M.D. With a Memoir and Glossary. Demy 8vo, 16s.

The Circle of Christian Doctrine;

A Handbook of Faith, framed out of a Layman's experience. By LORD KINLOCH, one of the Judges of the Supreme Court of Scotland. Third and Cheaper Edition. Fcap. 8vo, 2s. 6d.

Time's Treasure;

Or, Devout Thoughts for every Day of the Year. Expressed in verse. By LORD KINLOCH. Third and Cheaper Edition. Fcap. 8vo, price 3s. 6d.

Devout Moments.

By LORD KINLOCH. Price 6d.

Studies for Sunday Evening.

By LORD KINLOCH. Second Edition. Fcap. 8vo, price 4s. 6d.

The Philosophy of Ethics:

An Analytical Essay. By SIMON S. LAURIE, A.M., Author of 'The Fundamental Doctrine of Latin Syntax: being an Application of Psychology to Language.' 1 vol. demy 8vo, price 6s.

Supplemental Descriptive Catalogue of Ancient Scottish Seals.

By HENRY LAING. 1 vol. 4to, profusely illustrated, price £3 : 3s.

Life of Father Lacordaire.

By DORA GREENWELL. 1 vol. fcap. 8vo. Price 6s.

A Memoir of Lady Anna Mackenzie,

Countess of Balcarres, and' afterwards of Argyle, 1621-1706. By LORD ALEX-ANDER LINDSAY. Fcap. 8vo, price 3s. 6d.

The Reform of the Church of Scotland

In Worship, Government, and Doctrine. By ROBERT LEE, D.D., Professor of Biblical Criticism in the University of Edinburgh, and Minister of Greyfriars. Part I. Worship. Second Edition, fcap. 8vo, price 3s.

The Clerical Profession,

Some of its Difficulties and Hindrances. By ROBERT LEE, D.D. Price 6d.

The Early Races of Scotland and their Monuments.

By LIEUT.-COL. FORBES LESLIE. 2 vols. demy 8vo, profusely Illustrated, price 32s.

"This learned and elaborate book presents the closest and most satisfactory investigation of the character of the primitive races who inhabited the British Islands yet given to the public. Whether the readers agree with Colonel Leslie or not, they must of necessity allow that he has produced the most complete book on this subject that has ever been published."—*Daily News.*

Life in Normandy;

Sketches of French Fishing, Farming, Cooking, Natural History, and Politics, drawn from Nature. By an ENGLISH RESIDENT. Third Edition, 1 vol. crown 8vo, price 6s.

Specimens of Ancient Gaelic Poetry.

Collected between the years 1512 and 1529 by the REV. JAMES M'GREGOR, Dean of Lismore—illustrative of the Language and Literature of the Scottish Highlands prior to the Sixteenth Century. Edited, with a Translation and Notes, by the Rev. THOMAS MACLAUCHLAN. The Introduction and additional Notes by WILLIAM F. SKENE. 8vo, price 12s.

The Development of Science among Nations.

By BARON JUSTUS LIEBIG, F.R.S., President of the Royal Academy of Science, Member of the French Institute, etc. etc. Price 1s.

Little Ella and the Fire-King,

And other Fairy Tales. By M. W., with Illustrations by HENRY WARREN. Second Edition. 16mo, cloth, 3s. 6d. Cloth extra, gilt edges, 4s.

Love and Duty.

A Novel. By the Author of 'Basil St. John.' 1 vol. crown 8vo, price 12s.

Macvicar's (J. G., D.D.)

THE PHILOSOPHY OF THE BEAUTIFUL; price 6s. 6d. FIRST LINES OF SCIENCE SIMPLIFIED; price 5s. INQUIRY INTO HUMAN NATURE; price 7s. 6d.

Heroes of Discovery.

By SAMUEL MOSSMAN, Author of 'Our Australian Colonies,' 'China: its Inhabitants,' etc. 1 vol. crown 8vo, price 5s.

Medical Officers of the Navy.

Everthing about them. For the information of Medical Students, and of the Parents of Young Gentlemen intended for the Medical Profession. Price 1s.

The Correct Form of Shoes.

Why the Shoe Pinches. A contribution to Applied Anatomy. By HERMANN MEYER, M.D., Professor of Anatomy in the University of Zurich. Translated from the German by JOHN STIRLING CRAIG, L.R.C.P.E., L.R.C.S.E. Fcap., sewed, 6d.

The Herring:

Its Natural History and National Importance. By JOHN M. MITCHELL F.R.S.S.A., F.S.A.S., F.R.P.S., etc. Author of 'The Natural History of the Herring, considered in Connection with its Visits to the Scottish Coasts,' 'British Commercial Legislation,' 'Modern Athens and the Piræus,' etc. With Six Illustrations, 8vo, price 12s.

The Insane in Private Dwellings.

By ARTHUR MITCHELL, A.M., M.D., Deputy Commissioner in Lunacy for Scotland, etc. 8vo, price 4s. 6d.

Ancient Pillar-Stones of Scotland:

Their Significance and Bearing on Ethnology. By GEORGE MOORE, M.D. 1 vol. 8vo, price 6s. 6d.

North British Review.

Published Quarterly. Price 6s.

Reflections on the Relation of Recent Scientific Inquiries

to the Received Teaching of Scripture. By JAMES MONCREIFF, Esq., M.P., LL.D., Dean of the Faculty of Advocates. Price 1s.

The Extension of the Suffrage.

By JAMES MONCREIFF, Esq., M.P., LL.D., Dean of the Faculty of Advocates. Price 1s.

Biographical Annals of the Parish of Colinton.

By THOMAS MURRAY, LL.D., Author of 'The Literary History of Galloway, etc., etc. Crown 8vo, price 3s. 6d.

A New-Year's Gift to Children.

By the author of 'John Halifax, Gentleman.' With Illustrations, price 1s.

Man: Where, Whence, and Whither?

Being a glance at Man in his Natural-History Relations. By DAVID PAGE, LL.D. 1 vol. fcap. 8vo, price 3s. 6d.

'At the Seaside.'

Nugæ Criticæ; Occasional Papers written at the Seaside. By SHIRLEY. Crown 8vo, price 9s.

The Bishop's Walk and The Bishop's Times.

By ORWELL. Fcap. 8vo, price 5s.

Popular Genealogists

Or, The Art of Pedigree-making. 1 vol. crown 8vo, price 4s.

Reminiscences of Scottish Life and Character.

By E. B. RAMSAY, M.A., LL.D., F.R.S.E., Dean of Edinburgh. Fifteenth Edition, price 1s. 6d.

"The Dean of Edinburgh has here produced a book for railway reading of the very first class. The persons (and they are many) who can only under such circumstances devote ten minutes of attention to any page, without the certainty of a dizzy or stupid headache, in every page of this volume will find some poignant anecdote or trait which will last them a good half-hour for after-laughter: one of the pleasantest of human sensations."—*Athenæum.*

*** The original Edition in 2 vols. with Introductions, price 12s., and the Sixteenth Edition in 1 vol. cloth antique, price 5s., may be had.

Memoirs of Frederick Perthes;

Or, Literary, Religious, and Political Life in Germany from 1789 to 1843. By C. T. PERTHES, Professor of Law at Bonn. Crown 8vo, cloth, 6s.

Scotland under her Early Kings.

A History of the Kingdom to the close of the 13th century. By E. WILLIAM ROBERTSON, in 2 vols. 8vo, cloth, 36s.

Doctor Antonio

A Tale. By JOHN RUFFINI. Cheap Edition, crown 8vo, boards, 2s. 6d.

Lorenzo Benoni;

Or, Passages in the Life of an Italian. By JOHN RUFFINI. With Illustrations. Crown 8vo, cloth gilt, 5s. Cheap Edition, crown 8vo, boards, 2s. 6d.

A Quiet Nook in the Jura.

By JOHN RUFFINI, Author of 'Doctor Antonio,' etc. 1 vol. extra fcap. 8vo, price 7s. 6d.

The Salmon

Its History, Position, and Prospects. By ALEX. RUSSEL. 8vo, price 7s. 6d.

Horeb and Jerusalem.

By the REV. GEORGE SANDIE. 8vo, with Illustrations, price 10s. 6d.

Our Summer in the Harz Forest.

By A SCOTCH FAMILY. 1 vol. fcap. 8vo, price 6s.

Twelve Years in China:

The People, the Rebels, and the Mandarins, by a British Resident. With coloured Illustrations. Second Edition. With an Appendix. Crown 8vo, cloth, price 10s. 6d.

A Handbook of the History of Philosophy.

By Dr. ALBERT SCHWEGLER. Translated and Annotated by J. HUTCHISON STIRLING, LL.D., Author of the 'Secret of Hegel.' Crown 8vo, price 5s.

John Keble:

An Essay on the Author of the 'Christian Year.' By J. C. SHAIRP, Professor of Humanity, St. Andrews. 1 vol. fcap. 8vo, price 3s.

The Sermon on the Mount.

By the Rev. WALTER C. SMITH, Author of 'The Bishop's Walk, and other Poems, by Orwell,' and 'Hymns of Christ and Christian Life.' 1 vol. crown 8vo, price 6s.

On Archaic Sculpturings of Cups and Circles upon Stones

and Rocks in Scotland, England, etc. By Sir J. Y. SIMPSON, Bart., M.D., D.C.L., Vice-President of the Society of Antiquaries of Scotland, etc. etc. 1 vol. small 4to, with Illustrations, price 21s.

The Law and Practice of Heraldry in Scotland.

By GEORGE SETON, Advocate, M.A., Oxon, F.S.A., Scot. 8vo, with numerous Illustrations, 25s.

*** A few copies on large paper, half-bound, 42s.

'Cakes, Leeks, Puddings, and Potatoes.'

A Lecture on the Nationalities of the United Kingdom. By GEORGE SETON, Advocate, M.A., Oxon, etc. Second Edition. Fcap. 8vo, sewed, price 6d.

The Roman Poets of the Republic.

By W. Y. SELLAR, M.A., Professor of Humanity in the University of Edinburgh, and formerly Fellow of Oriel College, Oxford. 8vo, price 12s.

The Four Ancient Books of Wales,

Containing the Kymric Poems attributed to the Bards of the Sixth century. Edited, with an Introduction and Notes, by WILLIAM F. SKENE. 2 vols. 8vo, with Illustrations.

My Life and Times, 1741-1813.

Being the Autobiography of the Rev. THOS. SOMERVILLE, Minister of Jedburgh, and one of His Majesty's Chaplains. Crown 8vo, price 9s.

Life and Work at the Great Pyramid

During the Months of January, February, March, and April A.D. 1865; with a Discussion of the Facts Ascertained (Illustrated with 36 Plates' and several Woodcuts). By C. PIAZZI SMYTH, F.R.SS.L. and E., F.R.G.S., F.R.S.S.A., Hon. M.I.E. Scot., P.S. Ed., and R.A.A.S. Munich and Palermo, Professor of Practical Astronomy in the University of Edinburgh, and Astronomer-Royal for Scotland. 3 vols. demy 8vo, price 56s.

Dugald Stewart's Collected Works.

Edited by Sir WILLIAM HAMILTON, Bart. Vols. I. to X. 8vo, cloth, each 12s.

Vol. I.—Dissertation. Vols. II. III. and IV.—Elements of the Philosophy of the Human Mind. Vol. V.—Philosophical Essays. Vols. VI. and VII.—Philosophy of the Active and Moral Powers of Man. Vols. VIII. and IX.—Lectures on Political Economy. Vol. X.—Biographical Memoirs of Adam Smith, LL.D., William Robertson, D.D., and Thomas Reid, D.D.; to which is prefixed a Memoir of Dugald Stewart, with Selections from his Correspondence, by John Veitch, M.A. Supplementary Vol.—Translations of the Passages in Foreign Languages contained in the Collected Works; with General Index.

History Vindicated in the Case of the Wigtown Martyrs.

By the Rev. ARCHIBALD STEWART. Price 1s.

Natural History and Sport in Moray.

Collected from the Journals and Letters of the late CHARLES St. JOHN, Author of 'Wild Sports of the Highlands.' With a short Memoir of the Author. Crown 8vo, price 8s. 6d.

Christ the Consoler:

Or Scriptures, Hymns, and Prayers for Times of Trouble and Sorrow. Selected and arranged by the Rev. ROBERT HERBERT STORY, Minister of Roseneath. 1 vol. fcap. 8vo, price 3s. 6d.

Shakespeare.

Some Notes on his Character and Writings. By a Student. 8vo, price 4s. 6d.

Works by Professor James Syme.

OBSERVATIONS IN CLINICAL SURGERY. Second Edition. 1 vol. 8vo, price 8s. 6d.
STRICTURE OF THE URETHRA, AND FISTULA IN PERINEO. 8vo, 4s. 6d.
TREATISE ON THE EXCISION OF DISEASED JOINTS. 8vo, 5s.
ON DISEASES OF THE RECTUM. 8vo, 4s. 6d.
EXCISION OF THE SCAPULA. 8vo, price 2s. 6d.

Lessons for School Life;

Being Selections from Sermons preached in the Chapel of Rugby School during his Head Mastership. By THE RIGHT REVEREND THE LORD BISHOP OF LONDON. Fcap., cloth, 5s

What is Sabbath-Breaking?
8vo, price 2s.

The Dynamical Theory of Heat.
By P. G. TAIT, Professor of Natural Philosophy in the University of Edinburgh. 1 vol. fcap. 8vo.

Day-Dreams of a Schoolmaster.
By D'ARCY W. THOMPSON. Second Edition. Fcap. 8vo, price 5s.

Ancient Leaves;
Or Metrical Renderings of Poets, Greek and Roman. By D'ARCY W. THOMPSON. Fcap. 8vo, 6s.

Sales Attici:
Or Proverb Wisdom of the Athenian Drama. By D'ARCY WENTWORTH THOMPSON, Professor of Greek in Queen's College, Galway. Fcap. 8vo, price 9s.

Antiquities of Cambodia.
By J. THOMSON, F.R.G.S., F.E.S.L. Sixteen Photographs, with Explanatory Text. Imperial 4to, handsomely bound, half-morocco. Price Four Guineas.

An Angler's Rambles among the Rivers and Lochs of Scotland. By THOMAS TOD STODDART, Author of "The Angler's Companion." 1 vol. crown 8vo, price 9s.

Travels by Umbra.
8vo., price 10s. 6d.

Hotch-Pot.
By UMBRA. An Old Dish with New Materials. Fcap 8vo, price 3s. 6d.

Life of Dr. John Reid,
Late Chandos Professor of Anatomy and Medicine in the University of St. Andrews. By the late GEORGE WILSON, M.D. Fcap. 8vo, cloth, price 3s.

Researches on Colour-Blindness.
With a Supplement on the danger attending the present system of Railway and Marine Coloured Signals. By the late GEORGE WILSON, M.D. 8vo, 5s.

Dante's—The Inferno.
Translated line for line by W. P. WILKIE, Advocate. Fcap. 8vo, price 5s.

Westfield.
A View of Home Life during the American War. 1 vol. crown 8vo, price 8s. 6d.

ODDS AND ENDS—*Price 6d. Each.*

Now Ready, Vol. I., in Cloth, price 4s. 6d., containing Nos. 1-10.

1. **Sketches of Highland Character—**
SHEEP FARMERS AND DROVERS.

2. **Convicts.**
By a PRACTICAL HAND.

3. **Wayside Thoughts of an Asophophilosopher**
By D'ARCY W. THOMPSON. No. 1. RAINY WEATHER; or, the Philosophy of Sorrow. GOOSESKIN; or, the Philosophy of Horror. TE DEUM LAUDAMUS or, the Philosophy of Joy.

4. **The Enterkin.**
By JOHN BROWN, M.D.

5. **Wayside Thoughts of an Asophophilosopher.**
By D'ARCY W. THOMPSON. No. 2. ASSES—HISTORY—PLAGUES.

6. **Penitentiaries and Reformatories.**

7. **Notes from Paris; or, Why are Frenchmen and English-**
men different?

8. **Essays by an Old Man.**
No. 1. IN MEMORIAM—VANITAS VANITATUM—FRIENDS.

9. **Wayside Thoughts of an Asophophilosopher.**
By D'ARCY W. THOMPSON. No. 3. NOT GODLESS, BUT GODLY; A TRIANGULAR TREATISE ON EDUCATION.

10. **The Influence of the Reformation on the Scottish Character.**
By J. A. FROUDE, Author of the 'History of England.'

Now Ready, Vol. II., in Cloth, price 4s. 6d., containing Nos. 11-19.

11. **The Cattle Plague.**
By LYON PLAYFAIR, C.B., LL.D., F.R.S., etc.

12. **Rough Nights' Quarters.**
By ONE OF THE PEOPLE WHO HAVE ROUGHED IT.

13. **Letters on the Education of Young Children.**
By S. G. O.

14. **The Stormontfield Piscicultural Experiments. 1853-1866.**
By ROBERT BUIST.

15. **A Tract for the Times.**

16. **Spain in 1866.**

17. **The Highland Shepherd.**
By the Author of 'The Two Queys.'

18. **The Doctrine of the Correlation of Forces: its Develop-**
ment and Evidence. By the Rev. JAMES CRANBROOK, Edinburgh.

19. **'Bibliomania.'** ———

20. **A Tract on Twigs, and on the best way to Bend them.**

CPSIA information can be obtained
at www.ICGtesting.com
Printed in the USA
LVOW02s0456011215

464800LV00013B/225/P

9 781294 970811